WHERE DO I

Where Do I Belong?

by

IAN NICHOLAS MANNERS

Ian Manners.

TWO HUNTERS PUBLISHING

Published in Great Britain by Two Hunters Publishing,
Stokes Farm, Binfield Road, Wokingham, Berks. RG40 5PR.

Typeset in 9.5pt Baskerville
by Columns Design Limited, Reading, UK

Printed in England
by Cox & Wyman Ltd, Reading

ISBN 0-9543263-0-X

This book is dedicated to my two daughters
Hannah and Akinyi

Acknowledgements

I would like to thank everyone who has helped me with this book
and in particular my late father Norman Manners who was
a great source of encouragement to me.

Special thanks must also go to Gwen Schwalb,
Craig Gilbert and Brian O'Gorman.

CHAPTER 1

Sean Aloysius Cameron was six feet tall and weighed 190 pounds. His muscular body was perfectly honed from regular weight training and physical exercise. He had very straight, blond hair that curled slightly over his collar. He had piercing blue eyes that contrasted with his pale skin. His square jaw supported a well-formed bone structure, which showed no sign of physical damage, with the exception of a small two-inch scar above his left eye. A former Scottish international rugby player, he had retired five years earlier in 1985 shortly after Scotland won the Rugby Five Nations Grand Slam, defeating France, Ireland, Wales and then England. That was the pinnacle of his rugby-playing career. He was the hero of Scotland on that euphoric day at Murrayfield. Head to head with England for the punishing Grand Slam Five Nations decider. The memory of that day would never leave him.

The score was 12–12. Sean had picked up a loose ball in a defensive position, just inside his own 22-metre line. The safe course, with only five minutes remaining, was to kick the ball into touch. But not for Sean. He dummied and shimmied past the English left wing on the outside and slipped a pass to his fellow inside-centre Duncan Macrae. Macrae, a powerfully built man, ran straight at the fast-converging English back row forwards as he raced up the right touchline to the halfway line. Just before he was going to be tackled into touch he made a one-handed inside pass back to Sean who was following up in text book style.

From there, Sean could see the English goal posts. He had a few options: time, space, kick, run, pass.

Sean sensed a rare opportunity as he swerved; it seemed clear ahead but there would be a hectic chase. With an explosion of speed and the fullback to beat, he feinted left and again swerved to his right. He raced past the fullback and then found himself diving over the line. In that thudding instant he scored a try. Four points – the try. A Grand Slamming, incredibly breathless, try. One of the most memorable tries ever seen at Murrayfield. The roar from the crowd was deafening. When he picked himself up he was surrounded by a triumphant Scottish team mobbing him en masse. As he ran back to the halfway line he heard the crowd chanting his name: CAMERON ... CAMERON ... CAMERON! A huge grin spread across his handsome face as he watched Rutherford, the Scottish fullback, kick the ball between the posts for a further two points for the conversion: 18–12 to Scotland. Sean felt such joy, such relief as the referee blew the whistle for 'no side', and the game ended. The rest is history.

As they walked from the pitch towards the tunnel his team lifted him shoulder high and carried him back to the dressing room to the resounding words of 'Scotland the Brave'. Then it was a round of interviews for radio and TV and the international media before attending the after-match celebration dinner.

It had all been worth it, from what Sean could remember. He awoke the next morning with the most monumental hangover ever. In the quiet of his hotel room that afternoon he replayed the video over and over again. His winning try was a moment he would relive time and time again for many years to come. In that one millisecond he had made the right move and succeeded. He could have fumbled the ball, mis-kicked to touch and handed the English a try. But he'd taken his chance and now he was a hero. That was life.

It was at this defining moment that Sean decided to retire. He was 32 years old and as a world-class international rugby player he knew that many doors would be open to him. Wherever he went in Scotland he was famous. It might be said he was the George Best of rugby football. Very soon, product endorsements, after-dinner speeches and TV chat shows followed, all of which allowed him to lead an even more comfortable lifestyle than the one he already enjoyed.

At that time rugby was still an amateur game, but Sean and a few other top-class players had been helped with under-the-counter expenses and the opportunity to be employed by blue-chip companies. These jobs were really no more than an endorsement for a particular company, and involved attending sales and marketing conferences and giving after-dinner speeches in return for the chance to train and play in international matches.

Although Sean did not live in the lap of luxury, he was not short of the material things in life owing to the generosity of his sponsors. He had been divorced some years earlier – the pressures of work and the demands of international rugby had taken their toll on his marriage.

He now lived alone in a fashionable town house in Richmond, Surrey.

Despite its dramatic end, one good thing had come out of his marriage. He had a beautiful seven-year-old daughter, Louise, who was the most important person in his life. She had long blond wavy hair and deep blue eyes. When she smiled it melted his heart. He was fortunate that he was able to see her every other weekend and during the school holidays, despite having to make a round trip of about 200 miles to collect her and take her back to her mother's home near Bristol. After a busy fortnight of working and training for long hours it was a real effort to make the journey, but he always did. He was determined to minimize the effects of a broken home and to bring her up to live as normal a life as possible.

However the strain on Louise was also immense. To go from one environment to another required some adjustment and it would take her until the Saturday evening to feel totally comfortable and relaxed in her father's home. Of course, by Sunday night she wouldn't then want to go back to her mother! Despite this she remained a happy and cheerful child, but Sean didn't know what went through her mind and often wondered what effect her parents' divorce and separation would have in later life and whether the scars would prove to be too much.

Sean thought deeply about this. He was racked with guilt about leaving Louise when his marriage broke up and that feeling of guilt never left him, but his relationship with Sally, his ex-wife, had reached the end of the road. Her affair with the tennis coach at the local sports club had just proved too much for Sean, in what had been a pretty stormy seven years. He hadn't only divorced his wife; he felt that he had partially divorced his daughter, too.

He missed her growing-up, helping her with her homework and all the normal things a parent and child experience in those early and very influential years. It hurt Sean deeply. He recognized that, insofar as it affected Louise, he and his ex-wife had been selfish, but at least she would no longer have to hear the endless arguments and live in such a hostile atmosphere.

Sally, who was an attractive blond woman, with an extrovert personality, had since remarried. Her new husband was a wealthy guy called Joe, who seemed to be a calming influence on her, despite being 15 years older.

In the meantime, Sean had remained on his own. Although he had fallen out of love with Sally, the wounds had not yet healed. He had loved her in his own way, but he was a quiet man and liked his own time and space. He had done the best he could to provide her with a pleasant lifestyle, but she had always wanted more and eventually her behaviour destroyed any love he had for her. Like a bereavement, a divorce is a very sad time. It had taken him two years to lose the hurt and bitterness.

It was strange, really. He woke up one spring morning and it was as if a great weight had been lifted. He felt free. It was as though someone up above had pressed a release valve.

Sean wasn't a particularly religious man but that day he went to church and prayed, something he hadn't done since leaving school.

The time had come for him to start his life again. Although he had had a few brief affairs since his divorce, there had been no one special. He had had no intention of introducing Louise to any new woman in his life unless there was a distinct possibility of a secure and stable relationship.

CHAPTER 2

It was 19 February 1990, a day that would change his life forever. Sean was due to attend an international sales conference in Cologne for a client company launching ultra innovative football boots. Since his retirement from international rugby, nothing much had had a great influence on him. He had been leading a pretty normal life in the UK, working hard as a consultant for a sales and marketing company, and had achieved above average success for a man of thirty-seven back in the fast and furious business environment of the 1980s.

It was a bitterly cold winter's day, which Sean had spent preparing for the sales conference at the Messe Hall, checking all the usual pre-event things like delegate lists, catering arrangements, and so on. The product displays were in place and at seven o'clock he looked around the huge hall, feeling some satisfaction that everything was going to plan.

He had now only to meet his German interpreter, brief her on her role over the next four days and convey the essential product information. Heidi, his usual interpreter, was not available. However, she had suggested a friend as a replacement. She had also drawn his attention to the fact that her friend, Akinyi Ouko, was black. She explained that Akinyi spoke absolutely perfect German, held a master's degree in the language and was Kenyan.

Sean told Heidi that the colour of someone's skin did not bother him. He took the simple view that everything was fine as long as Akinyi was properly qualified and had good language ability. Heidi pointed out that some Germans had strong racist attitudes and might not deal with a company that was represented by black people. Although they wouldn't come right out and say it, they wouldn't place any orders.

Sean felt strongly against this attitude. Personally, he would rather lose an order than compromise himself. After all, his best mate James was black. They had been to school together and he knew that he would never be able to look him in the eye again if he had rejected a qualified black person in order to secure business. There was no question about it and, although he had never met her, he knew he wanted Akinyi Ouko to work for him.

Sean left the Messe Hall and hailed a taxi to take him on the ten-minute drive across the city to his hotel. It was a small hotel run by a pleasant German family. It was homely and Sean had stayed there several times before. He never liked staying in big anonymous international hotels full of salesman and reps away from home. Their behaviour generally appalled him. He didn't feel he had the right to moralize; he knew that many of them used hookers or escorts while they were away from their wives and families, but he, personally, wanted no part of this.

The traffic was heavy and the journey to the hotel took an extra fifteen minutes. Despite the delay, Sean had time to have a quick shower and change before meeting Akinyi for dinner. He chose a pair of jeans and a loose shirt, thinking it would make her feel relaxed and more at ease. He didn't want her to feel that she had to stand on ceremony. He left his room and walked down the stairs, through the glass doors just to the right of reception, eventually reaching the bar.

Hans, the regular barman, was on duty and they exchanged the usual pleasantries, asking each other about their day. Sean ordered a cold beer and sat down close to the bar to await Akinyi's arrival, positioning himself so that he would have a good view of the doorway.

Shortly after eight o'clock the glass doors opened and a vision of loveliness appeared before him; he saw a beautiful, slender black woman, approximately five feet seven inches tall with long, braided hair. Her eyes were almond-shaped and deep brown in colour, her nose was quite small, and her lips full. She had finely shaped cheekbones which emphasized the dark colouring of her skin. As she smiled, a slight dimple appeared between the left side of her mouth and her cheek. She looked stunning.

Sean rose from his chair to greet her. He had quite rightly assumed that it was Akinyi Ouko. After all, on previous visits, he hadn't seen many black women in that particular hotel in the heart of Cologne.

The woman moved towards him, gliding effortlessly across the room. Sean was transfixed; it was like watching a gazelle in slow motion. Her elegance and natural grace were a sight to behold. She extended her hand and with no trace of an accent, in flawless English, said, 'Mr Cameron, I presume?'

He reached out and took her hand, saying, 'Don't worry about the formalities. You can call me Sean.'

As their hands touched it was as though an electric shock had run through the entire length of his body, and his heart missed a beat. Sean always felt a clumsy shyness in the company of women that he was attracted to, and this was no exception. It seemed like ages before he finally withdrew his hand. 'I suppose I can call you Akinyi?' he stammered. Then he added, almost immediately, 'May I get you a drink?'

'Just a soda water with ice, please.'

They sat down and began to discuss the new product launch, how questions should be dealt with and the usual detail of taking business cards, and so on. They talked for about half an hour and then it was time for dinner.

As they walked in the direction of the restaurant Akinyi found herself to be attracted to Sean's masculine good looks and his down-to-earth manner. She thought he was a very handsome man, as blond as she was dark. She looked forward to the next four days.

After their meal was ordered and the appropriate wines selected, they began to discuss all sorts of topics, in particular, Africa and the developing world.

Sean was mesmerized by Akinyi's stories. He had never really considered very much outside his own environment. He had, of course, travelled quite extensively on business and on various rugby tours, but he had never spent much time discovering the different aspects of the many varied cultures around the world. He had been to Australia and New Zealand with the Scotland rugby team, but had refused to go on a rebel rugby tour to South Africa in 1983 as he disapproved of the apartheid regime. Beyond that, his holidays had consisted of tours to Spain and the Spanish islands and other parts of Europe. There was one holiday in the Caribbean where he had stayed with Sally in a typical tourist hotel but, even then, he had not ventured far. The truth of the matter was that he had experienced very little of the local life.

The starters arrived. They had both chosen melon with Parma ham. Akinyi began to tell Sean about the more recent history of Kenya. She explained that British interest in East Africa at the end of the nineteenth century had resulted from the European power struggles for Africa. The 1885 Berlin Conference of European nations had split the continent into arbitrary areas. Germany, for example, had been awarded Tanganyika, later to become Tanzania. Britain was 'given' Kenya and Uganda. These decisions were entirely political, albeit aligned to economic benefits, and although Germany had designs on Uganda, as it was strategically important for control of the River Nile, Britain's claim to Uganda was in danger of lapsing if it could not properly be garrisoned and supplied. Kenya was at the time devastated by drought, locusts, rinderpest and civil war, but the British established a series of trading forts at fifty-mile intervals from Mombasa, the main port in East Africa, to Uganda.

The waiter interrupted the flow of information to clear their empty plates.

Sean automatically filled Akinyi's glass with Chablis. He was not a great lover of German wines; they were too sweet for his taste.

'Oh that's enough thank you,' she protested, raising her hand to her glass. 'I don't normally drink much and we have to be up early in the morning.'

'Two glasses won't hurt you,' Sean chuckled, encouragingly.

The waiter returned and served their main course. Sean had chosen a peppered steak, his favourite food. Akinyi had selected trout with almonds. They both had mixed salad and baked potatoes.

'Guten appetit,' said the waiter.

'Thank you,' said Sean in response.

Akinyi smiled and began to eat. Sean tucked into his steak. 'The only things I remember learning at school about African history were Cecil Rhodes and the Boer War, and we probably only learned about the Boers because Winston Churchill was involved,' he explained, somewhat ashamed at his lack of knowledge.

Akinyi sighed. Sean was not alone in his ignorance of African history. She continued to outline the facts. The Imperial British East Africa Company (or IBEAC as it was known) was formed in 1885 to establish the trading posts but went bankrupt. The British government formally took control after this and declared a protectorate over Kenya and Uganda. As a result, a railway was built along the route linked by the old trading posts, and thus Uganda became only a month's journey from Europe by sea and rail.

'Did the colonials use the Kenyans to build the railway?' asked Sean.

'No. The Maasai refused to cooperate because the railway cut through Maasai lands.'

'Well, did the colonials build it?'

'No, of course not. They wouldn't get their hands dirty,' chuckled Akinyi. 'They brought in many Indians to work as labourers.' She hesitated for a moment. 'More importantly, the railway physically divided the Maasai. Kenya became a country of opportunity for white settlers, who took over the best land.'

'But how did they manage that so easily?' queried Sean. 'Surely the natives fought to keep their land?'

Akinyi reacted angrily. 'What could they do against the guns and fire-power of a highly organized army?'

Sean reddened, realizing his naivety, and stopped before he made himself look more foolish.

Akinyi continued without looking up from her plate. She explained that by 1916 nearly half the land worth farming was owned by white settlers. The Kenyan people were soon pushed aside into 'native reserves', or became squatters on the land without rights. The British then appointed 'Chiefs' from among the African population, whose job it was to collect taxes on every hut or house owned by the indigeneous people. As there was virtually no money economy, the only way the Kenyans could pay their taxes was to work on the white settlers' farms. A system of forced labour had been created and, following on from the hut tax, a poll tax was added. Cash cropping on African plots was discouraged or banned. Coffee licenses, for example, were restricted to white farmers. The highlands were strictly reserved for white settlers, while African land became Crown Land and its African owners became known as 'tenants at will' of the Crown and were liable to eviction at any time.

Akinyi took a sip from her wine. Sean by this time had demolished the remainder of the bottle. They had both finished their main course.

Sean felt he could continue listening to Akinyi for ever. He couldn't take his eyes off her.

Then Akinyi interrupted his thoughts. 'Please tell me something about yourself. Here I am, going on and on about Kenya. It would be nice to hear about your life.'

'Oh, I think what you've been telling me is far more interesting than my mundane little life,' laughed Sean.

The waiter returned to clear their plates, enquiring politely: 'Would you like a dessert or coffee?'

'Just coffee for me, thanks,' said Sean. 'And what about you, Akinyi?'

'Tea would be very nice, please.'

They sat in silence for a few minutes. Sean, in the meantime, watched another couple across the restaurant having what appeared to be a heated argument. Probably happily married he thought, rather cynically. All of a sudden he began laughing and grabbed Akinyi's arm. 'Don't look now,' he whispered, 'but that woman over there just stood up and slapped the guy around the face.'

Akinyi turned slowly to see the woman storming out of the restaurant, leaving the man sitting on his own looking very angry and embarrassed.

'Sorry to interrupt you,' said Sean. 'It's just my childish sense of humour. Please carry on and tell me more about Kenya.'

Akinyi giggled quietly before continuing. 'The First World War had a profound effect on Kenya. Although there were few battles in Kenya itself, something like 200,000 African soldiers and porters were conscripted and sent to Tanganyika to fight the Germans. Incredibly, about 25 per cent of them were killed or died of disease. Those who returned at the end of the war had been deeply influenced by the fact that white European people had been at war with each other. They had experienced European fallibility and had seen how to exploit it. At the end of the war Germany lost Tanganyika to the British, whose commitments in East Africa had suddenly multiplied.'

'What happened to the soldiers who returned after the war?'

'The African soldiers returned to their homes.'

'What about the white Kenyans? What happened to them?'

'The Governor of Kenya began a soldier settlement scheme for them so as to double the European settler population in Kenya.'

'Did it work?' queried Sean.

'Oh yes, but the scheme excluded all Africans, who bitterly resented it.

As a result, many ex-servicemen formed political associations. Harry Thuken, a Kikuyu and Secretary of the Young Kikuyu Association, realized its potential and began to recruit on a nationwide basis.'

'Did it work?'

'It certainly did. Another major grievance, the hated registration law, under which every African had to carry a pass, galvanized them into action, causing a spread of nationalism and the lobbying for the return of alienated land, the lowering of taxes and for elected African representatives to be on the Legislative Council. In reality, a system of apartheid had been created by the white settlers.'

'So, it was just like South Africa?'

'I suppose you could say that, but the Second World War had seen a large recruitment of Kenyans into the British army. Thousands of young men were drafted to fight in the Italian-held Ethiopia and also in Burma. Military operations in Burma and Ethiopia owed much of their success to African troops, but after the war a new awareness, similar to that felt by the ex-soldiers of the First World War, was felt again by returning Africans.'

'I suppose it was comparable to the huge social change that was experienced by us in Britain after the Second World War,' suggested Sean.

'Well . . . not quite. The most important thing was that the returning Kenyans, who thought that the white tribes of the world had fought the Second World War on the basis of self-determination, felt that almost every part of their lives was being demeaned and humiliated by white settlers.'

'You make it sound as if the Kenyans were treated really badly,' said Sean.

'They were!' replied Akinyi.

For the first time Sean detected a real iciness in her voice. He realized he had hit on a raw nerve.

'I'm sorry,' he apologized.

'There's no need to apologize,' Akinyi said, and left the conversation at that.

'I need to go to the little boys' room.' Sean stood up. 'When I come back you can tell me all about yourself.'

Akinyi studied him carefully as he walked out of the restaurant, wondering how on earth she could get him to tell her something about his own life.

CHAPTER 3

Sean was gone for about five minutes. 'Sorry I kept you waiting but I was just organizing an early morning call,' he said.

'Did you book me one?' asked Akinyi, rather shyly.

'I certainly did. I booked it for 6.30. Now tell me about yourself,' Sean commanded.

Akinyi began telling her own story. She was Kenyan and her people were Luo from near Lake Victoria. She explained that the Luo are the second largest ethnic group and one of the most united peoples in Kenya. Their language, Tholuo, closely resembled the Nuer and Dinka languages of Southern Sudan, from whence their ancestors had migrated south at the end of the fifteenth century. They found the shore of Lake Victoria sparsely populated by hunter-gatherers and scattered with Bantu-speaking farmers who had settled over previous centuries. Other than those people the region was one of wild, untouched grasslands and tropical rainforests teeming with wildlife.

She continued with her story:

'The Luo were swift invaders who brought their cattle with them, and within a few decades of their arrival had driven the Bantu speakers away from the shores of Lake Victoria.'

'What happened to the Bantu?' questioned Sean.

'They settled close by and, despite the fighting, intermarriage between the peoples was commonplace. This mostly took place through the buying of wives. The Luo were influenced greatly by their Bantu neighbours who were ancestors of the present-day Luyia and Gusii. The modern-day Luo are best known as fisherman, but they also cultivate the land and keep livestock. Traditionally, children had four or six teeth knocked out from the lower front jaw to mark their initiation into adulthood but nowadays this is rarely carried out.'

'So what's the difference between you Luo coming down from the Nile region and taking over the area around Lake Victoria and the way the colonials took over all around the world later in history?' said Sean, rather indignantly.

'It is different.'

'How is it different?'

'I'll explain that later, but first let me tell you about my family.'

'OK then, but I won't let you get away with what you've said without a proper explanation.'

'My family come from Kisumu, which is the third largest town in

Kenya. I was born in 1963, the year of independence.'

Sean quickly calculated that she was twenty-seven years old. He studied her closely. She looked much younger.

'By Kenyan standards I had a childhood of opportunity, being educated at one of Nairobi's best boarding schools. Before independence, it was for European girls only, but since Kenyatta came to power the country has changed and Kenyans are allowed entry to the school.'

'How did you manage an education like that?' Sean said, with an edge of challenge.

'My father had a good job with the government. He was Minister for Education and Cultural Affairs,' Akinyi said, with great pride in her voice.

Sean noticed her waver slightly.

'He also served five years as the Kenyan High Commissioner in America. He was a well educated man, having obtained a master's degree in law at Harvard Business School in Boston, Massachusetts, but he was also a very troubled man. He had grown up in pre-independence times under British colonial rule and saw many things that disturbed him, particularly how his people had been treated by the colonial government. He had supported Jomo Kenyatta and the KAU leadership in their fight against the colonialists. The Kenyan African Union (or KAU as it became known) was formed in 1944 to liaise with Eliud Mathu, who was the only African member of the Legislative Council, the colony's local government.'

'How did Kenyatta become the leader?'

'Kenyatta returned from England in 1946, where he had studied anthropology at the London School of Economics. At about that time the KAU was transformed into an active political party, campaigning for African political rights.'

'Wasn't it dangerous to be involved in such political campaigns?' Sean shook his head as he said this, still not really understanding the contemporary conditions in a British colony.

'The radicals within the party wanted sweeping changes in land ownership, equal voting rights and the abolition of the pass law for Africans. The moderates wanted negotiation, educational improvement, multi-racial progress and a gradual shift of power.'

'Where did Kenyatta figure in all of this?' Sean interrupted again, hoping she wouldn't mind.

'I'm surprised you're so interested in our history,' Akinyi replied, with a touch of sarcasm. 'Most Europeans only want to talk about their holiday experiences on safari.'

'I studied European history at school and I'm always keen to learn something new.' Sean paused. 'Besides, you are definitely far more attractive than my history master ever was,' he added.

Akinyi smiled and the dimple appeared again. She liked a man who could make her laugh. 'Although Kenyatta tried to steer a middle course, the KAU became increasingly radical and was dominated by Kikuyus. Kenyatta tried to create a multi-tribal profile to appease the white settlers. He also managed to dismiss some moderates to create stronger party unity, but some of the radicals, led by Dedan Kimathi, broke away and formed an underground movement which took oaths of allegiance against the British. Those who betrayed the movement, or collaborated with the government, faced execution. The infamous *Mau Mau*, from the word *muma*, a traditional Kikuyu oath, was formed and it attracted many young men from towns like Nyeri, Fort Hall and Nairobi.'

'I remember hearing about the *Mau Mau* when I was a very small boy,' said Sean.

The brief interruption did nothing to stem Akinyi's flow.

'They used Kenyatta's name in their propaganda and the *Mau Mau* oath-takers called themselves the Land and Freedom Army. Kenyatta was careful politically to condemn strikes and oath-taking, but he was waiting for his chance to exploit the situation. In 1952, the white settlers pressured the government into declaring a state of emergency and the *Mau Mau* and all African nationalist organizations were banned.'

'What happened to Kenyatta and the other KAU leaders?'

'They were all arrested, including my father.' Again Akinyi paused.

'What happened to your father?'

'They kept him in a concentration camp for three months then released him without charge.'

'What do you mean by a concentration camp? Surely such places only existed under Hitler and the Nazis?'

'Well I am sorry to disillusion you, Mr Cameron, but I assure you the British *did* run such places. They actually started them in the Boer War. You should know that!'

Sean took a slow sip of coffee.

'You studied the history of that war, didn't you – or didn't they tell you that in school either?' she questioned. Sean put his hands up. He knew when to back off. He let Akinyi continue.

'Thousands of British troops were sent to Kenya and a guerrilla war followed. Under the state of emergency a policy of villagization was enforced, and thousands of Kikuyu were relocated to secure villages or detained in barbed wire concentration camps. Dedan Kimathi, the commander-in-chief of the Land and Freedom Army, was eventually captured and executed. The Western media made a great deal of the *Mau Mau* atrocities. However, a total of only thirty-two European civilians and about fifty soldiers and police were killed, compared with an estimated 13,000 African men, women and children.'

'Why was there such a difference in the numbers that were killed on each side?' asked Sean, not sure whether he was going to be put in his place again, for Akinyi was certainly a feisty character.

'How could we possibly compete against the heavily armed soldiers of the British Army? Let me tell you something. I met a former British soldier in Nairobi shortly after I left school. He did his National Service in Kenya and told me about some of the atrocities that went on. When he and his fellow servicemen arrived in Kenya they were told that they had to protect white farmers and the indigenous population from the *Mau Mau* wildmen led by Jomo Kenyatta.'

Sean interrupted. 'I told you earlier that I remember stories about the *Mau Mau* and I vaguely remember as a boy listening to radio reports on the atrocities committed by the *Mau Mau* – and how they butchered white settlers, including children.'

'I don't deny that probably happened,' she said, 'but did you know that some British Army officers organized inter-regimental competitions to see who could kill the greatest number of blacks? The prize for the winners was a long weekend at a hotel on Nyali beach in Mombasa.'

Sean frowned. 'I find that a little difficult to believe.'

Akinyi was surprised at Sean's naivety. 'That sort of thing goes on in all wars. Targeting the "kills" was easy; they only had to be black for the whites to assume that they were members of the *Mau Mau*. The dead were then taken back to the camp for enthusiastic sergeants to count.'

'Can you prove that this ex-soldier was telling the truth?' queried Sean.

'Well of course I can't, but what reason would he have to lie? When I did a little bit of research myself I discovered that the original *Mau Mau* Association has, in the last few years, catalogued thousands of cases of rape, execution and land seizure by colonial authorities during the uprising. Even now they are putting together a claim for compensation against the British government.'

Sean was subdued. 'I never realized that such atrocities went on. We were always brought up to believe that the British never put a foot wrong and that it was only people like Hitler and the Nazis who committed such heinous crimes. Surely we weren't to blame for all 13,000 killings?'

'Well, I concede that the *Mau Mau* were responsible for the killing of some black people who supported the British but during my research I also met a former district officer who sympathized with the *Mau Mau* association and their claim for compensation. He described the *Mau Mau* period as one of the most sordid chapters in his experience of British colonial rule. He told me there was an outright abuse of power and that some of the crimes committed were horrific. He said that in one neighbouring district a British police inspector lined up six *Mau Mau* suspects against a wall and shot them without even a trial.' Akinyi's voice was in obvious distress. She paused, regaining her composure.

'In another case, a group of soldiers threw a phosphorous flare into a thatched hut with a family sleeping inside.' She paused again. 'If that's not a human rights abuse, I don't know what is.'

Sean looked at Akinyi. He could see she was becoming emotional, so he didn't pursue the conversation. Instead they sat in silence for a minute or two.

By now the restaurant was almost empty. Sean called the waiter over. 'One more coffee and the bill, please,' and almost as an afterthought he turned to Akinyi. 'And would you like another tea?'

'Yes please but that'll be my last. After that I must go to bed. We have an early start in the morning.'

Sean realized there would be a few more minutes for conversation and gently prompted Akinyi to resume her story.

'What happened to your father after independence?' His voice was low and even and he displayed genuine concern.

'In the early 1960s he was sponsored by the US government to study at Harvard. He got a scholarship, along with several other Kenyans.'

'Why was he selected in particular?' asked Sean.

'Well, I guess he was just one of the smart ones,' she said, with obvious pride, a fleeting smile appearing on her lips for the first time in about half an hour. Sean couldn't help but notice the gamut of emotions that gripped Akinyi as she recounted her story: her agitation, her pride, her bitterness and her sheer frustration with her country and its current problems.

'So how did your father like America and, as a black man, what was the reaction to him there?' asked Sean, gingerly.

'When my father was in America he saw the terrible way African Americans were treated. The history of slavery and the legacy that remained was a basic abuse of human rights. America had produced, and was deliberately encouraging, a black underclass. For example, he could not understand why black people were not allowed to be educated to the same standard as white people. He was able to draw parallels between the black American experience of segregation and the suffering his people had endured under colonialism. However, in spite of this, he wanted to adopt a conciliatory approach to the legacy of colonialism in his own country. For example, when he was President, Jomo Kenyatta displayed no desire for retribution. He welcomed all races.' Akinyi reached for the white china cup and drank the remains of her tea.

'While in America my father attended speeches by both Martin Luther King and Malcolm X, prior to their assassinations. He told me that although they sometimes appeared to have conflicting views in their approach to the civil rights problems suffered by black people there, they both shared some common ground. They wanted to move closer to their goal of "justice for all". My father was determined that when he returned to Kenya he would try and ensure an equality for all Kenyans, whether they were black or white. His first campaign was to seek to ensure that white colonial Kenyans held Kenyan passports only. He did not believe they should continue to hold British passports as well. He openly encouraged white Kenyans to stay and work in the country. He needed their expertise to help Kenya to develop into a stable economy with education for all. However, if the colonials were not prepared to relinquish their British passports and opt for Kenyan ones, they could leave the country and return to England or, indeed, go to South Africa where they would be welcomed into the apartheid structure of that country. Some of them stayed and agreed to keep Kenyan passports only, but secretly they kept both.'

'What happened to the ones that stayed?'

'Oh, they kept very much to themselves.'

'In what way?'

'Oh it's too long and complicated to tell you now,' Akinyi sighed, 'I'll explain another time. Let me finish telling you what happened to my father when he was in America.'

'All right then,' said Sean, glancing at his watch.

'Well, he fell in love with a white American woman. He decided that he wanted to marry her. Obviously he had to divorce my mother first, which he did on his return to Kenya in 1971. The suddeness of the divorce and the associated trauma of having to accept a complete stranger as my "new" mother led to me having a very unhappy childhood. In all the ten years of my schooling, during which time I grew up with my stepmother, I was never once kissed or hugged or shown any affection. By any standards that was emotional neglect. My stepmother had been raised in the American Deep South and had grown up surrounded by racial prejudice. It was ironic, really, that she fell in love with a black man. She felt that her relationship with my father was on a different level to normal black-white relations. However, she still couldn't accept that black people should be treated in any way other than the way many black servants were treated by Southern whites. She simply could not bring herself to touch another black person. Her justification of her love and attraction for my father was that he was African and not a black American, which made him somehow different.'

Sean couldn't come to terms with the fact that such entrenched racism actually existed.

'I know I didn't grow up with many black people except at school, but my parents taught me and my sister and brother to treat everyone equally, regardless of race, creed or colour. It's not a problem that I've ever really thought about, except when I was asked to go on a rugby tour to South Africa. Until one is able to experience problems at first-hand it's so hard to understand other people's suffering.'

'I could not talk to my father about this,' Akinyi continued. 'Although I know he loved and cared for me, he was a strict and private man and completely unapproachable about such an intimate subject. The other great scar that remained with me was that my best friend at school, up to the age of thirteen, was a white European girl called Emma. She was also my next door neighbour. In the changing times after independence, government officials and professional black people had moved into what used to be predominantly white neighbourhoods. Emma had lived next-door to me for five years, but suddenly, because I was black, her parents forbade her to play with me. I felt all alone. I just needed someone to share my innermost thoughts with. Although I have four older brothers they were brought up to be very much like their father. I didn't see much of my mother, who lived up country in Kisumu, except during school holidays. Even when my father was away on business, there was never enough time – or perhaps encouragement – to get to know her. In addition, my mother had kept very much to a traditional African Luo lifestyle, whereas I was now experiencing a cross-culture between the African and European ways of life. Thirteen was a very confusing age for me. At boarding school I was taught in the traditional English way. I learned about English history and the standards and method of teaching were very English in an old fashioned, Victorian style. Everything was based on the old English public school system. I became very Anglicized, but I was nevertheless extremely conscious of my African culture. I wanted to rebel against the pressure of British influence in my country.'

'Did that make a difference to you at school?' asked Sean, remembering his own childhood. 'When I had other influences at school that were more interesting than work, I began to rebel.'

Akinyi smiled.

'That surprises me, Sean. You strike me as though you were a bit of a teacher's pet.'

Sean laughed, revealing a row of white, even teeth. He had a lot to thank his dentist for.

'Nothing could be further from the truth. I was definitely a rebel in my time.'

Akinyi was not convinced. Her seductive brown eyes glinted mischievously.

'Okay then, tell me about your time at school.'

For the first time since they met Sean was the focus of attention and he didn't like it one bit. He leaned back in his chair and folded his arms across his broad chest.

'You're forgetting I'm the boss,' he said, tongue in cheek. 'I want to know all about you, before I tell you about me.' He laughed out loud and gave Akinyi a huge smile.

Akinyi smiled back, and at that moment found her attraction to Sean grew stronger than ever.

'So tell me about school. Did you do well?' Sean was determined to steer the conversation on to safer ground.

'In spite of everything I did reasonably well. By the time I left at the age of eighteen with ten O levels and three A levels – all at 'A' grades – I was head prefect and had also captained my school at netball, hockey and swimming.'

'It sounds to me as though *you* were the teacher's pet,' chuckled Sean, trying to lure her into battle. But Akinyi did not take the bait; instead she continued her brief. In addition to her academic success she had also been selected to swim for Kenya in the 50 metres breaststroke event at the All African Games and also at the Commonwealth Games in Auckland, where she finished a very creditable fourth in the final against strong opposition. As a result of her A levels she gained a place at Guy's Hospital in England to study medicine. Akinyi coasted through the first year but quickly become bored. She decided that a career in medicine was not for her. She then applied for a scholarship to study German at the University of Heidelberg in West Germany.

Typically, she won a place to study for a master's degree and started in October 1982. The five-year course presented some financial difficulties, despite the scholarship award which covered tuition and residence during term time.

'When I arrived in Heidelberg I got a part-time job working in a bar at night. From time to time I lectured at seminars for German businessmen, who needed to know about the cultural exchange between Europe and Africa. It was during these seminars that I was able to start putting together ideas for a thesis that I wanted to undertake after I completed my master's degree. I also worked as an interpreter/translator, as I am doing now.'

While Akinyi related this further chapter in her eventful life Sean sat entranced. He was overcome not only by the poignancy of her story but also by her strength of character and her rare, dusky beauty. He hoped his intense scrutiny of her was not obvious. She had perfect bone structure and he imagined her skin to have the soft, smooth, touch of velvet. Her smile was just enchanting and it accentuated her high cheekbones. Her face was slightly oval in shape. She wore red lipstick and her brown eyes sparkled as she fluttered her long eyelashes at him. Her

18

dark skin contrasted with the palms of her hands which were considerably lighter in colour. Sean couldn't help noticing her long, elegant fingers and her perfectly manicured nails which she had covered with a bright red nail polish that matched her lipstick. He had never been so mesmerized by a woman in his life. It seemed as though they had been there for only five minutes and when he glanced at his watch he couldn't believe the time. It was 1.30 in the morning and they were supposed to be making an early start. They had to be at the Messe Hall at eight o'clock. It was time to go.

They rose from the table and walked from the dining room towards the main lift in the reception area. Akinyi was staying on the third floor. After a short wait they heard the familiar swish as the lift came to a halt and the doors opened. As she entered, Sean had an overwhelming urge to kiss her. It took all his strength to resist. Instead he bade her goodnight and arranged to meet her for breakfast at 7.15 a.m. He climbed the short flight of stairs located off a narrow corridor to his room and lay down on his bed. It seemed ages before he fell asleep; his heart was racing and his mind was working overtime. He couldn't remember ever being so excited, not even when Sally gave birth to Louise, or when he had scored that try for Scotland to win the Grand Slam. He knew he was going to travel to Kenya and he knew he would experience an African sky at night. He had only read about an African sky in Wilbur Smith's novels, but he was already dreaming about what it was going to be really like.

He couldn't wait. Akinyi had ignited a fire inside him, the like of which he had never known.

CHAPTER 4

Sean awoke to the incessant buzzing of the alarm clock. He rolled over and yawned; it was 6.45 a.m. He felt tired but, as his thoughts returned to the previous night, his tiredness soon changed to a feeling of elation. He climbed out of bed, showered and dressed quickly, putting on his dark-blue pin-striped suit, light-blue shirt and a Scottish Grand Slam tie. He only wore that tie at sales functions as he knew it would help drum up business. Although German businessmen weren't keen rugby fans, there would be many others on that day from other countries who were. The tie was always a great talking point. Sean was a quiet man and often found it difficult to initiate conversation. The tie helped, as inevitably someone would spot it and ask why he was wearing it. Businessmen always liked to tell their mates at the bar that they had met so and so – especially if it was an international sportsman.

The day proved to be very busy and passed quickly. About two-thirds of the 1,200 invited guests turned up. It was a good success rate, but Sean knew the real yardstick would be when the contacts were made with the promise of further appointments. That's when he would hope to close the deals.

During the day Sean watched Akinyi carefully. She was professional in her approach to work and was skilled at handling people. She had a natural charm that broke down many barriers, including colour – which was significant in Germany. Sean did notice, however, that some of the businessmen tended to avoid talking to Akinyi and preferred to approach him. Whether it was a question of colour, or just an old fashioned male chauvinistic attitude, he didn't know.

Six o'clock, and the end of the working day. After the last of the guests had gone they packed up the displays and agreed to meet for dinner along with two American delegates from Atlanta.

After showering and changing, Sean met Akinyi in reception at 7.30. It was a cold, clear evening and the walk along the banks of the Rhine to the city centre took about half an hour. It was a refreshing change from the Messe Hall. They didn't say much during the walk, other than to briefly discuss the day's work. It was as if they were silently savouring each other's company without making any comment at all. Sean again felt a strong attraction towards Akinyi. He wondered if she felt the same.

Shortly after eight they arrived at the Dome Restaurant. The two Americans, Charlie Wilson and Geoff Bates, were waiting at the bar and had begun sampling the local ale. Sean ordered a rosé wine for Akinyi and a beer for himself. He was surprised at her choice because she had previously admitted that she didn't normally drink much alcohol. Sean wondered whether she needed a glass of wine to calm her nerves. The four of them then moved to a table in the restaurant. The evening passed quickly, and Charlie and Geoff explained that they were in Cologne to look for new products for various soccer sales promotions that they were running in America. They said that soccer had never really caught on in the States and that a consortium for the North American Soccer League had approached them to find ways of relaunching the game and repackaging it to achieve a greater appeal.

'When we read about the launch of a new style football boot, we decided it could be a way of promoting the game on the back of a new product,' said Geoff.

'Yes, we reckon we can provide displays that the NASL could use at the 1996 Olympics if Atlanta succeeds with its bid. With the huge numbers expected, it could be an ideal opportunity for us,' added Charlie.

'We're looking to put together a history of the game, and how it has developed over the years into such a global phenomenon,' continued Geoff.

'Not only that, you have also got the soccer World Cup shortly taking place in the States for the first time,' interrupted Sean.

Charlie went on to explain how the two of them ran a small sales promotions company in Atlanta. Although the venue for the 1996 Olympics had not yet been awarded, they wanted to be ready in the event of a successful bid. They saw it as a massive opportunity to expand their business from small players into the big time.

It turned out that Charlie was of English origin and had married the daughter of the owner of one of the largest plantations in Savannah. Although he could have sat back and waited for his wife's father to 'pop his clogs', as he described it, and share in the family inheritance, he had set up his own business with Geoff and wanted to succeed in his own right. They had so far achieved a fair degree of success.

Sean found the Americans to be fairly laid back and the evening was enjoyable. The restaurant had a lively atmosphere, the food and wine were good, and they soon became positively merry, if not drunk. Charlie arranged to meet Sean the next day for lunch at the Messe Hall, to discuss a possible agency agreement. Sean knew the two Americans recognized this as a great opportunity and would most certainly be open to negotiation. After Sean paid the bill they decided to go on to a nightclub. Akinyi suggested an African club called The Safari; she had been there on several occasions with a friend who lived in Cologne. It was a popular place for African and reggae music.

They arrived shortly after 11.30. It was already busy. Straightaway, Charlie took Akinyi off to dance and Sean and Geoff moved to a table in the corner. After three or four numbers Charlie and Akinyi returned. The atmosphere was relaxed. The four carried on general conversation with a few jokes thrown in. Geoff in turn asked Akinyi to dance and they went off and bopped to a couple of fast numbers, returning quite breathless.

Sean was contemplating dancing with Akinyi. He had been somewhat reticent until then, partly because of their working relationship but most of all because he felt shy and awkward in her presence. Then the mood of the music changed. UB40's 'Red, Red, Wine' struck up, a favourite of Sean, and this gave him courage. They took to the floor and began swaying slowly to the music. The next song, 'Move Closer' by Phyllis Nelson, couldn't have been more appropriate, so they did. Sean could feel the warm, slender contours of her body as they gyrated to the music. His heart raced and he sensed a tightening in his groin. From the waist down he had no control over his own body which seemed to respond instinctively. He felt the cool touch of her skin and could smell the intoxifying, heady scent of her perfume. It was Opium, his favourite, and one of the few he could actually smell, for he had broken his nose several times playing rugby and as a result lost some of his sense of smell.

Sean wasn't aware that the music had stopped until Akinyi whispered in his ear that they should rejoin the others at the table. The night continued in a light-hearted manner and it was 2.30 before Sean finally collapsed into bed, the worst for wear with far too much beer inside him, and drifted into a fitful sleep.

It was another early start the following morning and the next three days passed in a similar way. Business was brisk and Sean was pleased with the response to the product. Each evening he took Akinyi out to dinner, either on her own or with potential customers.

Sean thought he had fallen in love. At least he believed it was love, because he had never felt like he felt before now. If this was love, he wanted more of it. But there was a slight problem. Akinyi told him she used to have a German boyfriend, Hans, whom she had met at Heidelberg University. They had been together for six years but towards the end of 1988 the relationship had begun to falter. It was only recently that they had broken up. Hans came from a small village in Germany and while at University, where student life had a more cosmopolitan feel, he was able to adjust to being with Akinyi. However, he was very conscious of her being black. With the rise of nationalism in Germany he became increasingly embarrassed about Akinyi, especially when he returned to his home village. His friends and family told him that he should marry a white girl. If he married a black girl, they said, it would not help his future career as an accountant in Germany.

'He began to bend to peer pressure and eventually we split up,' said Akinyi. 'I was very upset as I loved him and felt that my colour should not have been an issue. If he loved me as another human being, he should have been strong enough to overcome other people's prejudices and accept me.'

'You seem very hurt,' sympathized Sean.

'Of course I am. I loved him very much.'

'I'm so sorry.' He touched her arm in a gesture of reassurance.

'I felt so let down again. I really thought I'd found that special someone who could give me the love and affection I craved.'

Sean found it a bit unnerving that she was telling him all this. He sensed she was still grieving over the breakup of her relationship, and knew a romance with her was out of the question at the moment. He wondered why she had confided in him. Perhaps it was because she hoped he would have the objectivity of a stranger.

On the final day of the conference Sean took Akinyi to Cologne railway station to catch her train back to Heidelberg. It was there that he gave her a small momento: a solid gold chain. Ostensibly, it was to thank her for her work, but, more than that, he wanted to convey his feelings towards her. He had never given a woman anything like that before. It was a spur-of-the-moment thing. He had only ever given Sally flowers on her birthday or anniversary. He had broken new ground, and he felt good.

They stood on the railway platform and exchanged telephone numbers. It was the usual 'If you're ever in England or Germany again, contact me'. They shook hands. The familiar electric feeling coursed through Sean's fingers and radiated all over his body. They let go, and Sean turned and walked slowly down the platform, raising his arm in a backwards wave. He didn't expect he'd ever see Akinyi again.

CHAPTER 5

Sean returned to England a changed man. He knew he was unlikely to contact Akinyi in the immediate future. He was too busy over the next few months with more sales conferences for other clients with other products.

He was restless. Meeting Akinyi had unsettled him. He wanted to experience a different environment, a new culture, and Akinyi's stories had captured his imagination. He knew Africa was the place he wanted to be most of all.

Days and weeks passed by, until one evening, after he had returned from a five-mile run in the cool of a summer's evening, the telephone rang. Sean guessed it was probably his daughter Louise; she hadn't called him that week – or even someone from the tennis club wanting to arrange a game. He picked up the phone and said, 'Hello'.

An unmistakable voice on the other end said, 'Hello Sean. How are you?'

Sean was momentarily taken aback. He had pushed all thoughts of contact with Akinyi to one side. There was a sudden rush of adrenaline; his body began to tingle.

'Hi, it's good to hear from you – and how are you?'

Akinyi was well and had been attending a few seminars. Other than that she was continuing with her studies.

'I am currently writing my thesis on "A Comparison of the Black Holocaust through History with the Jewish Holocaust",' she said.

They indulged in small talk for a while before Akinyi said suddenly, 'This may seem like a strange request but I would like you to come and spend a weekend with me in Frankfurt. I have a friend who lives there and we can stay at her place.'

Sean was completely taken aback. In fact he was surprised beyond belief. But it only took him a few seconds to say 'Yes'. Normally a Mr Cool, he just couldn't stop himself. They talked some more and arranged to meet in Frankfurt on 19 June, exactly four months to the day after they had first met. Sean said he would contact Akinyi again after he had arranged his flight. He was very excited when he put the phone down and took a deep breath. He then went to the kitchen, pulled a cold beer from the fridge and sat in the garden contemplating the telephone call. Even then he couldn't begin to realize how much it was going to change his life.

That night he couldn't sleep properly because of the excitement. He ended up cat napping, until he awoke to the sound of the alarm clock. He had the feeling he had only just gone to sleep and was trying to work out why the alarm had gone off so soon. Perhaps he had miscalculated the setting, but he hadn't; it really was seven o'clock in the morning. He dragged himself from bed, showered and went down to breakfast. The first thing he did after he had eaten was to visit travel agents in Richmond where he booked a flight for 18.55 out of Heathrow on the 19th. He then drove to his office. That night he phoned Akinyi to let her know his flight arrangements. They talked for maybe ten minutes and Sean promised Akinyi that he would telephone again on the 18th to confirm his arrival time.

The next three weeks seemed like three years. Although Sean tried to concentrate on his work it was difficult. He found the best way to relax was to go for a five-mile run or spend a couple of hours at the gym. Although he no longer played rugby he still kept in pretty good shape. Lots of thoughts went through his mind. He thought about his life to date; the things he had done wrong and the things he had done right. He didn't know what to expect of his forthcoming weekend in Frankfurt, but he was looking forward to it just the same.

Eventually Thursday 18 June arrived and he telephoned Akinyi that evening. Their conversation was very short and matter of fact. They both seemed nervous, yet it was obvious there was much anticipation – if not expectation – on both sides. Strangely, Sean slept well that night.

CHAPTER 6

Sean had taken the day off work so that he would feel fresh for his weekend. He packed a few things in his holdall, as it was only going to be a short trip, and at 5.30 headed for the airport, about twenty minutes away. He went to the long-term car park and hopped on the bus to Terminal 2. He was flying with Lufthansa. After checking in he went through passport control and still had time to have a quick look in the duty-free shop. On the spur of the moment he decided to buy Akinyi a bottle of Opium perfume. He remembered the night they had danced in Cologne and, although perfume might be too intimate a gift on this occasion, he would chance it.

The flight to Frankfurt was just under two hours, so with touch-down at 21.50 local time Sean spent the flight reading *Time Magazine* while downing a couple of large whiskies to calm his nerves. He had a strange feeling. It was like the hour before a major international rugby match: a mixture of nerves, fear, anticipation of the future and a certain confidence that everything was going to be okay.

As he carried only a small holdall he was through passport control and customs within fifteen minutes of landing.

The automatic doors opened at the end of the customs hall and he strode through looking left and right. He didn't see Akinyi straight away. She, however, was watching him from halfway behind a pillar, some twenty yards away. She moved slightly to one side and then he spotted her. His heart raced – it was that feeling again. Remembering Tom Cruise and Kelly McGillis in *Top Gun*, he imagined he could hear the soundtrack of 'You Take My Breath Away'. He moved a bit quicker now and as he reached Akinyi he took her hand. At the same time he self-consciously kissed her on the cheek, flushing a little with embarrassment, his awkwardness more acute than ever.

They stood and looked at each other for a minute or two saying nothing – but still holding hands. Akinyi looked very stylish in a body-hugging, black jump-suit that highlighted her hour-glass figure. She wore a pair of elegant black patent shoes. She looked even more beautiful than Sean remembered. He had dressed very casually in a pair of Khaki Chinos with a pale blue shirt unbuttoned at the neck. Although he wasn't scruffy, he momentarily wished he had made more effort to look smarter.

It was Akinyi who spoke first. 'It's really good to see you, Sean,' she said in a hoarse whisper.

'So where are we staying?' He was secretly hoping for a double room in a hotel.

'Oh, I thought I told you. We're staying at a friend's place. She's away this weekend but she said we could use her apartment.'

Sean realized that he had embarrassed her by bringing up the subject so abruptly.

'As you've arrived so late, Sean, I've prepared a meal for us. It's a chance for you to try some Kenyan food and get a taste of Africa,' said Akinyi, jokingly.

It broke the ice a little and they headed for the car park where they jumped into Akinyi's battered VW Beetle. As she drove towards the city, Sean filled her in on what he had been doing for the last couple of months. A business trip to Italy and one to America for a further meeting with Charlie and Geoff, to discuss an agency agreement. Both trips had been successful and he expected a lot of business to follow.

'What's your friend's name?' asked Sean.

'Her name is Muthoni. She is of the Kikuyu people. Like you, Sean, they are business people and she is usually away on business.'

Akinyi drove well on the way back to the apartment. It was almost midsummer night and was still very light. There was little traffic on the road from the airport, but as they neared the city centre the roads became busier and the sounds of the traffic became noisier. It was a warm evening and they passed several bars and cafes where people were still sitting outside drinking and eating. As they arrived at the private apartment block, Akinyi parked the car in Muthoni's allocated space. Sean removed his holdall from the boot and Akinyi led him through the reception doors. Muthoni's apartment was on the third floor. The lift wasn't working, so they climbed the three flights of stairs and entered the property. It was a small two-bedroomed apartment, quite modern and well furnished. Akinyi offered Sean a beer which he gratefully accepted. He needed a beer. She poured herself a glass of wine and together they went and sat in the living room. Akinyi leaned over to switch on the cassette player – the first bars of 'Red, Red, Wine' struck up and Sean was taken back to their first dance in Cologne. It was at this moment that he remembered the perfume in his bag. He reached across, pulled it out and handed it to Akinyi.

'Just a little something for you,' he said.

Akinyi smiled, reached up and kissed Sean on the cheek, at the same time placing her right hand on his left shoulder. 'Oh thank you Sean,' she gushed excitedly as she withdrew her hand quickly and opened the bottle. She sprayed a small amount of the perfume on to the back of her hand and raised it to her nostrils, breathing in gently.

'Oh it smells lovely Sean, thank you,' she repeated as she stepped forward again and gave him another kiss on the cheek. She turned, placing the bottle of perfume on the table near her.

The next song was 'Move Closer'.

'That's a coincidence,' said Sean. 'A touch of déjà vu. Haven't we been here before?' He smiled.

Akinyi moved closer. She placed her arms around his shoulders and fixed her gorgeous brown eyes on him, saying softly, 'Dance with me, Sean.'

They both rose and Sean took her in his arms; it was a good feeling to be holding her again. She was wearing a black, zipped jumpsuit and looked stunning. He breathed deeply, taking in her sweet, intoxicating scent. He could feel the contours of her womanly body under the close-fitting garment, which clung to her in all the right places. She was conciously pressing against him. His pulse quickened. She raised her head and he kissed her lightly on the mouth. Her eyes were closed and a soft smile played across her lips. He bent further, kissing the velvet smooth skin at the base of her neck and sucking gently on the soft, swollen lobe of her left ear. Her chest heaved, and she groaned aloud, 'I love you Sean.'

The music had come to an end. They walked entwined into the bedroom . . . Her hands flicked deftly at the buttons on his fly and they both fell down on the bed together. They began kissing in earnest, long and deep, his hands urgently seeking out and undoing her zip to reveal firm, round breasts with dark protruding nipples that stood to attention as he tweaked them gently. His temples were throbbing now, and tiny beads of sweat glistened on his forehead. He reached out to kiss her breasts, soliciting a low moan. It was not long before they were both naked and wrapped in each other's arms. Akinyi could feel the warm touch of Sean's practised hands beneath her ample buttocks as he gently encouraged her hips upwards, kissing her tenderly all the while . . . As he entered her, she moaned softly and gasped for air. He thought his heart would burst with the emotion that swelled up inside him. His movements were gently rhythmical, becoming more earnest as they reached orgasm and climaxed together. A moment or two of silence followed, before he looked deep into her eyes and bent to kiss her gently, ever so gently, on the lips.

'I'm in love with the most beautiful woman in the world,' he said. His mouth lingered on hers.

Akinyi's eyes filled with joy; she had never been happier. 'You know, Sean, from the first moment I saw you I knew I could love you.' She stared longingly at him.

Sean rolled over on to his side and put a finger to her lips to silence her. 'Let's savour the moment,' he said, and pulled her closer to him.

Akinyi quietly reflected on her discovery. She had been attracted to Sean from the first moment they had met but wasn't sure if she had fallen in love. She admired the way he conducted himself quietly with other people; his easy-going manner contrasted well with his extrovert personality. She could no longer contain herself.

'Sean, you have an inner energy and strength that I have never before seen or experienced in a man. I have fallen in love with you,' she stammered.

'Steady on', he replied, 'I'm just an ordinary guy.'

'No Sean, you are not. I fell in love with you the night we danced in Cologne without knowing it. Now I give you all of my love for 365 days of the year – for the next 100 years.'

'I bet you say that to all your boy friends,' Sean joked.

But Akinyi was deadly serious. 'Please don't mock me.'

'I'm sorry, I didn't mean to sound flippant. I really was only joking.'

Akinyi accepted his apology and they both laughed nervously. Eventually they drifted into a tired but contented sleep and made love again when they awoke. For the second time Sean felt that exploding, floating, falling feeling. He suddenly realized that he had never before truly made love to a woman. His affairs, both before and after marriage, didn't compare with his early love of Sally. But he had never had this depth of feeling for anyone; the all-consuming love that now burned within him for Akinyi.

He wrapped his arms around her and held her tight. He would never let her go.

That weekend they never left the apartment. They slept, they ate and most of all they made love. Sean was a very fit thirty-seven-year-old while Akinyi's appetite was unrelenting.

During periods of rest Akinyi continued her life story which she had begun in Cologne. When she had first arrived in Heidelberg she lived for two years in halls of residence but in her third year she decided to move out into a flat of her own. She explained how she had had great difficulty in finding one.

'I used to respond to newspaper adverts for accommodation by telephone. I was told that the flat or room was available, but within the fifteen or twenty minutes it took to travel to the place – I would find that it had been mysteriously let. On the phone there would be no trace of a foreign accent in my voice, but on arrival the landlord would see that I was black – a 'Schwarzer' as they say in Germany – and that's how it usually ended.'

She went on to explain that on another occasion when she found a place owned by a famous German socialist politician, she actually moved in. When she arrived the place was in a disgusting state so she spent every night and the first weekend cleaning it from top to bottom. When she finished, she felt she had at last got her own home. But sadly there was a bombshell. The neighbours didn't like living next door to, or in the same block of apartments as, a black person and put pressure on the house agent to force Akinyi to leave. On her tenth day in the apartment, there was a knock on the door early one evening. It was the politician's lawyer and he served her an eviction order because she had thrown out an old doormat that had almost fallen apart. Akinyi couldn't believe it. The incident distressed her. Their prejudice really hurt.

The old doormat had just been a pathetic excuse to get rid of her. She had done nothing wrong. Although she wanted to fight, she knew the odds were stacked against her – and she would have to leave. She then had to start looking for another place all over again. As luck would have it, she found a flatshare within days with two other girl students.

Akinyi talked more about her experiences and the racial prejudices she suffered. For example, one day in a park in Berlin she was suddenly attacked by a well-dressed, respectable looking middle-aged man and his wife, walking their dog. They hit her and spat in her face, pushing her over and shouting a tirade of abuse.

'Schwarzers should get out of Germany,' they screamed. Nobody came to help Akinyi. Somehow she managed to get up and run away. With tears streaming down her face she ran to the edge of the park and lay down, sobbing uncontrollably until an elderly man came and sat with her. He asked what the problem was. Akinyi turned and looked up at him. He had a kindly face. She began telling him about the terrible unhappiness she felt because of the prejudice against her from some German people. He urged her to try not to worry and told her about the time he had spent in concentration camps during the war. He explained he was a Polish Jew and had been four years in Dachau before being released by the Americans.

'I still can't forget the satanic wickedness and ungodliness that my captors sank to in the way in which they treated me and my fellow prisoners.'

He still carried the number that had been tattooed on his arm, but worse still, he continued to carry the mental anguish and pain, even after forty-five years.

'I saw my mother, father and little sister being forced to walk into the gas chambers by their German guards,' he whispered.

Akinyi could see the tears welling up in his eyes and realized that he had suffered far worse than she had ever done. She vowed then that she would be strong and fought back the tears. She decided she would stand up for herself in the future. Even if people broke her bones, she knew they would never break her spirit.

The man took her for a cup of tea at a small Konditerei on the edge of the park. They talked for perhaps a further hour, before the old man unexpectedly got up from his chair, raised his hat to Akinyi and left some money for the tea on the table. He thanked her for her good company and turned and walked up the road. Akinyi called after him, thanking him for his kindness. She never saw him again, but she never forgot him.

Sean sensed the hurt that Akinyi suffered. She became very emotional and began to cry softly. He pulled her to him; he felt the warm tears running down her cheeks on to his chest. He let her cry. He felt powerless to help her. All he could do was comfort her in the best way he knew how.

It was two o'clock on Sunday afternoon and the phone was ringing. They still had a little more time on their own as Sean's flight home wasn't until 17.30.

'That was Muthoni,' she said, replacing the receiver. 'She will be here in two hours. Come on, Sean, it's time you got up!' She gave him a gentle nudge, adding, 'There's room in the shower for two.'

They showered together, dressed and Sean helped prepare a lunch of cheese, ham and French bread, which they enjoyed with the bottle of well-chilled Chablis that he had brought with him.

It was at this moment that he asked Akinyi to take him to Kenya. He was due some holiday and he could manage three weeks in August.

Akinyi was doubtful about Sean's intentions.

'So that's what you want from me. You just want me to take you to Africa.'

'No,' Sean retaliated, 'it's much more than that. I want to be with you – and if I can spend time with you in your own country it would be truly wonderful. Besides which, I need a tour guide,' he joked.

Put like that, Akinyi immediately agreed and they decided that they would stay in Mombasa for a couple of weeks and spend a further week in Nairobi, taking in a three-day safari in the Masai Mara Game Reserve. Sean said he would book it when he got home. Akinyi had no problem with dates in August as it was part of the university vacation.

Muthoni arrived at two o'clock and bounced confidently into the living room. She smiled at Sean and said something to Akinyi in a language he didn't understand. It caused Akinyi to giggle. Sean was momentarily embarrassed but offered his hand in greeting to Muthoni. He poured her a glass of wine and they all sat down.

Muthoni was smaller than Akinyi, with light-coloured skin and a soft complexion. She obviously took great care of her skin. Her hair was similar to Akinyi's in that it was in long, fine braids.

During the polite conversation that followed, Muthoni told Sean how she had been married to a German who had worked for the Goethe Institute in Nairobi for a couple of years. She had since settled in

Germany and was now working for an advertising agency.

It was not long before it was time for Sean to leave. It took him only a couple of minutes to pack his holdall. He said goodbye to Muthoni and together he and Akinyi went downstairs to her car.

The journey to the airport seemed to go by in a flash. Sean checked in and they headed to a restaurant for a coffee, where they sat looking at each other without saying much. The call for Sean's flight over the tannoy broke their silence. They got up and walked slowly towards the departure gate. They were both deep in thought.

'Goodbye Sean,' Akinyi said. 'I have just had the most wonderful weekend of my life. You have made me come alive.'

'Me too,' said Sean. He hated goodbyes. 'I will call you tonight when I get back.' As he walked through the departure gate he turned and waved to Akinyi.

Once on board Sean very quickly dozed off. He felt a mixture of elation and exhaustion. Akinyi had worn him out. He slept soundly until they arrived at Heathrow. He disembarked and went through customs – nothing to declare. He hadn't even bothered to buy any duty-free. Walking quickly out of the terminal he hopped on the bus to the long-term car park and collected his car. It was a black Porsche 911 Targa – one of his few material indulgences, and Sean liked it. Not only that, he liked driving fast. He decided that one day he would drive over to see Akinyi in Germany and find out how the car could really perform on the autobahns. Meanwhile he just dawdled through the dense traffic, back to his house in Richmond. It was shortly after seven and a beautiful summer evening, but the roads were busy with people returning to London after a weekend in the country.

The first thing Sean did when he got home was to dial Muthoni's number.

'Hello, Sean, I guessed it would be you. I'll just get Akinyi.'

Akinyi came to the phone and they talked for over an hour. Sean knew this would be the start of a series of hefty phone bills but he felt it was worth it. They arranged to speak again the following night after Sean had booked the holiday.

Sean wouldn't see Akinyi again until 2 August when she would spend a few days with him in Richmond prior to flying to Kenya. It was about six weeks away but seemed like an eternity.

At the travel agents the next day Sean booked a double room for three weeks at The Indian Ocean Hotel in Mombasa, where, it turned out, Akinyi had stayed as a child. He planned to take the overnight train from Mombasa to Nairobi and then travel by jeep to Masai Mara. However, he didn't raise this with the travel agent as he wanted to arrange that locally to get a better deal. Sean always enjoyed the fun of bartering, even if he ended up unknowingly paying more than he should; it was the sport of it and the wheeling and dealing that he liked.

CHAPTER 7

This time it was Sean meeting Akinyi at the airport. Like Akinyi, he too would wait behind a pillar, just out of sight of the arrivals door. He wanted to observe her for a few extra moments as she emerged from the customs hall. She eventually appeared and Sean watched as he remembered the first time he saw her. Again she seemed to glide, rather than walk. Her head was held high and slightly back. Her braided hair, decorated with bright coloured beads, swayed gently about her shoulders. She looked angry, but then a huge smile lit up her face as she saw Sean. She ran to him and threw her arms around him. He could feel her heart beating excitedly as she held him close.

Akinyi was bursting to speak. 'I've missed you *so* much, Sean.' Her smile faded. 'The immigration officer stopped me because of my colour.'

'How do you know that it was because you are black?' Sean was concerned.

'I watched all the immigration officials and the only people they stopped were black. I even suggested to the man that he had stopped me specifically because of my colour. He replied that he was only doing his job. I then asked him why he hadn't stopped any white people, and he seemed to have no answer.'

Sean sympathized with Akinyi's frustration. 'I know it's easy for me to say because I don't know, and will never know, how it feels to be black, but you must try and relax. Racism is ugly in all its forms. We can only hope that one day black and white people will learn to treat each other as equals. The more travelled and educated people become, the easier it will be to break down such barriers.' He sighed, and touched her cheek gently. 'Anyway, we now have four whole weeks together. Let's try and enjoy every moment,' he said, skilfully changing the subject.

They walked arm in arm to the car. Akinyi's suitcase only just fitted in the boot.

'Is this yours, Sean?' She seemed genuinely surprised. 'You never told me you had a Porsche! If only my friends could see me now.'

'Actually, it's not my car. I just nicked it from down the road,' Sean said, keeping a straight face.

Akinyi was shocked. 'You didn't really, did you Sean?' she said, gazing at him with big brown eyes.

'What do you think? Do you really believe I nicked this?'

Akinyi looked at him without replying, realizing he was teasing her.

'Would you like to drive it?' asked Sean.

'No, I couldn't,' said Akinyi. 'I'm far too nervous.'

They soon arrived at Sean's house. He had left a bottle of champagne in the fridge, in anticipation of Akinyi's arrival. He picked up two glasses and the chilled champagne and led her to the bedroom. For a while they sat on the bed talking and sipping the cold, bubbly liquid. Neither was used to drinking during the day so the champagne made them feel light-headed. They made love. It was a long time before they eventually fell asleep in each other's arms.

When they woke it was nearly dark. Sean had booked a table for 9.30 at a small Italian restaurant on Richmond High Street. It was only a short walk but as they were running late they decided to take a taxi instead. It gave them time to shower and get ready.

CHAPTER 8

During dinner Sean told Akinyi about his life. He had been born in 1953, the year of the Coronation of Queen Elizabeth II, and was the middle one of three children, with an elder brother, John, and a younger sister, Christina. Throughout his late teens Sean had been regarded as a bit of a rebel. He left school at eighteen in 1971 with eight O and three A levels. The late sixties and early seventies were a time of hippies and flower-power and Sean felt he was a product of the 'swinging sixties'. He had been given the choice by his parents to go either to boarding school or to the local grammar school. His decision hinged on his surprise success in the common entrance exams, which he passed with flying colours. Indeed, if he had applied for a scholarship before the exams he would have attained one easily.

His father, a journalist on the *Sunday Times,* had left the newspaper at the age of thirty-five to set up his own publishing business. He produced a selection of popular motorsport magazines as well as a local free advertising paper. In addition, he played the stock market, and made a number of successful investments in the mid-sixties which enabled the family to achieve a level of prosperity beyond their dreams.

Sean enjoyed school but had the severe challenge of following in the footsteps of his elder brother, who had been school captain five years earlier and had excelled academically as well as on the sports field. John had captained the school rugby and cricket teams and had also played hockey at county level for Surrey. He left school aged eighteen and won a place at Fitzwilliam College, Cambridge to read economics and politics.

Sean was a clever student and did just enough to achieve a pass with the minimum of effort. He was good at hockey and cricket but excelled at rugby. He played at fullback and, while still technically a member of the Colts XV, was selected for the First XV a month or two before his sixteenth birthday. In his first full year with the First XV he became the record points scorer of all time at the school, kicking fifty goals, three drop goals and scoring ten tries. In addition, he was selected to play for Surrey Schools. The following year he made it to the England Schools Trials and played for England Schoolboys against Wales, Scotland, Ireland and the touring Australian Schoolboy Team.

His future in rugby had looked rosy. When he left school he didn't go to university. His grades at A level had been rather poor, although through his father's connections he could have taken up a place at Bradford University to read Business Studies or gone to Oxford

Polytechnic. But deep down Sean knew he would be wasting his time at university so he opted to go on a banking course just to appease his father. He hated every minute of it. That way of life was too regimented for Sean. He was a free spirit and many people regarded him as anti-authority and rebellious because he didn't like to kowtow to anyone. He wanted to do his own thing. He left his banking job after a few months, and a lengthy period of unemployment followed.

At one stage he had attended an interview for a job as a merchandizing salesman for Mars. He had had all the qualifications for the job but was refused the post because of his long hair. Looking back, he now realized how arrogant and immature it had been of him to attend an interview for a salesman's job with such long hair. In the meantime he was playing club rugby for London Scottish 1st XV and, during his second season, he received a telephone call from the Scottish selectors to attend a trial.

Having turned out for England Schools he had always hankered after playing for England, but he was also eligible to represent either Ireland or Scotland, owing to his parents' nationality. Scotland's offer of a trial was very flattering and, after much deliberation, he accepted. He attended the final trial at Murrayfield on the first Saturday in January and was selected for the Whites (the Possibles) against the Blues (the Probables).

That day Sean played well. He was one of the best at the trial and was duly selected for Scotland for the opening Five Nations Match against Ireland at Lansdowne Road in Dublin. Again he played well, Scotland winning nineteen to thirteen in a hard-fought contest.

He had managed to get tickets for the entire family. His mother was so proud of him that day. He remembered watching his parents in the grandstand as the national anthems were being played. His parents were both quiet people. They didn't converse much but he knew his mother was always there for him. Sean was close to his mother. He remembered well the time he had come home to tell his parents that he was divorcing Sally. His mother, seeing his distress, had hugged him warmly and told him she loved him and her granddaughter, Louise, and that she would always support him.

Sean was taken aback by his mother telling him she loved him. She had brought him up well and cared for all her children but had never shown much outward sign of emotion. Her declaration was to have a lasting effect on Sean.

Conversely, he had never got on too well with his father. They were always arguing. Sean's father was a disciplinarian. He was a military man and had very old-fashioned principles. He found it difficult to accept that Sean was growing up in a different way to his own rigid lifestyle.

Sean liked discussion and debate, but he did not have any particularly strong views on anything. He was good at starting a discussion and getting others involved, but had an amazing ability to walk away, leaving everyone else in the midst of heated arguments.

Sean's father, on the other hand, had very strong views. Sean never understood this. He felt that if someone went too far in one direction or another, he or she could never make a completely sound judgement about anything, particularly with regard to religion or politics. It was the headmaster of Sean's school, though, who probably had the most profound effect on him. He was something of a liberal. Although he followed a strict moral code of conduct, he allowed a good deal of freedom of thought and expression, an attitude that would help Sean later in life. It was strange, but with this point of view Sean had been successful so far with almost everything he had ever done. He seemed to take most things in his stride. If he applied himself, he normally achieved more than the average amount of success, particularly in business or sport. There was, however, one exception – women. He had failed in his marriage and other relationships had never really got off the ground. He was probably too laid back. If he liked a woman and took her out a few times, he expected her to realize that he was content and happy in her company and would be pleased to continue or develop a longer-term relationship without being too assertive. Perhaps it was because he was normally attracted to – or was found to be attractive by – extrovert, bubbly women. On the face of it, this type of woman usually appeared confident, but deep down was often very insecure. Sean didn't help the insecurity of such women by his apparent indifference to their feelings.

Akinyi was not the first woman to mention this. Others had commented that he appeared to have control of himself and his life. He seemed to have achieved inner peace. Nothing much fazed him. It was very rare that he lost his temper. He would often sit and daydream, even in someone else's company. His daughter, Louise, saw these characteristics quite clearly and would often make fun of him, saying: 'Knock, knock, Earth to Mars. Daddy, is there anybody there?'

Sometimes, in conversation with someone, he often felt he wasn't really there; he was one or two steps ahead and thinking his own thoughts.

In spite of all this, Sean was fairly content in life. So far he had had a lot of fun. He had taken up Formula Ford racing one summer with mixed success. He enjoyed the excitement and thrill of speed and had actually managed three third places at Brands Hatch. Generally, though, he finished in the lower part of the top ten. He eventually decided that perhaps he didn't have what it took to be a top racing driver so, in his usual laid back manner, he moved on.

Sean devoted the few days before they left for Kenya to sightseeing with Akinyi. They visited various places in London as well as other places such as Windsor Castle and Hampton Court Palace. He had never felt so relaxed in anyone's company. With Akinyi he was able to talk freely and openly. He found her interesting and exciting and she had the ability to discuss a huge range of topics, some of which Sean had never really considered. She had a strong character and a strong social conscience, and he thought some of what she said sounded very left wing. He had always held fairly conservative views, mainly because he generally mixed with people with similar ideas. Previously he had dismissed anyone with left wing attitudes as being too radical but Akinyi seemed to put things in a way that he understood, and could even identify with to a certain extent.

CHAPTER 9

Sean's first impression of Kenya was on arrival at Moi International Airport in Mombasa, where they stepped off the plane at eleven o'clock on a lovely morning. He was hit by the most searing heat and humidity he had ever experienced. Once before, in Atlanta, he had felt almost total humidity, but this was different. By the time he had walked down the steps of the plane and across the tarmac to passport control, he was dripping wet. He was welcomed by the immigration officer with a huge friendly smile and the greeting 'Jambo', Kiswahili for 'hello'. The officer stamped Sean's passport and spoke briefly to Akinyi before they moved on to collect their luggage.

From there they met their tour guide, a very tall girl of about twenty years of age. Her name was Charity Waweru. She directed them to their bus, and within half an hour they were at their hotel on the north side of Mombasa. It was a small, friendly hotel built in traditional African style, with the main reception and bar area covered with *makuti* roofing. The *makuti* roofing made the building look rather like an English thatched house, except that *makuti* is made out of dried leaves from palm trees rather than straw.

Sean and Akinyi were tired after their long, eleven-hour flight but they were both excited. Sean, because this was a new experience, and Akinyi, because she was returning to her homeland. They went to their room which was in a little round house set in the gardens of the hotel. They showered and changed into shorts and T-shirts.

They decided to take a walk along the beach before exploring the hotel grounds. The tide was out and the sea was about one hundred metres back towards the reef. It was a beautiful sight. There was hardly anyone on the beach, which stretched for miles, except for a few beach boys selling their arts and crafts. They were the kings of barter. Their prices were always ridiculously high to start with, but after bartering with tourists the prices would drop dramatically. Sean enjoyed the cut and thrust of the bartering process and had soon purchased some wooden animals. He quickly realized that he would never be bored in Kenya. He could sit for hours looking at the blue waters of the Indian Ocean, thinking nothing much about anything – or he could stroll for hours along the beach stopping to chat to the beach boys or mamas selling their *kangas*. Unlike some of the tourists he was not bothered by the traders. Sean realized they were only trying to earn a living and normally a smile or a firm 'no' would stop them bothering him. He was on holiday and had plenty of time. He couldn't see the point of getting frustrated or uptight about anything.

Akinyi took Sean on the local buses, as well as on the *matatus*, which were small, privately owned public service vehicles. They could travel for ten miles for about ten shillings each, which was equivalent to about ten pence in England. He wanted to enjoy as much of the local life and customs as possible.

One day Sean and Akinyi listened with great amusement to two girls on the bus who were talking about men. One told her friend that she was busy trying to find a *muzungu*, Kiswahili for a European, to marry her and take her away to a better life. The other one said she had left her husband because he had complained she was no good at making love and couldn't give him babies. He told her to go away and get experience with other men. She had done so and was recounting to her friend that she had been with German, Japanese, American, Danish and English men and that she now felt ready to go home to her husband to make babies!

Akinyi explained to Sean that because she was with him her fellow Kenyans would think that she was one of the local girls who only went out with white men because of their money.

'They don't realize we met almost five thousand miles away and that I fell in love with you after a chance meeting.'

They weren't to know that she wasn't one of the local girls – who were known as butterflies – or, in Kiswahili, *kipepapeo* – who went with rich tourists old enough to be their fathers.

Akinyi was exasperated.

'Don't worry about it, we know different, don't we?' said Sean, teasing her.

'Of course,' snapped Akinyi, who didn't appreciate his sense of humour.

'You can't blame the girls,' said Sean. 'They are only doing it to survive. If the economy was stronger and there were decent jobs available, most of the girls wouldn't be doing what they are doing now.'

Some of the girls got lucky and married Europeans, who looked after them and took them back to Europe. Others, sadly, were less fortunate and were taken back to Europe and forced into a modern-day slave trade. Those who managed to escape often landed right back where they started, hoping for another chance.

Sean and Akinyi went to nearby bars and listened to the local music. He found the African musicians and African sounds incredibly exciting. It was lively, vibrant music with a good beat – and the dancing was fantastic. Everyone had such rhythm and could move to the music in a way that Sean had seen few white people do.

He was having a fabulous time in Kenya. It seemed that he was a million miles from home. Of course, there were things he saw that were disturbing. He saw abject poverty; he saw beggars on the streets; he saw the homeless, the like of which he had not seen before.

One day they took the ferry from Mombasa Island to the south coast. Sean's immediate impression of the Likoni Ferry was a mass of people packed tightly on board, surrounded by a few vehicles. He watched from a distance as they alighted. It was like observing an army of ants suddenly springing into life and dispersing in many different directions.

Sean and Akinyi ambled through the street markets, which were a hive of activity. He watched as people got on and off the *matatus*. These minibuses were designed to take twelve to fifteen passengers, but actually carried twice as many! There always seemed to be room for one more! It seemed like good business to have a *matatu*. Sean found out that within a year an owner-driver could afford to buy two more. It was the cheapest form of transport and, as most people could not afford to buy a car, it was the most flexible form of travel as the *matatus* stopped on request at almost any point along a route. Most were gaily decorated and painted, and throbbed to the sound of loud music, with a volume control that had one level only – loud! To travel on one was an experience not to be missed. In Sean's mind, the drivers would probably be better suited to the race track or rallying, such were their amazingly daring overtaking manoeuvres. Some wouldn't have been out of place on dodgem cars at a fairground. It was a way of life. Each *matatu* had a name such as 'The Rapper', 'Malcolm X', 'The Purple People Eater', 'The Lover', 'Shadow Fox', 'Funky Boy', 'Happy Time' and so on.

Akinyi took Sean to Tsavo East. It was a one-day safari before they went on their main three-day trip to the Maasai Mara. They rose at 4.30 a.m. and were on the road by 5.15 to make the two-hour drive to the edge of Tsavo. They were with other tourists and Sean and Akinyi were greatly amused by one particular girl from Birmingham. She was about twenty and her name was Tracey. She was a hairdresser and talked with that twangy sing-song Brummie accent that had always got on Sean's nerves. At the first stop for coffee at about seven o'clock Tracey, who was dressed in white high heels and a white mini skirt, decided to go to the toilet. Within minutes she rushed back to her boyfriend and told him that the door was locked. He very dryly said that someone was probably already in there and told her to go and try again. Seconds later she tottered back on her high heels saying that the toilet was a hole in the ground and that she couldn't possibly use it.

The next stop was at a game lodge at eleven o'clock in the middle of Tsavo National Park. By this time Tracey was crossing her legs in desperation. When the driver stopped she was the first to jump off the bus and run to the toilet. Again she came racing back within seconds, screaming that there was a snake in the toilet. By the time they reached Voi Lodge for lunch the poor girl was in a terrible state.

During the safari they saw elephants, giraffes, cheetahs, lions, wildebeest, and many other animals. Sean was overawed by the sight of all those animals roaming wild in their natural environment. He had been to zoos and the safari park at Windsor but this was different. The other thing that would remain imprinted on his mind was the view from Voi Lodge. It was set high up on a hill and you could see for miles across the plains. It was breathtaking and it was only then that Sean came to appreciate the vastness of the land. Coming from a small country like England, he found it hard to contemplate the sheer size of Kenya, let alone a continent like Africa.

Akinyi told Sean that Lake Victoria, where she came from, was bigger than Scotland.

He had not only fallen deeply in love with Akinyi; he had fallen in love with Kenya. He could sit and listen to Akinyi for hours, as he could sit and watch the tranquility of the ocean or listen to the sounds of the African night – the wind whispering through the palms, the bullfrogs croaking and the chatter of the crickets.

The eerie quietness of Africa by night contrasted starkly with the continuous hum or buzz that existed during the day. It was as though Sean could hear the sound of the local drums at play. There was a rhythm to the sound of the night. And the sky was mesmerizing. Its clearness and the bright yellow stars gave Sean the feeling that he was floating away into the great black void of outer space. Tumbling, sweeping and soaring into the distance, just like their lovemaking.

One night, as Sean and Akinyi sat in a little beach bar looking out across the ocean, they watched as the moon rose from behind a black cloud on the horizon. At first all they could see was a halo of flames surrounding something very dark and mysterious. For a while Sean thought it looked like a ship on fire, far out to sea. But as the cloud started moving upwards off the horizon, the moon appeared to move slightly quicker, and the red flame of the halo became larger and larger until it turned into a yellowish hoop around the darkness of the cloud. For a moment the cloud seemed to remain perfectly still, motionless, as the moon rose high above it, eventually turning into a huge bright, yellow disc that lit up the deep blue waters of the ocean below, reflecting light in all directions. Sean had never seen anything like it before.

CHAPTER 10

By the end of the first week, Sean and Akinyi had become very relaxed in each other's company. Akinyi was impressed by Sean's adaptability to Kenya and his new environment. Although he was a shy man, he was able to talk easily and freely with all kinds of people from all walks of life, regardless of their age. His quiet confidence and abundant personality endeared him to her. She knew she would never love another man like she loved Sean.

On the second Friday they took the train to Nairobi. They booked an overnight sleeper in a first-class compartment, which included dinner in the restaurant car. The train, if not quite the *Orient Express*, took Sean back a hundred years. Solid silver sugar bowls and cutlery were still being used from Victorian times. Waiters in white jackets with gold-braided epaulettes provided the excellent service. Sean and Akinyi ate at the first sitting at 7.30 p.m. and then retired to their sleeper-cabin for the overnight journey. They made love, both of them happier than they had ever been in their lives.

As he drifted off to sleep, the rolling and lurching of the train reminded Sean of an old black and white spy thriller he had seen as a child at the local cinema. He imagined people going in and out of their cabins and snooping along the train corridor. He fully expected a man in a trench coat and fedora hat to appear suddenly and start shooting at the police who were chasing him. Outside all was blackness.

At sunrise at around six o'clock, Sean and Akinyi were awoken by the train grinding to a halt. They peered out of their window and could see clusters of small villages dotted across the landscape. There were signs of life in the compounds as people started to go about their daily duties. Already some women were working in the fields.

The main journey from Mombasa had taken them on a steep climb from jungly coast to arid semi-desert through Voi on the edge of Tsavo East National Park, up through Tsavo to Mtito Andei, Kibwezi, Makindu and Emali, winding across the Athi plains and the National Park to Nairobi. As the train began moving again and they started to approach the city, the speed dropped. They passed dwellings made in the traditional fashion. They saw houses with stone walls interspersed with others made from wood and corrugated iron. As they drew closer to the main station, little children waved and called out to the many tourists leaning out of the train windows. Some tourists began throwing sweets and small mementos – pens and keyrings – to the children, who picked them up as they ran beside the train. When some tourists began throwing biscuits and food into the mud, Akinyi shouted at them to stop. She said it was an abuse and that they shouldn't encourage children to beg – but most important they should not throw food to the children as if they were animals. She asked whether they would do the same in Europe. The tourists became embarrassed and there was an uncomfortable silence. Many of them retreated from the windows, hiding in their cabins. Akinyi then shouted to the children to stop chasing the train and told them to go to school.

Sean was impressed with Akinyi's strength of character and her determination to do what she thought was right, despite what others might think.

Eventually the train came to a halt at Nairobi Station and Akinyi and Sean walked along the platform to the exit. They were met by one of Akinyi's cousins who had invited them to stay. Her name was Atieno and she was a Luo like Akinyi. She came from Kendu Bay alongside Lake Victoria.

Sean and Akinyi spent the next four days touring Nairobi before moving on by jeep to the Maasai Mara Game Reserve, considered to be the best in Kenya. The landscape was sometimes filled with an unlikely combination of animals. Sean surveyed the scene and could see a dozen different species, or more, at any one time, animals such as zebras, giraffes, buffalos and elephants. The Mara Reserve extends along a huge wedge of undulating grassland nearly 2,000 metres above sea level. It is a spectacular place with the Mara, one of Kenya's biggest rivers, running through it. Situated in the remote south-west of Kenya, it is even bigger than the Serengeti plains and game reserve that lie on the other side of the Tanzanian border.

It was while they were in Nairobi that Akinyi began telling Sean about her concerns for her country and the distress that it caused her. She told him that after her degree she had returned to Nairobi to teach at the university. Although she held a first-class master's in German, she was paid the equivalent of only £100 per month. In contrast, one of her European colleagues, a German, was paid the equivalent of £2,000 per month as an expatriate, including expenses such as accommodation. Akinyi explained that this was a common problem all over Africa and not only in Kenya. They had a brain-drain of talented African scientists and academics, who felt forced to work in Europe or America because they were not paid fair and reasonable salaries in Africa. She felt strongly that this was an injustice done to the indigenous people. Nairobi, for example, had a very high standard of living because of the many expatriates working for the United Nations and other non-governmental organizations. But educated Africans could not afford to maintain those standards on local rates of pay.

Akinyi said that one of Africa's great tragedies – in its unenviable catalogue of tragedies – was the historical plundering of its major resources by the colonialists. The mining of gold, diamonds, zinc, copper, and so on, was hugely profitable for the European and American developers because the major work in the mines was carried out by very cheap African labour.

'The early slave trade and the estimated export of more than one hundred million people over the last three hundred years, were among the greatest human tragedies of all time,' Akinyi's voice broke with emotion.

She explained that the continent of Africa had an acute shortage of qualified manpower, yet more than one hundred thousand of its most educated people were working overseas. The irony is that the continent imports a similar number of very highly paid expatriates to oversee its industries and development projects. Studies showed that one of the major problems was a lack of an enabling environment for the benefit of Africa and its professional men and women.

Akinyi said that universities, research institutions and industries which require their skills did not thrive in Africa owing to political instability. In East Africa alone there had been a civil war in almost every second country. Uganda suffered turmoil for almost two decades during Amin's bloodthirsty regime, in which the then middle-class was either killed or forced into exile. Even now, Uganda had problems in attracting professionals back home.

In 1987 the Kenyan government sent a mission to Europe to try to persuade Kenyan professionals to return home to teach in state universities, which were short of staff mainly as a result of significant expansion. The mission came back virtually empty-handed because the pay being offered was very low – what the Americans would call peanuts.

Akinyi was one of the few who returned, but the low salary was insufficient to support her – and after a year she had to return to Europe.

'The employment of expatriates in Kenya has always been a controversial issue, and we claim that in most cases they are not needed,' continued Akinyi.

'Are you sure they're not needed?' queried Sean.

Akinyi laughed. 'Most jobs done by expatriates can be done by locals. But the major problem has been the strings attached to the aid from donors. They insist that use of their funds must be supervised by their own people, as they are fearful of corruption and of the money going astray.'

'Isn't that a perfectly reasonable view?' said Sean. 'If I was funding a project I would expect to be able to choose who I was employing.'

'Of course, that's perfectly reasonable,' she replied. 'But the irony is that some of the expatriates are ripping off their own organizations. In addition, they are highly expensive and end up taking a large chunk of the aid money in their salaries and living expenses.'

'But surely there's a rate for the job, regardless of who gets it, whether it's a local or an expat?' asked Sean.

'It's not as easy as that,' said Akinyi. 'The problem is that Africa is soliciting aid and therefore has to accept the associated conditions. Ultimately, the solution to the brain-drain and wastage lies with the African leaders. It is not simply a matter of economics. Unless they guarantee peace and create stable democracies which respect basic freedoms, the best brains will continue to be under-employed and thus will go overseas in search of greater opportunities.'

Akinyi said she was a great supporter of the ANC in South Africa. Sean had always understood from the media that the ANC was a terrorist organization. In fact, he learnt from Akinyi that its members were freedom fighters who were standing up for their human rights. The apartheid regime in South Africa was another of the worst examples of whites abusing black people. Sean had always been wary of organizations which seemed to have extreme views, but he now had a better understanding of many aspects of the problem of racism in the developing world. Akinyi's view was that human rights were an absolutely fundamental aspect of citizenship.

'A human being devoid of human rights is just a shell or a zombie. Human rights are colour blind and, contrary to the views of some African leaders, they do not differ from country to country.'

'I suppose you must maintain basic human rights in order to provide an environment with a sustainable political system,' said Sean.

'Yes, you're absolutely right. Human rights should not threaten political leaders if everyone is treated equally, regardless of race, creed or colour.'

Akinyi was pleased that Sean was seeing things from her perspective although, in reality, this was probably the first time in his life that he had thought deeply about such issues. He had come to realize that there were many things more important than his own little world. He listened intently to Akinyi and admired her. He gave her views great consideration.

'Sean, you always seem to have such a balanced view of things. Perhaps one day I will become less stressed about these matters.' Akinyi admired his even temperament. Now, she too began to think of her problems and her concerns from a slightly different perspective.

After their trip to the Maasai Mara, they returned to Nairobi and took the night train back to Mombasa. They arrived at Tsavo National Park just in time to watch hundreds of animals moving across the bush as the sun rose. It was an incredible sight. Sean was overjoyed to have come to Kenya, if for no reason other than to experience the beauty and diversity of the wild life in its natural habitat. He also felt fortunate to be with someone he loved and cared for so deeply.

When they finally reached Mombasa they relaxed for a few more days. During this time Akinyi told Sean about the thesis she was writing: 'A comparison of the Black Holocaust through History with the Jewish Holocaust'. It was a subject that was being debated widely in Africa and in black America in response to a movement demanding reparations from Western countries for black people. This was comparable to the billions of deutschmarks that post-war Germany had paid in restitution to the survivors of concentration camps and to Israel for the millions of Jews who had been exterminated both prior to and during the Second World War.

Akinyi had attended a world conference in Nigeria about this topic and now she was developing many new ideas. Behind the demands of black people for reparation was a conviction that black suffering throughout history had been equal to, or more than, that of the Jewish experience. The argument was whether anything in history could be compared in scale or criminality with the crime of the Nazi Holocaust.

'Those who have experienced the Nazi Holocaust will say that nothing compares with it. My argument is that the world has forgotten, or has chosen to forget, the crime against humanity by all those nations involved in the slave trade, colonialism and neo-colonialism. Such terrorism against the human race must at least have been the equal, over hundreds of years, of the Nazi tyranny,' she said.

'I've never thought about it in that way before,' stated Sean.

'I also feel that many Africans or African countries have not raised the spectre of their suffering as the Jews did. My argument is that if Africans don't raise monuments to victims of the slave holocaust then how can they expect reparations.'

Sean nodded in agreement.

'Africans didn't hold annual rites or gather at shrines to remind themselves of such humiliation and despoliation. The Jews, however, do hold annual gatherings and have erected shrines, not to prolong the suffering but to remind the world that such a thing should never be allowed to happen again.'

'Yes,' said Sean. 'I take your point.'

Akinyi, on the other hand, realized that not all victims of the Nazi Holocaust claimed reparation from the Germans. She also understood that not all black people agreed that reparations for slavery and colonialism was a realistic demand. But she felt strongly that black suffering over the centuries was something that could be compared as an experience of Holocaust proportions. It was a matter that should be pursued. It was important that humanity should ensure that people whose lives and culture are brutally and systematically destroyed by the oppression of others could seek reparations in the future. She realized that young Europeans and Americans should not be held responsible for the actions of their forefathers but also that it was most important to educate them about the history of slavery and the terrible crimes that took place against black peoples. Akinyi proposed that monuments should be erected in memory of these terrible events to remind people of evils that should never happen again. Like her father before her, she felt that a conciliatory approach would be the most effective.

Again it was something that Sean had not considered before. Like most people who hadn't experienced suffering, Sean found it hard to comprehend quite how much the Jews and black people had suffered in the past.

He learned a lot during the time he spent in Kenya, not only about the history of Africa but also about Akinyi in particular. He learned about Akinyi's strength of character. At times she was strong willed but at other times she displayed a vulnerability that made Sean feel very protective of her. He found her traditional Luo values and standards to be similar to the traditional family values he had been brought up with. At first he wasn't sure whether it was the English boarding school style of education that she had had while growing up in Nairobi, but after meeting her family he realized that wasn't the case. By the end of the holiday he was probably one of the happiest men in the world and it was on the flight home that he asked Akinyi to marry him. While he may only have known her for a mere six months she had engendered feelings in him he had never experienced before, and he knew he wanted to spend the rest of his life with her. He had fallen in love with her because of her sense of humour and most of all because of her intellectual passion. Up until then he had been almost one dimensional and very focused on his own sport – rugby. He found her to be so different from the many women he had met during his rugby days, who seemed to be interested in him more for his celebrity status than anything else.

The proposal took Akinyi completely by surprise. She was glad she was sitting down. She could feel a weakness in her legs and her heart was pounding madly. She considered the proposal for all of twenty seconds before responding. To Sean it felt like an eternity but at last she spoke.

'Sean, my life to date has been lived in a vacuum. I have felt for some time now that I no longer belong in Kenya, but neither do I feel at home in Germany.'

'Perhaps now you can settle at last.' Sean was impatient for an answer but tried hard not to show it.

'Please let me finish,' she said, leaning forward and gently squeezing his hand. 'In addition, I have felt emotionally unfulfilled. My six-year relationship with Hans was fun but we never got close and I felt somehow that a vital ingredient was missing. It wasn't until I met you, Sean, that I realized what it was like to be in love; truly in love. You make me feel safe and secure.'

She paused, keeping him in suspense even longer.

'Mr Cameron,' she continued, 'the answer is most definitely yes.'

Sean was elated. She belonged to him at last. He had not doubted that she would consent to be his wife, but the suspense had nearly killed him. Immediately he called the stewardess and ordered some champagne. He threw his arms around Akinyi and kissed her. The stewardess returned with the champagne and they toasted their happiness and their future at 35,000 feet and looked forward to many years together. By the time they arrived at Heathrow they were on a high, from a mixture of champagne and exaltation.

CHAPTER 11

It was now the end of August and Akinyi flew back to Germany to continue her studies. Sean was also very busy. They knew they wouldn't see each other for another four months, at which time they planned to marry with a quiet ceremony and fly back to Kenya for a reception with Akinyi's family in Kisumu. The next three months passed fairly uneventfully. Sean and Akinyi went about their respective business in England and Germany, and although they communicated by letter from time to time, neither one could say that they wrote regularly. Apart from the occasional romantic card, they managed to speak to each other on the telephone perhaps three or four times a week. Sometimes it was for only five or ten minutes, but at other times their conversation lasted for an hour or more. Their relationship continued in this vein, until one day in November when Akinyi phoned Sean to tell him she was seven months pregnant and that she was having his child.

Sean was overjoyed at the news. Although at thirty-seven he had never really contemplated having another child, he was genuinely delighted, not just for himself but for Akinyi, too. He knew it was something that would bond them together forever. It would also be a younger sister or brother for Louise.

They talked excitedly for a long time about bringing a child into the world – particularly a mixed-race child. They agreed that skin colour would be unimportant as long as they could give their child a happy home and bring him or her up to be a well-balanced individual. What would be important, though, would be to educate the child into the culture of both parents. They discussed the possibility of arranging a scan to determine the child's sex before birth but decided they preferred to wait until the actual birth.

Sean was convinced it would be a girl and he jokingly said to Akinyi, 'Real men only have little girls!' In fact, he didn't mind much whether it was a boy or a girl, as long as he or she was healthy.

For Akinyi the news was wonderful. It had given her a greater purpose in life. She was concerned initially that Sean's reaction might be cold and negative, and was absolutely delighted that he took the news so well. She longed to see him. She just wanted to throw her arms around him and be with him forever.

In a month's time she was due to leave Germany for good and come to England. It seemed so far away. She could continue her studies in England when they returned from their honeymoon in Kenya – and she would also work part-time for the BBC World Service on a current affairs programme entitled 'Africa Today'.

Three weeks after Akinyi had broken the news of her pregnancy Sean received a phone call from her friend Muthoni. It was 6 a.m. on 11 December. She told Sean that the previous night Akinyi had been speaking on a television programme in Frankfurt debating the problems of modern-day racism in Germany. She had been talking of her experiences and also about Africa and the problems encountered as a legacy of colonialism. When the programme finished she had left the television studio and had started to walk along the main street in Frankfurt to catch a bus back to the flat. Muthoni began sobbing. It was at this point that Sean started to become agitated. He began to realize something terrible had happened.

'Muthoni, why are you telling me all this?' he asked, not realizing quite where the conversation was leading.

'Sean, you must come quickly,' she cried.

Sean paused as he sensed that Muthoni was close to breaking point on the other end of the phone. After a few seconds she composed herself and continued. Akinyi had been attacked by a gang of neo-Nazis who had followed her from the studio. According to a witness, she realized she was being followed and had begun to run. But the gang chased her. In blind terror she ran up a side street into a dead end. There was no way she could escape from the by now chanting mob of about ten thugs. They attacked her and beat her unconscious with iron bars.

The witness, a woman, had in the meantime raised the alarm and called the police – but they arrived too late to catch the perpetrators as they ran off. The police had found Akinyi's crumpled body lying in the side alley. Her clothes had been almost torn off and she was covered in huge welts and bruises. Her arms and legs had been broken and she was suffering from internal bleeding. Akinyi was now on a life support machine and was not expected to live.

Sean said he would get the next available plane to Frankfurt. He hung up.

By this time he was worried sick. He checked his watch – it was 6.35 a.m. He jumped from his bed, threw on some clothes and dashed downstairs. He grabbed his wallet and passport and ran down the drive to his car. He reversed quickly out of the drive. He floored the throttle and screeched off up the road, tyres smoking, wheels spinning. He was at the long-term park at Heathrow in fifteen minutes. He parked and ran to the bus, jumping on just as it was moving off. At Terminal 2 he located the Lufthansa sales desk. It was now 7.05 a.m. and the clerk had just opened the counter. Sean breathlessly explained his story and asked for the first available flight to Frankfurt. The 7.55 was fully booked – the next one was at 10.30. Sean knew it might be too late. He asked the clerk whether any other airline was going to Frankfurt. She said she would check. She first tried British Airways, but they were fully booked. She tried Philippine Airlines who did a stop over at Frankfurt on the way to Manilla, but they were also full. The only available seat was on the Lufthansa 10.30 flight. Sean resigned himself to the three-and-a-half hour wait and handed over his credit card. With so much time to kill, he went off to get some breakfast. He ordered a coffee. He couldn't eat, his stomach was tied up in knots. He felt like crying out. There was nothing he could do. He slumped back in his chair and closed his eyes, trying to control his emotions. He tried to relax and remain calm. His mind was racing. What could he do? He sat there in a daze. The next thing he heard was an announcement over the tannoy system asking for a Mr Sean Cameron to go to the Lufthansa desk. It was 7.40 a.m. He walked quickly to the counter. The clerk looked up and smiled as he approached her.

'Mr Cameron, it's good news. One of the passengers has failed to show up, so if you hurry you may just catch the flight.'

Sean leaned across the counter and kissed her on the cheek. She smiled and handed him his boarding pass. He thanked her and headed for the departure gate through passport control and began running to Gate 12. There was no way he would miss this plane. He ran as fast as he could and arrived just as the last passenger was boarding.

'Mr Cameron?' enquired the stewardess.

Sean nodded.

'My colleague on the sales counter has told me your story. She telephoned to say you were on your way. I wish you the very best,' she said. 'Have a good flight.'

Sean boarded the plane and slumped into his seat. Nearly two hours to go. He wished he was on Startrek so Scottie could beam him up. Still, he had to try and be patient. He began thinking of Akinyi and the little time they had spent together. He wished he could have spent more time with her. A sudden shock wave hit him. What about their child? He hoped they would both be okay. He ordered another coffee. He was still too nervous to eat. He started to fidget in his seat. He began drumming his fingers on the pull-out table in front of him. He could feel beads of sweat running down his back. He started clicking his fingers, twisting the napkin in front of him, agitated, itching, turning in his seat. He looked at his watch. They had only been flying twenty minutes. Christ, thought Sean. How am I going to get through the next 90 minutes?

He got up to go to the toilet, came back, and sat down again. His anxiety was getting the better of him. He picked up the in-flight magazine and flicked through the pages. He didn't read it; he just couldn't concentrate. He kept looking at his watch. It was almost as if time had stopped. Watching the second hand was like watching an action replay in slow motion. It could have been going backwards, for it certainly didn't seem to be going forwards. He looked up and saw the stewardess standing by him. She leaned down and quietly told him that they had arranged for him to go through VIP customs and passport control on his arrival. She asked him to move to a seat at the front of the plane, usually occupied by a stewardess, so he could be first off when they landed. Lufthansa had even arranged for a special car to be waiting to take him to the hospital in the centre of Frankfurt. Sean couldn't believe their kindness and he thanked her.

He got up and moved to the front of the plane. Not long now, he thought. He would be with Akinyi soon.

They started their descent and he looked out of the window. He could see Frankfurt below. He heard the undercarriage dropping as the pilot prepared to land. He looked out of the window again. He could see it was just starting to rain. It was a dull, grey day in Frankfurt but nothing could be as grey as the way he was feeling at the moment. His head ached.

They made a perfect landing and taxied along the runway to the stand. 'Doors to manual,' the pilot announced. Shortly afterwards Sean exited the aircraft. He was first off and was met by a member of Lufthansa's staff who said that he should follow her. They walked quickly and soon reached passport control. Sean had no baggage so they went straight through customs out to the main entrance where there was a car waiting. It was a white Mercedes. Sean thanked the stewardess and climbed into the back of the car.

By this time it was raining heavily so the driver moved cautiously through the traffic. Within twenty-five minutes they had reached the hospital and the driver took him right up to the main door. Sean jumped out, thanking him as he ran up the steps and through the big revolving doorway.

He could see Akinyi's friend Muthoni waiting for him at reception. She looked tired and drained. She had been crying. He walked quickly to her and embraced her. She told him that Akinyi was in intensive care, which was on the third floor. They took the lift and Sean was finally at her bedside.

Akinyi was lying still with her head swathed in bandages. Her face was purple and swollen and he barely recognized her. He leaned over and kissed her gently on the lips.

Muthoni said she would wait outside and walked quietly out of the room, shutting the door behind her.

Sean was all alone with Akinyi now. He sat at her bedside and very carefully took her hand and squeezed it gently. He felt so helpless. What could he do? There was nothing he could do but sit and wait. He wondered whether Muthoni had contacted Akinyi's family in Kenya.

Sean was churning up inside. He had to be positive. 'You must have faith,' he said to himself. 'You have to believe everything is going to be okay.'

He leaned back in his chair and shut his eyes. He began to think of the wonderful times they had had together – all too short. How much Sean regretted that. He wished he hadn't been so busy at work.

Perhaps if he had been with Akinyi for that television debate she wouldn't be here now. How he wished he hadn't placed such importance on his work. He had done that with Louise, his daughter. Now he felt he had failed Akinyi, too.

When would he learn? When would he relax and give the people who loved him more time?

He looked up as Muthoni came back into the room.

'Sean, the police inspector wishes to talk to you, Kriminalhauptkommisar Meissner is waiting outside.'

Sean raised his eyebrows, exchanged places with Muthoni, and left the room.

In the corridor the inspector introduced himself. He told Sean that they were doing everything possible to find Akinyi's attackers. They had a good idea who they were and currently had about two dozen suspects under observation. However, as they had very little evidence to go on, there was not much they could do.

The eye-witness was too terrified to commit herself to appearing at an identification parade and giving evidence, because of the suspected neo-Nazi involvement. They just had to wait and watch, until maybe one of the suspects got drunk and started to boast about the attack to their friends. Sean thanked the inspector, who said the police would keep him informed of any progress.

Sean returned to intensive care and whispered quietly to Muthoni that he wanted to be alone again with Akinyi. Muthoni said she would be back shortly. He bent down again and kissed Akinyi on the lips. 'I love you,' he said, quietly.

At that moment Akinyi's eyes flickered just slightly and Sean moved closer. He began praying like he had never prayed before. If only, he thought. He had a million thoughts running through his mind, but not one of them would make Akinyi any better.

Time passed slowly. Sean had now been with Akinyi for nearly two hours, watching and listening to her breathing, which seemed to be getting slower. He began counting the intervals between the breaths. He felt her pulse. It was very faint. He began to get concerned.

'Muthoni, Muthoni,' he called. 'Get the nurse quickly, I think there's a problem.'

Muthoni had been waiting just outside the door and heard Sean cry out. She called the nurse who rose quickly from her desk in reception and ran to Akinyi's bedside. She felt her pulse. It was by now very faint. She pressed the buzzer to call for assistance and another nurse bustled into the room.

'Call the doctor,' she said. 'And tell him to come quickly.'

Sean by now was frantic with worry. 'What's happening?' he asked.

'I'm sorry Mr Cameron,' it was the first nurse who spoke, 'but it doesn't look good. I don't think she has long to live. We're just waiting for the doctor; he should be here any moment now.'

Sean felt the tears welling up in his eyes. He fought to hold them back. He had to stay in control. What would he do without Akinyi? He didn't know what he would do.

The doctor arrived and immediately took Akinyi's pulse. He lifted her eyelids and looked into her eyes. Then he turned to Sean and put his hand on his shoulder. 'I'm sorry,' he said. 'She's slipping away. I'm sorry but there is nothing I can do.'

Sean stared at him wide-eyed. He wanted to say something to the doctor, but the words wouldn't come. He looked back at Akinyi and the tears just flowed. They started rolling down his cheeks. He took her hand. It was still warm but there was no life in it. Akinyi just slipped away. She had gone. Sean's lips were trembling and he could taste the saltiness of his tears. He bent slowly and kissed Akinyi one last time. He looked at her. She looked so childlike, so peaceful. The pain had left her face. He gently touched her cheek with the back of his hand. What have I done in life to deserve this? he wondered. I have lost the only woman I really truly loved.

Muthoni took his hand and led him from the room. He leant heavily against her as they left. She didn't say anything.

When they got outside she took him in her arms and hugged him. He held on to Muthoni as though his life depended on her. He felt numbed. He felt so empty. At last he let go of Muthoni and told her he must telephone Akinyi's father to tell him the appalling news. I must be strong, thought Sean. He felt it was his duty to tell Akinyi's father. They had met once in Kenya. He liked the man. He was a good man, strong and proud. Sean had an affinity with him. They had a mutual respect. Muthoni was with him when they reached the phone booth.

Suddenly it dawned on Sean – 'What about our child?' he shouted to Muthoni.

She shrugged her shoulders, not knowing quite what he meant.

He ran back to Akinyi's room. 'Where's the doctor?' he asked the nurse in desperation.

She went to get him and they returned almost immediately.

'Doctor,' Sean said. 'What about our child?'

'I'm sorry,' said the doctor. 'We were monitoring the child's heartbeat but we dared not induce her because it would almost certainly have killed her mother sooner. She did not have the strength to give birth, or even to miscarry. I'm so sorry, Mr Cameron, but when Akinyi died your baby died as well. It would have been a girl.'

Sean just stood there and looked blankly at the doctor. He seemed to be frozen to the spot. He felt weak. It was as though the blood had drained from every inch of his body. He swayed slightly. He didn't speak for a few minutes. He could see everyone staring and knew they were talking to him, but he couldn't hear them. He was in a trance. Then something inside his head told him to snap out of it; he had things to do. He half stumbled forward but just managed to keep his balance. He struggled to collect his thoughts. He had to speak with Akinyi's father. He whispered a 'thank you' to the doctor and nurse and turned and headed back to the phone with Muthoni.

He knew Onyango Ouko's number off by heart and slowly pressed the buttons on the phone. It rang for about a minute before it was picked up. It was now about seven o'clock in the evening in Nairobi.

'Hello, this is the Ouko residence,' said a voice. It was the maid. Sean asked to speak to Mr Ouko.

'Hold on a minute please.'

How am I going to tell him? thought Sean. It was the shortest minute he had ever experienced.

'Hello, this is Onyango Ouko.'

'Hello, this is Sean Cameron. I'm sorry, but I'm afraid I have some bad news. I would like to have seen you personally but at the moment we are just too far apart.' Sean paused, taking a breath.

'I am so sorry Mr Ouko,' he stammered, 'Akinyi is dead. She died about half an hour ago.'

There was silence on the other end of the phone. Then Sean heard a great racking sob.

'NO!' Onyango cried. 'Not my beautiful Akinyi!'

Sean paused while Onyango composed himself.

'How did it happen?'

Sean explained how Akinyi had been attacked and how she had died. He felt terrible giving the news to her father like this but there was no other way. Sean said he would contact Onyango again when the flight arrangements to take Akinyi's body back home were in place and that he too would be coming to Kenya.

Sean put the phone down and looked at Muthoni. She was crying. The tears were rolling down her cheeks. He took her in his arms and tried to console her.

'Come on,' he said. 'Let's go home.'

They took the lift to the ground floor and walked through the revolving doors into the car park. Before they could call a taxi they were besieged by pressmen. The press had heard about the attack on Akinyi and were following the story closely because it had been a racist crime and, prior to the reunification of West Germany with East Germany, there had been a number of racially motivated attacks. Someone had tipped off the press that Akinyi's boyfriend was in fact quite a well-known international sportsman.

A barrage of questions were directed at Sean. Flashlights were popping on cameras. Sean recognized some of the sports press in attendance. To them it was a story for the sports pages as well as general news on the front pages.

'Mr Cameron, Sean,' they called. 'How is your girlfriend, Akinyi? Is she badly hurt?'

Sean felt a lump in his throat. He looked blankly at them. 'Akinyi died only a few minutes ago. I need to go home, to be on my own for a while to collect my thoughts. If I have something further to say I shall let you know. Now, please, let me go.'

He could see the compassion registering in their faces and they stood aside in silence forming a clear passageway for Muthoni and Sean.

Sean hailed a taxi. They climbed in and Muthoni gave her address. The car pulled out and moved slowly away. Sean asked the driver to stop at the next liquor store, where he got out and bought a couple of bottles of Glenmorangie, his favourite malt whisky. He climbed back in the taxi; it wasn't very long before they were at Muthoni's flat.

As soon as they got inside Sean poured two very large measures. One for Muthoni and one for himself, which he downed in one hit. He poured another; it was going to be a long night. He sat down and they began to talk. Sean asked all sorts of questions about Akinyi. He wanted to know as much about her as he could. He wanted to cherish all his memories of her.

Muthoni told Sean that since Akinyi and he had met she had never been so happy. She had a liveliness and bubblyness about her that she had never had before. Akinyi had confided in Muthoni that she at last realized where she belonged. She wanted to be with Sean forever.

Sean felt a terrifying numbness. He could not believe Akinyi had died, although he had seen it with his own eyes.

He couldn't help thinking about her distress and despair over certain parts of her life. A particular irony was that having finally found the true happiness she craved, she wouldn't be there to enjoy it.

At around midnight Muthoni and Sean finished the first bottle of Glenmorangie. Muthoni was feeling drunk and decided to go to bed, leaving Sean in the lounge. Sean said he would follow shortly; of course he didn't. After Muthoni left, he opened the second bottle and poured himself another large slug of whisky. He was tired and drunk but he knew he wouldn't be able to sleep. He wandered around the flat, filled with memories of his first weekend there with Akinyi.

He began to think about the bastards who had murdered her. He wanted to kill them. He began plotting his revenge. If the police were powerless to do anything, then he would track them down himself. Sean didn't really know where to start. He was neither a detective nor a killer. He knew he would have to seek professional help. He began to mull over in his mind how he would deal with the problem. He could either employ a private detective to help him find out who the killers were, and then bring them to justice through the courts, or he could hire a professional hit-man to deal with them. His mind was becoming muddled through drink. What was he thinking? He knew he had to bring them to justice through the courts; he could not take the second option. He had been brought up to respect authority and realized he couldn't take the law into his own hands. But he would speak to Hauptkommisar Meissner to find out what progress had been made.

He decided he would give the police one year to find the killers. If they failed in that time to bring a prosecution, he would have to find them himself, but he would need help. He immediately thought of James, his best friend at school. James was a captain in the army and, it so happened, a member of the SAS. He was a weapons expert and a martial arts instructor, specializing in unarmed combat. He would speak to James about getting some specialist training. When he returned to Richmond he would phone him and discuss how they might go about tracing the killers.

Sean put that thought to the back of his mind and began drifting into an alcoholic haze. He was getting more confused; the empty feeling returned. He felt so alone, but he was so numb he couldn't even cry. He had stifled his emotions. Sean wondered whether he would ever recover. He poured another whisky and slammed it down in one. He poured another and this time just held the glass between his cupped hands and sat staring blankly into it.

CHAPTER 12

It was 8 a.m. when Muthoni awoke. Her eyes were red and puffy – she had cried herself to sleep the previous night. Akinyi had been her best friend for fifteen years. She felt nauseous and her head ached; she wasn't used to drinking. She was dehydrated and needed some water. She got up and walked to the kitchen, where she poured herself a large glass of water and drank it quickly. She poured an orange juice and switched on the kettle to make coffee. She figured Sean was still asleep in his room. She didn't want to disturb him so she walked into the lounge. To her surprise Sean was slumped in a chair still clutching an empty whisky bottle and sound asleep. Poor man, she thought. She could see the pain and distress in his face. He was unshaven and his clothes were crumpled. He looked a mess. Muthoni knew that before long Sean would need help to get over Akinyi. She was aware he was a silent type who bottled up his emotions. She thought perhaps she might be able to help him, but she knew it was unlikely. He needed time on his own to come to terms with Akinyi's death. She looked at the empty bottle of whisky and wondered how many more bottles he would consume in the next few months. She wouldn't try to stop him. If that was his release then let him deal with it in his own way, she thought. She left the room and quietly shut the door.

It was a good four hours later when Sean ambled through into the kitchen. Muthoni was writing a letter to one of Akinyi's school friends.

She looked up and smiled briefly. 'My God, Sean, you look terrible.'

'Yes, and I feel a thousand times worse than I look. It's as though a steamroller has just trundled over my head. I need some water.' He went to the sink and ran the tap until the water was cold. After a long drink he went and sat with Muthoni.

'I've got so much to do today,' said Sean. 'First, I'm going to take a shower, then I need to go and buy some clothes; in my rush to get here I didn't bring any with me. Then I must go to the hospital to arrange for Akinyi's body to be flown back to Kenya. After that I hope to see the police inspector.'

Muthoni offered to accompany Sean. He couldn't speak German so he'd need her help.

He got up to have a shower. 'I'll be ready in fifteen minutes,' he said.

In fact Sean took about half an hour longer than he'd estimated. His head ached and he felt sick, so he stood under the shower for twenty minutes trying to clear his head. Never again, thought Sean, but he knew those bottles of whisky were going to be the first of many over the coming few months.

It was 2 p.m. when Sean and Muthoni reached the hospital. They went to reception and were directed to the mortuary office down two flights of stairs in the basement. There they met Dr Petersen, a large and pleasant looking man. He had carried out a post mortem on Akinyi's body that morning and handed Sean a copy of his report, saying that the body would be ready to be taken to Frankfurt airport the next morning for the onward flight to Nairobi. He also gave Sean the death certificate. Sean thanked him and said he would let him know when he had arranged all the flight details.

As it turned out, Sean flew back to Heathrow on his own on Thursday 13 December. He arranged for Akinyi's body to be flown back on a cargo flight via Heathrow, Terminal 4, and from there he arranged for her body to be flown back to Jomo Kenyatta International Airport in Nairobi. He booked the night flight out of Heathrow on the following Saturday, 15 December, after he had arranged with the Lufthansa Airways Office in Frankfurt the journey back to England.

His next port of call was the police station. He arrived at about seven o'clock that evening and asked at the main desk to speak to Hauptkommissar Meissner. When he appeared he greeted Sean and shook his hand firmly.

He was a tall, slim man with dark, wavy hair that was well-groomed. He had a very distinctive Roman nose and wore pince nez spectacles which were perched on the end of his nose. He peered over the top of them as he studied Sean. He had many frown lines on his forehead, and the lines around his eyes aged him considerably. Sean estimated that he was about 55 years of age. He wore a dark suit with a sharply pressed white shirt and black tie. His black shoes were highly polished. He walked in a very upright manner which gave Sean the impression he had previously been in the military.

They went to an interview room, where he explained to Sean that there was a neo-Nazi cell in Frankfurt and that the police now had them under 24-hour surveillance. The woman, the main witness to the attack, had been to see him. She had looked at dozens of photographs but was unable to give any positive identification. She had pointed out possibly seven of the ten men who had attacked Akinyi, but because it had been dark she could not be absolutely certain that they were the right ones. It was not enough to secure a prosecution. Meissner explained that in these circumstances they would wait a little longer before pulling the men in for questioning, in the hope that one or more actually admitted to the attack. It was a very slim chance but that was all he had to go on.

Sean was exasperated at this news. He just couldn't believe that so little had happened. Surely someone else must have seen the attack? Perhaps if they put out appeals on the radio or television it might encourage someone to come forward. Meissner explained that unfortunately many people were scared to provide information for fear of reprisals. This was particularly true in cases involving neo-Nazis. It was at this point that Sean lost his temper.

'You know, Meissner, it appears that you are not trying hard enough to find Akinyi's killers.'

'How dare you!' Meissner shouted. 'I am a professional doing my best, I promise you.'

'Mark my words,' replied Sean, regaining his composure and lowering his voice. 'There are other ways of reaching a conclusion.'

'What exactly are you implying?' asked Meissner, trying to contain his anger. 'I hope you are not threatening us.'

Sean didn't reply but looked directly at the policeman.

Meissner saw a glint of pure steel in Sean's eyes. He knew then that this man had the strength of character to carry out his threat. He shifted uncomfortably. Finally, he said that he would do his utmost to find Akinyi's killers.

Sean wished Meissner good luck in his search and gave him his business card. He wanted Meissner to contact him when he returned to England if there were any new developments. At that point Sean turned and left the office. Muthoni had been waiting outside.

'Come on, let's go and eat,' he suggested.

They were both tired and still suffering from the previous night's drinking binge. Sean knew he needed the hair of the dog, but also knew that it would be the start of a few drinks too many. They found a little Italian restaurant and each demolished a large plate of pasta carbonara, washed down with a couple of bottles of Barolo, and followed by very large brandies. When they got back to the flat they were both the worse for wear. However, Sean still had room for a nightcap. Not wishing to mix grain with grape he forsook his favoured Glenmorangie and opted for a couple more large brandies to comatose himself.

He was very tired when he climbed into bed, and was soon asleep. The drinks helped to start with, but after a couple of hours he woke and spent the rest of the night tossing and turning, unable to sleep properly. He kept seeing images of Akinyi's face. In his mind's eye he could see clearly the beautiful smile radiating across her whole face.

It seemed as if he had been awake for hours but shortly before dawn he drifted off into a deep slumber, his mind still working overtime. He dreamt of meeting Akinyi's family again. How could he face them? He was not responsible for her death but felt guilty that he had not been with her on that fateful night.

CHAPTER 13

On Thursday 13 December, Sean flew back to London. Akinyi's body was flown separately on a cargo flight out of Frankfurt and would arrive that afternoon at the cargo terminal at Heathrow Airport. Sean wanted to be there to ensure that all the paperwork was correct and that there wouldn't be any problems in Nairobi. In the meantime, he had arranged to meet Muthoni again at the funeral in Kenya.

Back home in Richmond Sean telephoned his brother, John, and asked him to come with him to the funeral. He needed the support. He needed someone to talk to. He hadn't been particularly close to John because of the five-year age gap, and he had never really discussed any deeply intimate problems with him before, but John immediately said he would come. He could tell from Sean's voice that he was crying out for help. He would do the best he could in his hour of need.

Sean then phoned his parents. His mother answered the phone. 'Hello,' Sean said. 'I'm sorry I haven't contacted you before now, but my life has just been turned upside down. Everything has happened so quickly.'

Sean's mother had read about Akinyi's death in the newspaper. There had been a front-page story in all the nationals. She hadn't known where to contact Sean but she knew he would eventually turn up or phone her. So she had waited for him to call in his own time.

In the meantime she was beside herself with worry about him. She knew how much Sean bottled up his emotions. She didn't have favourites, but she had a very soft spot for Sean. Probably because they were so alike. He had a quietness and gentleness about him, although on the outside he often appeared hard and uncaring. Occasionally, she too was a little abrupt, just like Sean. Their abruptness was probably born out of their shyness. She asked him to come to dinner on Friday, before he flew off to Kenya. Sean said he would do his best to be there, but he had lots to do before he left. He had plenty of loose ends to tie up because he wasn't sure whether he would come back to England for a while. He needed to talk to Ian, his business partner, about taking a sabbatical after the funeral.

He also needed to drive down to see his daughter, Louise. He had to explain to her how he was feeling and to tell her that, even though he loved her very, very much, she might not see him for quite a while. He knew she would be distressed and upset. He knew she loved her daddy very much. As it turned out, his mother invited Louise and Sean's ex-wife, Sally, to dinner on the Friday night. Sean was very grateful because he actually wanted Sally to be with him when he told Louise that he would be gone for a while. Fortunately, Sean's parents were still very fond of Sally, despite the divorce. They had kept in contact, mainly for the sake of their granddaughter.

Their open attitude had certainly helped to create a more relaxed environment for Louise as she grew up, without the usual recriminations of families involved in divorce cases.

On the Friday night, when Sean arrived, Louise and Sally were already there, having drinks in the conservatory overlooking the garden. His brother John and his sister Christina had also arrived. Sean poured himself a cold beer and sat down to explain to Louise his heartache and that he was going to Kenya to bury Akinyi. He explained to her that he needed time to himself and that after the funeral he intended to stay there for a while, maybe a few months. He thought it would help to put his life back in order. Louise reacted badly. She was hurt and found what her father had said hard to accept. Silently she was challenging his decision. Suddenly Sean realized that Louise was growing up. She had become a little adult overnight, with increasing maturity.

After dinner he and Sally found themselves alone in the garden.

'Sean,' Sally began. 'You must understand that Louise understands more than you give her credit for.'

'What do you mean?' said Sean, immediately going on the defensive and flushing a little. 'Of course, I know that.'

'I don't think you do. You really have no idea how much she misses you.'

Sean remained silent and shuffled from side to side, knowing full well that he was in for another lecture from Sally.

'I know how much you love and care for Louise, but she needs you to spend more time with her. She knows how much you loved and cared for Akinyi. She told me that you were a changed man after you met her. She so wants you to be happy, and she's so sad that Akinyi is dead. She really wanted you to have a partner and get married again. She's seen how lonely you've been over the years and I know that although you've cared for her financially, it's not the same as spending quality time together.'

Sean was taken aback at what Louise had told Sally. 'I promise you that I will be back as soon as I can,' he said rather lamely. He assured her that he would write to Louise and phone her whenever he could.

Sally thought his response was weak and indefinite.

At this point his mother called them to dinner and they headed for the dining room. Sean saw that she had cooked all his favourite foods. Although he wasn't hungry he ate everything she gave him, because he knew she would be very hurt if he didn't. As always, the food was delicious. As the evening went by everyone's mood became more sombre. Sean was very conscious that his family took care not to say anything that might upset him, especially with regard to Akinyi. Christina's husband and two children were also there and she did her best to cheer him up, reminding him of a few fun things they had done as children. It was obvious that everyone was a little anxious and at the end of the meal Sally announced that she was going to drive Louise home.

Sean's mother wanted them to stay but Sally was adamant that they would leave. They all said their goodbyes. Louise became tearful, but Sean consoled her with a big hug and she cheered up. Sean felt a huge pang of guilt as he waved goodbye to her. It was at this point that Sean excused himself. He wanted a reasonably early night. He had a busy day ahead before he took the overnight flight to Nairobi. John, who lived in Edinburgh and had flown down that morning, went with him. He would stay the night at Sean's before they journeyed together to Nairobi.

CHAPTER 14

As always, the Kenya Airways flight was very comfortable. Sean and John had four seats between them and were able to stretch out and relax, in-between consuming vast quantities of beer. Sean knew it was not very sensible to drink too much alcohol because of its dehydrating effects, but on this occasion he didn't care. What had he got to lose? They made a one-hour stop-over in Athens to refuel and by nine o'clock local time next morning they had touched down at Jomo Kenyatta International Airport.

Akinyi's father, Onyango, and her four brothers were there to meet them. They looked sad and grim. Onyango in particular appeared to be very distressed. Akinyi had been his only daughter and he had been particularly proud of her achievements. Onyango was above average height but smaller than Sean had remembered. He reminded him of Sidney Poitier, the actor, although his face was slightly slimmer than Poitier's. He had a small beard and his tight, closely cropped, curly hair was flecked with grey, making him look rather distinguished.

It was a Luo tradition to accompany the coffin when it was brought home. Onyango took them back to his house in Nairobi. They were due to take Akinyi's body on the evening plane to Kisumu. From there they would travel by road to the family home about fifteen miles out of town. Traditionally, bodies were transported at night in Kenya and not during the day.

They took the 6 p.m. flight, and just after seven landed at Kisumu Airport. There they were met by Mr Okoko from the Lee Funeral Parlour, whose undertakers would take the body home, where arrangements had been made in advance to receive the coffin.

Shortly before ten o'clock the parlour car arrived at Onyango's home. Akinyi's brothers had made a space in the fence around their compound. It was Luo tradition that a body could not be taken through the main gates as it was not actually going home. It would be there only temporarily before she was buried.

Some of Akinyi's girlfriends and female relatives between the ages of eighteen to twenty-five were already there to welcome the body, and it was their job to open the coffin and dress the body in white. Before they dressed her they had to clean her and embalm the body again. Even though this had already been done in Germany, it was tradition to do this at her home. Her parents and family then stayed at the house for three days, during which time everyone had a party. There was dancing and a lot of fun. It was the celebration of a life and an entry into a new life. Sean felt desperately sad, but he knew he had to observe the local customs and honour the family by taking part in the festivities.

The fourth day was the day of the burial. After midday, her four brothers and two cousins carried the coffin in slings to the family burial ground behind the compound. At the graveside the village chief and Akinyi's father paid their respects in short speeches; then it was Sean's turn. He spoke of his sadness and despair but also of the joy that Akinyi had given him in the short time that they had known each other. Her death was a wicked tragedy, he said.

John stood next to him while he spoke and gently placed a hand on Sean's shoulder as he leant forward to throw in some soil after her brothers had lowered the coffin into the grave. As Akinyi's boyfriend and future husband, it was Sean's duty to throw in the soil first. He was followed by her parents, brothers and close relatives.

That night there was a big party at Onyango's house. It was then that Sean saw Akinyi's family and friends cry for the first time. Although it was difficult for them, family tradition did not allow them to cry before she was buried. Now was the time for mourning.

Sean stayed up that night. He had drunk a lot and he spent the few hours before dawn sitting on the verandah of the Ouko home listening to the sounds of Africa by night. The music had stopped at about 2 a.m. and Sean sat alone just staring at the sky. Kisumu was chilly at night, not at all like Mombasa. John had said he would stay up with him but Sean wouldn't hear of it. He preferred to be alone.

As dawn broke and Sean heard the cockerels welcoming in the day, Onyango appeared on the verandah with a pot of tea. They sat together and discussed Akinyi. The tears flowed down his cheeks as her father recounted stories to Sean about her childhood.

'She was such a beautiful child, Sean, with such big eyes and the most wonderful, endearing smile.'

It was all Sean could do to keep his emotions in check. He could say nothing. Onyango continued talking. They discussed Sean's future. Onyango said that he would always be welcomed at their home. He was impressed with Sean. In spite of his quietness, he sensed Sean had an honesty and an integrity about him that could be found in few men. He had been happy with Akinyi's choice of a husband; he was aware of his daughter's love for Sean and her respect for him. He knew of her disquiet and lack of certainty about her future until she had met Sean.

After a couple of hours Sean knew he needed to sleep. He was jet-lagged and tired. He excused himself and went off to the room he was sharing with John, who in fact was just waking up. He slept until six o'clock in the evening. When he awoke he showered and dressed and wandered outside to sit with Onyango and the family.

Dinner was at eight and by the time it arrived Sean was ravenous. It was traditional Kenyan food: *ugali*, a type of maize cake and *sukuma wiki*, made from green vegetables, onions, spices, tomatoes and fish in a rich sauce. It was delicious and Sean soon demolished two helpings, followed by fresh pineapple. At the end of the meal he told Onyango that he would go back to Nairobi with John the next day. John had to return to work but Sean was going to Mombasa, where he wanted to spend some time before returning to England.

After breakfast the next morning, Onyango drove the two brothers to Kisumu for the flight to Nairobi. At the airport they shook hands and Sean promised he would keep in touch. They had a quiet flight down to Nairobi and on arrival booked into the Suncourt Inn on University Way, close to the Norfolk Hotel. It wasn't really a tourist hotel, which was why Sean preferred it, but it was clean and very welcoming. John's flight back to Heathrow was at midnight so they had dinner together that evening in the famous Thorn Tree Café at the New Stanley Hotel. It had originally been an Edwardian hotel, very popular as the downtown base for foreign travellers in Nairobi. After dinner they had a few more beers and then took a taxi to the airport. John checked in and Sean walked with him to the departure gate. Just before John went through Sean shook his hand and gave him a brotherly hug.

'Thanks, John, for coming with me. I don't think I could have managed without you. When I have a place to stay, I'll let you have some contact details, but in the meantime give my love to mother and father when you see them. Also, will you do me a favour and call Louise when you get back? Tell her that her dad's okay and that I'll be in touch. Have a good flight and thanks once again for your TLC.'

'No problem,' said John. 'I hope you never have to do the same for me one day.' At that, he walked through the departure gate, waving his boarding pass at the security guard. Sean turned and walked briskly to the exit. He knew he was all alone now, and a rising feeling of fear and trepidation began to creep into his mind. He shivered spontaneously. He walked out of the airport and hailed a taxi.

CHAPTER 15

The next morning Sean phoned his partner, Ian, in Richmond. He explained that he was staying on in Kenya for much longer than he had originally intended. He thanked him for his compassion and understanding and said he would let him know his address and phone number when he got to Mombasa. They agreed that Ian would employ a salesman temporarily to help out in Sean's absence. It was also agreed that this cost would come out of Sean's share of profits for the year. When he put the phone down he packed his bag and checked out of the inn. He called a taxi to take him to the bus station. The buses travelled three times a day to Mombasa and, as Sean had previously flown and taken the train to Mombasa, he thought it would make a pleasant change to go by bus.

It was an experience he would never forget. The early part of the main highway passed through fairly monotonous landscape. He had been advised to sit on the right of the bus as he would be able to see the finest scenery; fortunately it was a clear day, offering the best views. Beyond Tsavo train station he was lucky to experience the magnificent sight of Mount Kilimanjaro, striking majestically skywards, 5,895 metres, the highest mountain in Africa.

As they approached Mombasa the sun began to set.

The appearance of the landscape had changed significantly, from long areas of scrubland to banana and coconut trees. Shortly after dark they arrived in the centre of Mombasa, travelling over Nyali Bridge to the bus station on Jomo Kenyatta Avenue. Sean recognized the places he had been to before and as he got off the bus he hailed a taxi to take him on the twenty-minute drive to the Indian Ocean Hotel, where he had stayed with Akinyi. On arriving he paid the driver 300 shillings and carried his cases to reception. It was now eight o'clock at night. The day shift had changed; he didn't recognize any of the receptionists. He asked for a room for one week.

While the receptionist was making the booking, he nipped into the round bar, next to reception. He recognized the barman, Gary. He seemed like an old friend. He greeted Sean with a huge, friendly smile. He shook his hand enthusiastically and asked where Akinyi was. Sean became agitated and bowed his head slightly. He could feel the tears welling up in his eyes and he whispered quietly to Gary that Akinyi was dead. Later, he said, he would explain what had happened.

'Sean, my friend, I am so sorry. My heart goes out to you,' Gary said, as he saw the suffering in Sean's eyes.

Sean told him that he would return later for a drink, but that first he needed a shower. He went back to reception to pick up his key and walked quickly to his room, which was situated in a small block set in tropical gardens. Sean tipped the porter who carried his bags 20 shillings. His room was on the second floor of a small 12-room unit and had a balcony that looked out across the ocean. He walked on to the balcony, stared up into the sky, took a deep breath and let his mind wander. He was back in the Kenya he knew, his home away from home. He had plenty of time on his hands. He didn't know when he would return to England. He had to try and let the scars heal, but how long that would take he didn't know. He would never forget Akinyi, but could he ever let another woman get close to him again? He didn't know the answer to this. Tomorrow was another day and he had to look forward. But it was difficult for him not to dwell on the past. He closed his eyes briefly and then turned and went into his room, shutting the balcony door behind him.

After showering he went down to the bar and ordered a cold Tusker beer from Gary. It was now 9.30 in the evening. Most of the guests had finished dinner and were in the bar, drinking and chatting about the day's events, waiting for the evening's entertainment to begin. That night, a group of traditional Giriama dancers would be performing. The Giriama, one of the largest ethnic groups of the coastal region, were famous for their acrobatic dancing. They traditionally performed to the accompaniment of superb, fast, rhythmic drumming.

The dancing began and Sean, half watching, began talking to Gary. He started by telling him what had happened to Akinyi and why he had decided to spend some time in Kenya. Her violent death had disturbed him almost beyond reason and he felt that by staying in Africa he was closer to her. He didn't know when he would return to England. At this point in the conversation, the hotel manager, Mr Juma, arrived and greeted Sean. He offered his condolences. Word travelled fast in that part of the world. In a way Sean was grateful, because he didn't want to keep explaining to everyone what had happened. He was thankful that people showed their care, consideration and interest, but he believed that grief was a personal and private matter. He had to deal with it himself, in his own way, although he was aware that some people who suffered grief needed to share their innermost thoughts with others.

Tiredness was setting in but that night Sean was on a mission – to get drunk. Tusker followed Tusker and was soon pursued by whisky chasers. Sean sat alone at the bar in a world of his own, oblivious to what was going on around him. The African music was becoming a dull, thumping sound in his head. Gary knew that this was not the time to talk to Sean, but he was becoming worried that he was getting too drunk. By midnight he told Sean he was shutting the bar and wasn't going to serve him any more. Somehow Sean persuaded him to serve one more large whisky. Sean downed it quickly. He knew he would have to use all his powers of concentration to rise from the bar stool. With both hands on the bar, he lifted himself up from the stool, rocking forward slightly.

'Goodnight Gary,' he slurred.

With that he turned and staggered off in the best tradition of all drunks, who try desperately hard to walk straight but over-compensate and end up weaving a crooked line. Picking up his key from reception, Sean headed for his room through the tropical gardens. The path was narrow but normally two people could walk side by side. On this occasion Sean made it an art form and seemed to stumble from bush to bush. After what seemed an age, he finally reached his room. He struggled to put the key in the lock. After several attempts he finally opened the door and, after closing it with a bang that must have woken up all his neighbours, he staggered towards the bed. Half reaching to remove his shoes, Sean collapsed in a heap on the floor. His head was spinning and the last thing he remembered was lifting himself on to the bed, head first, and falling fully clothed into an oblivious sleep.

CHAPTER 16

The next few months of Sean's life were spent cruising the bars and clubs of Mombasa. Nearly all the barmen and doormen got to know him very well. They knew the story of his life: his rugby-playing days, the death of Akinyi and how he had come to be in Kenya. Although Sean was a fairly quiet person he had a natural charm and his easy-going manner endeared him to the locals. Everywhere he went he was greeted warmly by someone who knew him.

Each day Sean would rise with a massive hangover. He was on a bender to try and forget what had happened to Akinyi. He knew deep down he could never forget; he just hoped that time might dull his senses. Usually, after a late breakfast or lunch, Sean would walk for a couple of miles along the shore or sit and watch the ocean. Occasionally he would kick a football about with a few of the local lads on the beach for an hour or so. In spite of the copious amount of drink Sean consumed he was still capable of playing a pretty fair game of football. Maybe his reactions were a little slower than they had been, but his level of skill compensated for his temporary lack of fitness. Usually, by mid-afternoon, he would wander along to the Jolly Tar Bar situated on the beach not far from the cottage he had rented next door to the Indian Ocean Hotel. He got to know Rene and Johans, the owners of the bar, very well. They were Dutch and had come to Kenya about two years earlier after travelling the world on cruise liners. They ran a good bar and welcomed tourists and local people equally. The atmosphere was great, the music was good and there was almost always a funny or bizarre incident between either a local girl and a tourist or between tourists.

One day Sean watched as a Kenyan woman came rushing into the bar and attacked a white guy. Apparently he had not paid her for the sex they had had the previous night. It caused a scene. The guy grabbed his crash helmet and put it on to protect his head and face from the woman's violent fists. He tried to run away to his motorbike, but in his panic he only succeeded in tripping over a table, spilling everything and ending up in a crumpled heap on the ground. The woman stood over him. By this time a large crowd had gathered and were greatly amused as the man pulled a wedge of Kenyan notes from his pocket and handed them to the woman, shouting that it was all the money he had. By this time the woman was laughing at him – and he ran off. As she walked back to the bar to buy a drink, the crowd were cheering and laughing. One of the beach boys started a book on how much money the white man had given her; he was taking bets thick and fast. Nobody ever found out exactly how much money had changed hands because the woman wouldn't say. The beach boy disappeared quickly before he had to pay anyone.

Another time Sean arrived at the bar just as Rene was manhandling a middle-aged German out of the bar. Sean had missed the fun and games but Carmen, one of the waitresses, filled him in. Two drunken Germans had started fighting each other and Rene had stepped in to break up the fight. He punched each of them once, at the same time asking them if they wanted to be punched again. Rene was a big powerful man and they both declined, realizing how much he could hurt them. To see two Europeans fighting each other caused a great deal of amusement among the locals.

Sean spent many an afternoon and evening at the Jolly Tar. He was one of their best customers and would drink until about 7 p.m. before going back to the cottage to sleep off the day's booze. Late in the evening he would get up again and hit the bars around Mombasa Town. His first port of call was normally the Castle Hotel in Moi Avenue. The patio was much like The Thorn Tree Café in Nairobi, a busy pick-up joint, full of sailors. Some of the hookers got to know Sean but gave up hassling him after they realized he wasn't interested in doing business.

Occasionally he would buy some of the girls a drink and sit and talk to them. He often found them to be very amusing and pleasant company. They told him some amazing stories of their experiences, most stranger than fiction.

There was only one occasion when Sean ended up with one of the local girls. He had been on yet another binge and in the morning had woken up to find a black woman in his bed.

'Who the hell are you?' he had enquired, very embarrassed. 'And how did you end up here?' He couldn't remember a thing about the previous evening, least of all bringing someone back to his cottage.

'My name is Lucy, and we were drinking together in the Florida nightclub. You were very drunk so I brought you back here in a taxi.'

Sean shook his head in disbelief. 'Well you might as well stay for breakfast. Come on, you can have a shower while I make it.'

As he rose from the bed he realized he was naked and quickly grabbed a pair of shorts to cover his manhood.

Lucy climbed from her side of the bed and deliberately flaunted her nakedness, seductively wiggling her hips as she walked to the bathroom. Sean could very easily have been tempted but he shook his head and made for the kitchen to prepare breakfast.

He worked in silence and it was not long before he sensed that his every move was being watched. He turned around. It was Lucy. She was dressed in one of his big baggy T-shirts and shorts and a pair of his flip flops.

'How long have you been there?' he asked.

'Not long, but long enough to notice you must have once had a lovely body, Sean.'

He felt his cheeks redden. It was true he used to have a good physique, but the way he was abusing his body he was all too aware that it wouldn't be long before any sign of toned muscle would be gone. He gestured to Lucy to sit down.

'Help yourself,' he said, pointing to the food on the table.

As they ate their breakfast and sipped hot tea, Sean eventually broke the silence. 'Okay, Lucy, did we or didn't we last night?' he asked sheepishly.

'You mean did we make love?' giggled Lucy. 'Yes, Sean, we did, and you were very, very good. You surprised me, particularly as you were so drunk.' This time she laughed loudly.

'Not as much as it surprises me,' puzzled Sean, trying to remember how he could have managed anything considering the state he was in. Sean reasoned that he probably hadn't made love to Lucy; she was just after his money. They finished their breakfast in silence and Sean gave Lucy some money for the taxi.

'Thank you, Sean. Can I come and see you tonight? We can continue where we left off.' She laughed again.

'I don't think so,' said Sean, ushering her out of the door and along the path.

'I will make you a good wife,' she teased, swinging her handbag as she went. Sean closed the door slowly after her.

From the Castle he sometimes went to the Istanbul, just across the road, or up to Saba Saba, a local bar with very good live music on the corner of Jomo Kenyatta Avenue and Ronald Ngala Road. Usually, the bands would play until two in the morning, at which time Sean would take a taxi back to the Bush Bar up at Shanzu on the north coast. Sean's capacity for drink was becoming legendary in the bars he frequented, and it was not long before he was sampling the local marijuana or grass. Although a non-smoker, Sean occasionally dabbled in marijuana. He liked it because it relaxed him, but sometimes he would become completely incapacitated once he had smoked a joint. This often happened in his cottage during the early evening, and he would collapse in his verandah chair while watching the ocean or listening to the sounds of Africa at night.

The one saving grace was that when he dabbled in marijuana he tended not to drink afterwards, except perhaps a few beers towards the end of the evening.

Normally he bought the grass from the boys on the beach but one time in Shanzu village with Mary, one of the local girls who had befriended him, they bought some from the Rasta Man, the local dealer. When they left his house they were stopped by a plain-clothes policeman. Mary told Sean that they needed to bribe the policeman to avoid arrest. If found guilty of possession of drugs in Kenya, they could be sentenced to up to ten years in jail or face a 100,000 shilling fine. He was shocked to find that he had only 100 shillings on him and, for a few seconds, was overwhelmed by the risk he was taking. There was only one thing to do. Offer the money. To his enormous relief the policeman accepted the bribe and sent them on their way. Sean couldn't believe his luck – ten years or a fine of 100,000 shillings and the guy accepts a hundred! He would be more careful next time and never deal direct with a dealer. He considered the only safe source to be the beach boys.

On many a morning Sean awoke in his room with a hangover. He found the best way to feel better was to have another drink. However, two or three beers with breakfast was not really a good idea. Slowly he began to realize that he was becoming an alcoholic, but there seemed to be nothing he could or would do about it. Some days he tried hard to stay off the drink, but by early evening he would drift along to the Jolly Tar and after his first bottle of coke would quickly change to something stronger. His life was on a downward spiral. He was becoming gaunt and scruffy. He had let his appearance deteriorate, often not shaving for days on end and growing his blond hair to shoulder length. Frankly, he was a mess. On the rare occasions when he thought long and hard about doing something about his condition, he would end up with his head buried in another bottle of whisky or Kenya Cane.

He was losing all purpose in life and lacked the motivation to do anything. He realized he couldn't stay in Kenya forever but didn't feel he had much to go back to England for. He had written regularly to Louise, as promised, and she had sent him numerous letters telling him about her progress and adventures at school and what she had been doing in her holidays. He had promised that he would send her some money to join him in Kenya for a holiday, but he knew he couldn't possibly let her see him in his present state. His despair grew greater by the day and he was soon consuming at least two bottles of spirits a day. Some of his Kenyan friends tried to talk to him about his problems, but he wouldn't listen. He thought he could sort things out himself.

Eight months had passed since Akinyi's death and Sean was slowly poisoning himself with drink. After one of his three-day binges he ended up in the Istanbul Bar in Mombasa. It was very late on the third night. He was so drunk he had problems balancing on a bar stool and gave this up as a bad job, finally managing to half lean on the bar in a corner against a wall. The bar was crowded and all Sean could see was a mass of faces. He couldn't work out where he was. He knew he had to get home but he had run out of money and didn't have even his taxi fare back to his cottage.

He could see activity around the bar and could hear music and the babble of voices, but he couldn't focus on anything specific. Everything was just a blur of movement and sound. Then his head began to spin. He did his best to stand still but it seemed that the room and the whole bar was moving. It was like a slow motion replay on television. The last thing Sean could remember was slowly sliding down the wall at the edge of the bar. His last thought was that this time he had really overdone it.

CHAPTER 17

The next morning Sean awoke to the sound of African music. He opened his eyes and looked up at the inside of some *makuti* roofing. He was lying on his back. He tried moving his head but it hurt. Where am I? he thought. Slowly he looked around the room. He knew he wasn't back at his cottage, but where was he? He was lying on a big double bed stark naked. The room was quite large. It was well decorated, with the walls painted white. There were African paintings and a big mirror on one of the walls. In a corner there was a big antique wardrobe. The door was half open and he could see that it was crammed full of women's clothes.

His eyes were bleary but he managed to sit up on his elbows and look directly into the huge mirror opposite the end of the bed. He barely recognized himself. He looked ill. His face was grey and gaunt, he was unshaven, his hair was an unruly mess and his eyes were bloodshot. He felt sick. He needed a drink. His mouth was dry and his lips were cracking from the lack of liquid. Slowly he rose from the bed and looked around the room in search of his clothes. He couldn't see them. He felt very conscious of his nakedness in this strange house and grabbing a colourful *kanga* that hung on the back of the door he wrapped it around himself. His whole body ached. The pain in his head was almost unbearable and he was shaking uncontrollably. Slowly he opened the door and stepped out into a corridor. He saw doors left, right and straight ahead.

The corridor was dimly lit by a single overhead bulb. He tried the handle on the door to his left, but it was locked. He moved slowly along the corridor and tried the one to his right. It was the bathroom. He moved further along to the door straight ahead and carefully opened it. The sound of music grew louder. It was a sitting room, with a TV in the corner, a couple of settees and a coffee table. It was also well decorated and there were fresh flowers in a vase on a Welsh-style dresser. He followed the sound of music and walked through an archway which led into the kitchen. The music was coming from a big ghetto blaster perched on one of the shelves. The back door was open. Sean stepped out into the sunlight. The brightness hurt his eyes. He blinked and stood on the top step for a few seconds while his eyes adjusted. It was a very hot, humid day.

As he looked up he saw a tall black woman with her back to him. She was hanging clothing on the line. Sean recognized his own shirt and the jeans that he had been wearing the day before. As he stepped down on to the terrace the woman looked round and smiled. In spite of his hangover Sean noticed she had a beautiful figure. She was about 5 feet 6 inches tall, with rather large breasts for her otherwise hour-glass shape. Her hair was in a short rasta style which suited her pretty face. Her skin was quite light in colour, with a small scar on her right cheek. Sean momentarily wondered how she had got it.

'You've woken at last,' she said.

'Excuse me, but who are you?' asked Sean. 'And where am I?'

'My name is Njeri,' the woman said. 'I was in the Istanbul last night and I watched you pass out by the bar. You were obviously the worse for wear and you didn't seem to have any friends.'

Sean frowned. He didn't say anything because he was embarrassed by his appalling behaviour. He shuffled uneasily from one foot to the next.

'Sammy, the manager of the bar, is a friend of mine. He carried you to a taxi and I brought you here. This is my home; you looked like you needed a friend.'

'I don't need your help. I'm perfectly capable of looking after myself, thank you,' said Sean rather ungraciously.

'I know your name is Sean and I've seen you around Mombasa a few times. You look like a man who has big problems,' said Njeri.

Sean was a little taken aback and boorishly said, 'I've got plenty of friends and I don't have a problem. Why didn't you just put me in a taxi to my place? Why bring me back here?'

'First of all,' said Njeri, 'I don't know where you live. You had no identity card or passport on you. Not only that, you had no money and I had only enough for my taxi fare home – so I thought the best bet was to bring you with me.'

'I'm sorry,' said Sean, suddenly coming to his senses. 'Forgive me for my rudeness and ingratitude. It is inexcusable.'

'That's okay.' Njeri didn't take offence. 'But you look like you need a shower and some food. There's a fresh towel in the bathroom.'

'I could do with a drink first,' said Sean. 'Have you got a beer? I need the hair of the dog.'

'You just get in that shower,' Njeri commanded. 'You've had enough drink to last you the next ten years, so forget about having any more while you're in this house.'

For a second Sean thought of responding but he knew that discretion was the better part of valour. He looked sheepishly at Njeri, then turned and went to have the shower he so obviously needed.

As Sean entered the bathroom he could see the razor and shaving foam that had been left out for him. He leant on the basin briefly and looked in the mirror. At close distance he looked ghastly, much worse than that first sight of himself in the bedroom mirror. A shave and shower would revive him. It would also make him look more presentable. He shaved slowly and precisely. His hands were trembling so he took care not to cut himself. When he finished he splashed his face with water and then climbed into the shower. It was cold and the initial shock made him shiver and jump out quickly. He gingerly stepped back in again, giving his body time to adjust to the cold. He washed his hair twice and stood under the water for five minutes. His senses were beginning to be revived and he began to feel refreshed. He dried himself slowly and carefully, examining his body in the mirror. His muscles were beginning to loosen. He knew he had put on weight and was generally in poor condition. One day I'll do something about that, thought Sean, but at the moment I could do with a drink. He went back to the bedroom and put on the *kanga* he had worn earlier, plus a T-shirt that Njeri had left on the bed.

He could smell the food as he neared the sitting room. Njeri had set the coffee table for a meal and as he entered the room she emerged from the kitchen carrying a large plate containing an omelette with beans, tomatoes and some hot chapattis. He sat down and attacked the food with a relish he hadn't felt in a long time. It was delicious and in no time he had finished. He downed a large glass of fresh mango juice and then poured himself a cup of Kenyan coffee that was brewing in the pot. He felt better than he had done in a long time, but still felt nauseous from the previous three days' drinking. When he had finished, Njeri came back into the room and sat down on the couch opposite him.

'Well, Mr Sean,' she said. 'I think you and I need to talk.'

'What do you mean, we need to talk?' said Sean sounding more aggressive than he intended. 'I really don't see that we've got much to say, other than for me to thank you for your hospitality. As soon as my clothes are dry I'll be out of here and I won't trouble you again. Besides which, if you won't give me a drink I'll go down town and get one myself.'

Again Njeri assured Sean that he would do no such thing and said that in the best interests of his health he should stay with her for a few days to recover and 'dry out'. She told him that she was going shopping in Mombasa and would be back in about three hours. He could relax and read a magazine or a book, until she returned. It seemed she was placing her trust in him.

However as soon as she had gone Sean went to the garden and fetched his clothes. His shirt was dry but his jeans were still a bit damp. He desperately needed a drink so he climbed into them anyway. They felt cold and rough against his skin, but he thought they'd soon dry out if he found a little bar with a patio. He shut the back door and window and went through the front door, dropping the deadlock as he left. The house had a little front garden that only extended a few paces to the gate. As he walked through the gateway he looked around and could only see other houses. A Maasai who was obviously guarding the house opposite waved and grunted something he couldn't make out. Sean waved back.

He was clearly in quite a good residential area and he turned right into a narrow road, hoping he was heading for somewhere that sold drink. Reaching a crossroads he turned right again into a slightly larger street and walked for about two hundred yards. At the T-junction he made another right turn into a much wider road, which had a small group of shops up on the left. There was bound to be a bar among that lot. In less than a minute he had reached one and walked in confidently. In his best Kiswahili he asked the barman if he could speak to the owner.

'Just a minute, sir, I'll go and get him.'

Shortly afterwards a big, jovial man appeared through a doorway behind the bar.

'Good morning. My name is Jimmy,' he said to Sean. 'How can I help you?'

Sean quickly explained his predicament. He was staying with a woman called Njeri and had no money until she changed some for him at a bank in Mombasa. In the meantime he needed a couple of drinks to keep him occupied until she returned from town. 'My credit is good,' said Sean, adding 'I'll square up with you when she gets back.'

'*Hakuna matata*,' said Jimmy. 'No problem. Have what you like and you can pay me later.'

Sean smiled and thanked him. 'In that case I'll have a Tusker and a large whisky – and one for you as well, Jimmy.'

It was only 2 p.m. The barman served the drinks and Sean quickly downed the Tusker followed by the large whisky.

'Same again,' said Sean to the barman.

For the next hour he drank continuously. Mostly Tuskers, but with a few large whiskies thrown in for good measure. He was soon high again. By six in the evening the bar was beginning to fill up with locals returning from work. It was not long before Sean was holding court with several of them and talking of his rugby days. There was much laughter and leg pulling and soon there were about a dozen men, including Sean, involved in a heavy drinking session. The evening wore on and Sean was slowly approaching the condition he had been in the previous night. The bar began to move of its own accord, the chatter and conversation had become a babble, and he had begun to talk incoherently. He was sitting on a stool at the corner of the bar. His favourite position.

He noticed Njeri walk in. He smiled as she moved quickly towards him.

'And what do you think you are doing, Mr Sean? She demanded. 'I told you to stay at home and wait for me. I have been looking all over for you, and how do I find you? In a drunken state again, same as last night.'

He began to protest, but before he could say anything she asked Jimmy how much Sean owed.

'10,250 shillings.'

'How much?' she almost screeched. 'What's he been drinking?'

She turned to Sean and started shouting at him. 'You're such a stupid man, Sean. You have just made another problem for yourself. Your bar bill is ridiculous. What have you been doing? Buying the whole bar a drink, or what?'

'Well, actually I have,' said Sean with an inane grin on his face.

His friends at the bar laughed, which made Njeri even more angry.

She turned to Jimmy and said: 'Well, 10,000 is all I have, so that will have to do.'

'Don't worry,' said Jimmy. 'Your credit is good here.'

Njeri was furious. 'What do you mean, *my* credit! It's Mr Sean's bill, not mine. You'll have to get the rest of the money off him another time.'

At that she turned and shouted at Sean. 'If you want a bed for the night you had better come now, or you'll be out on the street.'

Sean climbed down from his stool and stumbled across the floor. 'I'll be in tomorrow to pay you the rest, Jimmy,' he called, as he was leaving.

'That's okay, Sean. You'd better get a move on and catch up with your wife,' said Jimmy laughing.

'She's not my wife,' said Sean. 'I only met her last night.'

'Soon will be,' said Jimmy chuckling, and at that, the rest of Sean's new-found friends began to laugh and poke fun at him.

Sean opened the door and hit the street. It was dark but he could just make out the tall figure of Njeri striding up the road. He half ran and half shuffled to catch up with her and, as he did so, she turned sideways and said, 'And don't you say a word, Mr Sean.'

They walked the remaining half a mile in silence. It was only when Njeri unlocked the door that she said, 'You can sleep in the same room as last night. I'll see you tomorrow.'

With that she unlocked the door to the room that Sean couldn't get into earlier, and closed it quickly behind her. Sean went to his room and fell on the bed fully clothed. He was soon fast asleep.

CHAPTER 18

Sean awoke the next morning with a throbbing head and a raging hangover. He lay on the bed thinking that his present way of living really had to stop. He would have to fight his depression another way and stop trying to drown his problems in drink. He contemplated this for a few minutes, then got up and went to the bathroom. After showering he went to the kitchen. Njeri was already at the stove preparing breakfast.

'Njeri,' said Sean, 'I need to talk to you. I'm sorry about my behaviour last night but I'm trying to get over a few problems. I thought I could deal with them on my own but now I realize I can't. When you saw me the other night in the Istanbul I was in a terrible mess. I had been drinking for three days.'

'It looked like it,' said Njeri, curtly.

'My troubles began when my fiancée was brutally murdered about nine months ago. Her death was tragic, sudden and violent. I came here to bury her in her native soil and stayed on for what has become a journey of pure escapism. Now, understandably, my business partner in England has phoned to say that he wants to sell up. He has shown great compassion towards me, but he can no longer run the business on his own.'

Sean went on to tell Njeri about his problems in more detail. He explained that the business was beginning to make huge losses. The market place had changed during the latter part of the eighties. The country was in deep recession and Ian had decided that it was better to stop trading before the inevitable happened and the business went bust.

'He has already sold my Porsche, which was one of my prized possessions,' he said. 'It is unlikely that a buyer will be found for the business at short notice, but he wants to quit while he's ahead. He also has the opportunity of a well-paid job for himself. I can't argue with his decision. I have been no help to him in the last nine months and am unlikely to be for the foreseeable future.'

Sean paused for a while. 'My life is at rock bottom. It has turned into a nightmare. Basically, I am an alcoholic. I have fought off admitting it to myself for a long time, but there, I've done it. I can't look at myself in the mirror any longer. I have let my family down, in particular, my daughter, Louise. She is pining for me because she hasn't seen me for nearly a year. I keep meaning to phone her, but rarely get round to it.'

Sean shuffled in his chair. The sweat began to drip from his forehead.

His hands became clammy. He was very self-conscious about revealing his innermost thoughts to Njeri.

'I don't want to bore you with my problems, but I have begun to hate myself. I hate myself so much that I have had to drink to stop the hate, to try and forget everything. When that doesn't work I turn to drugs. I know it's only marijuana, but when will that lead to something else? I am just a shell of a man. I am lying to you even now. It wasn't just marijuana, there was cocaine on occasions. It has been a steady decline for the last year. It's only a matter of time before I kill myself. I have lost my self-respect and my self-esteem. I know I go through the motions of talking to people about my glory days of international rugby, but they are just a dim and distant memory for me now. When I'm sober I'm lost.'

Njeri was very matter of fact. 'Well, Sean, you are just going to have to start again,' she said. 'At least try to do it for the sake of your daughter. You owe her that much.'

Sean felt ashamed. The mention of Louise had shocked him. He ran his hands through his hair and nervously brushed some fluff off his shirt.

'The last time I spoke to Louise on the phone she was crying. She begged me to come home.' Sean bit his lip and Njeri noticed his eyes watering.

'I just couldn't. My daughter of ten was crying for me, but I couldn't bring myself to go home to her. What sort of a man am I? It is unlikely that she would even recognize me. I've been kidding myself for too long. I need someone to help me, Njeri. I can't do it on my own. I'm at rock bottom. I've put on a brave face and pretended to be strong. I've fooled myself into believing that I can deal with anything that life throws at me. But I guess I'm just an ordinary Joe with the same weaknesses as other men. For the last year I haven't slept properly. I've passed out with drink and drugs for a few hours at a time, but when I wake up I find it hard to sleep again. Sometimes I've laid awake for hours, tossing and turning, trying to work out where I can get the next drink from. If I've drunk everything in the house and been unable to buy more in the middle of the night, I've smashed up the house through temper and frustration.'

Njeri sat impassively, listening to Sean. She said nothing. She was deliberately trying to get him to rid himself of the fears he had bottled up for so long.

'Sometimes I've woken up in my own vomit and urine.'

Njeri made a face that registered disgust.

'I've been through hell and back. I don't think my life will ever be normal again. I fear that I will never again have a relationship with someone else. Maybe I've put my girlfriend on a pedestal, but to lose someone you love so much, so deeply, is heart wrenching. There is a big void in my life and I doubt if I shall ever be able to fill it.'

Sean stopped talking and breathed a sigh of relief. It was as though a great weight had been lifted from his shoulders. He could feel his hands trembling and made an effort to control them by clasping them together. He looked at Njeri and waited for her to speak.

She pondered for a few minutes and observed Sean closely before she spoke. 'Well, Mr Sean, it appears that you have many problems, but if you want me to help, you must do as I say. You must observe a strict set of house rules, otherwise we will simply be wasting each other's time. If you want me to help you fight the evil of drink and drugs, you must stay here for a few weeks. You must not go back to your house and you must definitely not go to any bars. This is a dry house. I do not have any drink in it.'

Sean looked at her quizzically. 'Why's that?' he asked.

'There's no need for me to explain that now. The front door is there and if you want to continue with your bad old ways you can walk out of it at anytime. But if you do, don't come crawling back to me for help a second time around, because I won't let you in. And don't ever forget, you are not the only person who has suffered terrible tragedy. Remember, the good Lord only helps those who help themselves.'

Sean was surprised at Njeri's sudden religious comment, and he was equally taken aback by her toughness. But he didn't have much choice. It might be his last chance and he had to take it.

The next six weeks were hell; the most harrowing of Sean's life. He stayed at Njeri's house and didn't touch a drop of alcohol. The nights were the worst: cold sweats, hot sweats, hallucinations and finally the shakes as the poisons and toxins of the drink and drugs began to leave his system.

He found it hard to sleep. He tried to take his mind off drink, but it was very difficult to concentrate on anything else. The first two weeks were the worst. He had terrible nightmares, and on occasions was violently sick. He was dehydrated and had to drink gallons of water. After a fortnight Sean felt completely washed out.

He started training again. He began to run three miles in the mornings, often getting up as the sun was rising so that the most vigorous exertion was in the cool of the day. When he got back from his run he did a series of exercises to get his body back into condition. In the evenings he ran another five miles. Although his appetite had started to come back, by the end of six weeks he had lost a stone in weight. His muscles had become more taut and his whole body felt better.

Throughout this time Njeri was incredibly patient with him. She showed compassion and firmness in equal measure. Above all, she encouraged him, but Sean did not always see it that way. As far as he was concerned, she pushed him ruthlessly and cajoled him into finding the single-minded determination to kick the drink and drugs habit. On the other hand, she looked after him with great generosity. She did his washing and fed him.

She never said much about herself but was a wonderful listener. This gave Sean the confidence to tell her about his brief time with Akinyi, and, repeatedly, about his grief and sadness.

Towards the end of the six weeks, Sean began to notice how attractive Njeri was. She was a tall, beautiful young woman who carried herself with great poise. She gave the impression of arrogance, but Sean suspected it was more to do with a natural shyness. On the other hand, she seemed to have a worldliness and wisdom beyond her twenty-three years.

During the day Sean helped around the house. He painted the outside and kept the garden in good condition. Njeri had cut his hair and he began to look like the Sean of old. A smile was coming back to his face. His body was becoming tanned from the sun. It had been a long, hard haul. He realized he had to take one day at a time. He still thought about drink and he often felt like a beer. Above all, he knew he had to resist the temptation. One would lead to another . . . and another . . . and he didn't want to take the chance of slipping back into old, potentially fatal, habits.

After dinner in the evenings he sat on the verandah with Njeri and they talked about all sorts of things. She told him about Kenya and the different traditions of its peoples. She told him about her people, the Kikuyu. She explained how she had come to Mombasa four years previously at the age of nineteen in the hope of finding work. Her parents and brothers lived in Nairobi. Her father was a legal clerk in a lawyer's office and her mother used to be a nurse until she and her two brothers were born. One brother was at university in Nairobi and the other was at school. She explained that she had left school at sixteen as her parents couldn't afford to send her to university. Their money was all going on her brothers' education because they still had an old-fashioned view that a girl would just get married and not pursue a career. Njeri struggled to survive. She was a skilled seamstress and made ends meet by making clothes which she sold to local boutiques or tourists. But there was little evidence of her work in the house.

This puzzled Sean. He wondered how she could afford a house of such quality until one evening she explained that she had had a Norwegian boyfriend who had helped to pay the rent. However, they had split up three months previously and she was now living off some savings that she had. She was also looking for a better paid job, but it was difficult because she had no qualifications.

By ten o'clock most evenings Sean was in bed. It was about this time that Njeri used to change into her dancing clothes and go out. Sean would ask her where she was going, but she told him to mind his own business. She often didn't return until morning.

One day Njeri returned from a night out just as Sean had finished his early morning run. He was feeling good and while on his run had decided that the time was right for him to move back to his own place.

'Njeri,' he said, 'I feel ready to go home. I cannot thank you enough for the help you have given me and, when I can afford it, I would like to repay you for your kindness. I also want you to know that if you ever need help or get into difficulties, I would feel privileged to assist. I hope you would not fail to contact me. I will do anything humanly possible to help you.'

When he finished speaking, Sean paused for a moment reflecting on what he had said. He suddenly realized how stiff and formal he must have sounded to Njeri, but he was overcome with embarrassment because he now felt so beholden to her.

Njeri looked stunned. 'Sean, you don't have to leave yet,' she protested. 'I think you need a little bit longer before you go.'

'Ah, get away with you!' he said. 'I feel fitter than I've felt in years and it's all thanks to you. I am going to have a shower now and plan to leave after breakfast. Perhaps you would be kind and call me a taxi for ten o'clock.'

He turned and walked off, leaving Njeri speechless.

By the time he joined Njeri for breakfast, he found a huge meal set out in front of him. They sat in silence. Njeri just picked at her food while Sean ate the ham and eggs with relish. He was hungry after his run and was looking forward to returning to his cottage by the beach. He hadn't seen the ocean for six weeks and longed for a swim.

Njeri meanwhile was feeling very sad. She had enjoyed Sean's company and knew that she would miss him.

'*Hakuna matata*, no problem,' she said all of a sudden. 'Don't lose contact while you are in Mombasa and please let me know if you decide to return to England.'

The taxi arrived punctually at ten and Sean once again thanked Njeri for her kindness. As he walked to the front gate he turned and gave her a big hug. It was the first time he had touched her and, momentarily, he realized again what an attractive woman she was. Briefly the thought struck him that they might have an affair, but he quickly dismissed it. He was almost old enough to be her father. Sean withdrew from their embrace and turned and walked to the taxi. He climbed in beside the driver, who introduced himself as Joseph. As Joseph put the car into gear and began driving away, Sean turned and waved back at Njeri, who was standing at the gate. He could have sworn she was crying, but he wasn't close enough to be sure.

As they drove towards Mombasa, Joseph began telling Sean his life story. Sean didn't really pay much attention. He was sort of half listening. His thoughts were about Njeri and the kindness she had shown him. Without her he would probably be dead by now – or close to it. It was strange but he already felt a little homesick for her. It reminded him of when he used to return to boarding school at the beginning of a new term. It was a feeling of trepidation, of not knowing what to expect of the term ahead. Now it was a case of not knowing where his new life would take him. It was as if he was starting all over again.

Joseph drove slowly because of the bumpy roads, but within half an hour they had arrived at Sean's house. Sean paid him and climbed out of the taxi.

Rather than go into the house straightaway, Sean decided to walk down to the ocean. His house was set approximately 50 metres back from the edge of the beach. It was the first time in six weeks he had seen the sea. He looked out towards the horizon. There were a couple of windsurfers riding the waves. He gazed at the expanse of water and watched in wonderment at the serenity of the scene before him. He took a deep breath and the smell of the salt water filled his nostrils.

There were a few tourists ambling along the shore and the silence hit him. He realized this was part of the world he loved. Although he was Scottish and Irish by birth and had lived all his life in England, he felt very close to Kenya. One day he knew he would settle there. But first he had some business back in Germany. Another six weeks and it would be a full year since Akinyi's death. He remembered his conversation with Hauptkommissar Meissner. He decided then that he would return to England in a month's time at the beginning of December. He needed to spend a bit more time on his own to see if he had conquered his drink problem. After all, he wanted to be fully recovered when he saw Louise.

Sean soon settled back in his house. After going for his evening run he took a short walk along the beach to the Indian Ocean Hotel. His friend Gary, the barman, was on duty. When he saw Sean a big smile lit up his face.

'Mr Sean, it's good to see you again. You are looking so well, just like you did when I first met you. What'll you have to drink? A beer, or maybe a whisky?'

'Neither thanks,' said Sean. 'I'll have a lime and soda with lots of ice. I've kicked the booze, Gary. It's been a struggle but I seem to have managed it. If it hadn't been for a woman called Njeri I might not be here today.'

'Yes, I had heard you were staying with her,' said Gary. 'You be careful,

Sean. She's a wild woman, that one. Always with different men. She's well known in some of the bars, night clubs and hotels along here. I don't mean to talk out of turn, but the word is she's been telling everyone that you're her new boyfriend.'

Sean laughed nervously. 'That's ridiculous,' he said. 'I've never as much as laid a finger on her, let alone become her boyfriend. She's just helped me get over my drink problem. She never asked anything of me or from me. Not even money.'

'Mark my words,' said Gary, 'that one is a cunning woman. She's like so many of the bar girls around here. They're devious and they never do anything to help anyone unless there's something in it for them. Girls like her are past masters at trapping a man. Many of them are brilliant actresses. They get lonely, gullible men who come from Europe to take them back there and then, when they see a better opportunity, they're off. Admittedly, they are often abused by some of the old *muzungu* tourists along the way. But they will persist until they 'capture' one who is genuinely soft-hearted and feels sorry for them. I know some of the girls are not like that but most are. Just watch out for yourself, Sean.'

'Thanks Gary, I'll bear that in mind, but I have a lot to thank her for. She has a generous spirit and has helped me most unselfishly.'

Sean was angry with Gary for running down Njeri but he didn't say anything. He thought that Gary's description of Njeri was in complete contrast to what he had seen of the woman at her house. He had found her quiet, seeming to go about her business in a sensible way, never saying much and certainly never gossiping to him about other people. Altogether, she was a mystery.

Sean daydreamed for a while, not paying much attention to what was going on around him.

'I've decided to return to England, Gary,' he said, hardly realizing he was giving voice to his thoughts. 'I need to get back to earn some money. Next week I will go up to Kisumu to see Akinyi's grave and visit her family. I hope to spend some time there before I return. It may be a while before I see them again. I must pay my respects. It is nearly a year since her death; I didn't know it would take me so long to get over it. Actually, I doubt if I ever will. My heart is still tearing every day, but I must get on with my life. While I've been here I've reached rock bottom and nearly destroyed myself in the process. That won't bring Akinyi back. There will always be a place in my heart for her, but I have come to realize that life is for the living. I've just been feeling sorry for myself. Still, let's talk about something else. How's your family?'

'Oh they're all very well, Sean. My youngest daughter, Julie, started school the other day and she was very excited. She woke at six o'clock in the morning and was dressed in her school uniform hours before she had to get the bus. By the end of the day she was completely exhausted and fell asleep in class during the last lesson,' said Gary.

Sean laughed. 'That's just the sort of thing my daughter Louise did when she was younger. I probably won't recognize her now, she will have grown so much.'

Sean finished his drink and bade Gary goodnight. 'I'll see you before I leave for Kisumu next week.'

The following Monday Sean took the train to Nairobi on his way to Kisumu. At Nairobi station he phoned the airport and booked his flight to Heathrow five days hence. He still had his return ticket.

He continued his journey by train to Kisumu, where he met Akinyi's parents. Onyango was at the station and greeted him like a long-lost son. Fortunately, Sean was now back in good shape so Onyango didn't see any of the ravages he had suffered in the last few months.

During the drive to their homestead Onyango and Sean chatted generally. He asked Sean what he had been up to and Sean talked around the point. He didn't fully enlighten him. He recognized that his alcoholism was a part of his life that he had to try to put behind him. It would be difficult because he knew deep down that he would always be an alcoholic. The problem would never leave him, even if he never touched another drink. He had to take each day at a time.

On arrival at the homestead Sean went immediately to Akinyi's grave. He had brought bougainvillaea flowers with him and he knelt and placed them gently by Akinyi's headstone. It was dusk and there was no one else around. Sean began talking quietly to Akinyi. He felt her presence all around him and told her what had happened to him. He told her that he was going back to England and that he would contact the Frankfurt police to find out what progress had been made in finding her killers.

So far Sean hadn't received any news, so he presumed that the police were no further forward in their investigations. He vowed again that he would seek the murderers out, no matter how long it took. Sean stayed at Akinyi's grave for more than an hour, and it was only when darkness fell that he returned to the house.

On the short walk back, the sounds of Africa at night began. A unique rhythm seemed to surround him. He heard bullfrogs croaking and saw fireflies flitting between the trees.

Occasionally he heard an owl hooting, and he could feel that unmistakable music of the night that he had only ever heard in Africa.

Akinyi's family were most hospitable and they looked after his every need. Although they offered him drinks during his stay, they didn't pursue the issue when he kept refusing. They knew the pain that he had suffered.

On 28 November Sean departed in time to catch the night flight to

Heathrow from Jomo Kenyatta Airport. When the plane touched down at 07.55 hours the next morning, Sean cleared customs as quickly as he could. His parents were meeting him and Louise would be there with them. He was a little nervous as he walked through the automatic doors into the meeting area. He looked left and right and then straight ahead. Then he saw Louise with his mother and father. She stood still for a minute and then a huge smile lit up her face.

'Daddy, Daddy,' she shouted as she ran towards him.

She jumped up into his arms and held him very tightly.

'I've missed you so much, Daddy,' she cried, the tears beginning to flow. 'I'm just so excited to see you. It's been so long.'

Sean put her down eventually and she grabbed his hand as he walked forward to give his mother a hug and a kiss. His father shook him firmly by the hand and said: 'It's good to see you, boy.'

On the journey home Louise never stopped talking. Sean was overwhelmed by her pleasure in seeing him, but deep down he wasn't sure how long he would be staying. He would probably have to break her heart again quite soon. What a father, he thought to himself.

He spent the next few days with Louise and his parents. He took her ice skating at Richmond, to the cinema and to McDonald's, and tried to occupy her with many of the activities that a father would normally offer his daughter. Louise loved every minute of her stay with her father and, on the drive home to her mother's house, they chatted about her hobbies and all the things that she was involved in. Next year she would be starting senior school and was very excited at the prospect.

On reaching Sally's house, Sean tried to warn Louise that he was likely to have to go away again for a while.

'But, Daddy, I don't want you to go away again! Why can't I see you just like a normal dad? I don't like it when you're not around. I get worried. At least when you're in Richmond I can always phone you. Please don't go abroad again.'

'I'm not sure that I will be going away again, but if I do, I don't think it will be for long,' lied Sean.

As always, Sally was waiting for them. 'Late again, Sean. Why can't you ever be on time? I'm meant to be going out and now I'm late.'

'I'm sorry,' he said. 'The traffic was bad.'

'Oh, don't give me that! And make sure you telephone regularly.' She turned to Louise. 'Say goodbye to your father, Louise,' she said, rather pointedly emphasizing the word 'father'.

They hugged each other and Sean reached into his pocket and gave her some pocket money. 'Don't spend it all at once, mind.' With that he jumped into his car, did a rapid U-turn and was off towards the motorway heading for home.

CHAPTER 19

On returning to his house in Richmond for the first time in a year, Sean was pleasantly surprised to find that it was warm and presentable. His mother had been her usual thoughtful self and had cleaned up for him or, at least, got her daily help to come in. He must remember to thank her, he thought. He turned on the gas log-effect fire and slumped in a chair. He would have preferred a real fire, but was often too tired to make one – or clean the grate afterwards. Sean didn't want to reflect on his past. He now had to be positive and think about the present. He had to phone Meissner in Frankfurt and he had to sort out a job. But first he had to call James to catch up on all the news and discuss his plans.

James had made captain at the age of twenty-five and had spent the last ten years or so attached to the SAS, undertaking all sorts of missions the world over. He had been awarded the Military Medal in the Falklands and had received the Military Cross for his work in Northern Ireland, plus a host of campaign medals. He never told Sean much about his job because he was governed by the Official Secrets Act, however Sean knew enough to realize it was dangerous work. No doubt James had cheated death on many occasions. But the last time they had spoken, James had expressed for the first time ever his dissatisfaction with the army. He was disillusioned. Although he had come up through the ranks and had been made one of the youngest captains ever in the British army, he knew that his colour would inhibit his progress up the ladder. He could not see many of the higher ranks open to him. He had already been overlooked several times for his majority in favour of less competent people.

Sean dialled James's number in Hereford. He wasn't sure whether he would be there or on one of his missions. He would probably get Yolanda, James's girlfriend. The phone rang briefly and James answered it.

'Hello,' said Sean, 'I didn't expect to catch you in but I'm glad you're there. I just phoned for a chat.'

'Good Lord, if it isn't a voice from the past!' chuckled James. 'I'd given you up for dead a long time ago. I figured you had disappeared off the face of the earth. Still, I guess bad pennies always turn up. How are things with you, Sean? We must get together for a beer. Why don't you come up for the weekend and we can talk about old times – and all your news.'

'That would be great,' said Sean. 'I've got a few things to sort out here, but I can make it on Friday evening.'

'I look forward to seeing you then.'

'I'll be there around six.'

'Bye,' said James. 'See you Friday.'

Sean replaced the receiver, thinking about all he had to do before Friday. The most important thing of all was to try to get a job. At the very least he had to earn some money. His former business had been sold in small tranches to keep the Revenue and VAT men at bay. In fact, Sean and Ian had been fairly lucky. They had ended up with about £5,000 each. It wasn't much for seven years' hard work but at least they didn't owe anybody anything. Fortunately for Sean he had a small mortgage. He had been lucky in the property market, buying and selling a house in a good area of Richmond just at the right time. At least it was a base for him, but it now felt much less like home than when Akinyi was around. Even though she hadn't been there much, she had brought a freshness to the place. A little bit of heart and soul, thought Sean.

It was time for Sean to contact former business acquaintances to try and get himself some work. He phoned a few who were pleased to hear from him, but they were struggling with the recession and couldn't offer anything at the moment. After four fruitless hours on the phone, Sean decided to call an old rugby acquaintance, Clive Smith. Smithy had been a prop forward when they played together at London Scottish and it was a team joke that he was Sean's minder. They went everywhere together and roomed on tour and for overnight away games. Smithy had set up his own sports marketing business some years earlier and was now quite successful. He had good business acumen and never openly displayed his wealth. He hadn't had a good education like Sean but had made it through hard work and sheer determination. He was a bit rough round the edges but very down to earth. He got on well with most people from all walks of life.

The phone rang four times before being picked up by Smithy's secretary.

'Good morning, this is ProSports, how can I help you?' she said cheerfully.

'Good morning,' said Sean. 'I'd like to speak to Clive Smith, please.'

'Just a moment, I'll see if he's available.'

Sean waited briefly.

'I'm sorry,' said the girl when she came back on the line. 'He's in a meeting at the moment. Can I take a message so that he can call you back, or will you call again later?'

'Just tell him it's Sean Cameron, please. I'll only take a couple of minutes of his time.'

'Hold on,' she said.

Seconds later Smithy came on the line. 'Well if it isn't my old mate Sean Cameron. Last I heard, you'd hit the hippy trail to Africa or India or some such distant part of the world. What are you up to?'

Sean explained briefly that he had been away for a year and was now back in England. His business had been sold and he was looking for a job.

'Well, as luck would have it,' said Smithy, 'I've just won a new contract and I need someone to run the account for me. It probably won't be your kind of money, Sean, but if you want to come and have a chat with me this afternoon, maybe we can fix up something. You know where I am now?'

'Just off Shaftesbury Avenue?' queried Sean.

'Yes, that's right. Make it five o'clock and perhaps we can go for a beer afterwards.'

'Sounds great,' said Sean. 'See you later.'

That afternoon Sean changed into a suit and tie for the first time in almost a year. It felt strange, after living in jeans and T-shirts for so long. He decided not to drive but took the train to Waterloo and then the tube to Piccadilly, from where he walked up Shaftesbury Avenue to Smithy's office. On arrival he was greeted in reception by a tall blond girl in a mini skirt. Smithy always did have good taste in women, thought Sean, as he admired her neat, trim figure.

'Clive will be with you shortly,' she said. 'In the meantime, please take a seat.'

Sean sat down in one of the low, comfortable chairs and picked up a copy of the current *Rugby World*. He flicked through the pages briefly. He was very out of touch and barely recognized any of the names mentioned except for a few of the older players who had just been starting out as Sean was coming to the end of his international career.

As he put the magazine down, Smithy walked in. He was six foot tall, dark haired, with a rugged face bearing the scars of many rugby accidents and perhaps even a few fights! He looked almost as wide as he was high. He had always been big during his playing days, but now he looked as if he were eighteen stone or more.

Sean stood up and shook Smithy by the hand. 'Great to see you, Smithy, and thanks for seeing me at such short notice.'

'Don't mention it. Come on into my office.'

Sean followed him into a plush, spacious room. Smithy walked behind a huge mahogany desk and settled down in a very large leather swivel chair.

He's certainly doing well, thought Sean, looking around the rest of the room and admiring the bookcases that lined the walls.

'Right,' said Smithy. 'Let's get down to business.'

He explained that he had secured a new deal to handle all the outside promotions for the Japanese electronics giant Sukimoto. They had just opened a new factory near Derby that would be assembling a new digital telephone system that they wanted to sell in the UK and Europe. Part of the marketing plan was to promote the product via sports sponsorship because of the young and clean image, and also to test-market the system at outside events. In addition, they wanted to organize one or two corporate hospitality days at venues such as Ascot, Twickenham and Henley.

'Sounds just up my street,' said Sean.

'The salary's not brilliant,' warned Smithy. 'I can only pay you thirty a year plus expenses and a car. I know it's not your kind of money, Sean, but that's all I've got in the budget. If this project is successful then maybe we can develop a closer and longer-term association. I can give you a six-month contract to set the whole thing up. I want you to employ an assistant who can take over the day-to-day running of it once the foundations are laid.'

'It's all fine by me,' said Sean. 'When do you want me to start?'

'A week on Monday would be ideal,' said Smithy.

They shook hands on the deal.

'I've got a few things to clear up here, then we can go and have a few pints and you can tell me what you've been up to. If you wait in reception, Emma will look after you until I've finished. I should only be about forty-five minutes.'

Sean got up to leave. 'Thanks again, Smithy, I am eternally grateful to you. You don't know how much I need this job.'

Sean waited an hour for Smithy to finish. In the meantime he chatted to Emma, the blond receptionist, about the various projects and clients that ProSports were involved with at that time. She was a pleasant, easy-going girl and Sean took an instant liking to her. Eventually Smithy came out of his office.

'Let's go, Sean. There's a nice little tapas bar on the corner of Brompton Road. It's not far from where I live.'

It was now seven o'clock and the London rush-hour traffic was beginning to tail off. It was raining, a typical light English drizzle that Sean hadn't experienced for a while. They hailed a cab to take them to Amigos. When they arrived, Smithy paid the cabbie and they entered the bar. It was quite busy with people stopping for an end-of-work drink before heading off for home. Smithy ordered a pint of lager for himself and turned to Sean, 'What'll it be?'

'I'll just have mineral water with ice.'

Smithy laughed. 'What, you, a mineral water? No way! I'm sorry, Sean, but I never thought I'd see the day that you'd be ordering mineral water in a bar. What's happened to the Sean who used to drink till he dropped? I'll get you a pint.'

'No, really,' said Sean firmly. 'I only want mineral water, please. I'll explain why in a minute.'

Smithy was about to protest but thought better of it. 'A mineral water for the girl here,' he laughed. 'And one for yourself,' he said to the barman.

'Cheers,' said Sean.

'Bottoms up, and here's to Sukimoto – and you'd better have a damned good reason for why you're not drinking, Sean. Explain yourself, my man.'

Sean related the last year of his life to Smithy. He explained that much as he would like to have a drink, he couldn't. He told Smithy of his alcoholism and his fight to beat the disease.

'I reached rock bottom,' said Sean grimly, recalling the effects of the worst of his excesses. 'It was only the intervention of a young Kenyan girl called Njeri that saved me. Without her help I probably wouldn't be here now.'

Smithy was stunned by Sean's story.

They talked of old times together, their rugby playing days and what the future held. Smithy still wasn't married. He was a larger than life personality who had plenty of girlfriends around him, but no one in particular. Like most of his mates he had considered settling down, but enjoyed life too much to commit himself to one person. He thought he would settle down one day, but he wasn't ready yet.

Sean told Smithy that he was going to see James the following day. He didn't tell him the purpose of his visit. He didn't want to jeopardize his new job.

Sean's thoughts wandered. He had to call Meissner the next morning. It was exactly a year to the day since Akinyi's death and he wanted a full report of the progress that had been made. The evening passed quickly. Smithy was still his bubbly old self and was soon a little merry from the drink. They ordered some chilli and tacos and Smithy demolished a bottle of wine on his own.

Sean looked on enviously, but knew he had to take one day at a time in his fight against drinking. Somehow it seemed a bit easier to be in a place that sold alcohol than sitting at home without any and wanting it. Although it was just an arm's length away, Sean found it easier to refuse. He knew one drink would be one drink too many.

They left Amigos shortly after eleven; Sean knew he had just enough time to catch the last tube home. He said goodbye to Smithy, adding that he'd see him a week on Monday.

He was pleased with his day and how things were working out.

Next morning Sean called Meissner. The police had hauled in ten people for questioning regarding Akinyi's death, all neo-Nazis and well known to them. Despite intensive interrogation, however, none of them had confessed to being involved in the attack. Even after twenty-four hours, the legal maximum anyone could be held in custody without charge or a judge's consent, Meissner could not establish sufficient evidence to bring charges. He said he had a gut feeling that six of the ten were definitely involved, but all of them appeared to be foot soldiers. He was sure the leader was not among them. Two of them, Rheiner Grunefeld and Wolfgang Schenkers, appeared to be more agitated and nervous than the others. Meissner felt they were weakening and resolved to pull them in for further questioning. They were summarily hauled in on their own about two weeks later but they still didn't break. Meissner thought he was getting closer and expected them to crack eventually. He kept hounding them. He pulled them in a couple more times and on each occasion he sensed they were nearer to breaking point. He knew that he would soon be there but shortly afterwards Grunefeld was found dead under suspicious circumstances and Schenkers had disappeared. Meissner put out 'most wanted' posters at all the German police stations in his search for Schenkers.

A year later and the police had drawn a blank.

'I've pursued every possible avenue, Mr Cameron, and I'm still no nearer. We will get there eventually and I'm sure we'll solve it, but you will have to be patient.'

'Thanks for your efforts, Inspector Meissner,' Sean said, a touch of sarcasm evident.

He didn't elaborate on his thoughts to Meissner. He hung up. He would be talking to James that night and they would decide on a course of action. Meissner was right about Sean needing to be more patient. He realized that he had to stay calm and focused if he were to pursue the killers successfully.

The drive to Hereford took four hours. It was a bright, crisp, clear day. The sun was shining and the temperature was almost zero. Sean marvelled at the spectacular views over the rolling hillsides of Oxfordshire and the drive through Cheltenham brought back memories of a day he had spent with Akinyi. It was an attractive English Spa town with Georgian architecture. He would like to have stopped for a while, but he needed to press on if he were to arrive in Hereford before dark. Nevertheless, although there was a certain something about England that he loved, he knew that he would eventually settle in Africa.

As darkness fell he arrived at James's house. Yolanda greeted him at the door with a broad smile. She was beautiful, tall, slim and with light-brown skin. In the early sixties she had escaped from Cuba with her parents and they had somehow arrived in England via Miami. She had been brought up in London and had met James when she was researching a report for the *Mail on Sunday Magazine* about his experiences in the Falklands War. The two had immediately been attracted to each other and had been together ever since. She still worked as a freelance journalist, mostly when James was away on one of his missions. Otherwise she was quite happy to stay at home and look after their two young children. Yolanda showed Sean to his room where he had a quick wash before joining her downstairs for a cup of tea. He sank into a big armchair beside the roaring log fire and they chatted easily about his experiences in Kenya over the past year, that Sean managed to keep as brief as possible. James had taken the afternoon off but had gone to collect their two children from games practice at school. He would be home later. Yolanda excused herself and went off to prepare dinner.

Meanwhile, Sean sank deeper into the comfortable armchair. He watched the flames flickering in the fire and his mind drifted back to Kenya, to the times he had gone tracking in the bush. He had often gone off for three or four days at a time with Olepesai, a Maasai guide, who taught him all sorts of hunting tricks. He would spend hours round a camp fire at night listening to old folk tales of the Maasai people.

Sean soon dozed off into a light sleep, to be eventually woken by the arrival of James and the two children. He stood up as James entered the room. His friend hadn't changed much, other than a slight greying of hair round the temples. He had a very dark complexion, almost black, and was six foot two inches tall with a strong, muscular body, just as Sean remembered him. There wasn't an ounce of superfluous fat to be seen. It was obvious that he still kept himself in superb physical condition. They shook hands and each took a step back to assess the other.

James's two children appeared by his side. Sean said hello to Mark, who was nine, and Maria, a year younger. They both grinned at Sean and said 'Hello'.

'Right, you two,' said Yolanda, briskly. 'I think a bath is in order, then your supper and then it's off to bed. Your daddy and Sean have lots of talking to do.'

'But Mummy,' they pleaded, 'it's Friday night and there's no school tomorrow. So why can't we stay up?'

'No arguments; be off with you,' said Yolanda firmly, as she followed them upstairs.

'We're off for a quick pint at the local before dinner,' James shouted as she disappeared out of sight. 'We'll be back in about an hour.'

'Dinner's at eight,' she called back. 'So don't be late.'

The pub was only six minutes away. It was a typical old English inn, characteristic of the area, and on entering it Sean felt immediately relaxed. He was desperate for a pint, but knew he shouldn't. He got to the bar first and ordered a pint of Guinness for James and a mineral water for himself.

'What on earth are you drinking?' asked James, amazed as they sat down at a small table in the corner near the fire.

'It's a long story.'

How many more times was he going to have to explain to his friends about his fight against alcoholism? He sat and talked to James about Kenya, telling him as briefly as possible about what had happened. He was becoming a bit bored with his own story, but he knew his friends wanted to know what he had been up to, especially as they had not heard from him for so long. Eventually, Sean broached the subject of Akinyi's death and the killers.

'You remember, James, when we talked a year ago about pursuing Akinyi's killers, I told you I was going to go after them myself if the police hadn't caught them. I spoke to Meissner of the Frankfurt police today and he's no nearer a successful prosecution. You promised me then that you'd help train me in unarmed combat and how to handle guns and so on. Well, I'm ready now.'

James looked at Sean briefly. 'I'd love to help you, but right now I can't. I have six more months in the army and, as a serving officer, I can't get involved with anything that might jeopardize my career record. I want to leave on good terms, even though I know I have been treated badly. I have struggled for years; I've had to do twice as well as the next man, simply to progress to where I am now. I intend setting up a security firm specializing in private investigation and the supply of bodyguards and surveillance teams. What I can promise you, however, is that in six months' time you can be my first client. I shall set aside three months of my time and I am sure we will find the killers between us. You have my word.'

'As luck would have it,' said Sean, 'I've just been offered a six-month contract by Smithy, an old rugby playing pal of mine, so the timing couldn't be better. I start a week on Monday and will be able to honour our agreement without letting him down.'

'That's great,' said James. 'But what we can do in the meantime is to put you through a special SAS crash course in basic training. You'll need to get yourself fit again – and I mean really fit, better even than the condition you were in when you were playing for Scotland. It's probably a tall order for a man your age,' he said jokingly, 'but if I can do it so can you.' Before Sean could respond he glanced at his watch. 'Come on. Let's get a move on. Yolanda will kill us if we're late.'

At dinner Sean told them about Njeri. He explained that he wanted to send her an air ticket to come to England as a way of thanking her for her help while he was in Kenya. He also explained that they hadn't had a physical relationship of any kind, but ... it had recently dawned on him that he missed her a great deal.

'Sounds to me like there could be a romance in the offing,' giggled Yolanda.

'Not at all,' Sean flushed, feeling embarrassed.

'Well it wouldn't do you any harm if it happened,' teased James.

Sean told them what Gary the barman had said about Njeri.

'Oh you shouldn't worry about local gossip,' said James. 'There are many good-time girls like Njeri in places like Kenya. They are not really prostitutes, just girls looking for fun and, they hope, a prince to carry them away from their tough life. Most of them have young children from teenage liaisons at school and struggle to make ends meet.'

'The situation of young unmarried mothers in the developing world is really no different to that in Europe or in America – or anywhere else, for that matter,' interrupted Yolanda.

'Well at least she doesn't fall into the category of an unmarried mother. I don't know much about her but I think she would have told me if she had children,' said Sean. He paused. 'At least, I saw no evidence of any children in her house.'

'You just be careful,' said James. 'I've seen many of our young squaddies fall for local girls when they have been abroad. They bring them back to England to marry them and usually end up with a whole heap of trouble. Most of the girls can't adjust to our way of life – and most of the lads are too young and stupid to be able to deal with the problems. Not that you fall into that category, Sean.'

'Have a good time by all means, but don't get yourself involved in something that will cost you a lot of heartache and money to boot,' added Yolanda.

'Is this a lecture?' said Sean, not fully realizing the potential problems he might create for himself by inviting Njeri to England.

The rest of the weekend passed uneventfully. Sean felt good being back with his friends. In some ways it was great to be home, but he still had a lot on his mind.

The following week, before Sean was due to start work with Smithy, he took the opportunity to sort out his house and his financial affairs. He also bought an open return air ticket for Njeri, which he sent to her together with a banker's draft for £500 to enable her to pay off her debts before she came to England. Sean never liked being beholden to anyone, and he felt a little more relaxed for now he had at least in part repaid his debt to Njeri.

CHAPTER 20

The following Monday Sean started work. Having been idle for so long, it came as a bit of a shock, but by the end of the first week his powers of concentration had improved and he was soon back into the swing of things. Emma, the receptionist, had been appointed as his assistant and he soon realized that she would be an absolute jewel in helping him set up their marketing and promotional strategy for Sukimoto. She had great organizational ability, was easy on the eyes and had a great sense of humour.

However, by the Friday night Sean was mentally and physically exhausted. He hadn't had a chance to get into a fitness regime as James had suggested, but he knew he would have to make a start at the weekend. He planned to alternate his training programme with a mixture of running, training in the gym and the occasional game of squash. He had six months to prepare himself for what would probably be one of the toughest challenges of his life.

On the Thursday of the second week at Smithy's, Sean received a fax from Njeri thanking him for the ticket and the money. She confirmed her flight and would be arriving on the morning of Saturday 16 December. However, she had had to pay some bribe money to get her passport application processed quickly and she needed another £100. Sean was incensed. He knew a passport only cost £14 or the equivalent of 1,500 Kenya shillings.

What really annoyed him was that everyone in Kenya complained of corruption in high places in government, but the problem was endemic and had spread right across Kenyan society. It had become a way of life for most people. He knew he had no right to criticize the Kenyan people because so much of their trouble was a deep-rooted legacy of the past. But it was also true that Kenyan politicians and businessmen dealing with the West had enriched themselves shamelessly, largely because they were encouraged to accept bribes by outsiders seeking business or political advantage.

As in any other culture, people want prosperity and the material possessions it brings. It is often said that the quickest way to achieve prosperity in Africa is to be a member of government, the civil service or in any other position of power. Hence, a clerk in the passport office could use his position to improve his standard of living. He could supplement his income by charging 'extra' for what, after all, was every Kenyan's right: to have his or her own passport. Sean didn't know how these problems could be resolved. He thought the answer had to come from within and only when outside interference and influences could be resisted on ethical grounds would Kenya be able to sort out its own problems.

Sean duly sent Njeri the £100. Shortly thereafter she got her passport and telephoned Sean to let him know the good news. She was ecstatic.

Sean, too, was excited. He was looking forward to her arrival in ten days' time.

Njeri's plane arrived at 7.55 a.m. and Sean waited at the meeting point, expecting her to be through the baggage hall within about forty-five minutes of landing.

However, after waiting an hour and a half, he became increasingly agitated. Perhaps she had decided not to come after all. Sean wasn't really sure what to do, so he went to the Kenya Airways desk to find out whether there was a problem. The girl at the desk confirmed that the plane had landed on time and suggested that Njeri might have been detained by Immigration. She proposed that Sean phone them from the special phone sited near the meeting point. He soon found it and dialled the number as instructed by the sign near the handset. After a long ring, the phone was eventually answered. Sean introduced himself and explained the situation.

'I am waiting for a friend called Njeri Mwangi, who should have arrived on the 7.55 from Nairobi. I've been advised by the Kenya Airways desk to check with you.'

'Just a moment please, I'll see if we have her here.' Sean waited for the person to come back on the line.

'Yes, we have Miss Mwangi here. She is being interviewed by the Immigration department at the moment and we will call you shortly when they have finished. Someone will be down to collect you, so stay near the phone.'

After a further hour's wait Sean became even more agitated. He decided to call the Immigration department again.

'Hello,' he said. 'This is Sean Cameron. I phoned over an hour ago and someone said they would be down to collect me. Is there a problem?'

'Oh no, Mr Cameron, I'm sorry, but we have been very busy. My name is Mrs Patel. I will be down in five minutes.'

Mrs Patel was a short, fat woman who had squeezed herself into a tight-fitting black suit with a ridiculously short mini skirt. She was heavily made up and Sean wanted to laugh, but managed to stifle it.

'Mr Cameron? You had better come this way. I would like to ask you a few questions about Miss Mwangi. It's just routine, so there is nothing to worry about.'

'I'm not worried,' said Sean. 'I have come to meet Miss Mwangi, who is here for a holiday at my invitation. I must say, I find it somewhat irritating that she has been kept for questioning and I am left wondering about her whereabouts. Wouldn't it have been better to put a call out over the public address system requesting me to go to the information desk? Then I could have been told what's going on, as presumably she's told you that I was meeting her. I find it a lack of consideration on your part.'

'I'm sorry,' said Mrs Patel, apologizing again. 'But we have hundreds of immigrants arriving every day.' She glanced at her watch. 'We couldn't possibly put out a call for everyone,' she said, rather patronizingly.

When they reached the second floor Sean was shown into a small office.

'Just wait there, I'll be back in a minute.'

Sean sat down. The office was stark and drab. It reminded him of George Orwell's *1984*. This really was like Big Brother watching, Sean thought. He was in England, for God's sake, not some Eastern Bloc police state.

Mrs Patel returned and sat down in front of Sean, opening a file she had brought with her. 'Right, Mr Cameron, this is just a formality, but we'd like to know where you met Miss Mwangi?'

'I met her when I was on holiday in Kenya this year.'

'How long were you there?'

'I was there for nearly twelve months. I took a sabbatical after the death of my fiancée last December.'

'I'm so ...'

Sean interrupted her before she could finish. 'There's no need to be.' he said aggressively.

'Where exactly did you meet Miss Mwangi?'

'I met her in a bar.' He didn't want to elaborate on his condition at the time. 'We became friends and I stayed at her house for a while.'

'Did you sleep with her?'

'What business is that of yours?' Sean said, calmly.

Mrs Patel looked at Sean and saw that he was angry. 'Do you know what work she did in Kenya?'

'As far as I know she was a seamstress, and occasionally she danced in a few of the tourist hotels.'

'Why did you ask her to England, Mr Cameron? And how can a young girl in her early twenties from Kenya afford the flight to England?'

'Listen,' said Sean, becoming increasingly angry. 'She became my friend and I am expressing my gratitude to her by paying for a holiday in England as a thank you for her friendship. I was down on my luck for a while and she helped me enormously, that's all there is to it.'

'Have you noticed how beautiful Miss Mwangi is, Mr Cameron?'

'Yes, of course, I would be blind and stupid not to!'

'May I suggest to you, Mr Cameron, that you picked up Miss Mwangi in a bar and you had a relationship with her?'

'How dare you,' said Sean. 'As I have already said, we have a friendship, a very good and warm friendship – but not a relationship as you mean it. Anyway, what right have you to ask me these questions?'

'We are concerned to know how Miss Mwangi will support herself while in England. She has arrived here with very little money.'

'I am going to support her,' said Sean. 'I've paid for her return air ticket and she will stay at my house for up to six months.'

'How do I know that you can afford to support her? What exactly do you earn and where do you live?' Mrs Patel asked.

'I live in my own house in Richmond and I am currently earning £30,000 per annum. Before I went to Kenya I had my own business and was earning £50,000 a year,' he said.

It suddenly dawned on him what Mrs Patel was implying.

'Miss Mwangi is not a prostitute, if that's what you're implying. She comes from a good family in Kenya. Her father is a solicitor's clerk in Nairobi and her mother is a nurse.'

'I'm not suggesting she is a prostitute,' said Mrs Patel. 'I have no more questions for you. If you'd like to wait here I'll fetch Miss Mwangi.'

Five minutes later she returned with Njeri, who looked very tired and obviously scared. When she saw Sean she ran to him and threw her arms around him.

'Oh, Sean, it's great to see you. I was so scared that I would be sent back without seeing you.' She hugged Sean tighter. 'I am sorry to have caused you all this trouble.'

'It's no problem,' said Sean, soothingly. 'Let's go home.'

As they left the interview room, Sean turned and thanked Mrs Patel for allowing Njeri a six-month visitor's visa. He tried not to sound sarcastic and felt sick about having to be so nice to her. Although it was better not to cause a scene and complain about the way they had been treated, he knew that he should have done so. But he just wanted to get the hell out of the place. He felt it was petty bureaucracy gone mad.

Sean picked up Njeri's case and she unexpectedly grabbed his hand. He felt a little self-conscious as they walked slowly back to the car park in Terminal 3.

It was obvious he was quite a lot older than Njeri, and he could see people staring at them. He was more conscious of the difference in age than of colour. It crossed his mind that people would be thinking there goes another rich white man taking advantage of a vulnerable young girl from the Third World. It was strange, really, because Sean had always been at ease with himself, and in the past a thought like that would never have crossed his mind. He dismissed it.

They reached his car, a three series 'M' BMW that came with his new job. It was okay, but nothing like his old Porsche. Still, beggars can't be choosers, he thought.

It was Njeri who broke the silence.

'Sean, before we go any further I cannot thank you enough for bringing me here. When you left for England without saying goodbye I was so upset. I missed you so much. Gary from the Indian Ocean Hotel told me that you had gone. I really thought I would never see you again. It was then that I realized how I felt about you. In spite of your problems. I have met many men in my short life but no one such as you, Sean. I'm in love with you and have been for a long time.'

Surprise registered all over Sean's face. He didn't know what to say. He paused for a minute, trying to take it all in.

'Come on, Njeri. This is not the place to talk,' he said. He opened the nearside front door to the car. 'We can talk later at home.' He shut the car door, walked round to the boot and deposited Njeri's case. He was shaking a little as he climbed in beside her. He put the key in the ignition and pressed the throttle, bringing the engine to life. There was a dull throaty roar.

On the way to Richmond Sean asked Njeri about her family, and how they felt about her travelling to England to stay with a strange man.

'They don't mind. My father is a keen rugby follower. He played for Nairobi Harlequins in the days when he was a student. He remembers watching you on TV in the Five Nations Championship matches. They used to watch recorded videos at the rugby club. Just think, Sean, he's only ten years older than you! He's quite impressed and feels sure that you will look after me. My mother just wants me to find a nice husband and settle down and have children. Perhaps you will be that man, Sean?'

'Steady on,' responded Sean. He could feel himself going a deep scarlet colour. 'We'll be home in a few minutes. I think you need a rest after your long journey and then we can go out to dinner tonight. I know a perfect little Italian restaurant in the centre of town that you'll enjoy.'

'That sounds nice, Sean, I shall look forward to it.'

Sean sensed that Njeri was watching him closely. He felt a bit awkward and was pleased when they got home. Sean opened the front door and gestured for Njeri to go inside.

'After you,' he said.

At that, Njeri turned and kissed him on the cheek. Again he felt himself turning a deep scarlet colour.

'Your room is the spare room,' he stammered. 'It's up the stairs, first door on the left. The one opposite is for Louise, my daughter, and mine is at the end of the landing, next to the bathroom. Make yourself at home. There are towels in the airing cupboard, so help yourself. If you want to lie down that's not a problem, I've got some paperwork to keep me busy this afternoon.'

'Thank you, Sean,' Njeri said. 'I'll have a shower and then I think I'll sleep for a while. I'm so tired after the long journey. I didn't sleep at all last night, I was too excited, but I feel I could sleep for a week now.'

Sean woke Njeri at seven, and by 8.30 they were sitting in Rossi's Italian restaurant in the centre of Richmond. Sean couldn't bring himself to take Njeri to Mario's, where he had dined several times with Akinyi. The atmosphere was less formal at Rossi's and the clientele were somewhat younger. The place was very busy and lively and he thought Njeri would enjoy it, especially the main attraction of the waiters singing as they walked between the tables. The evening passed quickly. Sean and Njeri never stopped talking. She was a great conversationalist and was obviously very excited about her first night in England. Sean felt very comfortable in her company. By 11.30 he could see that Njeri was getting a little drunk. How he wished he could share that experience with her, but he knew he daren't. By midnight they were back home.

'Tomorrow I'll take you to Windsor Castle,' Sean suggested, as they climbed the stairs to bed. 'You'll enjoy that. Sleep well, and goodnight.'

'Thanks again for everything, Sean.' They had reached the landing. Njeri leant over and kissed him full on the lips.

Sean blushed, but something stirred deep within him and he realized again how attractive she was. 'No problem,' he said. 'See you in the morning.'

With that he went to his room and closed the door behind him. He undressed quickly and was soon in bed, thinking of everything that had happened over the last couple of years. He realized that his life had changed completely. He thought of Njeri and realized how attracted he was to her, but he didn't want any involvement, not yet at any rate. He had to deal with Akinyi's killers before he could get on with his life, and he didn't want any distractions.

He was drifting off to sleep when he heard his door opening quietly. He could just make out Njeri's form as she crossed the darkened room and slipped into bed beside him.

'Don't say anything, Sean, and don't argue.' Her fingers moved to his lips to silence him. She took him in her arms and hugged him, whispering, 'Sean, I will take care of you and love you forever.'

Sean felt uncomfortable. His body was telling him one thing, and his mind another. It would be unfair of him to take advantage of Njeri. 'I am very, very fond of you, and I know I am physically attracted to you, but I don't love you.' He paused. 'I don't know whether I can ever love anyone again.'

But Njeri could not be dissuaded. 'Live for today, Sean,' she said. 'Just go with the flow. You've been honest and I know you don't love me, but perhaps one day you will love me as I love you.'

Sean took Njeri in his arms, and as he did so he felt her left hand slide up his right thigh touching him between his legs. As she did this he became even more aroused, and as much as he tried to fight it he was unable to resist her. Her hands moved expertly all over his body and they were soon kissing passionately. He responded by moving his hands over the contours of her perfectly rounded buttocks. Her skin was as smooth as silk and her perfume smelt fresh and strong as though she had only recently applied it.

The wetness of her lips was similar to the moistness he felt between her legs. She ran her hands through his hair and as she did so he dropped his head and buried his mouth between her ample breasts, moving it deftly across to her left nipple which was already hard and erect. Her body began to react beneath him. She moaned in appreciation of his moist tongue stimulating her nipple even more, and when his fingers began to caress her gently between her legs, she responded instantly to his touch. She could feel the wetness increase, and she pushed him on to his back and mounted him. She could wait no longer As she thrust down on him he drove up deeper into her, causing her to moan louder. Their rhythm increased almost to a frenzy and her feelings for him intensified. Sean began to completely lose control as he felt her climaxing. Her juices felt like a waterfall as he climaxed in turn with such ferocity that they both cried out.

It had been a long time since he had had a woman, but with Njeri he found it to be a very enjoyable experience. She certainly knew how to make a man feel good. That night they made love several more times. Then they drifted off to sleep.

Sean awoke first. He had a strange feeling that something was different. Turning over, he saw Njeri lying peacefully next to him and remembered what had happened. Oh no, what have I done? he thought, smiling to himself. As he gazed across at Njeri, admiring her dusky beauty, she awoke. She looked at Sean and smiled. Her eyes sparkled.

Sean couldn't help sounding overly formal. 'Good morning Njeri. How about some breakfast?'

'Yes please.' She was still smiling languidly.

As Sean showered he planned what he would say to Njeri at breakfast. He had to explain to her that his mission and aim in life was to find Akinyi's killers. He felt he had to be frank and tell her that he was only working on a six-month contract for his friend Smithy and that then he would be off with James to hunt down Akinyi's killers. He didn't want to build up Njeri's hopes of a long-term relationship and then disappoint her. He got out of the shower and dressed. While he was making breakfast Njeri showered. He remembered his time at her house in Kenya and was faintly amused that the tables had turned. It seemed he was now looking after her.

They sat in the conservatory next to the kitchen, overlooking the walled garden. It was a typically cold December day, but bright and sunny.

'It's a bit different to Mombasa,' said Njeri, observing the gaunt, bare, deciduous branches that overhung the east side of the dividing brick wall, and the silvery white patches of ice slowly receding from the edge of the paved walkway. There were precious few flowers to be seen.

'Well, it'll be staying like this for at least the next three months, so you'll have plenty of time to get used to it,' laughed Sean.

Over breakfast, Sean explained that he wasn't a rich man and that times were a bit harder than when he used to run his own business, but that she was very welcome to stay. He would look after her in terms of her household expenses, but he couldn't afford to pay for everything else and he was sure she would want to earn some money of her own. He told her that she could apply for a Working Holidaymaker Visa which allowed her, as a Commonwealth subject, to live and work in the UK for up to two years part-time or one year full-time if she wanted to stay as part of a working holiday. He said he would take her to Croydon during the next week to arrange such a visa.

Njeri appeared a little confused. 'But, Sean, I thought you said you would take care of me?'

'Of course I will,' said Sean. 'As I've said, all your basic living expenses will be taken care of, but you must see your visit here as an opportunity to give yourself a better chance for when you eventually return to Kenya. You're a smart lady, Njeri, you're attractive and you've got plenty of self-confidence. You can go on a computer course, if you like, and learn about word processing. Once you know how to use a computer you can always find yourself a job. The sky's the limit for you. You don't need to rely on me. Last night was terrific and I really enjoyed myself, but you know I'm not looking for a long-term relationship, or to get married. Sure, we can have some fun and maybe things might change, but just at the moment I don't want to make any commitments.'

Njeri looked visibly hurt. 'But, Sean, I love you and I want to marry you.'

Sean was momentarily taken aback. 'Look, I don't want to sound like your father, but quite frankly you're too young to get married. After you've spent some time here the chances are that you'll meet a guy nearer your own age and start a relationship.'

Once again, Njeri would not be detracted. 'But I don't like younger men, they are too childish for me. I need a more mature man like you. I will be patient and, mark my words, Sean, one day you'll be mine.' She spoke with such determination that it caused a shiver to run down Sean's spine.

CHAPTER 21

The following week Sean took Njeri to the Immigration Office in Croydon where she was issued with a two-year Working Holidaymaker Visa.

'Well that was easy, wasn't it?' said Sean, as they came out of the building and were walking down the steps. 'All you have to do now is get yourself a job. With your skills as a seamstress I'm sure you'll find one quickly. It might be a good idea to try one of the small boutiques in Richmond. The money won't be brilliant, but I'm sure you can get yourself extra freelance work by making up special designs for some of the rich customers who go in there. You can try tomorrow and see what happens.'

But Njeri was reluctant. 'I don't know that I can, Sean. I'm scared of working here in England. Everything is so strange to me.'

'There's no need to go through a confidence crisis,' retorted Sean. 'Your natural personality and looks will help you get a job easily. Once you do it, you won't look back, I assure you.'

The next day Njeri got a job. At several boutiques she was told that there were no vacancies and that they would not need anyone else until the beginning of April in preparation for the summer season. However, at the sixth boutique she visited, they offered her a job starting immediately after Christmas. It would be for thirty hours a week initially, with the possibility of full-time work as the season progressed. It was a start and would also give her an opportunity to make clothes in her spare time, not only for herself but also for sale commercially.

When Sean returned from work that night Njeri had made dinner and he could see that her temperament had improved. As he looked around his house he noticed fresh flowers beautifully displayed in vases. He could smell the cooking. It was good to be home and he hadn't felt like that for a long time.

Louise came to stay for the first time at Christmas and Sean wanted to make it extra special for her. They spent Christmas Day with Christina, his sister, and fortunately Louise got on well with Christina's two children, Sara and Ben. Christina's husband, Donald, was a pleasant, steady guy. An accountant by profession, he was a tad conservative but, surprisingly, appreciated Sean's dry sense of humour.

It was a family gathering, typical of those taking place in a million English homes, with the added luxury of Christina's cordon bleu cuisine. Sean watched Njeri carefully to see how she fitted in. Generally, he was impressed at the way she conducted herself. Not unnaturally, she was somewhat nervous to be among Sean's family for the first time but she was a good conversationalist, entertaining them with stories about Kenya. She didn't say much about herself; it was almost as if she was avoiding the subject, and she became a trifle guarded when Christina and Donald began asking her probing questions about her family.

Sean felt uneasy with some of her answers and the way she answered them, but he consigned his thoughts to the back of his mind. It wasn't the moment to pry into her life. He would wait and quiz her when he felt the time was right.

After high tea at seven o'clock they played several games of charades and by ten o'clock Sean could see that Louise was getting tired. It was time to go. They said their goodbyes and returned home. It was only a twenty-minute drive from Christina's house in Weybridge and, being Christmas night, there wasn't much traffic on the road.

Boxing Day lunch was a typical Kenyan meal cooked by Njeri. It was the first time Louise had had *sukuma wiki* and *ugali* served with chicken in a spicy sauce. She turned her nose up at the food at first, but after a few mouthfuls soon realized how delicious it was and ate heartily. After lunch they took a walk around Richmond Park and during the afternoon played Scrabble in front of a roaring fire.

The next day Sally collected Louise. The festivities were over and Sean settled into the serious business of combining his work at Smithy's with getting himself fully fit for basic training with James. He would have preferred to concentrate on training rather than work, but not only did he need the money, he also didn't want to let Smithy down after he had helped him in his hour of need.

He knew the job would be demanding and the training probably more so, but if he found the right balance he reckoned he could fit both in without one or the other suffering. The only part of his life that might suffer would be the growing relationship with Njeri. He found her to be quite demanding of his time and attention.

This irritated him somewhat because it indicated a basic insecurity. It wasn't so much to do with the strange environment she found herself in, but she seemed desperate to be loved. It was almost as if she was trying too hard to please him. Still, once she had acquired her own friends she would, he hoped, become more independent, and less obsessed with him. It wasn't that he didn't want her to be about; it was simply that his mind and heart were elsewhere.

CHAPTER 22

The next couple of months flew by. Sean left for work every morning at six and would return at seven in the evening. The project for Sukimoto was going well. It was fairly intense, but with Emma's help they were well ahead of their targets for implementing all the forthcoming promotions. They were also well within budget, which was always a criterion Sean tried to achieve. He was pleased with the progress they were making, particularly in staying ahead of targets because, when his physical training with James started at the end of February, he would more than likely exhaust his mental capacity for work.

He ran three miles every evening and played squash every Tuesday and Thursday night, with circuit training on Monday and Wednesday. He already trained with the Richmond Rugby Club on Mondays and at London Scottish on Wednesdays. He thought the rigorous demands of first-team training would prepare him well for the surprises that James had in store.

Things were going fairly smoothly with Njeri. She was enjoying her work, although she complained she wasn't being paid enough. She was earning about £150 a week and, as far as Sean was concerned, it was all pocket money because he paid all the household bills. It consequently annoyed him that she never seemed to have any money when they went shopping on Saturday afternoons, and used this as a lever to persuade him to buy her new things. She always did so with a smile and Sean didn't have the heart to say no. However, by the time he had paid the mortgage, gas, electricity, and so on, he didn't have much left either and it was certainly less than Njeri's pocket money of £150 per week.

One evening, when Sean arrived home from work, he noticed that the phone bill had come. He was shocked to see it was for £400 that quarter. He hardly used the phone and his average bill before he met Njeri had only ever been about £70. He checked the itemized billing. Njeri had been phoning Nairobi two or three times a week. As he walked into the kitchen where she was cooking, he felt anger rise in him.

'What the hell is this, Njeri? Our phone bill has just arrived and it's over £400! All these calls to Nairobi have got to stop. I can't afford it.'

Njeri was indignant. 'I have been homesick and I needed to talk to my mum. You told me it would be okay.'

'Yes, sure I said it would be okay, but I thought you would call two or three times a *month*, not two or three times a *week*!'

'But, Sean, you are a rich man. You can afford it,' she said with a thin smile.

'I'm not a rich man and I cannot afford it. I am happy to pay for £60 worth of calls per quarter, but no more. If the bill amounts to more than that, you can pay the difference yourself. That gives you a five-minute call each week, which is perfectly reasonable, to let your family know you are okay. Beyond that, you can write to them or pay for your own calls. After all, you have about £150 a week pocket money, so you can easily afford it. Anyway, what the hell do you do with your money?'

'That's my business not yours, Sean.' She paused. 'But since you ask, I send it to my children.'

'What do you mean your children? You told me you didn't have any children!'

'No, sorry, I meant my family not my children. I told you, my mother has been sick and my brother needed some money for university.'

'But it's your father's responsibility to look after your mother and brother, not yours! He's a solicitor's clerk and by any standards he's well paid for his job.'

'We do things differently in Kenya, Sean. I have to help my family.'

'All right then, since you started work you've earned over £1,200. Where is it? Have you saved any?'

'No. I've sent £1,000 back home!' shouted Njeri.

'What?' Sean looked incredulous. 'I just don't believe it! I give up, I'm going for a run.' He stormed upstairs and got changed, slamming the back door behind him.

Njeri was shocked. She had never seen Sean quite so angry before.

When he got back from his run, having worked off his anger and frustration, he found Njeri sitting in the lounge crying.

'What's the matter?' he said gently. Maybe he had been a little too hard on her.

Njeri looked up. She was dabbing her eyes with a damp tissue. 'Sean, I do my best for you. I love you more than enough. I cook, I clean and I look after you, but you just don't respond. You are completely indifferent to me because you are still obsessed with your old girlfriend. She is dead, Sean, and nothing will bring her back. Stop living in the past. Please try and make it work for us.' Another flood of tears threatened.

Sean's voice softened. 'I know you look after me and the house well enough. But I've always been honest and told you repeatedly that I'm not able to fully commit myself to a relationship at the moment.'

'But you're committed enough to screw me,' shouted Njeri. 'You treat me like a whore, to be used when it suits you. I don't only want a physical commitment, Sean, I want more.'

Sean was angry. 'I don't treat you like a whore. I've looked after you well since you came here – at my invitation and expense. I've given you advice and help, I've given you a comfortable home and I've picked up the tab for almost everything you have. So don't tell me I treat you like a whore. I'm the first man who has shown you some respect. Don't think I don't know what went on in your life in Kenya. I'm not completely stupid, Njeri. People have told me things about you but I chose to ignore the idle gossip and gave you the benefit of the doubt.'

Njeri reached for another tissue and blew her nose, keeping her eyes downcast.

'I found a different Njeri in Kenya to the one described by some people in Mombasa. If I've treated you like a whore it's because you've occasionally behaved like one. I see the way you flirt with those men in Oscar's discotheque, and while I'm at it, what about that jerk, Barry the doorman, whom you've been meeting recently at the local swimming pool? Don't think I don't know about that, either. Don't forget, a lot of people know me around Richmond and they've told me things which, again, I've chosen to ignore.' Sean could feel himself getting angrier.

Njeri went on the defensive. 'I've only met Barry a few times,' she replied. 'I knew you'd find out. I deliberately met him in a place where we could be seen together so that the gossips would tell you. I hoped to make you jealous. Anyway, he treats me properly and at least he tells me he loves me. Not like you.'

Sean laughed. 'Tells you he loves you? That's a joke! He just wants to get inside your knickers. I know that creep, he's a real headbanger. He's beaten up loads of his girlfriends, so don't think he's going to change just for you. Guys like that don't respect you. The trouble is you don't know the difference between respect and lust, because you haven't known anything different. Yes, I respect you because I think you're a smart lady and you've had a tough life. Also, you were good enough to help me when I was down on my luck, but I can't be beholden to you forever, or you to me.'

He stopped and drew a deep breath.

'If you want to you can continue to live here for the time being, but please move back to the spare room for a while. Let's not rush our relationship. Akinyi might be physically dead, but to me she is still very much alive, and will always be. She is a part of my life I cannot forget. Quite simply, Njeri, you can take it or leave it,' said Sean. He sighed with relief. He had felt for a few weeks that things had been building up and he was glad that now they were out in the open.

Njeri looked longingly at Sean. It was the first major disagreement they had had, and she felt wretched. She had badly underestimated the depth of feeling he had for Akinyi. How could anyone fight a ghost, she wondered? She bowed her head, and in a whisper said, 'I'll stay where I am for the moment, thanks.' She got up and walked to the kitchen in silence.

Sean turned and climbed the stairs to the shower. When he came down, dinner was on the table. He was hungry after his run and tried to ignore the tension between them by concentrating on his meal. He was eating well to build up his strength, and finished quickly. His body had responded well to the physical demands he made of it over the last couple of months; he had developed muscles that he hadn't had since he last played rugby at international level. He was again becoming supremely fit. He didn't know his ability and stamina beyond five miles, but he felt he was fitter than most people. It remained to be seen whether he was fit enough to withstand James's training regime.

That night Sean was surprised to find Njeri in his bed but didn't insist upon her moving into the spare room. He certainly didn't feel like making love, but as he turned out the light he leant over and kissed her goodnight.

'Whatever you think, Njeri, I am truly very fond of you,' he said.

'And I love you Sean.'

For all the worldliness and toughness that Njeri sometimes portrayed, deep down Sean sensed that she was a troubled soul.

CHAPTER 23

It was the last weekend of February and Sean was due to travel to Hereford on the Friday night for a weekend of initial training with James. He left work early and, after collecting Njeri from Richmond, they were soon on their way up the M40 towards Oxford. Njeri was learning to drive and James had suggested that she came along so she could drive Sean back to Richmond after his arduous weekend. James knew the sort of condition that he would be in by then.

They missed the worst of the London weekend traffic heading for the country and with some fast driving arrived in Hereford by 7.45. James and Yolanda were there to greet him. Sean introduced them to Njeri. It was the first time they had met her and Sean thought it would be a good opportunity for her and Yolanda to indulge in 'girls' talk.

After dinner, James took Sean to his study to run through his training schedule over the next four months. During this first weekend James wanted to cover the typical army Basic Fitness Training, so they would start at 6 o'clock in the morning on the Brecon Beacons.

They rose at 5 a.m. and drove out of Hereford to the grid reference that James had pinpointed on the map. It was a bitterly cold morning and heavy, grey mists were swirling around the foot of the hills. Sean shivered as he climbed out of the car, gasping as the shock of cold air hit his face. What had he let himself in for? he thought. He was glad of the T-shirt, waterproof jacket and thick army trousers and boots that James had given him the night before, together with an army kit bag, known as a bergen, that he had to carry. This was filled with a spare set of clothes, a sleeping bag, water bottles and some food. Finally he gave him a compass and a map of Brecon Beacons with grid references, just in case they got lost. Sean knew how to read an ordnance survey map from his geography field trips at school.

He pulled on his bergen and felt the straps biting into his shoulders. It weighed nearly 50 lbs and Sean suddenly realized that although he was fit to run three or four miles in tracksuit and trainers, this would be a completely different kettle of fish.

James pulled on his bergen and they synchronized their watches. 'We'll run together this morning,' he said. 'It's very foggy and I don't want you to get lost on your first day. It's safer to run with me. I'll allow you fifteen minutes to run the first mile and a half and after that we have to cover the remainder in twelve minutes – otherwise we'll have to do it again.'

Piece of piss, thought Sean to himself. I'll do that easily.

'Okay let's go!' said James and they broke into a trot.

Although they hit their target of fifteen minutes for the first one and a half miles, Sean thought his lungs were going to explode. Already his body ached and he kept looking across at James, who hardly seemed to be breaking sweat. Sean's breathing became erratic and by the end of the run he thought his lungs would explode. They reached the next grid reference and James slowed to a halt, throwing his bergen down on the ground next to him. Sean was bent double. He had used all his determination to keep up, but no way was he going to give in now, even though he could feel the blisters on his feet where his boots were rubbing. The two pairs of socks that James had suggested did not seem to be making much of a difference. He wasn't used to running in army boots and the straps on the pack had cut into his shoulders. He struggled to lift the bergen from his back and slumped to the ground.

'Don't do that,' said James. 'Stand up and get your breathing going evenly. You've got ten minutes rest, then we'll do the run again in reverse, to the same time pattern. If you want a drink, sip the water from your bottle slowly and try to keep moving about, otherwise you'll stiffen up.'

Sean began to feel cold. His T-shirt was soaked through with sweat but as he only had one spare he thought he'd wait and change it at the end of the next run. The ten minutes were soon up.

'Okay,' said James. 'Let's hit it.'

Sean wished he had had some padding for the shoulder straps as he put the bergen back on, but said nothing. James set the pace.

Although they managed the same time on the return journey, to Sean it felt like they had travelled twice the distance. When they reached the car he was puffing and wheezing like an old man. James still looked as though he had been for a Sunday afternoon stroll in the park. Sean's shoulder muscles felt like they were being ripped away from the bone.

'Is that it, James? Can we go home now?' Sean had had enough.

'What do you mean, is that it?' James replied. 'It'll be four o'clock at least before we get home. We've got lots more to do. If you are serious about finding Akinyi's killers you need to be pushed to the limits of your endurance and stamina. Remember, to track them down you may have to infiltrate a neo-Nazi cell. I can tell you those guys are very, very tough and will show no mercy. They won't mess around if they discover that you are spying on them and, if they think you are trying to get some of them arrested or killed, God help you. I know guys who have been tortured and kneecapped by them.'

Yes, thought Sean, sarcastically. I know exactly how they feel.

James continued his pep talk. 'You must be aware of your limitations before you venture into an unknown world. Quite simply, Sean, you will have to adopt a killer instinct. It will be the survival of the fittest. I for one don't want to end up dead in a dark alley. I'm sure you can imagine what will happen to me as a black man if they find us out. I need you to give me the same protection that I will be giving to you, Sean.'

What he didn't tell Sean was that he would have to learn both unarmed and armed close-quarter combat fighting. He'd leave that till later.

'Anyway, enough of that,' he concluded. 'We'll have a quick brew, and then we'll move on to the next exercise.'

James had brought a flask of tea with him and he filled Sean's mug. The tea was still piping hot and Sean was well pleased to get something warm inside him. They sat in silence for a while. Sean was contemplating what James had just told him.

'James, you've known me since we were kids. Do you think I've got what it takes to do this job?'

'I don't know yet, mate, time will tell. I've spent almost half my life in the army and I've been trained to kill. I'm a professional soldier and I know nothing else. I've had some good friends killed in action, tougher men than you, Sean. So at this stage I just don't know the answer to your question. Any time you feel like pulling out, just tell me. There's nothing to be ashamed of if you do. In my case, I look upon it as an aptitude or skill.'

James looked at his watch. They had been talking for over half an hour. It was now nearly nine o'clock and the mists were beginning to lift. A watery sun was trying to break through and the temperature had risen a few degrees, but Sean was still cold. He changed into his other T-shirt. 'We'll leave our bergens in the car,' commanded James. 'All we'll need are maps and a water bottle. Next up is a five-mile run, done in intervals.'

Every mile they would stop and do sets of one hundred press-ups and sit-ups, followed by one hundred metre runs on piggyback and then one hundred metre fireman's lifts. 'No prisoners on this one, Sean.'

They set off. Without the bergen Sean found it easier, and kept a steady pace close to James. The press-ups and sit-ups were no problem. The circuit training was beginning to pay dividends. But the fireman's lifts and piggybacks were a struggle. James weighed well over 200 lbs and at six feet two inches was a big man to carry. Sean drove himself on. He looked upon it as a necessary part of his future mission, but really he wished he was elsewhere. As he laboured on he sang to himself, dreaming of sunnier climes. By the end of the five-mile sets Sean was once again struggling. He could feel more blisters on his feet. The witchhazel he had rubbed on his feet the night before didn't seem to have hardened the skin enough. He wanted to take his boots off, but James insisted he should wait until the end of the day. They jog-trotted back to the car.

'We'll stop now for something to eat and then we'll finish with an eight-miler with bergens on,' said James.

James had brought some soup and bread rolls which they quickly devoured and washed down with the last of the tea. As they sat on the ground, leaning against their bergens, Sean asked James about his army experiences.

He had trained originally with the Light Infantry based at Winchester and then transferred to the Grenadier Guards.

'It was with them that I had a really tough time. As a private – or Guardsman – I had to go through a 'blacks only' initiation ceremony. It was all unofficial, of course, but my section commander told me that from then on my name was to be Mandingo and he gave me a spear to carry. He said it was a tradition in the Guards' regiments that blacks had to carry a spear as a personal weapon. None of the other recruits were allowed to call me by my proper name and neither did any of the training staff. I was made to carry the spear everywhere. I was regularly called a black bastard. Although humiliated frequently, I toughed it out.'

'Why didn't you complain to your commanding officer?' Sean asked, mystified.

'That would have been a waste of time. Most officers turned a blind eye to it and pretended that nothing like that went on. My size helped me because on a one to one basis I was able to stand up for myself if I was ever forced into a fight. The problem was to deal with the ten guys who came for me the night after I had been awarded the prize as best recruit. The training staff didn't want me to win it, but they could do nothing when I came first in nearly all the exercises and assessments. The company commander insisted I receive the award. He felt it would be good for the recruitment of other ethnic minorities into the army. I had just fallen asleep when ten masked guys dragged me out of bed. They punched and kicked me, and then bog-washed me by putting my head down a toilet full of urine and faeces. They deliberately flushed it so it went all over my face and head. Of course I vomited and nearly choked on my own vomit as they dragged me back to my room. In the meantime, others had urinated on my bed. "That's what we do to sassy black nigger bastards who steal the prize from good white men," they chanted, as they left.'

A look of shock and sheer disbelief appeared on Sean's face.

'On that occasion I did complain to my CO, but he told me that it was typical of army life and that I would have to live with it. I knew at least two other black guys in other regiments who suffered so much they left the army completely broken. I also knew black guys who suffered abuse and jibes that were utterly tame compared to what I suffered. On more than one occasion I received scribbled notes with the chilling message that there was "No black in the Union Jack". I resolved to fight the abuse, because I was determined to pursue a career in the army. Fortunately, I made some good friends who weren't racist and I managed to get through. When the opportunity came to be considered for selection to join the SAS (the Regiment), I grabbed it with both hands. The Regiment is the least racist of all the units in the British army. It has to be, of course, as we are often on attachment in other countries with people of many different races, creeds and colour, and so we have to be able to deal with everyone regardless of their ethnic origin. I was delighted to be selected first time and then I transferred to Hereford. I bought a small house and was happier than at any time since I joined. Within a couple of years I had made sergeant, and it was after I was awarded the Military Medal for rescuing five Welsh guardsmen from a troop of Argentines in the Falklands that I was recommended for a commission.'

'Surely things improved for you then?' asked Sean.

'They did a little, but it was ironic, really, because two of the Welsh Guards I rescued were two of the ten that had attacked me all those years before. They were very embarrassed to be rescued by a black man – and I was told later by three others that they were so humiliated they couldn't bring themselves to thank me. I didn't want their thanks. All I wanted was their respect.' James paused.

'I had earned it. I met one of them again on exercise in the Malaysian jungle and he very quietly and humbly thanked me. He told me he didn't want to lose face in front of his mate and that's why he had never thanked me before. His colleague, apparently, was a member of the British National Front and vowed he was never going to thank a nigger for anything, even though I had saved his life.'

While they were sitting, Sean watched as other small groups of men ran past. James told him some were just out on a training run while others were on selection proper. Some looked to be struggling while others seemed to be cruising. James explained that many wouldn't make it.

'Isn't it about time we made a move?' said Sean.

James was taken aback. 'You're a bit keen aren't you?'

'Eight miles round here will seem like a lifetime, I'd rather get this over and done with. I can't wait to get back to your place and have a long soak in the bath. I feel like a steamroller has driven over me.'

They pulled on their bergens and went on their way. The fog had lifted but the sun still hadn't fully broken through. It was bitterly cold and the wind had picked up. In those conditions the Brecon Beacons was not a place for the faint hearted. Sean managed to stay with James while they covered the first three miles in good time, but he was beginning to struggle. His pace slowed considerably. It was not so much that James began to pull away, it was that Sean was slowing almost to a jog walk. The 50 lbs in his pack seemed to get heavier, if that were possible. The fourth mile was even harder. Sean was well off the pace and watched as James went striding out about half a mile ahead. There was no way he was going to catch him, but he had to make up the lost time. He looked at his watch. He had twenty-eight minutes left to reach his target time. That meant seven-minute miles. No way could he do that in his condition. He tried picking up the pace, but when he reached the final rendezvous he was still over by three and a half minutes. James by now had removed his bergen and was doing some cool down exercises.

As Sean half stumbled in, James looked up. 'Well, Cameron, you've just failed selection. If we have a target time you have to make it. It's no good turning up late for battle. Others will be relying on you and your lateness is no good to anyone. You do at least get points for finishing, but you will have to pull your finger out over the next few weeks. Your general fitness isn't bad, but running in boots and carrying a bergen uses all sorts of different sets of muscles. It'll take you time to adjust. When you go on your training runs in Richmond, wear these boots and carry a pack with about 20 lbs weight. That'll help you.'

'Thanks,' said Sean. He felt despondent at failing the first test. Maybe he would pick up extra points over the next few months.

When they arrived back at James's house, Sean showered first and then soaked for half an hour in the bath. When he had finished he inspected his feet which were covered in small blisters, and his shoulders which were red raw. James suggested he pop the blisters with a hot, sterilized needle. As he did so, he watched the clear pus come out. When he dabbed them with iodine he nearly hit the roof. He wondered how he would be able to run the next day. He finished his repairs, slipped on a tracksuit and went downstairs. Yolanda and Njeri were sitting by the fire drinking tea. He went over and kissed Njeri.

'Hi everybody,' he said. 'Yolanda, that husband of yours is a real hard taskmaster. I can't believe how someone of his age is so fit. What do you feed him on?' he said, jokingly.

James finally arrived downstairs. He, too, had had a long soak. He appeared fresh in comparison to the exhausted-looking Sean. The four sat and talked, joked and laughed. They had dinner an hour before the usual time, because James and Sean would be up early the next day for another five or six hours on Brecon Beacons. Sean didn't remember climbing into bed and falling asleep, but when he woke the next morning at six he struggled hard to leave Njeri's warm body. She hugged him and looked at him through sleepy eyes.

'Take care, Sean. Yolanda tells me it can be dangerous where you are going.'

'Don't worry about me. There's plenty of life in the old dog yet. I'll be okay.' He grimaced as he said it, his body aching like nothing before. 'See you later.'

The day passed with a series of map-reading exercises. James would give Sean a map reference and a time to rendezvous. The distances and terrains varied, but Sean managed to reach all his targets. They finished at one o'clock and returned to James's house.

'Not a bad day's work, Sean,' he said, as they walked to the front door. 'Next weekend we'll run through some combat survival techniques. So be here by 10 p.m. next Friday. We'll leave at eleven to go on an overnight exercise. I'll show you how to survive with very little. I'll teach you how to make shelters, find food by setting snares and how to light fires by rubbing two sticks together – just like boy scouts.' James laughed.

'Sounds like fun, James, but how will all these things help me catch Akinyi's killers?'

'Listen,' said James. 'These exercises teach you endurance, stamina, determination and initiative. There's lots more to come that you've never thought about, but I assure you it's all relevant. Not only that, but I've got to feel confident about you as my partner. Since I joined the Regiment, I've had to kill many people in the course of my duty. It's not something I've relished, and the first time was particularly tough, but now I am hardened to it. In the Army we operate within the law of the land wherever we go, but for us in Germany we will be operating outside those laws so you have to be prepared for every eventuality.'

'Okay,' said Sean. 'I'll take your word for it.'

After Sunday lunch, Njeri drove home. The journey was slow but Sean was relieved that he wasn't behind the wheel for he was exhausted. Njeri drove well, and as Sean kept dozing off it gave her the opportunity to experience different roads and driving conditions almost entirely on her own. Njeri told Sean that she had enjoyed her time with Yolanda. They had been shopping and had gone to a small art gallery in Hereford. Njeri found it different from Richmond but an interesting experience nonetheless.

CHAPTER 24

The next two months were tough on Sean. His work commitments were substantial and his contract with Smithy would soon be up. He was grooming Emma to take over from him and was confident she would do the job well.

Sean had also made substantial progress in his exercise and training programme with James. He had passed the Combat Survival Technique course, but he didn't know how he would have handled it on his own, without James' guidance. He was surprised, though, that they had had to spend two consecutive nights and one day learning to survive out in the open air. He had geared himself up for one night living off the land, and when James had sprung the second night on him he almost reached the depths of despair.

The weather had been bitterly cold. There was about three feet of snow on the ground in certain parts of the hills and to find shelter, and keep dry and warm, was exceptionally difficult. He had never known coldness like it. It seemed as though he had shivered for forty-eight hours non-stop. He was very glad when that particular session came to an end.

One weekend he did enjoy was weapons training. James taught him to use a variety of weapons, including a 5.56 mm M16 and the self-loading rifle, and the GPMG standard army machine gun. It was reliable and powerful. This was followed by a selection of hand guns, a Browning, Colt 45s and a number of different semi-automatic weapons.

Sean preferred the Browning, which was in fact the Regiment's most popular pistol. He tried out some shotguns. He had used a couple of twelve-bores on clay pigeon shoots in the past and he liked the feel of the Federal Riot Gun. It was a pump-action shot gun with a folding stock. Sean fancied that he could use it in anger if the need ever arose. He hoped, however, that he wouldn't have to use any weapons but if he did he knew the ones he preferred.

Although James said it was unlikely they would have to use mortars, he showed Sean an assortment – 81 mm, 60 mm and 40 mm – to demonstrate the fire power they might be up against. James went through a variety of Eastern Bloc weapons: Russian, Czech and Chinese AK47s and a number of different pistols, such as the Austrian Steyr which was apparently favoured by neo-Nazi factions. The AK47s were good to fire, but as James explained, if you had to lie down to shoot you couldn't get the weapon in the shoulder because the big thirty-round magazine hit the ground.

James taught Sean to shoot on the range in the standing position at targets one hundred metres apart at varying distances. It turned out he was a good and accurate shot. Firing at a target on the range was easy, but whether he could kill another human being was something that began to trouble Sean. He could see at first hand the damage the bullets caused; James explained that a 7.62 mm bullet could almost blow a man's shoulder away. The image of heroes in the movies was a far cry from reality.

One weekend was spent learning close-quarter battle techniques. To follow up on the pistol training, James explained that the pistol was most likely to be their most important weapon. It was easy to conceal and he taught Sean how to draw it, how to fire it quickly and how the weapon became an extension of the body. Sean was surprised to learn that the unarmed combat training was not more closely related to karate. James explained that karate was a sport in which one man was up against another, using similar techniques and abiding by certain rules. He told Sean that close-quarter battle was learning how to put someone down as quickly as possible: to drop him and run away, or kill him. It depended on the circumstances at the time.

'Sean, you need to know how to sort out a threat within closed environments. You could be down an alley, getting out of or into your car, or in a pub packed with other people,' James said. 'If a bigger person hits you, it's going to hurt and you're likely to go down. If we get involved in a fight outside a bar in Germany, the other guys aren't going to fight clean. You must understand that you may need to kick, head butt, bite or gouge them. You've got to learn to fight dirty.'

'So it's speed, aggression and surprise,' said Sean.

'Absolutely right, but you've got to know when you need to apply maximum aggression and get the job done quickly and efficiently.'

'Got you,' said Sean.

James showed Sean how to use his pistol while being pushed against a wall. He learned how to use the gun as it was pulled out of the shoulder holster without shooting himself and how to avoid being shot at close quarters. James explained that if, for example, someone drew a pistol on you at close quarters, it was relatively easy to knock it out of the line of fire and drop the attacker.

By the end of the weekend Sean was covered in small cuts and bruises, but he had learned a huge amount about close-quarter battle.

The following weekend they spent two days shooting, mainly firing pistols from different positions. They practised until Sean could hit a target from thirty five metres, and then fifty metres with both eyes open. James was a crack shot and could hit the bull almost every time. Sean managed a few centres, but generally his aim was scattered in comparison.

Each weekend Njeri accompanied Sean and would inevitably drive home on the Sunday evening. Her driving skills were rapidly improving.

CHAPTER 25

One weekend Sean got a quiet moment on his own with Yolanda and asked her what she thought of Njeri.

'She's a strange one, Sean,' Yolanda said. 'She seems a nice enough girl, but she's a bit of a mystery. It's as though she's hiding something. I think she loves you, or so she says, but I don't think she understands what true love is. She seems to have a fairytale idea of what it's about. I suspect she's been abused in the past.'

'It's funny you should say that, but I feel exactly the same myself,' said Sean. 'We had an argument a few months ago and, in the heat of the moment, she said she was helping her children by sending money to Kenya. When I picked her up on what she'd said, she told me she meant her family and not children. Do you think she's got kids?'

'It's certainly possible,' said Yolanda. 'Perhaps she's got a child and is embarrassed to tell you. Maybe she thinks you won't want the burden of her and a child. You should tackle her about it. You should also sort out the money problems she claims to have. She says you're mean, Sean!'

'Mean? That's outrageous!' cried Sean. 'She never has to spend a cent in the house, for food or anything, and I'm forever buying her clothes. I also pay £60 a quarter for her phone calls to Kenya. The first quarter after she arrived it was over £400 with calls to Nairobi and I picked up the tab for that. I would hardly call all that mean, would you?'

'Well, no I wouldn't, Sean, but something's troubling her. I think you should talk to her sooner rather than later.'

'Yeah, maybe you're right, I'll speak to her one evening next week. Thanks Yolanda.'

Sean didn't tell Yolanda that he had been having other problems with Njeri. She had shown a strength of character in Kenya that seemed to wane when she came to England. It was almost as though she wanted Sean to take full responsibility for looking after her. She had become very childish with her demands. Secondly, she had started to go out on her own to discos during the week. She never said who she was going with, but Sean thought it was probably girls she knew from work. It was strange, though, that she never mentioned anyone by name. Sean thought that was distinctly odd. On the drive home from Hereford he made up his mind. He would confront her on Tuesday.

When he returned from work that Tuesday evening, he decided not to go for his usual run. He walked into the house and could hear music, but Njeri was not downstairs. He called upstairs for her but got no reply.

Getting worried, he ran up the stairs, just in case something had happened to her, but she was nowhere to be found. He looked in all the rooms and finally went to his bedroom. She was not about, but on the bed were some magazines lying open. He glanced at them casually, and did a double take as he realized they were hard core pornographic magazines. What the hell are these doing here? he thought. Sean was not a prude but he was pretty shocked at some of the content. The next moment he heard the front door slam. It was Njeri.

'Sean, where are you.'

'Up here,' he called back.

As Njeri ran into the room, she stopped suddenly as she realized what Sean had in his hand.

'I think you've got some explaining to do,' he said, his voice dangerously low.

Njeri paused for thought. 'I was simply interested in reading them.'

'Well, where did you get them? These look way beyond the usual top shelf stuff at your ordinary paper shop!' challenged Sean.

'Well . . . , Tony gave them to me.'

'And who is Tony?' queried Sean.

'He's the fashion photographer I told you about who came into the shop the other week. He said he could get me a job in a modelling agency.'

'I warned you to steer clear of him.' Sean's anger was turning to frustration. 'But that still doesn't explain why you have these magazines. Or perhaps it does. He deals in pornographic photography doesn't he? They're disgusting, Njeri. You're not keeping them in this house. What happens if Louise finds them by mistake when she comes to stay?'

'Well, if they're hidden away she won't find them.'

'Yeah, but I found them sprawled on the bed. If you are that careless, how do you know you won't make the same mistake again? They're out of here and that's it. And while I'm at it, I've got a question to ask you – and I want an honest answer.' Sean looked very serious.

'Ask away,' said Njeri. 'I've got nothing to hide.'

'Well I think you have.' Sean was blunt and to the point. 'Do you have any children?'

Njeri had been dreading this moment. She looked at Sean and the tears began to flow. 'Yes I do,' she sobbed. 'I have twins; a girl and a boy, and they're seven years old.'

Sean was stunned. He didn't quite know what to say.

Countless questions were flashing through his mind.

'I suppose that's why you're sending all this money back to Kenya, then,' said Sean. 'Where do they live?'

'They live in Nairobi with my granny. She looks after them but she's now quite old and needs a maid to help her. They've started school recently and their school books and clothes are very expensive.'

'Why the hell didn't you tell me about this when we were in Kenya? It wouldn't have made any difference to me if you had one, two or three children. Here we are, supposedly in a relationship, and you've never told me!'

Njeri looked at Sean. 'I've been meaning to tell you for ages, but I've been too scared. I thought you would send me home.'

'But why should I do that?'

'Sean, I was so ashamed of having children while I was still at school. I was only fifteen and their father ran away when he found out I was pregnant. I've had to support them on my own. My mum helped me a bit but my father refused to have anything to do with me, he was so disgusted. I've had it tough, Sean, and I've struggled ever since.'

'What do you mean by not telling me?' said Sean. 'What would have happened if we had decided to get married? You surely couldn't have kept it a secret then?'

'I promise I was going to tell you, Sean.'

'Njeri, for a long time I haven't been able to trust you. That's no foundation for a relationship. If you haven't told me about that, which is fundamentally important, then what else might you be hiding? I admit I've not made a full commitment to you because of my feelings for Akinyi, but I've been totally honest and have really tried to help you. To be frank, Njeri, I think that you've been seeing other men behind my back. If you have, you'd better tell me now. You may as well bring everything out into the open. And I want to know who Tony is.'

Njeri was cornered. She had no alternative but to tell the truth. 'Sean,' she paused. 'Tony's not a photographer. He runs an escort agency and wants me to work for him.'

'A *what?*' said Sean, nearly apoplectic with anger. 'Am I hearing things? You said an escort agency? Don't you know that an escort is just a polite name for a hooker? You can't be so naive that you didn't know.'

'It's not like that, Sean,' Njeri responded. 'Tony says I only have to go to dinner with them, and I can earn £100 an hour just for going out to dinner.'

'Don't be so ridiculous. It's not just dinner that's involved. I tell you quite clearly now, Njeri, that if you as much as go near this man again, you and I are finished – and you can leave this house straight away. Whatever you do, Njeri, don't think you will outsmart me on this one. There's no way I'll have a hooker living in my house, because that's exactly what you will be.'

Njeri was contrite. 'I'm so sorry Sean, I'll tell Tony that I'm not interested in working for him. I'll call him tomorrow.'

'No you won't,' said Sean, barely able to contain his anger. 'You'll call him right now and you'd better make sure he stays away, or I'll have to do the convincing for you. Go and get his number.'

Njeri could see that Sean was furious. She was frightened and knew better than to argue. She did as she was told. She went to her handbag and took out her diary.

'What's his number?' said Sean, and he began to dial as she recited it to him. It was a mobile number. It had to be, thought Sean. He waited as the phone rang.

'Hello, Naughty but Nice Escorts,' said a man's voice.

'It's him,' whispered Sean, passing the receiver to Njeri.

'Hello, is that Tony?' said Njeri. 'I'm calling to say I'm not interested in your job offer. This is Njeri, by the way.'

It took a while for Tony to link the voice with the name. He had been expecting her call. 'What do you mean you're not interested? You said you would do it. I'll tell that boyfriend of yours that you've worked for me already!'

Sean had put the phone on monitor and could hear Tony's every word.

Tony continued, 'I know he's a famous ex-rugby player. How do you think the papers will respond to a story that he's living with a call girl? It'll make good headlines, don't you think?'

'Don't worry,' she said, 'I've already told him about you and your job.'

Tony was incensed. 'Don't mess with me little girl,' he rasped. 'I've got some very heavy friends who might just ruin that pretty face of yours.'

'Listen asshole,' Sean interjected. 'Don't you threaten my girlfriend. I'll break you in two if you come anywhere near her in future, and while we're at it, I've got some very heavy friends as well. So be careful who you're threatening, you scumbag. I am warning you to stay well away.'

At that, Sean pressed the monitor button to hang up.

'There, that tells you what sort of a man your little friend Tony is. You just tell me if he gives you any more hassle in future. In the meantime I'm starving, so how about some grub. Your turn to cook, I think,' smiled Sean.

Njeri turned to leave the room.

'Wait a minute,' said Sean. 'You can take these and burn them on the fire,' he said picking up the offending magazines and handing them to Njeri. 'I hope we don't have to raise this subject again,' he called after her.

While Njeri was busy in the kitchen, Sean picked up the phone in the bedroom and dialled James in Hereford. The phone was answered almost immediately.

'James, I have a problem that you may be able to help me with,' said

Sean. He told him about his most recent conversation with Njeri and her 'friend' Tony.

'Leave it all to me,' said James. 'I've got a colleague who's just left the Regiment. He's a former sergeant and completely reliable. I can trust him with my life. We've seen plenty of action together and he's going to join me in the security firm I'm setting up. He's down in London now. I'll get him to tail Njeri for a few days to see what she's up to. I need you to send a recent photo of her to John so that he knows who he's following.'

'I'll put one in the post tomorrow,' said Sean. 'Thanks, James, I owe you another one.'

'Don't mention it,' said James. 'I'd help you anytime, and besides, it's a good opportunity for John to practise some surveillance in his spare time. It'll keep him out of trouble, if nothing else. I'll keep you informed and will contact you again in about a week.' He hesitated. 'Oh, and by the way, I can't make it this weekend for training. I was going to call you; something has come up.'

'No worries,' said Sean. 'I could do with a weekend off, anyway. Speak to you soon.' He hung up.

The next day Sean duly despatched a couple of photos of Njeri to John in London, including details of the boutique where she worked. He felt bad about putting Njeri under surveillance but he had to make certain she could be trusted if they were to have any future together.

CHAPTER 26

It was dark when Sean finished work the next day. It was Friday night and, for a change, he was looking forward to an idle weekend. His recent workload and training weekends in Hereford were beginning to take their toll. As he ambled to his car in the multi-storey car park off Tottenham Court Road, near his office in Shaftesbury Avenue, he suddenly sensed he was being followed. He looked around him but could see nothing except a few vehicles left in the car park. It was 7.30 p.m., and most of the people who regularly used it had already made the usual early Friday exodus from London for a weekend in the country.

Sean reached his car, and as he was bending to put the key in the lock he detected a movement behind him. As he turned he received a sharp blow to the back of his head. He crumpled to the ground and began to lose consciousness.

Sean awoke to find himself on a cold floor. He tried to move but his hands and feet had been tied together behind his back. He was blindfolded and there was a numbing throb at the back of his head. His mouth was dry, and as he tried to call out only a painful croak emerged from his throat. He wet his lips with his tongue and shouted out to attract attention.

Almost instantly he heard a door open behind him. He could feel himself being picked up and dragged along the cold floor. As he tried to struggle the grip strengthened, so he gave up, thinking it would be better to conserve his energy. After being dragged for what felt like ages, he was unceremoniously dumped on the floor and his hands and feet were untied. The ropes had already chaffed his skin bare and he rubbed his wrists to try and ease the pain. His blindfold was removed and he was ordered to strip off all his clothes. He refused. Instead he shouted. 'Where am I and who are you?' Looking around the gloomy room he could see it was small, with one brown table and three chairs.

'Maybe this will help you strip,' said a voice, as he was hit across the knees with a long cane. Sean buckled at the pain and collapsed to the floor. Slowly he stripped to his underpants.

'And your boxers,' the voice commanded.

Sean sensed a slight accent. He did as he was told.

There were two men in the room. One stood against a wall watching Sean. There was only one man doing the talking who suddenly threw Sean a pair of overalls. He put them on. The man was very tall with close-cropped hair. His head was almost shaven. He was about sixteen stone and very solidly built.

Both men then stepped forward and blindfolded and handcuffed Sean. This time to the front. He was made to stand up and was pushed against the wall. He couldn't see who pushed him, but he guessed it was the tall, solid man. His breath smelt of stale tobacco. He told Sean to stretch out his hands and lean against the wall. He then kicked his legs out and back so that he was leaning at an angle. Very quickly his hands went numb, so he moved them from side to side to readjust his position. Immediately, both men grabbed him and put his hands back in position. Within a few hours his whole body was aching. The two men appeared again and forced him to sit cross-legged, with his hands behind his head and with a straight back. The stress was unbelievable and each time he bent to relieve it the two men forced him upright.

After what seemed like hours, Sean was dragged out of the room and across a surface that felt like tarmac. He could feel his bare feet being cut and the pain was immense. Sean was deposited in a chair and the blindfold came off.

He was temporarily blinded by a beam of strong light aimed directly at him and he quickly shut his eyes. As he readjusted to the light he could just make out two figures on the far side of a table. Both men were in their early thirties with short-cropped hair and were dressed in black army uniforms. Sean noticed they both wore the Iron Cross around their neck.

'Where the hell am I?' asked Sean. 'And who the hell are you two?'

'Shut up!' said one of the men. 'What is your name?'

This time, Sean recognized the crisp, guttural Germanic tones.

'My name is Sean Cameron but I guess you know that.'

'Where do you live?' said the man on the left.

'I'm not telling you.'

'What do you mean you're not telling us? You'll bloody well do as you're told, you cocky bastard!'

'Who the hell are you, anyway?' said Sean, as he began to stand. He hadn't noticed a man behind him who now grabbed his shoulders and pushed him hard back into the chair.

'Where do your parents live?'

'I'm not telling you.'

'Where does your daughter live?'

'I'm not telling you.'

'Listen, I've said it before, you cocky bastard, we're asking the questions so you'd better give us some answers, or you'll really be in the shit. We've been watching you for a long time and unless you can give us an assurance that you will cease your mission to avenge your girlfriend's death, the rest of your family will be in deep trouble.'

'Touch them and I'll kill you, you bastards.'

Again Sean tried to rise but was quickly pushed back into the chair.

'Can I have a drink, please?'

'No!'

'Listen, I've been in here hours and I'm tired and thirsty. I need a drink.'

'You can have a drink when you give us some answers.'

'This is bloody silly. You've asked me where I live and where my family lives. You probably know already, so I'm not telling you. And I wouldn't tell you anyway.'

'Get him out of here,' screamed the smaller man on the left.

They jumped up and Sean was grabbed from each side and blindfolded again. The door opened and he was dragged out of the room back across the tarmac and dumped into what he thought was the original room. It had the same musty smell so it was a reasonable assumption. He was put straight up against the wall and made to adopt the sitting position. This alternating process went on for what seemed like hours, constantly changing between the two positions.

Later, he was dragged back to the interrogation room, and questioned over and over again about where he and his family lived. The same two men were sitting behind the desk. This time the man on the right began to speak.

'What is it about you, Cameron, and the fact that you love niggers? We had to deal with one mouthy nigger bitch, and now you're living with another one.'

Instead of trying to get up, Sean kicked out with both feet and sent the table sprawling. In the commotion he leapt forward and aimed a double-fisted punch at the man on the left. He connected and heard the man scream in pain. He had broken his nose and blood splattered everywhere.

'You fucking kaffir-loving bastard,' a voice shouted. 'I'll get you for that.'

Sean tried to double up in a ball on the floor, but it didn't prevent the boots smashing into his ribs from all sides. After a few minutes the kicking stopped. Sean was winded and the pain in his ribs and legs was excrutiating.

'A stupid thing to do, Mr Cameron. If we have to dispose of you, we will, make no mistake about that,' said the smaller man. Sean noticed he had a nasty scar on his left cheek, about one inch below his eye.

Sean was dragged away again and dumped back on the floor of the first room. The lights had been turned fully on. He lay there for a while and soon fell into a deep sleep, only to be woken by a guard who threw a bucket of cold water over him and then hosed him down with even colder water. The shock was almost too much to bear. He was picked up and dragged out again across the tarmac. He was dog tired. All his energy had gone. He was back in the interrogation room. This time there was a plate of food on the table and a glass of water.

'Now,' said the man on the right. 'I'll give you one last chance to answer my questions – and then you can eat.'

'I've told you before, my name is Sean Cameron, and other than that I'm not telling you anything. You can go to hell,' Sean said, shivering in his wet overalls.

'How long do you think you've been in here?'

Sean thought for a few minutes. He could only guess. 'About thirty hours.'

'Oh, so you are answering our questions.'

'I'll answer any question that doesn't affect my family.'

'If we told you that you've been here forty-eight hours, what would you say?'

'I don't know. I guess I would have to believe you.'

'Well, Mr Cameron, you'd better believe it. You can take a drink of water now and then we'll tell you who we are.'

Sean grabbed the glass of water and gulped it down. It didn't quench his thirst. His lips were dry and cracked. He could feel the stubble of his beard. His whole body ached.

'Ok, so who are you then?'

'Actually, Mr Cameron, we work for your friend James . . . '

'James!' gasped Sean. 'What's he got to do with this?'

'Well, rather than spend the weekend at Hereford, he thought it would be better to catch you by surprise at a time when you were least expecting it. We've tried to give you a little experience of what it might be like if the neo-Nazis get hold of you in Germany – or Combat 18, a wing of the National Front in England. You came through very well. James said you were a stubborn bastard. We weren't exactly gentle with you, especially when you broke Clive's nose. It serves the bugger right. He should have anticipated your moves more quickly.'

Sean couldn't believe his ears. 'Wait 'til I get hold of James. I'll kill him.' he rasped. 'I'd been looking forward to a quiet weekend and I get to spend it with you bunch of nuts.'

'You can have your food now and, by the way, my name is Angus McLean. I'm a friend of James from Hereford. Just helping a pal out when needed,' he smiled, as he offered Sean his hand.

In no time at all Sean had wolfed the food down. 'I need a shower and some clean clothes, if you don't mind.'

'Just through the door on the right. Give us a shout when you're ready and we'll take you home. We've already delivered your car there,' said Angus.

Sean got up and left the room.

That night he called James. He was pretty angry at the way he'd been treated and wanted to give James a piece of his mind. Yolanda answered the phone and told Sean that James wouldn't be back until the following Thursday. I bet he's there, thought Sean. He was probably keeping a low profile while Sean's anger subsided. As much as Sean realized that James was trying to help him, he thought this time he had gone too far. Would this training really help to find Akinyi's killers?

CHAPTER 27

It was 9.30 a.m. when Sean woke the next morning. He was late for the first time since he had been working for Smithy. The weekend had taken its toll. Although he had slept soundly his whole body ached. He struggled out of bed and looked at his face in the mirror. His eyes were puffy and there were a few small cuts on his face. His body hurt like hell. A legacy of the kicking. He winced in pain as he touched his bruised ribs.

There was no sign of Njeri. Sean figured she had already gone to work. He called Emma and told her that he was running late, and asked her to tell Smithy that he would like to see him at five. Sean showered as quickly as he could, considering his injuries. He dressed, had a quick cup of tea and headed off to work. He left a note for Njeri, saying he would be back at about seven o'clock and that they would go out to dinner.

Sean arrived at the office at midday and got an update from Emma on the Sukimoto project. As before, things were running smoothly. Emma could handle the account on her own, thought Sean – and he would tell Smithy this.

At five he went to Smithy's office.

'Ah, come in Sean, it's good to see you. But, Christ, you look as though you've been brawling.'

'It's nothing really, just a little trouble I had at the weekend.' He hadn't told Smithy about his training. The fewer people who knew, the better.

'What can I do for you, Sean? How's the Sukimoto project?'

'It's going well, and that's why I'm here to see you. I've got a full report in this file for you. It runs through all the budget breakdowns and a proposal for the future. I'm sorry to tell you this, Smithy, but I need to leave in three weeks time.'

Smithy was surprised. 'I know your contract finishes then, but I was hoping you would stay and develop new business for us.'

'In normal circumstances I would, but I've got some unfinished business to deal with – and I'm not sure how long it will take. However, Emma is super efficient and will have no problem in handling Sukimoto. Promote her to account manager, Smithy. She's perfectly capable of it. She's been trained by an expert,' grinned Sean.

'OK, Sean, I can see there's nothing I can do to persuade you to stay. I won't insult you by offering you more money, because I know that's not your beef. I know you need to exorcize past ghosts. Still, when you've sorted yourself out there's always a job here if you want it.'

Sean was pleased that Smithy had taken it so well. 'Thanks for everything, Smithy, I really do appreciate all that you've done for me. I'll tie up all the loose ends before I go.'

He got up to leave and offered Smithy his hand. They shook firmly.

'You'd better send Emma in so I can tell her the good news,' said Smithy.

Sean left Smithy's office and went to look for Emma.

'Smithy's in a fearful mood and wants to see you at once. I don't know what you've done, but I think you're in deep trouble,' he said jokingly when he found her.

'But Sean I've done nothing wrong,' Emma said, nervously.

'You'd better get a move on, or he'll be even more angry if you keep him waiting.'

Five minutes later Emma returned with a big smile on her face. 'You bastard, Sean. You were just winding me up! You knew Smithy was going to give me your job,' she said, as she playfully went to slap Sean around the top of his head.

'You deserve it,' he said. 'I'm leaving in three weeks, but you might as well run things from now on.'

Sean returned home to tell Njeri his plans over dinner. He had booked a table at one of the Italian restaurants in Richmond which they often frequented. He told Njeri that he was leaving Smithy's in three weeks and that he was going to Europe on a new project.

'I'm not sure how long I'll be gone, but you can stay on at the house for as long as you like,' he said.

'What about us?' asked Njeri.

'Well, I guess the break will do us good,' he replied. 'Anyway, I'll be back as soon as I can.'

'I'll miss you so much, Sean. It will be the first time we've been apart. I really do love you, Sean.'

'At times I think you have a funny way of showing it, but I guess dealing with me can be pretty difficult. Perhaps my quietness is not too helpful at times. I know I don't express my feelings very much, Njeri, but I do care for you a great deal. I suppose I need to tell you that more often.'

'Yes, you must try, Sean. It helps my confidence.'

They sat in silence for a while and Njeri finished the bottle of wine she had been drinking. Sean stuck to mineral water. He had found it tough on occasions not drinking, but he knew he had to get through one day at a time. He was already thinking of his trip to Germany.

'What are you thinking?' interrupted Njeri.

'Oh, nothing,' mused Sean.

'Come on, then. It's time to go.'

He paid the bill and they left.

Sean eventually got hold of James on Saturday morning when Njeri was out. Either he was hiding from Sean or he really had been away on a mission.

'Hello, James, you son of a gun. I'll just warn you now that surprises can come from all quarters,' chuckled Sean.

His anger had subsided.

'You did very well under interrogation, Sean. Still, that was a picnic compared with what it will be like if you get captured interfering in Nazi business. Remember that.'

'I'll make sure I'm not caught,' said Sean confidently. 'If I've got a decent partner watching over me, I'm sure I'll be okay. But that's up to you, James. It'll be *my* turn to find out what *you're* made of.'

'Don't you worry about me,' interjected James. 'We'll soon find Akinyi's killers and then I can get on with my future plans. I haven't told Yolanda what we're up to, so don't breathe a word to her. In three weeks I'll be out of the army and back in civvy street. Imagine!'

'Changing the subject, James, have you had any news from John in London about Njeri?'

'Ah, I wondered when you would come to that. That Njeri is a dark horse. John has kept her under almost constant surveillance. She's been a naughty girl, Sean, and I've been wondering how to tell you this. She's definitely gone 'on the game'. She is working for that arsehole Tony Valvoni who runs Naughty but Nice Escorts. By all accounts, she's well in demand from the regular customers.'

'Jesus Christ!' gasped Sean. 'And she's been living here while doing it. Come on, James, how long has she been at it?'

'Oh, not long. According to John only about three weeks, but she's been busy all right.'

'Whereabouts? Not in Richmond I hope.'

'No, no, mostly around London hotels and around the airport. It's certainly big business and an area I'm not familiar with. John's done a good deal of research. Most of the girls employed are middle-class who work as secretaries or sales reps during the day. Most of them hold down good jobs. They want to supplement their income. Also, there are many students at it who want to pay for their education.'

'It's hard to believe, James. I can tell you I'm shocked. How can she do this to me?'

'Well, Sean, you're just going to have to get rid of her as soon as possible.'

'Don't you worry, I will,' said Sean. 'Thanks for the information. Although I've suspected it myself for a while, I didn't want to believe it. I'll deal with it in my own way.' He hung up.

Sean was absolutely stunned by James's news. He sat for a while staring blankly and trying to collect his thoughts. Njeri would be home soon and he would have to confront her. His breathing was shallow and he had a lump in his throat. *What have I done to deserve this?* he thought.

'Sean?' Njeri shouted as she slammed the door behind her. 'I'm back. Where are you?'

'I'm in the lounge,' Sean croaked, trying to clear his throat.

Njeri bounced in and went to kiss Sean. He turned his face away.

'What's the matter, Sean?'

'I think you've got some explaining to do again. Now, just tell me about that scumbag Valvoni, and I want a straight answer for once.'

'There's nothing to say, Sean. I haven't spoken to him since the telephone call you made with me.'

'Don't lie. I know all about your activities. I know you are no longer working at the boutique. I know you are working for Valvoni.'

'I promise . . . '

Sean interrupted. 'Stop lying, Njeri. I know you're on the game. I've had you followed.'

Njeri began to cry.

'Don't waste your tears. I want you out of here as soon as you have packed your case. I really don't care where you go, but you can damned well get out of my house. I don't want a whore like you living here,' he shouted.

'Sean, I'm sorry. I needed the money for my family. You are so tight and you just didn't send them enough. How do you expect my two children to live on £80 a month?'

'Listen, it wasn't my responsibility to pay anything for them – but I did. Not only that, you sent money yourself. What about all the money you earned? Explain that!'

'School fees are expensive in Kenya and, besides, you didn't care for me. You never told me you loved me. What sort of a man are you?'

'I didn't tell you I loved you because I haven't been able to make up my mind yet. Also, I couldn't understand how you behaved in the way you did. What about the time you went out to dinner with another man on my birthday? That's no way to behave. You said you were trying to make me jealous, but it didn't work. It just made me angry. How do you expect me to tell you I love you when you behave like that?'

'At least he gave me money for my kids.'

'You mean you were taking money off him as well? I don't want to hear any more. Get the fuck out of here!'

'But, Sean, I love you more than enough,' Njeri said, mixing up her words.

'Listen,' said Sean. 'You don't know what true love is. Think about it

138

for a minute. Look at the difference in our ages. How many twenty-three-year-olds in England end up with a man my age? Not many. Yes, it's been nice being with you and very flattering – but I think that you wanted to marry me just to get your papers to stay full-time in England and then move on.'

'It wasn't like that, Sean, I promise you.'

'You promise a lot but rarely deliver. Get out now. You've got twenty minutes to pack your belongings and leave.'

'But, Sean, please,' she protested.

In his wrath he waved her away.

Njeri left the room. Sean tried to suppress his anger and hurt. His breathing was heavy. He sat watching the fire. The flickering flames cast wild shadows beyond the enclosed confines of the red-brick fireplace. How could he bring himself to ever trust anyone again?

Sometime later he heard Njeri on the telephone. She was calling a taxi. A few minutes later the front door slammed shut. He got up and went to the drinks cupboard. He pulled out a bottle of Scotch. It was a new one. He broke the seal and went back to his chair. He put the bottle on the table and sat watching it. He hadn't had a drink since Njeri rescued him in Kenya. He was sorely tempted. He knew he shouldn't have another drink, but this was an exceptional circumstance. He eventually relented. He poured the Scotch into the glass to a depth of two fingers and took a huge gulp. He felt the old burning sensation in his throat and swallowed. The smell of the whisky filled his nostrils. He poured another, then another.

Sean awoke to the continuous buzzing of the front door bell. It hurt his head. Someone was eager to get in. He tried opening his eyes. He was still in the lounge, slumped in his chair. The fire had long gone out and there were several empty bottles scattered on the floor. As he got up he stumbled over his shoes. 'Oh shit,' he cursed. He reached the front door and opened it. It was Emma from the office.

'What are you doing here?'

'I've come to see if you are all right. Do you know what day it is? It's Tuesday and I've been ringing you for the past two days. I was worried about you, so I thought I'd call in on my way home from work.' She pushed past him into the lounge. 'Look at you, Sean, you're a mess,' she said, staring wide eyed at the debris that covered the floor. 'I thought you didn't drink.'

'I don't,' said Sean, lying.

'It doesn't look like that to me.'

'Well, what I meant is, I don't normally. I've just had some bad news, that's all.' Sean knew he couldn't tell Emma the full story. 'Njeri's gone and she's not coming back.'

'What happened, Sean? Tell me.'

'Let's just say she's gone and leave it at that, eh?'

Emma realized Sean wasn't going to expand on his story. 'All right then, let's get this place cleaned up. You go and have a shower – you look terrible. I'll make some food.'

Where had he heard that before? he pondered, slowly climbing the stairs. As he went into the bathroom he glanced in the mirror. A touch of deja vu, he thought, remembering Kenya and the state he'd got into there. He really didn't want to fall into the same trap again. This session just had to be the last. It was a weakness that he had to conquer.

When he came downstairs, Emma had prepared some food and had cleaned up. He told her it was only a temporary aberration on his part. He was clearly embarrassed, so Emma didn't pursue the subject.

He didn't want to go back to work and finish the last three weeks at Smithy's. He would only have been marking time anyway. He spoke to Emma about it and decided to call Smithy. He would ask to be paid off immediately. His heart was no longer in the job and he had to be totally honest with the man. He didn't want to take his money under false pretences.

The next morning Sean telephoned Smithy and explained the situation. Smithy agreed it was the right thing for him to leave. He asked Sean to return his car and he could then collect his final pay cheque. There were no hard feelings.

CHAPTER 28

It was a struggle for Sean to stay off the booze over the next few weeks, but he punished himself with an intensive personal fitness training programme. He had agreed with James that they would fly to Frankfurt on 3 June. It would be nearly two years since Akinyi's death. He hoped the killers' trail had not gone cold. He phoned Inspector Meissner, the detective in charge of the case, and arranged an appointment with him for the morning after their arrival in Frankfurt.

Three weeks passed quickly. Sean had organized all his affairs and paid all the neccessary bills. He was ready to go. He had neither seen nor heard from Njeri. Some post had arrived for her but he had no forwarding address. He reckoned she would contact him soon enough.

He was very troubled by the lifestyle she had chosen. He enjoyed her company and missed her greatly. While he didn't love her, he felt a deep affection and fondness for her. He also felt he owed her a debt of gratitude for the help she had given him in Kenya. He was deeply saddened by the way things had turned out. He hated to think of her with different men every night. If nothing else, he had a fatherly love for her.

Two days before he left for Germany, Njeri contacted him. He was sitting watching TV late one afternoon when the phone rang.

'Sean, I need to see you. I have a problem and I need your help. I need to see you,' she pleaded.

'I don't think that's such a good idea.'

'Please, Sean, I'm desperate. Please!' Njeri implored.

'Okay. It's against my better judgement. But you're not coming here. Where shall we meet?'

'By the entrance to Richmond Park. You know, where we used to go walking sometimes. I'll be in a red Golf GTI. I'll see you in an hour.' She hung up.

Sean wondered what the trouble was. He knew he had to help her, even if it was only for old time's sake. He was down to his trusty old bicycle since he had returned his car to Smithy. However he didn't fancy riding there, so he decided to run instead. He changed into his tracksuit and trainers and set off. It took him fifteen minutes to run through the streets of Richmond. It was probably just as quick as driving as the traffic was particularly bad that evening, especially along the one-way system towards Richmond Hill.

As he arrived at Richmond Park, he spotted the car parked by the gates. He ran up and knocked on the window. Njeri wound the window down and told him to get in. She was wearing dark glasses, which he thought was strange.

'What have you got those on for?' he enquired.

'Because I like them,' sighed Njeri.

'Don't be silly, it's getting dark. Let me have a look at you.'

Sean grabbed the glasses and was shocked to see the state of Njeri's face. She had been crying; her eyes were all puffed up and badly bruised, and there were cuts on her cheeks. He also noticed a bandage on her left hand.

'What happened to you?'

'I just fell over.'

'What happened to you, Njeri? Who did this?' he asked again, tenderly caressing her cheek.

'I told you, Sean, I fell over.'

'Don't take me for an idiot. It was that bastard Valvoni, wasn't it?' Sean could feel the anger rising in him.

'Sean, I'm pregnant,' Njeri suddenly announced.

Sean's mouth fell open. 'What! I don't believe you! I . . . '

Njeri interrupted. 'I am, Sean, and before you ask who the father is, I'm going to tell you. It's you, Sean.'

There was a stunned silence.

'Really, Sean, it's yours. I'm five months' pregnant. I visited the doctor today for a test and he confirmed it. I've suspected for a while now, but I wasn't sure.'

'How long is a while?'

'About two months!'

'What? You've suspected you're pregnant with our child, and you've been sleeping with different men every night?' Sean exploded.

'Yes, Sean, but I needed the money. Last night I earned £900 and the night before it was £600. I can earn another £600 tonight,' she said with a hint of pride in her voice.

Sean looked at her. Distaste registered all over his face. 'What the hell are you doing to earn that sort of money?'

'I earn £900 for one and a half hours' work. Can you believe it, Sean?' she said, rather defiantly. 'It was terrible, Sean, with six men in that time, but I'm doing it for my kids.'

'And the £600. What did you do for that?' he snapped.

'Oh, that was four men but it was only for an hour,' Njeri said nonchalantly.

Sean couldn't believe what he was hearing. 'In one breath you tell me you are pregnant and in the next you say you are being gang banged by lots of different men. You're sick in the head, Njeri.' He moved to open the passenger door.

'Wait please, Sean, please,' Njeri sobbed. 'I'm now living with a bodybuilder. He comes home drunk at night and beats me up. He doesn't know what I'm doing, but he calls me a whore. Every night for the last week he's beaten me up.'

'But that's just what you are, Njeri, a whore.'

It hurt Sean to say that but he was so angry he was past caring. He wanted to kill the new boyfriend and all the other men. He wondered how she could go with these men if she knew she was pregnant with his child. She must have no respect for him, and none for herself or her body. They sat in silence, other than the sound of her sobs. Sean looked long and hard at Njeri. She looked in pain. Not just physical pain; there was an inner anguish that he could see in her eyes.

Very quietly, Sean began to talk to Njeri. He said she was plunging in to terrible depths by her life of prostitution; it was humiliating and degrading. He explained that all the money in the world wouldn't save her from the emotional turmoil – and, no doubt, physical damage – that she would suffer as a result of selling her body; it would haunt her for the rest of her life. He begged her to stop it.

Njeri argued that she couldn't make the same sort of money any other way, or so quickly. She told him she only intended doing this for another six months, during which time she would earn enough money to return to Kenya and buy a house and a car. She said it would be the new start she needed.

Sean persisted, telling her that it would ruin any chance of her having a normal loving relationship with a man in the future. She would never be able to trust men again, and she would always feel that they were only interested in her for sex. It would create incredible jealousies if and when she might settle down more permanently with a man, especially if he as much as looked at another woman. Her life was heading for disaster.

'I can't go on lecturing you, Njeri. Whatever you do must be your own decision. In the meantime, our immediate problem is your pregnancy. If we were still together, I would have been delighted with the news, but after what you've told me it's as though you have defiled our child. You'll have to get rid of it, and that needs to be done sooner rather than later.'

'But, Sean, can't we get back together?'

'Njeri, you are so naive. I don't think you have the slightest understanding of what is right or wrong. Frankly, the answer to your question is no. It's not something I would even consider after what you have told me. Anyway, I am leaving the country for a while and I don't know when I'll be back. In the meantime you are going to have to terminate your pregnancy,' he said uncomfortably, avoiding the term 'child'.

'I'll see the doctor tomorrow,' said Njeri, dejected. Her last-ditch attempt to salvage the relationship had failed. No matter how much she wanted this baby, she was not prepared to raise it on her own.

Sean climbed out of the car. 'Let me know how you get on. If you need to contact me in the next few weeks, call Yolanda and leave a message. You have her number. Good luck, Njeri. Despite your chosen path, I wish you all the best.'

He slammed the door and hurried off through Richmond Park. He ran and ran as hard as he could, trying to get as much air into his lungs as possible. He felt like screaming. It was drizzling slightly and the rain on his face substituted for the tears he felt like shedding. What had he done to Njeri to make her behave like that? Somehow he felt responsible, but realized it was not his fault. She had deceived him once too often. What she was doing was a far cry from playing around in bars and discos in Mombasa. There she was smart enough to deal with the elderly tourists who chatted her up over a drink; she wasn't selling her body, she was just having a good time like any European girl in the bars and discos of their own town. He did not want to believe that Njeri was now an expensive call girl in London. He ran on, eventually reaching home almost an hour later. He was mentally and physically exhausted. How was he going to deal with this latest upheaval in his life?

CHAPTER 29

On 3 June James and Sean flew from Heathrow on a British Airways flight to Frankfurt. James celebrated his leaving the army with a bottle of champagne; Sean toasted him with mineral water. He was apprehensive about their adventure. He wasn't sure whether he'd be able to cope adequately with the severe and dangerous challenge that lay ahead.

On the flight, he confronted James with the same question he had asked while training on Brecon Beacons.

'Tell me,' Sean said. 'Do you think I've got what it takes to kill a man in cold blood?'

James looked at him long and hard. 'Frankly, Sean, I don't. It takes a very special something to kill a man in cold blood. You are pretty damned fit and strong, but I don't think that you have that single-minded aggression that is required to kill a man. I'm worried that I am putting you in a very dangerous position, possibly even risking your life.'

'It's my decision,' said Sean, rather sharply. 'I kept up well in training, didn't I?'

'Sure you did, Sean, but a dozen training sessions on a crash course is a far cry from front-line action. I've got years of experience in all sorts of dangerous situations, all over the world. No one learns that overnight. Least of all a soft lad like you,' he teased.

'Bloody cheek, James, and I suppose you are Lord God Almighty.'

James could see that he had touched a raw nerve.

'Sean, you've been my closest friend for more than twenty years, but in all my time in the army anyone who has asked the same question as you – about being able to kill a man – hasn't been able to cut the mustard when it's come to the crunch. The guys that can do it, and can do it cleanly, never ask. They know themselves that they can do it.'

'Huh,' said Sean moodily.

They spent the remainder of the flight in silence while Sean contemplated what James had said.

When they arrived in Frankfurt they checked into their hotel on the edge of the city centre. It was a small, three-storey building with a restaurant and bar overlooking a neat town square.

The next morning Sean visited the main police station where he met Hauptkommissar Meissner. He rose from his chair to greet Sean.

'Good morning, Mr Cameron. It's been a long time. What can I do for you?'

'Well, first I would like to know how far you have got in tracking down Akinyi Ouko's killers.'

Meissner explained that very little had happened since their last conversation and that they were no further forward with their enquiries. They hadn't actually closed the case. The file was still open, but they had withdrawn active investigation. Unless new information or clues came to their attention, it would remain dormant.

'I suggest you just put it down to one of life's very tragic experiences,' Meissner commiserated.

It was an unfortunate statement, to which Sean reacted badly. Meissner seemed not to care much about the eventual outcome. On the other hand, Sean didn't want to reveal the depth of his own intentions.

'Well I guess you've done your best,' he said sarcastically. 'If you can't find the criminals, perhaps I can.'

'That's your choice, Mr Cameron, but just make sure you don't step outside the law to do so. If you break the law you will leave me with no alternative but to arrest you. You have been warned,' he said menacingly, a thin smile forming on his even thinner lips.

Sean turned and left the office, grunting a surly goodbye. Don't you worry, he thought to himself. I'll sure as hell do it my way, *and* I'll get a result.

James was waiting outside, reading the morning paper. He could see Sean was in a black mood.

'No joy then?' he enquired.

'Meissner's a waste of time. Operation Stormtrooper has just begun,' he said, as he carried on walking.

James followed a few paces behind. 'Slow down, Sean. We need to sort out our plan.'

'Don't worry, I know what I'm doing,' said Sean. It was only then that it dawned on him that he had no idea how he was going to start the investigation. He had no plan at all. He also recognized that he was being unacceptably abrupt with James, who, as his partner with most of the know-how, fully deserved to share in his thoughts.

'James,' Sean said sheepishly. 'I'm very sorry if I appeared to brush off your question. I was being both arrogant and stupid. We haven't a clue where we go from here.'

'You may not but I do. I know exactly what I'm doing, and indeed I know exactly what the next step is.' James was not pleased with Sean's brush-off and ignored his apology. 'In the meantime,' he continued, 'we've got to meet Dieter Beck in the Kaiserstrasse. I've arranged to meet him at noon in a pub called Zum Kaiser.'

'Who's Dieter Beck when he's at home?'

'Just a friend of mine,' said James quietly.

'Why is he important to us?'

'I didn't say he was.' James was still peeved. He glanced at his watch. 'Come on, Sean. We'll grab a cab, otherwise we are going to be late. We can't keep Dieter waiting; his time is precious.'

On the journey James updated Sean on the underground network of neo-fascist splinter groups that were springing up all over Europe. They arrived at the bar in ten minutes and Sean recognized Dieter Beck immediately. He was the man who had sat to the right hand side of the table during his mock interrogation. His hair was cut in short military style. He looked bigger than when they had met before, but Sean reckoned that was because previously he'd only seen him sitting behind a table.

Dieter rose from his bar stool and offered Sean his hand. 'Hello, Sean. At least this time we meet in more convivial circumstances. You certainly look healthier,' he smiled.

'Yes, it was certainly no picnic last time. But since James explained your mission, I've got no hard feelings. Mark you, that's not what I thought at the time.'

Dieter grinned. 'And you, James, you're looking fitter than ever. I don't know how you manage it. Come on, let's sit over there.'

He led them to a table in the far corner of the bar. It was a good vantage point and perfectly positioned to survey the main entrance in case they had been followed. It was also well sited next to the kitchen door, which made it easier if they had to make a swift exit into the back alley behind the bar. Dieter's years of experience had taught him always to be wary of the opposition and to expect the unexpected.

They sat down and ordered three coffees. The barman brought them over and when he left them Dieter began.

'I picked this place because I think we can remain fairly anonymous here.'

Sean glanced around. It was relatively quiet. There were a few hardened drinkers sitting at the bar and two guys playing pool in the far corner. There was a slight hum from the background music, which was barely audible but enough to drown out their conversation from eavesdroppers.

'James has told me all about you, Sean. Now, let me explain where I fit in. I am currently working under cover for an organization which is trying to flush out the neo-Nazi groups operating in Germany at the moment. It's an open secret that we are government backed, but official sources will not admit it and are trying to keep a low profile.'

Dieter went on to explain that the German government was concerned about the negative worldwide publicity the country was receiving, because of the increased number of attacks on foreigners and immigrants. Most of the personnel employed were ex-Special Forces or police who had been trained in covert operations.

'So far we have had mixed success. I was recently on a training course with your SAS and it was there that I met up again with James.'

James picked up the story. 'That's right. I first met Dieter some two years ago. We were both on a special assignment which I can't talk about, but we got to know each other pretty well. When he turned up on the course at Hereford recently we got chatting, and I told him about Akinyi and your determination to find her murderers.'

'Yes,' said Dieter. 'I had a free weekend and that's when we hatched the plot to organize your abduction and interrogation.'

'It was after that,' interrupted James, 'that Dieter contacted his boss about you and Akinyi. The government knew about her murder. After all, it was splashed all over the newspapers, so it didn't take them long to endorse Dieter's involvement. They were severely embarrassed by the manner of her death and they want results.'

'Yes,' said Dieter. 'First and foremost, they feel the police have dragged their heels somewhat and they are sure there are too many far-right sympathizers in the force. In particular, Rudy Meissner is suspected of attending neo-Nazi rallies and weekend training camps. We've got him under close observation.'

A look of shock registered all over Sean's face.

'They want to track down Akinyi's killers not only for your sake, Sean, but also because it would be a significant feather in the department's cap,' said James. 'The powers that be in Bonn have assured Dieter's boss that there would be a blaze of publicity if our operation were to succeed.'

'What do you call yourselves, then?' Sean asked Dieter.

'Justice 89 is the name we gave the department when we formed it in a small office in Frankfurt back in 1989, would you believe?'

'Very imaginative,' said Sean, and grinned.

'Justice 89 is here to help you. You must realize these Nazis don't play to the same rules as we do – and to embark on a mission on your own would be completely suicidal. I promise you we will get the men who killed your girlfriend. For the past year we have been making discreet enquiries. We believe we know who did the killing, but we need you to help us draw them out into the open and to arrest them. Then we have to find proof. For you, Sean, it will be very dangerous, and we'll understand if you choose to back out. We will always be in the background. You won't see us but you have my word we will be there when needed. Now, here's what we want you to do.'

Dieter explained that Sean was to go about openly, asking questions about the neo-Nazi cell in Frankfurt. He had to go to various known haunts of the Nazis and make himself look as plausible as possible.

Dieter wanted Sean to make it known who he was and why he was asking the questions. Dieter explained that the Nazis would obviously check him out and would find it hard to believe that he was a member of Combat 18. In this way, Dieter and James knew Sean would start to be followed wherever he went. Once he was followed they would have individuals to target and build up a dossier of the people involved. So far they had little information. The neo-Nazis were very clever. They constantly moved their people around from town to town and city to city. The only 'regulars' in each cell were the main controllers, who until now had managed to remain anonymous. They were very secretive and apparently never openly attended any of the public rallies. They operated underground and controlled things from afar by directing operations through their lieutenants on the ground via mobile phones and walkie talkies.

At most of the public rallies the 'troops' or troublemakers covered their faces with balaclavas or scarves, although they all tended to wear paramilitary uniforms. These were made up of Doc Martens boots, black army fatigues and black bomber jackets, which made their dress code instantly recognizable to outsiders. The irony was that although they tried to keep their faces hidden they actually quite openly displayed their allegiance by their uniform.

Dieter wanted Sean to infiltrate a cell by pretending he had realized the error of his ways in consorting with a black woman and wished to reform by joining the cause.

First, he had to cut his hair short in a crewcut style and to dress like the Nazis. Dieter had arranged for Sean to visit a barber that afternoon and for a Nazi 'uniform' to be delivered to his hotel. He was about to go through a metamorphosis.

Second, he had to visit a local bar frequented by Nazi sympathizers and make himself known as soon as possible. He had to tell them he had joined Combat 18 in England, a new organization, and that he had been sent by them to learn about the development and methodology of the German units, so that they could extend the cause in England. The Germans were not stupid and would check Sean's credentials with Combat 18 headquarters in the UK. Dieter had already prepared for this eventuality. He explained that during the past year one of his own men had infiltrated Combat 18's headquarters in London and was now in charge of their central records. When the Germans contacted London to check on Sean's credentials, the mole would verify that Sean was a new member of about six months' standing. The Germans would be asked to help him acquire new techniques and knowledge that they were willing to pass on to Combat 18, whose 'spokesman' would say that Sean wanted to become a fully fledged member and join one of their active service units when he returned to the UK. As far as Combat 18 was concerned, this would be a good test of Sean's initiative and commitment. It sounded fairly rational but Sean had a question for Dieter.

'If I'm supposed to be a neo-Nazi member of Combat 18, why should I be openly asking questions about Akinyi's killers? It doesn't make sense to me.'

'What we are really discussing, Sean, is your cover story,' said James, again stepping into the discussion. 'It is obviously complex and is not without risk. But it seems reasonable for you to mean that you are asking questions about Akinyi's killers for three essential reasons: first, that your attitudes have changed towards foreigners, especially black people; second, that, despite your conversion to nationalism, understandable sentiment makes you feel that you don't want to operate in a unit with guys who could possibly have killed Akinyi; and, third, that, in pursuit of your new crusade, you wish to find out more about neo-Nazi methods so that you can apply them to take up a more active role in Britain. You can say you now have an enthusiasm for, and a certain pride in, the crusade that has overtaken your life. Your new enthusiasm for extremist measures is partly because you suffered badly at the hands of the Africans during your period of alcoholism in Kenya. The locals treated you as a joke and now you have come to your senses you want revenge on all foreigners who come to Europe, particularly black people who settle in a European country and make you feel it is yours no longer.'

'Do you understand now, Sean?' asked Dieter.

'Loud and clear. I get the picture. But are these expressions of mine going to stand up against serious challenge? Will they really accept me as an envoy of Combat 18, without any prior consultation between the two organizations?'

'Frankly, we can't be sure,' said Dieter. 'That's the risk we've already brought to your attention. If you abandon the assumed link with Combat 18, are they more or less likely to confide in you? We suspect the latter. You would be regarded purely as a loner without any control.'

'Okay,' said Sean. 'Let's give it a try. But for God's sake, fellows, keep me in sight all the time – and pull me out if necessary.'

Dieter ordered more coffee. From his briefcase he pulled out and passed to Sean a selection of photographs.

'These are the guys we suspect of killing Akinyi,' he said as he handed over six photographs. 'The first one, Rheiner Grunefeld, is dead. The second, Wolfgang Schenkers, has disappeared, and we suspect that he, too, is dead. The other four are very much alive. Examine them closely, just in case they cross your path.'

Sean took the photos and studied them carefully one by one. He had never seen them before. Each one had the distinctive short-cropped hair common to most Neo-Nazi 'troopers'. Sean memorized their faces. He had a score to settle.

Dieter continued. 'We don't know their names, so it's up to you to find out. You will no longer be able to stay in the same hotel as James. If you're seen with a black man your cover will be blown, but James will be in charge of field operations. You will report to me on a daily basis. Here is my number. Memorize it and destroy the piece of paper. You could be risking your life, Sean. If the Nazis find out you are working for us they will definitely kill you. I repeat again, this operation is very dangererous. If at any time your cover is blown, walk into a police station and ask to see the local chief, who will contact me to come and get you. Do you understand?'

'Yes.'

'Right. First the barbers and then to your new hotel. It is not far from here and convenient for the Kaiserstasse where, it's hoped, most of your work will be done,' said Dieter. 'Good luck!'

'Thanks, it sounds like I'm going to need it.'

'Just one more thing,' said Dieter. 'I should explain the sort of operations we go on. In one of our first field exercises we raided a group of far-Right-wing youths gathering for survival training at the Wolletzsee, a large lake outside Berlin. We arrested twenty-seven people and siezed a huge cache of arms.'

Sean interrupted. 'Raiding rallies like that won't stop them. Surely it will drive them further underground?'

'Yes, you are partly right,' Dieter continued. 'The scale of the attacks against foreigners has increased by at least 10 per cent in the last twelve months. Since the Berlin Wall came down there are an estimated 45,000 extremists from the former communist bloc alone. Add to that the estimates of 30,000 in the old Federal Republic of Germany and you can see that it is becoming a problem on a massive scale.'

'Come on, we must go,' said James. 'It doesn't do to be seen in one place for too long.'

At that the three rose. James and Sean shook hands.

'Don't you worry, Sean. Your guardian angel will keep an eye on you,' said James, and he grinned.

As they left, the barman went to the phone and made a short call.

CHAPTER 30

Sean had his hair cut and returned to the hotel where Dieter had already arranged the delivery of his 'uniform'. He checked out of the hotel, leaving James behind. Dieter had already departed, but he left Sean with the address of his new hotel and the emergency contact. As he walked along the street he suddenly felt apprehensive about his mission. It was obvious that things would become dangerous and he wondered how he would deal with it.

It didn't take him long to reach his new hotel. He checked in and went to his room. Immediately he tried on his new outfit. As he looked at his reflection in the mirror, he felt very self-conscious and a little ridiculous in the black combat trousers and shirt. He had worn Doc Martens boots in his youth and they reminded him of the days of skinheads at football matches back in the seventies. The black bomber jacket was a little tight, but he guessed that was how it was meant to be worn to create a more imposing figure. His blondish hair had been cut very short. Again, it reminded him of a crewcut he had had when he was a boy of eleven, the last time he had such short hair. He contemplated his new image for a while and wondered whether he would be treated seriously. After all, he hadn't seen many men of his age dress in such a curious way.

It was five o'clock in the afternoon. He lay down on his bed to get some rest before he visited the neo-Nazi bar just off the Kaiserstrasse. He soon dozed off.

When he awoke it was 7 p.m. He looked out of the window on to the street below. There were a few cars parked outside, and one or two people walking along the pavement. He could hear the buzz of traffic and the sound of a police siren wailing. By now he was hungry. He needed to eat before he went to the Beerhaus. After a quick meal in the hotel café downstairs, he got up and headed off on the first leg of his mission. He had a street map in his pocket and studied it as he was walking along. Within five minutes he had arrived at his destination, all the time memorizing the return trip and also taking note of the side streets. He waited for a short while across the street from the Beerhaus, watching several people coming to and fro. Most of them were like kids, dressed in a similar style to Sean.

Finally he made his move and headed to the front door, trying to look as relaxed as possible.

'Tag!' said the doorman gruffly.

He was huge. Sean was almost mesmerized by his size. He was

wearing black combat trousers and a very tight black T-shirt that accentuated the well-developed muscles in his broad chest and arms.

'Just here for a drink,' replied Sean in English, trying to appear as cool as possible. He knew next to nothing of German, and he obviously looked so English it seemed silly to pretend he was anything else.

'Ein moment, Engländer. What are you doing here? This is a club for members only.'

'Oh really? A taxi driver told me I would be able to meet people like myself here. I'm from Combat 18 in England.'

The doorman recognized the name immediately and moved aside to let Sean pass. As he moved slowly down the corridor, he was hit by a wall of sound. It was a mixture of laughter and cheering, intermingled with a soundtrack of what he thought might be a newsreel of Hitler addressing a rally in pre-war Munich. As he pushed back the curtain to the bar, he was confronted by a huge television screen showing scenes of Hitler ranting and gesticulating. He had guessed correctly.

Several drinkers were chanting 'Sieg Heil, Sieg Heil' and standing to attention, raising their arms in the traditional Nazi salute. As Sean entered everybody turned and stared, fully aware of a stranger in their midst. The noise died down slightly as Sean pushed his way to the bar. In one corner two guys had passed out, slumped across a table, drunk.

'Ein grosses Bier, Bitte,' he said to the barman, and waited as his drink was poured, all the time sensing the eyes that were upon him. He paid for his drink and leant against the bar feeling awkward. Someone pushed into him, spilling his drink.

'Pardon me, Engländer.'

'No worries,' said Sean, not wanting to get into a confrontation with anyone too quickly. He downed the remainder of his beer and ordered another. He had almost gagged at the taste of his first beer for many months. He didn't want to take the alcohol but he felt it was more realistic than a soft drink. What now? he thought. He was in a sleazy bar in the centre of Frankfurt that he wouldn't normally have gone into in a month of Sundays. What next? He decided his best move was to drink up and come back the next day when he had worked out something. He drained his glass and turned to leave. The bar was very smoky. It began to affect his eyes. By now the place was so full he had to push his way towards the door. As he reached it he was confronted by the doorman.

'My boss wants to see you, Engländer.' He indicated a door on his right. 'Fritz will take you.'

Fritz, an ugly looking fellow and bigger even than the doorman, was also dressed in black fatigues and T-shirt. A swastika was tattooed on his shaven skull and his arms were covered in numerous other designs, including a skull and crossbones and an Iron Cross set above 'München

'76'. Probably a reference to the Israeli athletes massacred at the Munich Olympics, thought Sean.

Fritz moved forward and gripped Sean's arm. Sean brushed it off. 'No need for that,' he threatened. 'Let go.'

Fritz released his grip and muttered something under his breath, at the same time opening the door and beckoning Sean to go first down a flight of narrow stone stairs. It was dimly lit and the paint on the walls was peeling. Sean led the way, sensing Fritz breathing down his neck. At the bottom of the stairs he turned right and entered a small, brightly lit room.

The walls were covered in posters and Nazi memorabilia. A swastika flag was draped on one wall. There was a group of four men talking in the corner. They turned as Sean entered. One of them walked across to meet him.

'Tag, my name is Rudy Schneider. These are my colleagues.' He didn't introduce them by name but they all gave Sean a Nazi salute.

'Sieg Heil!' they cried in unison.

Sean looked at Schneider. He estimated he was in his late fifties as he had very closely cropped receding greyish hair. His face was pock-marked and weatherbeaten from the sun. Sean sensed a coldness about him. He was missing the tops of his index finger and smallest finger on his left hand, and part of the lobe on his left ear was missing.

'Jörg the doorman tells me you are from Combat 18 in England. No one told us you were coming. What's your name?' he enquired with a menacing voice.

'Cameron – Sean Cameron. You should have been told I was coming. I recently joined Combat 18 and they wanted me to come over and learn about your methods of operation.'

'Who sent you?' Schneider asked, suspiciously.

'Peter Brown. He's the head of recruitment in London and he thought I needed to come and see you.'

Schneider frowned, 'It's unusual you were sent on your own. Normally, new recruits are accompanied by their trainer. Can you explain that?'

Sean had to think quickly. Schneider's line of questioning was very abrupt. Sean shivered slightly as Schneider made him feel very uncomfortable. He shifted from one foot to the other. 'Well, no one could be spared. There was a rally coming up in Birmingham and they wanted as many people to attend as possible. I think they also thought it would be a good test of my initiative.' He nervously hoped his cover story would hold.

'It's strange you weren't sent on the trip to Birmingham first, to learn the ropes.'

'What's this, an interrogation?' protested Sean. 'Don't you believe me or something? You can phone Peter Brown in London if you like.'

Dieter had told Sean that their mole in London was called Peter Brown. He hadn't wanted to play his hand so soon but he had been left with no alternative. Schneider had got very quickly to the point. He clearly didn't trust Sean.

'I have his number in my hotel room. I'll bring it back to you tomorrow if you like.'

'Don't worry, that won't be necessary. We know the number for HQ in London. I'll speak to my friend David Owens about you. If you are who you say you are, he'll know you,' said Schneider icily.

Sean had no idea who David Owens was. He had never heard of him. He wished that his briefing had not been so superficial. He knew he had to live on his wits, but he began to doubt the effectiveness of his cover story.

'Okay, when will my training start? I'm only here for three weeks. I've got to get back for a weekend exercise on Salisbury Plain at the end of the month,' Sean lied.

'Come back tomorrow, Cameron, and don't forget that number.' He was testing Sean.

'I thought you said you already had the number,' responded Sean quickly. 'Can I go now?'

'No problem, you are free to go, but be here tomorrow at 11.00 hours. We have much to talk about.'

As Sean turned he found Fritz standing behind him, arms folded. He smelt of stale tobacco and alcohol. He moved aside to let Sean pass. 'We'll meet again,' he said menacingly. It was clear he didn't like Sean, who for some reason had made an enemy.

'No doubt we will,' Sean smiled, with a hint of sarcasm in his voice.

As Sean stepped out into the street he felt a sense of relief. Beads of sweat had congregated in the small of his back and his palms were wet. He had never before experienced quite the same fear. He moved quickly back to his hotel, glancing furtively around him, expecting all the time to find he was being followed. He reached his hotel. The night porter was on duty.

'Room fifteen, please,' said Sean.

The porter handed Sean his key. 'Oh, wait a minute, sir. I have a message for you. Mr White phoned. Please call him, he says it's urgent. Here's his telephone number.'

He passed Sean a small piece of paper with a number on it. Mr White was James's code name.

'Thanks,' said Sean. 'I'll call him as soon as I get to my room. What do I dial for an outside line?'

'Just dial zero and then the number. It's a Frankfurt number so there's no code to worry about.'

When he reached his room Sean dialled James's number. He was still in the same hotel. Lucky sod, thought Sean, it's a bit more comfortable than this. The operator put Sean through to James's room.

'Cameron here. What's so urgent?'

'I spoke to Yolanda tonight. She says Njeri called and wants you to phone her urgently. He gave Sean her number and they chatted for a couple of minutes. James was careful not to ask Sean what he had been up to. He knew he would receive a report shortly. Besides which, unknown to Sean, James had followed Sean to the Bierhaus just to keep an eye on him.

As he put the phone down he looked at his watch. It was eleven o'clock. Not too late to call Njeri. He got an outside line and dialled. Njeri answered and explained to Sean that she has seen a doctor about an abortion. She told Sean that because she was now twenty-four weeks' pregnant there was no medical reason to abort the child. The doctor refused her assistance on the National Health. He suggested she should try a private clinic if she was serious about the termination.

The doctor had tried to persuade her to keep the child but she explained that the father was not around and that she already had two children. He said the final decision was hers.

'What about us?' Njeri pleaded. 'Please let us try again and then we can keep the baby.'

'No chance,' responded Sean harshly. 'How can I even be sure that the child is mine? Not only do I disapprove of what you are doing, but how can you just move in with another man so quickly? If you're earning so much money, surely you can afford a place of your own?'

'I have to save the money for my children and if you want me to have an abortion, then you had better send me £1,100 to pay for it. Otherwise I'll keep the child.'

Sean had already thought Njeri might threaten this and he was prepared. 'Don't worry, I'll send you the money,' he sighed.

'I need it by tomorrow afternoon, Sean, as I made a provisional appointment at the clinic for Thursday morning.'

'There's no way I can organize a bank transfer that quickly.'

'Then you had better find another way,' she threatened.

'Leave it to me. I'll contact Smithy and get him to deliver the cash to you. You'd better give me your address.'

'I can't tell you where I am staying because of my new boyfriend. I'll arrange to meet Smithy somewhere.'

'No. It'll be easier for you to go to Smithy's office. Be there for midday, I'll phone him in the morning to arrange it.'

It was then that it dawned on him that it wasn't such a good idea to give Njeri cash. She could pocket the money and not have an abortion . . . and keep coming back to him in the future for more money.

'Wait a minute, I've a better idea,' he said. 'Tell me the name of the clinic and I'll pay them direct. Give me their telephone number and I'll call them in the morning.'

'What? Don't you trust me with the cash, Sean?'

'Frankly, no,' he replied.

Njeri protested but Sean was adamant. That was the way it was going to be.

'Okay, Sean, if that's the way you want it I'll go to the clinic as planned, but you'd better arrange payment or else.' She gave Sean the number and hung up.

Sean slept badly that night. He tossed and turned, worrying about the abortion. But he was even more concerned about going back into the lion's den at the Bierhaus. He catnapped throughout the night and eventually woke at eight o'clock in the morning. He had plenty to do. First, he had to phone the clinic. It was a better solution for him to deal direct with them. He didn't really want to get Smithy involved. He spoke to a Mrs Robertson in the administration department. He explained who he was, giving her all his bank details and so on. She accepted his word that he would pay and said that when Njeri turned up she would ensure everything was done correctly. She told Sean that the bill would be £1,100 and no more, unless there were unforeseen complications. At least Njeri hadn't lied about the cost, thought Sean. He hung up.

He sat in his room for a while. The names and photographs of the four men he had memorized were flashing through his mind. He could still picture them quite clearly. He kept repeating the names to himself: Manfred Roth, Ulli Müller, Herbert Bauer and Wolfgang Schmidt.

He had arranged a rendezvous with Dieter at 10 a.m. at another bar and didn't want to be late. Dieter never normally used the same meeting place twice. Sean needed to report on the previous evening's contact with Schneider and his cronies, about which he had some fears.

He arrived on time. Dieter was already there sitting in a corner. They greeted each other and Sean explained what had happened. He felt his cover story was weak because he didn't know the Combat 18 people and that Schneider had threatened to contact David Owens about him, which could, of course, blow his cover. Schneider also thought it was odd that Sean had been sent out on his own. Nevertheless, he had been ordered to return later today for a further meeting, which he hoped would lead to his request being granted for an introduction into their methodology.

Dieter said that the whole operation might take a few weeks and not to be impatient. It was important for Sean to obtain as much information, and as many names, as possible.

'It is likely that this is the last time we will meet openly, Sean. From now on, you will call me from a public phone each day at 10 a.m. and give me an update. We can't risk you being followed and seen to be connected with me. From now on, you're very much on your own unless I contact you to change this instruction.'

'Fair enough,' sighed Sean. His mind was still on the problem of Njeri's abortion. 'I'll report in tomorrow.'

They shook hands and Sean left. He was already dressed in his 'uniform'. He headed for the Bierhaus.

CHAPTER 31

Jörg was still on the door. This time he moved aside promptly and greeted Sean. 'Hello again, Engländer.'

'Morgen,' said Sean, as he descended the stairs.

'Schneider's not here yet, but he said if you arrived before him you had to wait in the cellar. I think you know the way.'

The cellar was empty. Sean recognized the German music playing in the background as a piece from Wagner's 'Die Walküre'. Sean studied the memorabilia on the walls. As he walked around the cellar he came across alphabetical lists of names on one of the walls. He figured they were names of Nazi soldiers who had died in the last war. Just typical German names on a roll of honour. Even though Sean didn't go along with their affiliations, he guessed there were some brave men among them.

While he was still looking, a group of troopers walked in and eyed him suspiciously. They didn't talk but promptly stood to attention when Schneider arrived.

'Morgen!' they chanted in unison, giving the Nazi salute.

'Ah, Cameron, Jörg told me you had arrived. Wait there a moment. I've got some business to attend to first.'

Schneider disappeared through a steel door at the back of the cellar.

Sean sat down with his back to the wall. He wanted to survey what was going on. He studied the faces of all the men in the cellar and those of other men arriving. The cellar was beginning to fill up and there was a babble of noise. Sean didn't understand much of what was being said, but there were obviously some amusing stories being told. After about twenty minutes Schneider returned. He beckoned to Sean to come over and led him through the steel door into a small office. Again the walls were decorated with Nazi memorabilia. There was a photograph of Hitler and one of Adolf Künzler, supposedly his son, who saw himself as the leader of the neo-Nazis.

Dieter had told Sean that there was a network of Nazis who were convinced that Hitler hadn't died in a Berlin bunker at the end of the Second World War. They were sure that he had escaped to South America with his mistress, Eva Braun, and that the bodies found in the bunker were doubles. In South America Eva apparently gave birth to a son, Adolph Künzler. Whether he was Hitler's son was open to debate. It was suspected in many quarters that he was just a self-styled dictator who had come to believe in his own publicity. Like Hitler, he was a megalomaniac and apparently anyone who crossed him or left the organization did so on pain of death.

Schneider returned. 'Well, Cameron, it appears that David Owens in London is away at the moment on exercise. He's not due back until next Tuesday so I can't check out your credentials until then.' He stared intently at Sean with his cold blue eyes. 'Looks like I'll have to take a chance that you are who you say you are. There's an exercise in the Black Forest this weekend. I want you to attend. Report back here on Friday afternoon at 16.00 hours.'

'OK,' said Sean. 'Is there anything I need to bring with me?'

'Just a change of clothes. You'll be issued with combat kit. Be here at 16.00.'

Schneider dismissed Sean; he didn't want him snooping around. He didn't trust him fully, but he was a patient man. He could wait until the following Tuesday when he would speak to David Owens.

CHAPTER 32

Sean had some time to kill that afternoon. He had gone back to his hotel to change. He felt conspicuous in his uniform and wanted to visit the hospital where Akinyi died. It wouldn't have been appropriate for him to turn up looking like an ageing skinhead. By coincidence he was back in Frankfurt for the first time since her death. He took a bus to the hospital and asked at reception if Dr Matthias was on duty. The receptionist directed Sean up to the third floor where Dr Matthias was working. Sean then asked the senior nurse where he could find Matthias. She said she'd check to see if he had finished his rounds. Just as she lifted the receiver, Matthias appeared through the swing doors. He hesitated briefly when he saw Sean, who recognized him immediately. Sean walked forward and offered his hand. Matthias looked surprised to see him.

'Mr Cameron, isn't it? I remember you well. You're the rugby player whose girlfriend died here about two years ago. I didn't expect to see you again.'

'I'm here on business and I thought I would drop in to see you. I never really had the chance to thank you for your efforts in trying to save my girlfriend's life. It was all so sudden and tragic, I haven't got over it yet.'

'Well, we tried our best. I'm just sad that we could do no more for her. I'm expected in theatre now so I can't stop, Mr Cameron, but thanks for coming to see me.'

He turned and walked down the corridor through the double doors. Sean thought it strange; he could see a sign for the theatre indicating that it was in the opposite direction. Still, perhaps he had to call in somewhere first or maybe he was going to the theatre via a special route. He dismissed the thought from his mind.

As Sean made ready to leave the ward, he saw a nurse he recognized. He smiled and raised his hand in acknowledgement. She smiled nervously back at him. He carried on walking. As he reached the lift he felt a tap on his shoulder and looked round. It was the same nurse. 'Hello!' said Sean. 'I'm sorry but I don't remember your name. What can I do for you?'

'Mr Cameron, I can't stop now because I don't want anyone to see us, but I must speak to you in private. I get off at six. Meet me after work.' She thrust a small piece of paper into his hand. 'The address of a café is on that; it's a safe place for us to meet. I'll see you later.' She was gone as quickly as she came.

Sean was bemused. He studied the piece of paper as the lift

descended. He wondered what on earth the nurse wanted to speak to him about. He was most intrigued. He looked at his watch; he had two hours to kill.

He didn't know where the café was, but he soon found the address on the street map. It was not far from the city centre. It was a warm, sunny afternoon and the walk would give him time to think.

He arrived at the café and ordered a coffee. Shortly afterwards the nurse arrived. She was a stout woman, about 5 feet 8 inches tall with thick, grey hair tied back in a bun. It made her look matronly. She was dressed in tweeds and brown brogue shoes.

Sean rose from his seat to greet her. 'I don't recall your name,' he said. 'However, I remember you from a couple of years ago.'

'My name is Stella Weitz. For the last two years I've hoped to see you again because I have some important information for you. I didn't know where to contact you and I was scared to get anyone else involved.'

'Go on,' said Sean, 'I'm listening.'

Stella Weitz proceeded to tell Sean her story. She had worked in the hospital for the last ten years. For much of that time it was for Dr Matthias on the maternity ward. She told Sean that there had been several unexplained deaths of supposed stillborn children. Matthias had arranged for Dr Peterson, the pathologist, to sign the death certificates. On other occasions, mothers had supposedly had abortions as late as eight months into their pregnancies. All the bodies of the babies had mysteriously disappeared. Stella had been troubled by these strange events and had decided to investigate for herself. Her investigations had come to nothing until Akinyi had arrived at the hospital. She knew from Akinyi's records that she was in her seventh month of pregnancy and although she might have given birth to the child prematurely at that stage, with the correct neo-natal care there was a good chance the child might have survived. From her years of experience, Stella figured that Akinyi was likely to die from her injuries. They were extreme and the stress of fighting for her life in such trauma was too much to expect, together with the additional complication of pregnancy. If she hadn't been pregnant she would possibly have survived. However, she thought that if Akinyi had given birth or was induced, the baby would most likely be born safely. That is exactly what Matthias had decided to do. The baby was induced and was definitely alive and well at the moment of birth.

'Just hold on a minute.' Sean raised his voice. 'You mean to tell me that my fiancée actually gave birth to our daughter and no one told me? I don't believe you. When could that have possibly happened? I was with her most of the time before she died.'

Stella interrupted. 'Well, when you thought your girlfriend had died, she actually hadn't.'

'What do you mean? I saw the cardiograph monitor or whatever you call it? It registered no sign of life.'

'When you were out of the room, Matthias tampered with it so that it gave a false reading.'

'How do you know he tampered with it?'

'Well, other than you and your friend, he was the only person who had access to the room for any length of time. He must have tampered with the machine and shortly afterwards it was taken away for repair on his orders. It was all too coincidental.'

Sean frowned, 'Go on.'

'When you thought your girlfriend had died, and you both left the room, Matthias got to work with Nurse Beatrix. They knew they only had about an hour to play with before she would actually die.'

'I can't believe you are telling me this. It's just a pack of lies! Do you realize the implications of what you are saying? Do you realize that, if this is true, Matthias and Beatrix could possibly be on a murder charge?' Sean almost shouted.

'Shhhsh,' whispered Stella. 'People are watching us and some of them may well understand English. Be careful.'

The café had begun to fill up while the two had been talking. Sean could see several people staring.

'Let me continue, please.' Stella implored. 'I realize you are upset and it's difficult to believe, but that is exactly what I am saying.'

Sean sighed deeply and looked into her eyes. He could see she was distressed. Perhaps she was telling the truth after all, he thought.

'Go on,' he commanded, lowering his voice and trying to control his emotions.

'After Matthias and Beatrix had succesfully induced the baby, another nurse immediately took her away to an incubator in the intensive care unit. It was a baby girl. The strange thing is that Beatrix made a point of coming back to tell me she had died almost immediately of respiratory difficulties. It was only later, when I was going off duty, that I saw Nurse Beatrix carrying away a small bundle. I suppose there is a possibility that it could have been a child. I saw her go down the fire exit to the car park at the back. I followed her downstairs and watched her from a window. Dr Matthias was waiting in his BMW. She climbed in and they drove off.'

Sean thought for a minute. 'Do you know much about this Nurse Beatrix?' he asked.

Stella didn't know Beatrix very well. She had appeared to be close to Dr Matthias. On further investigation, it turned out she had been having an affair with him for years. He was a married man with two children, but wouldn't leave his wife for Beatrix. In spite of this, Beatrix was very much in love with him and totally under his spell. On delving deeper, Stella had found out that Matthias and Peterson were running a small private clinic in a suburb of Frankfurt. She had never been there herself but had heard they specialized in gynaecological problems and abortions. Apparently, although on the surface they appeared to be running a perfectly legitimate business, the rumours were rife that it was a cover for an illegal child adoption ring.

'You mean you think our child was very much alive, and that she was taken there by Beatrix and Matthias and nursed until she was strong enough to be adopted?'

'Exactly that,' responded Stella.

'Can you be absolutely certain of this?' he asked, as he realized the implications.

'Well, I can't be totally sure, but I think that if you start a detailed investigation you might find a few answers.'

'Can you give me the address of this place? I've got a friend who can find out more for me. If I go snooping around, Matthias might get suspicious and cover his tracks, and I'll never find out if I actually have a daughter alive.'

Stella passed Sean a piece of paper. 'Here is the address and telephone number of the clinic, together with details of the directors' names and addresses which I thought might be helpful.'

'I really can't thank you enough. You've been very kind and helpful, but why are you doing this for me? You don't owe me anything.'

'Please, Mr Cameron. Please don't insult me. I am a human being. I saw your distress when your fiancée died and I've seen others suffer in a similar way. I always wanted to be a doctor myself but wasn't educated enough, so I had to settle for nursing as the next best thing. I'm disgusted with doctors like Matthias and Petersen who abuse their positions of trust in order to further their own gain. It is completely unethical.'

'I'm sorry. I really am. I didn't mean to insult you. I am truly grateful, but before I go please answer a question.'

'What is it?' she enquired.

'Are you prepared to give evidence to the police and to the court, if neccessary?'

'There's no question; of course I will.'

'The other thing is, I do remember Matthias telling me that Akinyi was carrying a little girl. I now realize that I should have questioned him about it. I should have asked to see the baby. But that's hindsight for you!'

'Mr Cameron, there's no need to be harsh on yourself,' said Stella sympathetically. 'He would probably have come up with some excuse, anyway.' She hung her head for a moment. 'I must go now, Mr Cameron. I wish you luck.'

Sean sat alone, totally bewildered, his mind in turmoil. He wondered if his life would ever be 'normal' again. From the time he had first met Akinyi, things had been happening to him over which he seemed to have no control. He was tired of this complicated, unhappy life. It was impossible to settle and he felt his life was in limbo. He wanted to achieve his goal of finding Akinyi's killers and then move from England for good. He had toyed with the idea of returning to Kenya but he still wasn't entirely sure that that country would be his final destination. He paid his bill and left the café. He needed a good night's sleep in preparation for the weekend ahead.

CHAPTER 33

At ten o'clock the next morning Sean telephoned Dieter Beck from a call box near his hotel. He had a lot to report – not least the latest development regarding Stella's information. He hoped Dieter would be able to help him with an investigation into Matthias's activities, although it was unlikely there was a connection with the neo-Nazis. Nevertheless, he explained the situation. First, he told Dieter of the planned weekend in the Black Forest. Dieter expressed his reservations about Sean participating. He had heard about some of these Nazi exercise weekends, at which it was thought fascist sympathizers were offered the opportunity of attending a 'course' in a remote part of the Black Forest. The quarry was usually black immigrants who were rounded up from cities like Munich and Stuttgart. They were abducted and used as bait to be hunted down and killed to satisfy the blood lust of white supremacists. Their bodies were easily disposed of.

As they usually had no relatives to report them missing, the authorities wouldn't even notice that they had disappeared. There were rumours that such weekends were happening in Germany, but until now Dieter and his department had no concrete evidence for this. Although it was risky to send Sean in, as he had been only partially trained in undercover work, Dieter had no choice but to take a chance on a long shot. If he could get to the source and centre of the organization, it would blow the lid on Nazi activities throughout Germany. This would drive the Nazis further underground but it would also make it harder for the perpetrators of racist hate and violence to spread their doctrines among Germany's youth. A team of Dieter's best agents would be assigned to follow Sean to the weekend camp. The whereabouts and exact location was still unkown. Dieter couldn't take a chance on equipping Sean with a tracking device in case he was searched. He had to rely on the experience of the surveillance team to determine the actual location of the camp. It was arranged that Sean would contact Dieter again on Monday morning at ten o'clock. However, if Sean felt his life was threatened during the weekend, he could abort his mission and somehow escape from the camp and the surrounding area. He was very much being left to his own devices.

In response to Sean's report on Dr Matthias, Dieter said that because he could not risk having James in the surveillance team, he would use him to investigate the clinic run by Matthias and Petersen.

'Finally,' said Dieter, 'we know that David Owens is away on exercise this weekend somewhere in England. Intelligence reports say he will be back on Tuesday but, as a safeguard, we have arranged for Special Branch to pick him up for questioning when he returns. It's a weak case and we will only manage to hold him for forty-eight hours. After that, you will have only until Thursday night before Rudy Schneider is able to contact him. So you have to find out as much as possible before your cover is blown.

Friday arrived and Sean went to Jörg's bar at 16.00 hours as agreed. He was dressed in his uniform and carried only a change of clothing, as advised by Schneider, who had told him that he would supply everything else. In the event of problems, Sean had strapped a short hunting knife to his right ankle. If he was searched and it was found, he figured it wouldn't matter. He would explain it away as something he always carried in England for protection. As he descended the stairs to the cellar, he could hear the now familiar music. The cellar was full, mostly with menacing looking youths, all wearing the same uniforms. They were seated in rows of chairs, cinema style. Sean looked around. Oh shit, he thought, there was only one seat left – next to ugly Fritz. The latter eyed Sean suspiciously and slapped a heavy arm around his neck.

'Na, my Engländer friend, you are my partner this weekend. I will take good care of you,' he said in clipped English and roared with laughter.

Sean could feel the strength of the man and hoped he would not have to fight him. He could feel the bruises already.

'Silence,' Schneider shouted above the din. 'This is not a holiday, we are here to work. Now listen carefully ... ' He proceeded to debrief them.

They would be picked up in one hour's time by coaches. There were almost one hundred men going on the exercise and they would be travelling under the guise of football supporters attending an end-of-season tournament near Munich.

Although they were all in 'uniform' they wouldn't be out of place as many German soccer teams attracted gangs of skinheads as their supporters. It was a Bundesliga tri-team tournament including Bayern Munich, VFB Stuttgart and Kaiserslautern. Fritz and his cronies would supposedly be supporting Bayern Munich. As was the norm on this type of exercise, the leaders travelled in separate cars so as not to be caught in association with any known far-Rightists. They travelled as respectable businessmen, some individually and some in pairs, careful not to take the same route. Some would go by way of the autobahn and some would take the slower roads, getting on or off the autobahns at strategic points to synchronize as far as possible the time the journey took for everyone. Meanwhile, the coaches would travel on the autobahns with football scarves in customary fashion trailing out of the windows.

'You will be fully briefed on arrival at our rendezvous, but in the meantime I would like to introduce you to one of our 'brothers' from Combat 18 in England. This is Herr Sean Cameron from England,' he said, pointing at Sean. And then he barked: 'Stand to attention when I address you.'

Momentarily shocked, and not expecting this introduction from Schneider, Sean rose slowly to attention and gave the Nazi salute. 'Sieg Heil,' he said weakly.

'Sieg Heil, Sieg Heil,' the other men chorused in unison as they jumped to attention, stamping their feet on the cold stone floor.

Schneider returned the salute and raised both arms in the air, dropping them to his sides slowly. As he did so everyone sat down.

'This is Herr Cameron's first trip to Germany so we must give him a warm welcome. To ensure that he learns well, I want all of you to watch his progress very carefully.'

Oh no, thought Sean. He wondered how he would be able to find out any information of interest and value to Dieter and his department. He still wasn't sure what he was meant to do.

'Ja, Ja, Herr Schneider,' they chorused and burst into laughter, all directed towards Sean.

A siren sounded suddenly and the men immediately stood to attention. They then turned and marched from the cellar in single file. It was their call to start the weekend. As they trooped out, Sean fell into line behind Fritz. Although Sean was six feet tall he could barely see over his shoulders. He had a thick, muscular neck, must have weighed twenty stone and stood at least six feet seven tall.

Within five minutes they were seated in the coaches, ready for the three-hour journey to Munich. Sean didn't know the exact details of their destination because the rendezvous point was known only to the drivers and the officers. This was a security discipline to minimize the risk of someone letting something slip in idle conversation.

As the two coaches moved away through the evening traffic, Sean leant back in his seat and shut his eyes. He hoped to conserve his energy. Try as he might he couldn't sleep. His thoughts drifted back to Kenya, to the time he had spent with Akinyi and the year he had spent there after her death. In the blink of an eye his life had changed from extreme happiness to the depths of despair. He had resigned himself to pursuing his current mission, but now his life had been thrown into greater turmoil by discovering he might have a daughter. If Stella Weitz was correct, how could he trace her? It was nearly two years since Akinyi's death. He tried to imagine what his daughter would look like. Would he be united with her by her next birthday? His private thoughts were suddenly interrupted by a chorus of song from the rear of the coach. Sean was one of the last to get on so he had been unable to study the faces of his weekend comrades as they boarded. So far he hadn't seen anyone he recognized from Dieter's photographs, but it was early days yet. The singing continued and now everyone was joining in. Sean couldn't understand the words but he sensed a certain menace about them.

Fritz nudged him in the ribs, 'Come on Engländer – Sing!' he commanded.

'How can I sing when I don't know the words, you fat bastard!' retorted Sean angrily.

The insult was wasted on Fritz.

'Well, sing us some Combat 18 songs then,' he taunted Sean.

'I don't know any of those, either. I told Schneider that I've only just joined.'

'Schneider doesn't believe you. He thinks you have another motive for being here. Anyway, we'll soon find out when he contacts David Owens on Tuesday.'

'Why are you telling me this?' queried Sean.

'Because you are my partner and partners should stick together,' and saying that, he roared with laughter again.

Sean looked at his watch. They had been travelling for over two hours. They would soon be at their destination. It was still light, a pleasant summer evening. He studied the countryside. They drove very fast and he occasionally saw signposts for Munich as they went past various inter-sections. So far, he had seen nothing unusual. He wondered whether James was managing to check out Matthias's clinic. He looked forward to a full report.

The coach started to slow. Sean peered out of the window. They were leaving the autobahn. Looking around, he could see no sign of urban life or buildings. It wasn't a proper exit; rather, it was one of those picnic areas set out at regular intervals along the autobahn. There were no service facilities, just a clearing with a few benches and seats.

Fritz stood up and moved to the front of the coach. He picked up a microphone and started to speak slowly in German. Sean understood little of what was being said, but everyone stood up and began to alight from the coach.

'What's going on?'

'Just a short trip,' grinned Fritz. 'You'll find out soon enough.'

As they stepped off the coach, Sean noticed the second coach pulling up beside them. As the fifty or so men got off he tried to study their faces. Most were unrecognizable as they had covered their faces with black balaclavas or scarves. He wondered why the remainder had not done so. Maybe some of them had a special reason for not wanting to be recognized. But the bottom line was that he had still not identified anyone.

They stood around in small groups chatting and laughing, some smoking cigarettes. They were a motley crowd. Sean didn't fancy meeting any of them on a dark night. All had crew cuts and a multitude of scars and tattoos, the likes of which he had never seen before. The tattoo parlours must have made a small fortune out of this lot, he thought.

Sean stood on his own with his back against a tree, trying not to look conspicuous. Although he had a crew cut he stood out like a sore thumb. There were men of Sean's age and a couple older, but most were between eighteen and twenty-eight. Sean wondered if any of them had jobs or whether they just lived on state hand-outs. He was sure most survived on petty thieving, car stealing and the like, and had probably served time in prison.

After about ten minutes, Fritz and the leader from the other coach raised their arms aloft and barked a command.

Sean moved towards the second coach and began to climb on board. As he did so he felt a firm hand on his shoulder pulling him back. 'Just a moment, Engländer, it's the wrong coach,' said a voice. It was Fritz.

'Oh, my mistake,' said Sean, innocently. Fritz was certainly watching him like a hawk. If he had to escape for any reason, he knew he would have to deal with Fritz first. This was a tall order. They had soon piled back on to the coaches. As they moved away, Sean noticed that they were not returning to the autobahn. Some two hundred yards away there was dense forest on all sides. One of the 'stormtroopers' had been ordered to open a five-bar gate at the entrance to a narrow single track leading to the forest. They drove slowly through and he carefully shut the gate behind them, before running to catch up with the second coach. Darkness had begun to fall. It was now over three hours since they had left Frankfurt. It was quiet on the coach. All that could be heard was the distinctive whooshing sound a vehicle makes as it moves between gaps in trees or barriers. They seemed to travel for miles as the coaches turned left or right at clearings in the forest. The driver didn't appear to have a map; it was obvious he knew the route well. After about half an hour the coaches slowed. They seemed to have reached their destination. It was a large clearing in the forest, surrounded by orderly rows of neatly cut twenty-foot timbers stacked in piles.

A fortress situation had been created. As they disembarked from the coaches, several of the 'stormtroopers' dispersed to the four corners of the clearing and climbed to the top of the higher stacks of logs. Sean guessed they were acting as lookouts. The coaches had been parked at the back of the clearing, and the remaining area was about the size of a typical army parade ground. If Sean had wanted to escape it would have been almost impossible without being seen.

Within a few minutes a lorry turned up and parked next to the coaches. The driver got out and went to the back and unhooked the tarpaulin. Two masked men jumped down holding sub-machine guns, which looked like the Austrian Steyr type that Sean had practised with James at Hereford. Fritz then barked a command pointing to the truck. At that, six 'troopers' from Sean's coach ran to the lorry and began off-loading into two separate piles. The first pile was obviously food provisions for the weekend, but the second looked remarkably like the steel canisters that Sean had seen during his training. They normally carried guns, mortars and grenades. The action was about to begin. Sean suddenly realized the crucial importance of his training in Hereford. He drew in a deep breath and wondered what would happen next.

Within half an hour the men had been split into groups of four. Sean had been assigned to Fritz and two others. The first introduced himself as Jochen and the second, Peter. Both were about Sean's build and, surprisingly, about the same age. Clearly Fritz was taking no chances and had selected two of the more experienced 'troopers' to keep an eye on Sean. They all sat and waited patiently.

CHAPTER 34

By now it was completely dark. The camp, however, was lit, partially by a number of small hurricane lamps, and with the main light source coming from a small generator which hummed away in the background. Its main use was to illuminate some powerful floodlights surrounding the food and weapons area. Sean was sitting quietly on the ground when he noticed some headlights in the distance, flashing through the undergrowth. What looked like a convoy of cars was moving quickly along the forest track. It wasn't long before he was able to tell that there were four cars, and now he could hear the whine of the engines as they got closer. The guards at the front of the compound moved aside to let the cars enter. They slid to a halt on the loose gravel.

The first car was a large Mercedes and carried a driver, Rudy Schneider, and two others whom Sean hadn't seen before. The second was also a Mercedes, out of which four men climbed, all masked, wearing Nazi officer uniforms, and each with an Iron Cross around his neck. The third car was a white Volkswagen Passat estate containing five masked men. The fourth was a black Golf GTI, from which two men got out. Sean recognized them as being two of Schneider's bodyguards whom he had seen at Jörg's bar. Schneider had his aides in what appeared to be a definitive order of seniority. One of the masked men from the second car walked up and stood alongside Schneider. On the shoulders of his uniform was silver braid. He was clearly one of the senior officers, but he remained masked. Sean watched him carefully, scrutinizing his movements. There seemed to be something very familiar about him, but Sean wasn't sure what it was.

By now all the men had fallen into ranks of ten. Sean positioned himself in the back row alongside Fritz, Jochen and Peter. Schneider began to talk slowly and clearly in German. He was giving the men their instructions for the weekend and Fritz whispered a rough translation to Sean in broken English.

They would shortly go on a night exercise and wouldn't return until 03.00 hours when they could get two hours sleep before dawn. Then there would be a series of exercises starting with square bashing, weapons training and, later, a ball game that Fritz would explain nearer the time. As the men were ordered into their groups of four, they were issued with a map showing grid references, a compass, a torch and a box of matches. They were also given a piece of paper with detailed instructions of what they had to do.

Each group of four left at intervals of five minutes. They were all on a target time to return to camp not later than 03.00 hours. The exercise was similar to the overnight runs that Sean had done with James over the Brecon Beacons, only this time the weather was much better. Sean, Jochen, Fritz and Peter studied their map with the grid references very carefully and headed off punctually at their allocated time. Sean had no trouble keeping up with the others. They were running at a steady pace and he easily managed to stay just ahead of the other three, although he wondered how he would have fared against some of the younger guys in the other groups. As they ran they kept mostly to the forest tracks, but if they caught up with any of the other groups they had to make a detour into the forest to avoid contact. Contact with the other groups was forbidden. Sean occasionally tried to go in a different direction to the grid reference, but each time he strayed Fritz grabbed him by the shoulder and ordered him back. It was a good try and, in spite of Sean's efforts to deviate, they only missed one target time. They soon caught up at the next two check points and finally arrived back in camp at 02.45 hours, fifteen minutes ahead of schedule.

They had acquitted themselves well and Fritz was particularly pleased with Sean's performance, not realizing he had deliberately tried to sabotage the exercise.

'You're a fit man, Engländer, but your map reading leaves much to be desired. There's still the weapons training and the game of tag to come. Then we'll see what you are really made of,' he said, roaring with laughter as he slapped Sean hard on the back.

By now Sean was very tired. His feet ached and he took care when he removed his Doc Martens boots. He had no witch hazel to rub on his feet so he doused them with water. The knife he had strapped to his ankle was still in place. When he finished he put his socks and boots back on, curled up on the forest floor and quickly fell asleep. Even though the ground was hard he slept well, but the two hours were not enough. Age was beginning to take its toll!

CHAPTER 35

Sean awoke to the feeling of cold water being splashed on his face. The shock made him jump. As he looked up he saw Fritz standing over him with a bucket.

'Hey, Engländer, time for some work,' and he roared with laughter as he walked away.

Sean sat up, resting back on his elbows as he surveyed the camp. Shafts of bright light were breaking through the surrounding trees. The sun was already up and the men were stirring. There was a murmur of voices as they went about their early morning ablutions.

On the far side of the camp several camouflaged tents had been erected. Nobody had appeared from them. Sean assumed that these were for the comfort of Schneider and the officers. Perhaps they weren't due to get up until later.

The cook had brewed up some coffee on a stove and was handing out mugs of hot, black liquid. Sean fell into line with the others and accepted a mug as it was offered to him. He didn't normally like coffee other than instant, so he sipped cautiously. It was very strong and bitter. In fact, it tasted horrible, but he needed something hot inside him. He picked up some brown German bread and dunked it in his coffee. If this was breakfast, he thought, what would lunch be like? The men began congregating in small groups. Sean sat alone watching the others, hoping he would recognize some familiar faces. So far there had been no sign of Roth, Müller, Bauer or Schmidt. He looked at his watch. It was 06.40 hours; still no movement from the tents. At 07.00 hours exactly, Fritz barked an order and the men jumped quickly to attention. Sean fell in line and Jochen and Peter suddenly appeared either side of him. They were obviously under instructions to watch him very carefully.

It was time for weapons training. Each line of ten men were grouped together. The first one in each line was issued with what looked like a Chinese AK47 automatic rifle. Sean had done well with this weapon on the range at Hereford. It was soon his turn to fire. He grabbed the rifle from Peter and lifted the stock to his shoulder. Taking careful aim he fired at the target one hundred metres away. All the bullets hit the target, although they were scattered mostly to the outer rings. Not as good as at Hereford, thought Sean. He was annoyed with himself, but he put it down to being a bit over anxious. He finished the thirty-round magazine and passed the rifle to Jochen, who was next.

Jochen's shooting was very good, all the shots hitting the target in a small group just to the right of the bull. Very soon everyone had completed the first round. The targets were moved outside the compound two hundred metres away. Each man ahead of Sean acquitted himself well. This time Sean's shooting was even more wayward, but he did at least manage to hit the target. It turned out he finished eighth in his group and eighty-second overall out of the hundred men shooting. All who were ahead of him were pretty crack shots. They were obviously well trained and took the task at hand very seriously.

During the course of the morning a number of weapons were used, including pistols. Sean knew the Austrian Steyr but he didn't recognize any of the others. They were probably Eastern Bloc weapons, sold on the black market after the Berlin wall came down. All the weapons were fired and Sean did moderately well. Afterwards the men repacked them in the steel canisters. They then had a fifteen minute break. It was during this time that the officers appeared. Fritz reported on his own to Schneider. They spent some five minutes talking, all the time glancing across at Sean. He wondered what they were saying.

Square bashing followed the break. Sean knew now why he had never joined the army; he was already becoming bored with the monotony of such a routine. He hoped it wouldn't be an entirely wasted weekend.

Lunch followed. It consisted of bread, sauerkraut and bratwurst. Sean managed to eat the bread and the sauerkraut, but the bratwurst made him gag. As a kid he had never liked the taste of frankfurters and the wurst was much stronger. He managed one mouthful and pushed the rest to the side of his plate. As he finished the sauerkraut, Fritz appeared.

'Time for Tag,' he grinned and gave Sean a gentle tap with his boot. 'Tag' was a derivation of rugby, although there was no ball as such and there appeared to be no rules.

Here, the 'ball' was human, represented by one of the men from each group of four. The idea was that the other three had to stop the fourth man from reaching the other side of a line marked out on the forest floor. There were no holds barred. Fists and boots were swung at random, and full-blooded tackles were used to prevent the fourth man from reaching the line. As a member of the defending three, Sean made all the tackles he needed without having to swing a fist or a boot, but the others seemed to enjoy kicking and hitting their opponent. Sean had already picked up a few bruises before it was his turn to break the line.

Fritz, Jochen and Peter faced him aggressively. Sean wanted to limit the damage to himself by getting to the line as quickly as he could. He crouched low, eyeing the opposition carefully and suddenly sprang forward to the right. He had decided that Peter would be the easiest to avoid. He reckoned that he could use his rugby skills and speed to take him on the outside. What he hadn't allowed for was kicking and punching. He sidestepped Peter easily, but just as he thought he had got away from him a fist crashed into the side of his head. He stumbled forward and a split second later felt the full force of Fritz and Jochen crashing on top of him, boots and fists flying. He winced in pain as the fists pummelled his ribs. He tried to roll away to protect his head with his arms, but as he did so the boots followed, raining in thick and fast, finding their target easily. Somehow Sean managed to scramble clear of Fritz and, as he was getting up, he swung a right hook straight at Jochen, smashing his fist into his nose as hard as he could. Jochen screamed in pain and arched backwards, crumpling to the ground clutching his face. Just as Sean was feeling very proud of himself, Peter jumped on him from behind and swung him round, to be met by a head butt from Fritz that floored him. As he collapsed on his knees he began to drift into unconsciousness. He tried shaking his head from side to side as James had trained him to do, but the pain was too great. An overwhelming wave of nausea engulfed him and he fell backwards to the ground.

As he came to, Sean tried to remember what had happened. He gingerly touched the bridge of his nose and winced; he could feel a ridge of broken skin and a trickle of blood running down his cheek. As he sat up, the pain from his bruised ribs was excruciating. The little finger of his right hand was broken and had quickly ballooned to twice its normal size; the rest of his hands were covered in welts and bruises. The attack had only lasted a couple of minutes; he couldn't remember the other three getting a similar beating like himself. He stood up and, as he did so, Fritz came marching towards him.

'What did I do to deserve that?' asked Sean.

'We were just seeing what you were made of. We always do that to new recruits. Jochen is none too pleased with you either,' he said, referring to his mate's broken nose.

'So what's next on the agenda and where has everybody gone?' said Sean, as he looked around the camp. There were just a couple of guards near the food and weapons area and half a dozen younger lads lying on the ground within the compound.

'What you see are other new recruits like yourself. The others have gone on a training run.'

'So we get to miss that, do we?' enquired Sean, hoping that that was it for the weekend.

'No way. When the six recruits have rested, you'll be going on a five-kilometre training run together. Only after that do we finish. The others will be back soon.'

As each new recruit recovered, Fritz ordered them to line up alongside Sean and himself in preparation for the run. Shortly after the others arrived back, Sean's group set out. It was a slow pace as all of them, with the exception of Fritz, were suffering from the damaging effects of 'Tag'. As they were running, Sean tried to assess his achievements to date. Thus far, nothing out of the ordinary had happened. He knew everyone was watching him like a hawk and they were careful not to pass on any useful information to him. Most of the recruits hadn't spoken to him. Fritz's English was half reasonable but Sean's German was hopeless. His opportunity to learn something valuable was very limited. His best chance was to see, rather than to hear, evidence of their criminal activities. And he still hadn't identified any of the men.

As he ran he began to drop back from the others. Soon a gap of about twenty metres had opened up. Fritz kept turning round and shouting encouragement to cajole Sean into catching up, but the more Fritz shouted the more he eased up. Soon there was some fifty metres between them. The forest track narrowed and every so often there was a break in the undergrowth. Just ahead of them Sean saw his chance. There was a slight clearing to the left with a bend shortly after it. As the main group turned the corner, Sean was out of sight of Fritz's prying eyes. He quickly upped his pace and darted off down the track to the left. He knew he had about ten seconds before Fritz realized that he was missing, then, if he was lucky, another ten seconds. A total of a twenty-second lead.

Sean had figured that if it looked like he was making a run for it, Schneider and his cronies would interrogate him when they eventually caught up with him. He raced down the narrow track and shot left again, doubling back in the direction he had come from. His heart was pounding as he raced through the undergrowth. He could hear Fritz shouting his name. 'Cameron, Cameron, where are you? It's no good running away, we will get you,' he called, laughing as he ran.

Sean glanced at his watch. Thirty seconds had elapsed. He ran on harder, zig-zagging as he went. As the track widened he saw more daylight ahead. He was coming to the edge of the forest. Ahead of him lay a big, open field and just beyond, on a slight ridge, was a tarmac road. He could hear the shouting behind him. Pounding feet were snapping the dry twigs on the forest floor. He was now almost sprinting. The grass in the field was quite long so he had to high step. He had almost reached the road when he heard the distinctive chatter of machine-gun fire. A hail of bullets kicked up a cloud of dust in a sweeping arc ten metres in front of him. He stopped and turned to face four black-clad masked gunmen.

'Halt now, Engländer,' they shouted.

Sean slowly raised his hands, but stood his ground as the men came towards him.

'Put the cuffs on him, Jurgen,' the lead man ordered.

Sean offered his wrists as Jurgen stepped forward and clamped the handcuffs shut.

'Right, let's go, Engländer.' he commanded. 'I'm sure Schneider wants a word with you.'

Jurgen gave Sean a push and they marched him back to camp where he was taken to Schneider's tent. The boss man was seated at a table, alongside the familiar-looking mystery man who was still masked.

'Search him first,' ordered Schneider.

Jurgen and his men stepped forward and began searching Sean. It was not long before they found the hunting knife strapped to his ankle.

Schneider beckoned Sean to sit down, saying, 'I think you have some explaining to do, Herr Cameron.'

CHAPTER 36

James arrived at Dr Matthias's clinic on the Sunday morning. It was a small, two-storey building, tucked away behind the Kölnstrasse in the eastern quarter of the city. As he reached the front door he pressed the intercom button and announced himself to the voice in reception.

'I am James Annan to see Dr Matthias. I telephoned yesterday and made an appointment.'

'Please enter when you hear the buzzer,' responded a woman's voice.

James pushed the door and entered. The room was air-conditioned, which was a relief after the humidity outside. It was a hot June day and James wished he was anywhere other than in the city centre. His thoughts drifted to Yolanda and his kids in Hereford. It would have been an ideal day for a picnic along the River Wye.

'Dr Matthias will be with you in ten minutes,' the receptionist said. 'In the meantime, please complete this application form with your personal details.'

James frowned and took the application form while reaching for a pen inside his pocket with the other hand. He had pre-planned his life history. He didn't include Yolanda's name, as he wished to avoid any risk of endangering her, so he entered Susan as his wife's name and used John's London address. John had already been briefed about what he was up to. He filled in all the details he could and passed the form back to the receptionist. She was a typically stout German woman, conservatively dressed, who wouldn't have been out of place in a consultant's surgery back in England.

'Herr Doctor will see you now.' She pointed to the door to the right.

'Thank you,' smiled James.

He knocked on the door and entered. Matthias was seated in a comfortable but well-worn leather chair behind his desk. He stood up when James came in and offered his hand.

'Welcome, Herr Annan, please take a seat.' He indicated the chair in front of his desk. 'What can we do for you and how did you hear about us?' he asked.

James had his story well rehearsed. He said that he and his wife were unable to have children of their own. They had tried unsuccessfully for years but had finally given up hope. Unfortunately, because of their ages, it was too late to go through the official adoption channels in the UK. Although James was thirty-nine, his wife at forty-six was considered too old to adopt. Second, and most important, James's wife was white and, as a mixed-race couple, it was even harder to adopt a mixed-race child. Their local council wouldn't let them have a black or a white child, and they had set their hearts on adopting a mixed-race child so they could bring him or her up as their own.

'I am being posted on attachment to the United States Air Force based at Ramstein. I'm in the British army and have come here for a week to sort out accommodation in readiness for a move in August. My wife and I will be at Ramstein for six months. I was in the Officers Mess last week and someone mentioned to me that you could arrange discreet adoptions for couples like us.'

'Yes we do,' replied Matthias cautiously. 'But to get a mixed-race child is very difficult. We did have one case nearly two years ago when we managed to place a newly born mixed-race child, coincidentally with an American couple based at Ramstein.'

'That's interesting,' said James. 'Are they still at Ramstein? If they are, perhaps I could talk to them to see if they could give me a few ideas of how we might be able to adopt more quickly.'

'I don't know. Once the adoption papers were signed I had no more contact with them.'

'What happened to the real parents?' enquired James.

Matthias hesitated for a minute. 'Oh, they were killed in a car crash,' he said unconvincingly. 'The pregnant woman was black and she went into premature labour as a result of the shock. Sadly, she died a short while after giving birth.'

'Well, do you think you can help us, Doctor?'

Matthias was pensive for a minute, slowly looking James over. 'I can't promise anything because of the colour problem, but give me a few days and I'll see if I can sort something out. In the meantime I will need a deposit from you. The whole process is expensive. The total cost will be about 80,000 Deutschmarks, and I require a 25 per cent deposit of 20,000 Deutschmarks. I must stress that the deposit is non-returnable as the initial costs of administration are very high. It must also be in cash. How soon can you get it?'

James was taken aback; he hadn't reckoned on this development. 'That's a tall order, I hadn't expected it to cost so much. I'm only on a captain's salary and my wife doesn't work. I doubt that I can lay my hands on that much immediately. Will you accept 6,000 Deutschmarks tomorrow? That much I can afford.

Matthias frowned and looked at James thoughtfully.

'Mr Annan, I am not a charity,' he pondered, 'but in the circumstances I will take the 6,000 tomorrow. However, I will need the remainder of the deposit in exactly two weeks. If by then you are unable to raise the money, I shall consider you not to be serious about your enquiry and I won't waste any more of my time. Agreed?'

'Agreed,' said James, thinking that within two weeks he would have all the information he needed to find Sean's daughter, although he didn't fancy losing six thousand marks to Matthias. Sean would have to cover that.

'So where do you normally get your children from?' James dared to ask.

Matthias bristled. 'You ask too many questions for your own good, Mr Annan. That's my business. Let's just say I have many contacts in the former Eastern Bloc states. There are many orphans and many very poor families that want to give their children a better life. For the right kind of money, anything is possible,' he ended.

James frowned. 'But aren't there laws in those countries governing the traffic of children? I seem to remember that an English couple were arrested in Hungary for trying to smuggle a child out of the country illegally. In any case, surely you are unlikely to get a mixed-race child from that source?' suggested James.

'Mr Annan, you are very naive. As I said, anything is possible for the right money. That couple you refer to must have been unlucky. The Eastern Bloc countries are not the only places I deal with. Don't you worry, I will find you a child with the right negroid qualifications,' he almost sneered. 'Anyway, I'm a very busy man.' He looked at his watch. 'My next appointment is waiting. You have already taken up too much of my time. Kindly deliver the money here tomorrow before noon and then I can start a search. Good day to you.'

James got up to go. 'I'll see you tomorrow then. Goodbye Dr Matthias.'

Matthias got up and escorted James to the door. As James was leaving he said, 'One last thing, Mr Annan. Remember our conversation is highly confidential. I do not expect you to discuss this with anyone, except, of course, your wife.'

'Yes, I understand,' said James, closing the door.

He was back in reception. The receptionist was still seated at her desk. She seemed intent on keying some data on to the computer that occupied the centre of her work space.

James smiled at her. 'Your boss is a strange man,' he said, as he was leaving.

'Really?' she replied, barely glancing up as she spoke.

'By the way, what's your name?' The smile was still on his face.

'Frau Riedle,' she retorted.

'That's very formal,' James gently provoked. 'What's your first name?'

'Mr Annan, here in Germany we are very formal, particularly in business when we don't know someone personally. But since you ask, it's Hanna,' she said rather haughtily.

'Okay, Hanna, see you tomorrow,' and at that he left, grinning widely.

As he descended the small flight of steps from the front door, James stopped and shut his eyes for a moment, drawing breath. He disliked Matthias's arrogance. He wondered what Sean would make of him. He also wondered how Sean was managing on his weekend expedition. He opened his eyes and headed back to the hotel.

CHAPTER 37

Sean sat down. His mind was racing. He had to be careful not to say the wrong thing and blow his cover.

'I've told you before, I've nothing to hide. I started carrying the knife for protection when I joined Combat 18 in England.'

'And that's the only reason?' countered Schneider.

'That's all there is to it.' Sean said no more. Silence was the best form of protection.

'So explain, if you can, why you ran away from your group. It seems a very strange thing to do.'

'I can't explain it. It was just a spur of the moment thing. I guess I got bored and wanted to run on my own for a while.'

'You expect me to believe that?' queried Schneider, searching Sean's face for signs of nervousness.

Sean remained deadpan.

'Well, Mr Cameron, our weekend is almost over. I will be contacting David Owens in London on Tuesday to check your true identity. Make the most of the time left to you, because if you don't get the proper security clearance you will be in serious trouble.' He smiled menacingly. 'We may even have to make you disappear.'

Sean swallowed hard, he knew this was no idle threat. 'I'm confident you will get the necessary clearance,' he said, praying that Owens would be picked up by Special Branch as planned before Schneider could speak to him. This would leave the way clear for Peter Brown to speak to Schneider and give Sean the all clear.

'Can I go now?' said Sean as he got up to leave.

'You can, but make sure you stay in the camp. We will be watching you even more carefully now,' said Schneider.

Nothing much else happened for the remainder of the day. At seven o'clock in the evening the lorries were loaded up with the weapons and the remaining food. A working party of about a dozen men swept the area with small branches to destroy as much evidence of their presence as possible. The men one by one, climbed aboard the coaches that then pulled slowly away from the compound on the long journey home. It seemed to take ages to travel through the forest, but eventually they reached the picnic area at the side of the Autobahn where they had entered on Friday night. They then travelled southbound to the next junction before turning back to Frankfurt.

The men were tired from their weekend activities and there was little conversation as most of them slept. Sean himself dozed off, waking only occasionally to check his watch and to look out of the window to see if he recognized any landmarks. Eventually the coach he was in reached the outskirts of Frankfurt, where the driver made several stops to let the men off in ones and twos. It wasn't long before the coach reached the city centre. Sean got off at the Bahnhof along with a couple of others, making sure he detached himself from them as quickly as possible. He hailed a taxi and was soon back in his hotel room.

Despite his exhaustion, the adrenalin he'd built up, together with the anticipation of his next progress meeting with James and Dieter, kept him awake for what seemed like hours. Finally his lids began to feel heavy, and in time he fell into a deep slumber.

CHAPTER 38

It was 10.30 in the morning and Sean was the first to arrive at the Junction Bar for their pre-arranged meeting to give a full report on his weekend away. James and Dieter arrived shortly after. They ordered coffee, but Sean asked for a full breakfast of ham and eggs. He had missed breakfast at the hotel and was feeling ravenous after his weekend exertions.

'What happened to you?' James said as he studied the cuts and bruises on Sean's face and hands. 'You look like you've gone ten rounds with Muhammed Ali. Seems I can't leave you alone for five minutes,' he chuckled.

Sean ignored the taunt. 'So tell me, how did things go with Matthias?'

James proceeded to tell them about his trip to the clinic. He explained that Sean's daughter – if it was indeed certain that his child had been born alive – might have been adopted by an American couple who, at the time, were stationed at Ramstein. Matthias didn't know whether they were still based there as he had had no further contact after the adoption papers were signed. James said that he intended to see the Commanding Officer at Ramstein to tell him Sean's story.

'It would be better if I go alone in the first instance, to try to extract as much information as possible about the American couple off the record,' he said.

'But why can't I come with you?' pleaded Sean.

'Because, as a civilian, it is almost certain that your enquiry will be treated formally, thus making any investigation official and involving a lot of red tape,' replied James. 'Believe me, I know how the armed forces work. I will appeal to the CO as a fellow officer. The thing is, Sean, the implications of this are very serious. If we can prove that the child is yours and Akinyi's, through DNA testing, you will still have to consider the American couple's legal position and, of course, their personal and emotional feelings.'

'But if I can prove she is my child, surely I have a right to take her back?' interrupted Sean.

It was Deiter who spoke next. 'I know I'm an outsider in all this, Sean, but you must also consider the child's feelings. She would be introduced to a complete stranger, claiming to be her father. How on earth could she be expected to understand that? By now she would have bonded with the two people whom she considers to be her parents. What will you do about that?'

Sean sipped slowly from his glass of orange juice. 'But I owe it to Akinyi, if not to myself, to claim her,' he exclaimed, feeling his heart race.

'As a father, Sean, I appeal to your better nature to forget this quest, once and for all,' said James. 'Why can't we just concentrate on tracking down Akinyi's killers and close that chapter of your life for good?'

'How could you expect me to do that?' responded Sean angrily. 'I thought you were my friend, James?'

'I am, but there is a possibilty that you could end up breaking two people's hearts and also traumatizing your own child.'

'Enough of this,' interjected Dieter. 'I don't mean to belittle what you must be feeling, Sean, but James is right. Your first priority must be to find Akinyi's killers, and then you can sort out the other things. Now, tell us what happened at the weekend.'

Sean knew they were right, but he also knew he couldn't stop, now that he had discovered he had a daughter. He proceeded to relate his experiences over the weekend in detail, highlighting his clash with Schneider. 'Not much of any great importance, but quite a few of the men – and in particular the officers – were masked, most of them for the entire weekend. Isn't that a bit strange?'

'Not really,' said Deiter. 'I suspect they didn't want you – or the others – to recognize them. After all, you have to remember they haven't checked you out yet.'

'I guess you're right. I certainly didn't recognize any of them from the photos you showed me the other day.'

James got up, went over to the bar and picked up a newspaper which he brought back and began to read.

'What the hell's the matter with you?' asked Sean. 'Aren't you interested in what I've got to tell you?'

James stayed behind his newspaper. 'Don't look now, but there is a guy to your right, sitting at the table in the corner on his own. Have you seen him before?'

Sean's instant reaction was to peer across at the man James was referring to, studying him carefully. He wasn't deliberately disobeying James's instruction, but it was a natural instinct. 'No. I've never seen him before in my life.'

'Okay, you can carry on now, it must be me. It's just that he looks familiar, but it might be my mind playing tricks. We can't be too careful; we can't afford for you to blow your cover just yet. Come on, tell us any other details that you think might be important.'

'Well, from my limited knowledge, I would say that they all appear to be very well-trained. They are highly disciplined, fit and strong, and about 90 per cent of them are experienced in the use of a variety of weapons. My shooting was very poor in comparison.'

'That's to be expected,' said James.

'What do you mean? I did all right at Hereford didn't I?' said Sean indignantly.

'Beginner's luck,' James teased.

'Will you two stop needling each other. We've more important things to consider than your childish rivalry,' scolded Dieter, irritated. 'You'll be pleased to know that Special Branch raided the headquarters of Combat 18 in Bromley last night and took David Owens in for questioning. He hasn't been charged yet, but your police are going for distribution of subversive and racially prejudiced literature.'

Sean interrupted. 'That doesn't sound very serious.'

'No it isn't, but your police will be able to hold him long enough to prevent Schneider from speaking to him tomorrow. He'll have to speak to Peter Brown instead.'

'By the way,' said Sean, 'I forgot to mention that there was one masked guy in officer's uniform who seemed very familiar.'

'Do you think it could be Meissner?' asked James.

'I don't know. I haven't met Meissner often enough to be certain. Don't you think that if it was Meissner he would have recognized me and perhaps even interrogated me?'

'Possibly, but he probably thought it was worth keeping a low profile to observe you in depth,' suggested James.

'I thought of grabbing his mask on one occasion, but that would have definitely blown my cover,' Sean said.

'It's a bloody good thing you didn't or you wouldn't be here now. I'll say again, never do anything stupid. Those guys don't play by the book. They will have no qualms about killing you and disposing of your body, very, very easily.'

'Surely they wouldn't risk that? They must realize that if I'm not genuine I would be operating with outside help – and if I disappeared then someone would come looking for me and start asking awkward questions.'

'Don't you believe it. The minute they kill you, that particular neo-Nazi cell will be broken up and dispersed to another part of Germany. It would be very difficult to trace anyone.' Dieter was deadly serious.

'Did you find out how often they run these camps?' James asked.

'I tried asking questions, but most people didn't know, or at least said they didn't know. I met a wall of silence,' replied Sean. 'Of course, my German isn't good enough to speak to many of them, but Schneider did say that if my credentials checked out there was to be an exercise of special significance next weekend. Do you think it might be one of those chases you told us about, Dieter, like the runs they do in the mountains of

Montana and the American Deep South?'

'Yes, very possibly. At our last meeting I mentioned similar runs in the Black Forest. We've heard rumours but, so far, have no conclusive proof.'

Sean began tapping his fingers on the table.

'So where do we go from here, Dieter?'

'Well, as soon as we know that Schneider has contacted Peter Brown – and he puts you in the clear – you can go to Jörg's Bar again and find out about next weekend's exercise.'

'In the meantime, why don't you lie low in your hotel room?' suggested James.

'Good idea,' said Dieter. 'You could do with a rest.'

'Yes, and I'm off to see the CO at Ramstein this afternoon,' said James. 'Mr White will call your hotel later and let you know the score.' As he got up to go, he shook Dieter's hand. 'See you the same time tomorrow then?'

'No, make it 16.00 hours, and you too, Sean.'

'Whatever you say, boss.' Sean's mind was in turmoil. He kept thinking of the child he had never seen. How would Louise react to a baby sister? he thought, perhaps prematurely. He got up and shook Dieter's hand.

The three men left the café separately, each going their own way.

CHAPTER 39

'There's a Captain Annan to see you, sir,' said General Sundberg's secretary on the phone to the CO of Ramstein, United States Air Force.

'Who is he and what does he want?' asked the General, rather offhand.

'He says it's of a very personal and confidential nature and that he will only take up five minutes of your time.' She paused. 'He looks a nice young man, sir.'

James grinned.

'You had better show him in, but five minutes is all I've got,' said Sundberg. He was a man who prided himself on giving anyone the time of day. He had come up through the ranks from a very humble background. His parents had raised him with good old-fashioned Christian values.

James was eyeing Sundberg's secretary. She was a very attractive woman, but not pretty in the conventional sense. Her uniform gave her a smart, handsome appearance and her dark hair was tied back neatly in a bun. He couldn't help looking her up and down, admiring her well-proportioned body.

'The General will see you now, Captain.' She saluted James.

'Thanks.' He returned her salute before marching into Sundberg's office. The General stood up and offered his outstretched hand to James who took it firmly in his grasp.

'I'll make an educated guess, Captain. I would say you are from Special Forces.' General Sundberg smiled.

'That's not for me to say,' replied James with a wry grin. 'You know the rules.'

He didn't want to tell the General he had left the Army two weeks previously – the General might be more helpful if he thought James was still a serving officer. In all probability he would have him checked out, but in the meantime James intended to disclose as much information to the General as possible.

'General, I need some information about an officer and his wife who might still be stationed here. I have a rather unusual story which you might find strange.' James went on to tell the General about Sean and Akinyi.

'That's an incredible story,' said the General. 'There was an officer here about 18 months ago who adopted a mixed-race child in Germany of all places. I guess we live in a more cosmopolitan society now.'

'Do you remember his name?' enquired James.

'I don't, but I can soon find out. I think he was posted to Mildenhall in Suffolk, England. Postings are normally for two years, so he's probably still there. Let me get my secretary, Sandra, to check. It shouldn't take long; everything is computerized these days.'

He lifted the receiver on his desk. 'Sandra, do me a favour. Get me a list of all the officers who have been transferred to Mildenhall in the last two years.'

They carried on with small talk while they waited for Sandra to come back with the information.

'So tell me about yourself, Captain. I bet there's an interesting story to your life.'

'There's not much to say, really. I joined up when I left school at 18 and have come up through the ranks.'

'That's quite an achievement,' the General paused. 'Particularly in view of your colour.' He paused again. 'I came up through the ranks myself. It was hard enough for me as a white man from a poor background, and I know it's even harder for a black man in the States. But at least we had affirmative action to give the blacks a chance. I've heard you have strong, positive discrimination against black men in the army in Britain with all your army traditions and prejudices, even though it may appear to be kept beneath the surface.'

'Yes, sir, it was hard for me. I came very close to giving up a few times, but I battled through, and I was fortunate that, in spite of the bigots and racists, there were a number of fair and open-minded people who were prepared to give anyone a chance. I have some good friends in the forces from all ranks.'

Just then Sandra entered the room carrying a buff file which she handed to her boss.

'Thanks, Sandra.' 'I'll call you if I need more information.'

She turned and left, her hips swaying gently, accentuating her ample figure. Pity I'm already spoken for, thought James, momentarily distracted.

Sundberg studied the file carefully for a few minutes before looking up at James. 'Well, I think this could be your man. Officially I am not supposed to divulge his name, but in the circumstances it seems your friend Sean Cameron is in need of some help. I can appreciate his dilemma, but I'm not sure he will gain anything by upsetting a happy family situation.'

'I've already told him that,' concurred James. 'But he's adamant he wants to find his daughter.'

Sundberg looked up from the file. 'The name of the man you want is O'Keefe, Major Adrian O'Keefe. He is serving at Mildenhall and has six months of his tour left. He is white and his wife is black. I remember them now. They are a nice couple. Apparently they were too old to adopt in the States and, according to the file, there are only three US states that have laws promoting race matching. Even then, it's very difficult for couples of their age to fit the criteria required. O'Keefe and his wife jumped at the chance when a mixed-race child became available here in Germany. The little girl is well loved and cared for by both parents. Captain Annan, I think you need to persuade your friend Sean not to interfere.'

James nodded.

'I'm giving you this information off the record because I think you are a man who would have found it out, anyway. It's probably better to get things over and done with as quickly as possible.'

'You are right, sir. My friend Sean is a really stubborn bastard at times, if you will excuse my French. He's got the bit between his teeth over this one and I don't think I can stop him. Thanks for your help, General. I really do appreciate it.' James rose from his chair to go.

Sundberg stood to attention and offered James his hand. Again James took it firmly in his grasp. 'I'm not a betting man, Captain, but I still think my first assessment of you is correct,' he said as he chuckled. 'Goodbye and good luck.'

'I don't suppose it will take you long to find out.' James grinned and marched slowly from the office.

Sandra was filing her nails at her desk, seemingly bored with what was going on around her. James approached her and hesitated for a moment, before saying, 'I'm in town for a couple more days. How about dinner tonight?'

Sandra looked up and smiled. 'That's the best offer I've had all day,' she said, in a pronounced Texas twang. 'I know a nice little Italian restaurant in the city centre. It's called Mario's, on the Mainzer Landestrasse. I'll see you there at eight.'

'I look forward to it,' said James smiling broadly.

As he wandered down the corridor, Sandra's eyes remained on him. She was admiring his powerful physique. She smiled to herself. As far as she was concerned eight o'clock could not come soon enough.

James reached the car park and reversed his hire car from the space. He drove slowly to the main gate and handed his visitor's pass back to the guard. The guard raised the barrier and James accelerated into the traffic. He knew Sean would be pleased with the latest information. He was also looking forward to his evening with Sandra. In all the years they had been together, he had never been unfaithful to Yolanda. He just liked the company of women and he had been away from home for quite a while. He needed a break from Sean's problems, at least for an evening.

He returned to his hotel, collected the key from reception and took the lift to his room on the fourth floor. He was soon stretched out on his bed. He lifted the telephone receiver and dialled Sean's number. He knew that as a security measure he should have used a call box, but on this occasion he was feeling tired. He would never have compromised a situation if he had still been in the Army, but he decided to take a chance and hoped he wouldn't regret it later. The telephone rang and the receptionist put him through to Sean's room.

'Mr White here, Sean. I've got some good news. My appointment went well today and I've got the name of the people you have been looking for.' He deliberately didn't use any names, just to be on the safe side.

'That was quick work,' Sean gasped.

'I can't tell you any more at the moment, but I'll explain tomorrow.'

'But I can't wait until tomorrow! I need to know now. At least give me the name.'

'I really can't give you the name over the telephone. I will tell you tomorrow.'

'If you can't give me a name, at least tell me where I can find him.'

'Put it this way, he is closer to home than you think. That's all I'm telling you for the moment. See you tomorrow. I've got to go now.' He promptly replaced the receiver.

Sean jumped up, punching his fist into the air. He was ecstatic. He didn't normally display emotion, but on this occasion a great deal was at stake. He sat down in the armchair in a corner of the room. Stretching back he closed his eyes, deep in thought. He began to relax, thinking of Louise. He hadn't been a rotten father to her, but his long absences on business and the year he'd spent in Kenya had caused her a lot of distress and heartache. How could he contemplate bringing up another child on his own? It was selfish even to think about it.

James and Dieter were right, but it was only natural for him to want to see his child. He would contact the couple and arrange a meeting to explain the facts. If it was true that his daughter was really happy with them, then he would let sleeping dogs lie. Perhaps he could send her birthday and Christmas presents in the future, and when she was 18 he could tell her the truth – that he was her father. However, if she was unhappy then he would do everything in his power to prove he was her father. He stretched further back in the chair and his thoughts drifted to the time he had spent with Akinyi in Kenya. He vividly pictured their walks on the beach. The times they had sat together, just looking at the ocean and watching the waves gently breaking on to the shore. How he wished he could turn back the clock. He wondered what name his daughter had been given.

His concentration was broken by the phone ringing. He lifted the receiver. It was James again. 'Hello, it's Mr White. Tomorrow's meeting is now today, same time, same place. See you there.' He hung up.

Sean shook his head. He wondered what was so important that couldn't wait until tomorrow. He looked at his watch. It was 3.45. He didn't have much time. It was too far to walk. He wasn't sure of the bus routes, so he hailed a taxi outside the hotel.

He arrived just as James was entering. He paid the taxi driver and ran across the road. There were quite a lot of people about. It would soon be rush hour.

The bar was empty except for Dieter and James. The staff were busily preparing for the expected rush of office workers calling in for a few drinks before returning home to their families. Dieter and James were seated at the usual table, deep in conversation.

'Hi guys,' interrupted Sean.

Dieter beckoned for him to sit down and carried on talking. Sean helped himself to a coffee from the pot on the table. He poured it slowly, steadily watching the steaming black liquid rise slowly to the rim of the cup.

'Why the change of appointment?' He looked at Dieter quizzically.

'There have been a few developments. Owens has been released on bail.'

'Oh shit!' exclaimed Sean. 'They'll be on to us now. Schneider will surely speak to him.'

'No, we've been very fortunate. Schneider did call but Owens wasn't there. He spoke to Peter Brown again. We've got a bit more time. Brown managed to bluff his way through. He told Schneider that Owens had been picked up by Special Branch and had been released on bail. But because it was prudent to lie low for a while, he'd gone away on a short holiday. He told Schneider that he would ask Owens to call him on his return. Of course, Brown will conveniently forget to tell him.'

'The other piece of news is that Njeri telephoned Yolanda last night. She was very distressed. Apparently she has been taken to Germany by a businessman she met in London. He promised her a good job in a club in Hamburg. I don't know how you manage it, Sean, but trouble seems to follow you everywhere. Not even pulp fiction would contain some of the stuff that's happened to you over the past couple of years.'

'What's the problem with that? What's so bad about working in a club?' Sean asked, looking agitated.

'Jeez, sometimes you are so naive, Cameron,' grinned James. 'You just don't see it, do you? It looks like Njeri has been lured into a prostitution ring. The businessman took her passport on the pretext of obtaining a long-term visa but what he's done is made sure she can't run away. If she does, she'll get picked up by the Police and will then be deported back to Kenya as an illegal immigrant.'

'I don't want to worry you, Sean,' said Dieter, 'but this type of prostitution ring is very typical in the larger cities in Germany. Girls, particularly from the former Eastern Bloc countries, are lured into the same trap. Their passports are taken away and they are kept as sex slaves in the more sleazy brothels. Black girls, normally brought in from North Africa, are an even bigger attraction. They are abused, beaten and threatened. They are actually paid very little. They don't even earn enough to send money home to their families. They have no one to turn to for help.'

'Well, where is she?' asked Sean.

'We don't know that,' said James. 'All she told Yolanda was that she was somewhere in Hamburg. She didn't give the name of the club or anything. Before she could finish the the conversation, the line went dead.'

'I'll have to go and help her,' said Sean.

'You can't. There's too much at stake here to jeopardize the operation now,' commanded Dieter. 'You were the one to insist on this operation, and you've involved James and me, so you can't chicken out now.'

Sean could see Dieter was very annoyed.

'Well, there must be something I can do for her.'

'Just a moment, Sean. I've already got John from London on the case. He has a photo of her, as you know, and as soon as he gets a flight organized he will go to Hamburg to check out the clubs and bars there. It shouldn't take him long to find her. It's more a problem to get her out of the country without a passport. We'll do that through the proper channels at the Kenyan High Commission in Bonn. We'll explain the situation and get them to issue her with a new one. That's relatively easy. The hard part is getting her away from her pimp. Those guys are merciless and totally amoral. Njeri represents an opportunity to make them a lot of money. She can earn them at least £1,500 a night, so they won't let her go without a fight. John is the best man I've got. He should be able to find her on his own, but after that much will depend on the heavies working at the club. He might need reinforcements and that's where we will come in later, if necessary.'

'But we're stuck here and may be here for a while yet,' argued Sean, momentarily forgetting the importance of their mission in Frankfurt.

'Don't worry. John will survey the situation. He'll make contact with Njeri and make sure no harm comes to her. It might take a little longer than we would like, but one way or another we will go in and lift her out of there. She won't be in danger for too long, I promise you.'

'Okay, okay,' said Sean exasperated. 'I'll do as you say, but tell me about the couple who might have my daughter. What's the story there?'

James outlined his conversation with Sundberg and all the information he had been given. 'He's a very simpathetic guy,' said James. 'He's helped a great deal and we can pursue the matter further when we get back to England. But first, let's complete our mission here.'

'Yes, back to basics,' said Dieter, taking control of the conversation again. 'I want you to go on the trip to the Black Forest on Friday night. We'll be watching you carefully.' He poured more coffee for himself and offered some to the others.

'No thanks,' said James.

'Nor me, thanks,' said Sean. 'I could do with something stronger, though.'

'But you know you can't have anything stronger!' scolded James. 'Don't do it just because you are feeling a bit uptight.'

Sean pursed his lips. 'I guess you're right,' he said, looking very depressed. 'You're *always* right.' However, his sarcasm was lost on James.

By now it was 5.30 p.m. and the bar had filled up. Although the three men looked less conspicuous than before, it didn't stop them from being scrutinized by the barman. As they got up to go he waved goodbye and went to the kitchen, where he made a call to his boss.

As the three reached the street they separated and went in different directions, backtracking and turning left and right down side streets as many times as possible to avoid being followed.

CHAPTER 40

On Wednesday morning, Sean was reading in his room. He needed some rest and an early night had been on the agenda for a long time. He needed to sleep in preparation for the weekend ahead. James had taught him that when he was on an operation it was best to follow the old army habit of getting as much sleep as possible whenever he had the opportunity. He had also told him that no one ever knew what might arise and that therefore it was always best to stay off the booze. Sean certainly didn't need to worry on that score. Although sorely tempted on occasions, he hadn't touched a drop – apart from a couple of beers in the Nazi bar – since his lapse in Richmond when Emma had found him comatosed.

He had an agreed check-in time with Dieter each day. All he had to do was call a number and give his personal PIN code to the operator. It was just a routine to confirm he was okay. So far it had been a formality. As usual he went to the call box down the road from the hotel. He dialled the number. The operator answered: 'Good morning, how can I help you?'

Sean's PIN code was 1215. He had deliberately picked that number because it was easy for him to remember. Numbers 12 and 15 were the shirts he'd worn when he played rugby at centre three-quarter or fullback. He gave his number to the operator.

'Just a moment, please. I'll see if I can connect you.'

As Sean waited he watched the street outside. People were going about their daily business. There was a queue at the local bakery. The other shops had only one or two people in them. Sean began whistling quietly. The operator eventually came back on the line.

'Mr Wulf is not available at the moment, but he says he will meet you in the usual place at midday. He says to tell you it is very important.'

'I understand, thank you.' Sean hung up. As he left the telephone booth he began to wonder what could suddenly be so important. He had only seen Dieter the previous evening. Surely there couldn't have been an important development so soon? He had two hours to kill. He couldn't understand how James had put up with so many 'ops' during his time in the Regiment; a lot of it must have been pretty boring work, hanging around waiting for something to happen. At least in his own business there had always been something going on.

He headed for the covered shopping parade just off Hermanstrasse. He disliked shopping at the best of times and window shopping was even more tedious. He ambled along aimlessly, not really taking much notice of the inviting window displays. In less than half an hour he was bored and very hungry. He decided to look for a McDonalds. He asked one of the security guards in the shopping centre where the nearest one was. The guard directed Sean along the parade. McDonalds had always been a saviour. He ordered a Big Mac and fries and a strawberry milkshake. He didn't particularly like the taste of the food, but it filled a hole. He carried his tray and took a seat in the top left-hand corner of the store where he could keep an eye on everyone coming and going. He wasn't really looking for anything or anyone in particular. He was just studying people's faces, the way they looked and dressed, the way they walked, any distinguishing marks. He had picked this up from James. It was a surveillance technique and a way of memorizing things that might later prove to be vital clues. He soon finished his burger and began fiddling with the straw. He looked at his watch; it was eleven o'clock. One hour to go before he met Dieter. He decided it wouldn't hurt to get there early. He slurped the last of his milkshake. He still had his book with him. It was an autobiography of Malcolm X. He enjoyed reading about famous people and what made them tick. This one was very interesting. As a child he'd remembered vaguely hearing about Malcolm X, but he hadn't really understood much about Black Power in the States. He had been too young and the British news reports were extremely superficial, although he'd remembered the poignant moment at the Mexico Olympics when Lee Evans and John Carlos had raised a black gloved fist into the air as they collected their medals. It'd seemed a cool thing to do at the time but he hadn't realized its full significance. The book was certainly an eye-opener to Sean. Malcolm came across as far more mellow and prophetic than he had previously been portrayed. He seemed a man ahead of his time.

Back at the rendezvous again, Sean took his usual seat. He ordered a soda water. A different barman was on duty. Sean hadn't seen him before. He opened his book and began reading. The remaining time passed very quickly.

'Good morning, Sean.' It was Dieter greeting him.

'Oh, hi. I didn't notice you come in.'

'I know,' said Dieter. 'It's unwise to be so engrossed in a book that you fail to notice what's going on around you. A newspaper's much better. You can read it without really reading it – if you understand what I mean. Anyway, on to more important things. James is in big trouble.'

'Why, what's happened?' asked Sean, never imagining that James would get himself into a situation that he couldn't handle.

Dieter explained that James had met Sandra, General Sundberg's secretary, the previous evening for dinner. 'She's okay and it's fortunate she's very well trained, otherwise we wouldn't have had a clue where James is.

Sean closed his book and placed it on the table, memorizing the page.

'Apparently they finished dinner at about 10.30 and parted company on the steps of the restaurant. Sandra's car was in the restaurant car park and James had watched her as she returned to it safely. As she climbed in she saw James move towards his hire car, which was parked about 200 metres away on the opposite side of the road. As he reached the car a transit van, or a similar vehicle, appeared from nowhere, and screeched to a halt. The rest is rather hazy, because it all happened so quickly, but Sandra reckons six men jumped out and attacked him. Fortunately, she had her mobile phone and quickly contacted the military police at Ramstein. It was all she could think of doing at the time. Meanwhile, James had been clubbed over the head and had gone down quickly, having been caught completely unawares.'

Sean sat listening wide-eyed. 'What happened next?'

'He had no chance as the six men bundled him in to the back of the van and sped off.'

'So what did Sandra do?'

'She kept her cool and followed at a safe distance, maintaining contact with Captain Stephens of the USAF police. The van travelled very fast, dodging in and out of traffic, but Sandra managed to keep up. She trailed the van for over 20 minutes and ended up outside a bungalow in a suburb of the city.

'Then what?' asked Sean.

'It was a fairly well-to-do suburb. The van pulled up in the drive and Sandra saw James being dragged to the front door. The door was opened from the inside, so they'd obviously been expected. James appeared to be semi-conscious. His legs trailed behind him as he was dragged to the front door. He had probably had a severe beating in the back of the van. The porch was badly lit, so Sandra couldn't get a clear glimpse of their faces. They got inside quickly and the door was shut behind them.'

'How come neither the security forces nor the police had caught up by this time?'

'Well, General Sundberg had been informed of developments and had contacted his counterpart in the German army, who'd very quickly got hold of me. It wasn't long before we had a full surveillance team surrounding the house and Sandra was relieved of her self-appointed task. She was taken back to Ramstein and was debriefed by myself and the General.'

'So, have you stormed the house yet?'

'No. While James is in there he should be safe. It is unlikely they'll kill him yet. They need him for the "chase", if that's the purpose of the kidnap. When they do come out we've got surveillance teams in place to track their movements, even if they separate.'

Dieter went on to tell Sean about Sandra. During the debrief she described what she could remember, but appeared to be in a state of low-level delayed shock. He was confident, however, that she would make a quick recovery.

'We catapulted monitors on to the roof and soon had listening equipment in place.

'Have you learned anything yet?' interrupted Sean.

'Not much. They are too well trained to call each other by name. No names means they will be hard to identify.'

'Do you know how many men are in the house?'

'Again we are not sure, but we estimate about nine. The only time they spoke to James was to tell him they had a surprise in store for him at the weekend.'

'So James is okay?'

'Yes, as far as we know, he's okay. He's tried questioning them, but they've been unresponsive other than to say they speak little English.'

'So what do you think their surprise is?' asked Sean.

'We're not sure of that, either, but my guess is they have him down for a "chase".'

'You mean the human chase you told me about?'

'Yes, the very one.' Dieter's voice sounded uncharacteristically ominous.

'I've really landed James in it this time,' said Sean guiltily, his face creasing into a worried frown. 'I should have left this job to the police, even though they were dragging their feet. Where do we go from here?'

Dieter told Sean that everything was under control. A surveillance team was ready to follow the minute James was moved from the house. A network of cars had been strategically located around the city, all in radio contact. General Sundberg had put his best MPs on standby, and there was a squadron of Special Forces ready as back-up if James was going to be used in a 'chase'. The squadron was already on its way to the Black Forest, on the assumption that it was the most likely place for the 'chase' to take place, and to set up rendezvous points in preparation.

'But how many men are in a squadron? The Black Forest is huge; surely they can't cover it all?' said Sean, thinking aloud. He was trying to fathom out all the possibilities. 'Can I help on this one?' he pleaded. 'I want to be in on the action.'

Dieter was firm. 'I'm sorry, but on this occasion you are not coming with us.' He then proceeded to make notes in a file.

Sean knew by the look in his eyes that he meant business and that it was pointless to argue. He had already learned that Dieter was autocratic and inflexible. An uncomfortable silence followed. Sean drummed his fingers on the table. The bar was filling up with the lunchtime trade.

When Dieter eventually finished writing, he looked up at Sean. 'We want you to go on your weekend exercise as planned. That is very important. I suggest that the two things are connected.'

Sean pieced together the evidence. 'You mean you think my exercise is going to be one of those human "chases" . . .? You think I'll be hunting down my mate, James? It doesn't bear thinking about,' he said, incredulously.

'That is a possibility, but if you are one of the team that has to hunt him down, he has a better chance of escape with you on the inside. You may be able to help him. You may well be his *only* chance of escape!' Dieter paused for a moment. 'Sean, I tell you again, this may be the most dangerous thing you will ever have to do in your life. You can't go in armed by us and it's not easy to wire you up. The chances are that, as a new recruit, you won't be entrusted with a weapon, and you will probably have a minder who will watch your every move. However, if there is a "chase" and James is caught, I suspect you will be one of the recruits chosen to kill him as a test of your true allegiance to the neo-Nazi brotherhood.'

Sean was silent. The implications of what he might have to do were too terrible to contemplate.

Dieter continued. 'If it comes to that, and you are given a weapon to shoot James, you will have to use it on your comrades in arms. Assuming it is an automatic with a reasonably large magazine, you'll have to be extraordinarily quick when you start firing. You won't get a second chance and you must hope that when you open fire your so-called comrades are fairly close together. James will know that if you are given a gun you are not going to use it on him – so he'll be prepared to make a move. However, if they don't give you the right kind of weapon you will probably both be doomed.' Dieter paused for his words to take effect. 'One thing James told me is that he didn't think you were capable of killing a man in cold blood. Are you?' asked Dieter. He hated asking the question, but he had to be sure.

Sean's reply left little room for doubt. 'If that situation arises, mark my words. I'll kill anyone who gets in my way,' he said, slowly and determinedly.

'I believe you would,' said Dieter, studying Sean carefully. 'When the shooting starts, James will jump into action and it'll be every man for himself. We hope it won't come to that, because as soon as the "chase" starts we will move in as quickly as possible. In addition to the Special Forces, we'll have every available member of our team in place. I will be controlling things from close by. In order to help us track your movements, we are currently fitting out a pair of boots with a homing device in each heel as a precautionary measure in case one fails. By the time our experts are finished they'll be undetectable. The boots will be delivered by courier to your hotel tomorrow morning.'

'Well, I hope they're not new,' said Sean, remembering the searing blisters on his first exercise at Hereford with James.

'We've allowed for that,' countered Dieter. 'They've already been worn in. I am sure they'll fit comfortably. Size nine, isn't it?' he said, and grinned, showing a bit of humour for the first time. He was beginning to feel slightly more confident that Sean wouldn't let them down. He would rather have used a professionally trained man but there was no immediate alternative.

'How did you know my shoe size?' puzzled Sean.

'Just a guess,' said Dieter, and grinned again, as he took a file from his briefcase, knowing that James, ever the professional, had supplied him with Sean's personal details before they had arrived in Frankfurt. He had briefed him fully on Sean, even down to his blood group. He had also given details of his next of kin, in case of an emergency. Dieter closed the file and returned it to his briefcase.

'Well, that's it, I suppose,' said Sean nervously.

'It certainly is. You're on your own now, Sean. Good luck, I think you'll need it. But if you want to pull out now, I won't think badly of you. This is the moment of truth.'

Sean stared hard at him. 'That doesn't warrant a response.' He got up to go and offered Dieter his hand. Dieter shook it firmly.

'Thanks Dieter, thanks for everything you have done so far.' For the first time in his life Sean was scared, really scared. He tried hard to block the fear out.

CHAPTER 41

Sean slept late, having spent a restless night tossing and turning. He finally awoke to the sound of a police siren ringing in his ears. He felt drained, as though he'd been up all night. He stretched out and yawned, lying back to look at the ceiling. A spider had woven its web around the pendulous light cluster suspended above his bed. Sean watched as it moved meticulously across the web feeding on the many small flies that had become trapped. He thought of James. He too was trapped. Sean wondered whether he would try to escape or wait for things to take their natural course and, he hoped, lead Dieter to the ring leaders of the neo-Nazi group. He suspected James would be biding his time and considering the options with his renowned objectivity. He would be in for a rough ride if he was going to be the human hare in the 'chase'. Sean shivered involuntarily. He felt a bead of sweat trickle slowly down his left temple. James's life might now depend on him – his strength of character and whether he was able to kill in cold blood. The thought troubled him greatly. He questioned his ability to live up to Dieter's expectations. His thoughts then switched to Louise. If anything happened to him he knew she would be well looked after. She was in safe hands with Sally and her husband. Sean also had several life insurance policies that Louise would benefit from if anything happened to him.

For a minute, a wave of emotion overcame him. He was becoming morose. He swallowed hard as he said to himself, 'Okay Cameron, pull yourself together.' At that he rose and had a shower, savouring the flow of tingling hot water as it ran down his body.

Soon afterwards he tucked in to a hearty breakfast of boiled eggs, ham, cheese, fruit and coffee. He ate well. He needed to fuel his body with as much food as possible. He remembered the meagre offerings on the last exercise, especially the bratwurst.

His new boots had arrived. They were a little newer than his other pair and slightly less supple. He prayed they wouldn't give him blisters. He had inspected them closely and there were no obvious signs of any electronic devices having been fitted. He wondered how they had managed to fit them so cleverly. He checked out of his hotel and headed for Jörg's Bar.

There was plenty of activity when he arrived. The doorman recognized him and let him pass. As he entered he could hear the now-familiar German marching music. The bar was quite full. He recognized a few faces from the previous weekend. There was a small group of men on a slightly raised platform to the right of the bar. Their tattoos, close-cropped hair, Levi 501s and braces likened them to English skinheads dressed to go to a football match. He moved closer to hear them speak. Sure enough they were English.

Sean hadn't bargained on meeting other Englishmen. He decided to keep clear of them in case they were real members of Combat 18 and blew his cover. He moved slowly away and took up a position near the back wall of the room, trying to look inconspicuous. He kept glancing around furtively, feeling self-conscious and thinking everyone was looking at him. The truth was that nobody was taking the slightest notice of him. They were just going about their own business, chatting noisily and drinking beer. Sean looked at his watch. As he did so, a whistle sounded. Lift off, he thought, as the men began to file out of the bar. He slipped in behind a couple of hefty Germans, making sure he kept a discreet distance from the group of Englishmen.

By now two coaches had pulled up outside the bar. At the first coach he spotted Jochen and Fritz directing operations. He tried to turn away but they saw him.

'Ah, Engländer, that coach please,' Fritz commanded, pointing towards the second one. 'I'll be with you in a minute, so save me a place next to you.'

Fortunately for Sean the other Englishmen had been assigned to the first coach. He swallowed hard. The thought of Fritz being his minder again didn't please him. He was hoping for one of the younger, more inexperienced, crew. He climbed aboard and took an aisle seat towards the back, leaving the window seat free for Fritz.

Fritz and Jochen were the last two to get on the coach. Jochen sat next to the driver and Fritz claimed the outer seat by the aisle, pushing Sean towards the window. As the engine started up, Sean noticed the first coach moving off in the opposite direction. He wondered why. He thought they might be using the ring road so they could meet again at a pre-arranged rendezvous. However, it was possible they could be going somewhere completely different to take part in another exercise. Sean hoped it was the latter as it would cut the numbers to 50 or so on the coach, plus any others that might join them by car. The fewer the better, which would increase his prospects of helping James if he was the target of the expected 'chase'.

He turned to Fritz. 'Where's the other coach going?' he enquired, casually.

'I've told you before, Engländer, you ask too many questions. It's not good for you. You will land yourself in trouble one of these days.'

Sean tried again. 'Are they meeting us later?'

Fritz didn't reply but began talking to a comrade in the seat in front of him. Sean didn't catch what was being said, but it was in German and he wouldn't have understood anyway.

It wasn't long before they reached the Autobahn. They turned south in the direction of Karlsruhe and the coach picked up speed quickly. Sean estimated they were cruising at about 120 kilometres per hour. If the rendezvous was the same as the previous weekend, it wouldn't take them long to reach it. He looked at his watch. It was 17.30 hours. He shut his eyes briefly. He couldn't sleep because he had to follow the route. If he fell asleep and the coach turned off at another intersection, it would be difficult for him to determine where they were going. James and Dieter had told him that any information on the routes would help future surveillance operations. The tiniest detail was important.

As they sped south along the Autobahn, Sean saw the signs for Darmstadt, Mannheim and Heidelberg. The route was different from the previous weekend. Within two and a half hours they had reached Karlsruhe on the edge of the Black Forest. From Karlsruhe they turned east towards Pforzheim, but it wasn't long before they turned off on to a minor country road. Sean had missed the signs through Pforzheim and began to panic. The coach slowed as the driver negotiated sharp bends and twisting country roads, then they began climbing. As they left the valley behind them the landscape changed quickly, revealing mountainous areas with dense forest. Eventually the coach slowed and the driver pulled into a layby. Jochen stood up and issued a directive. It was obvious that they had reached their destination. One by one the men filed off the coach and fell into three orderly ranks.

Sean took up a position at the rear, flanked by Fritz on one side and a man he hadn't seen before. 'What's your name?' he asked nonchalantly, in the best German he could muster.

'Kurt,' came back the icy reply.

'Where are we going?' he asked Fritz, expecting the usual rebuff.

'We will be there in another ten minutes,' said Fritz, glancing at his watch.

CHAPTER 42

When John arrived in Hamburg, he didn't know exactly where Njeri was working. All he had were the very sketchy details that Yolanda had given him. He quickly found the red-light district and began travelling from bar to bar, asking questions as to whether anyone had seen Njeri.

The first day had drawn many blanks. In the seedy red-light areas it was difficult to get people to talk. Even loosening their tongues with bribes proved difficult. Many people were scared to talk, in case they gave the wrong information to the wrong person. The Russian Mafia had set up many businesses in Hamburg since the Berlin Wall had come down and it could be a very dangerous place. Human life was cheap, and nobody fancied ending up in a dark alley with a knife in their gut. Even John didn't fancy his task working on his own. In the army he would normally have had back-up in a situation like this, but James had no one else he could call on. On this occasion John was most definitely on his own. He would much rather have been in the Black Forest with James. In 15 years together, John had owed James his life on several operations. He had great respect for him as a soldier and as a man. They had formed an almost unbreakable bond. James had always picked John as his right-hand man on many operations around the world. John had been looking forward to being on James's first civvy street operation, but this particular single-handed project in Hamburg was not quite what he had in mind. Nevertheless, he was confident in his own ability, and in close-quarter combat there were few men to touch him in the Regiment. He also had a good knowledge of German. He had served with the British Army in the Rhine and had attended German classes. His accent wasn't perfect, but he could get by.

Hamburg was very cosmopolitan. The low lifes that hung out in the bars and dives on the backstreets were of all nationalities – Dutch, English, Italian, Turks, Chinese, several of Arab origin and many Germans made up an interesting local population. Several drug addicts roamed the streets, but when John questioned them they proved to be the least helpful. Mostly they were off their heads, and the ones that weren't lied through their teeth to get money for their next fix. John spoke to many of the street hookers, but they, too, were unhelpful, thinking he was an undercover cop. He soon decided his best bet was to travel the 'Red House' bars and speak to the drinks hostesses and, he hoped, loosen their tongues with alcohol. This cost him a fair amount of money. Although he stuck to beer, most of the girls insisted on champagne. At upwards of 300

Deutschmarks per bottle he knew he would soon be in James's bad books for spending too much money on expenses. Sean would just have to pick up the tab if he wanted John to find Njeri.

On the second night he struck lucky. A black hostess called Angelique told him a girl answering Njeri's description had started work at the Beer Brezel, a no-holds barred 'Red House' that offered every possible sexual favour for its clients. According to Angelique, who was an illegal immigrant from Guadeloupe, the Beer Brezel was renowned for enslaving girls from North Africa or Eastern Bloc countries who had come on the promise of jobs in the film and modelling industries. When they arrived, with little more than a passport and the clothes they stood up in, they were vulnerable to the pimps who took away their passports and put them to work. Most ended up being gang raped by the pimp and his friends and forced to work in return for meagre payment, mainly food. They lived in appallingly squalid conditions in accommodation that resembled jails. They were watched constantly by armed minders, so they couldn't escape. They never saw the vast amounts of money they were earning for their pimps. The brothel Madam took care of that. Many of the girls drank excessively or took drugs to blank out the reality of what was happening to them.

Angelique was very helpful. She liked talking to John and flirted shamelessly. He could hardly be termed handsome, but at 48 he was still well muscled and in good shape, with hardly an ounce of fat on him. He continued to cut his hair in a military style and his rugged face had that lived-in look that showed that he had a strength of character and many tales to tell about life on the hard side of the track. John, too, was attracted to Angelique but he didn't have the time to be sidetracked by a liaison with her. Although twice divorced during his time in the army, and with a reputation for being something of a ladies' man, he stuck to the golden rule of never mixing business with pleasure, for he had seen too many of his colleagues fall into that trap, inevitably compromising themselves and often putting an operation in jeopardy.

Angelique gave John directions to the Beer Brezel. He tipped her 100 marks and, as he moved to leave, she slipped a piece of paper into his hand.

'That's my telephone number, just in case you are ever back in town,' she said as she giggled, fluttering her long lashes and giving him a huge smile. 'I would like to get to know you better.'

'Maybe I'll take you up on that one day,' said John, hurriedly pushing the piece of paper into his pocket.

He stepped into the street and pulled out a map. He studied it under the light in the porch. Angelique's instructions were good and he traced the route with his fingertips. He reckoned it would be a five-minute walk. He memorized the route and pushed the map back into his pocket. Turning his collar up against the chill of the night air he headed in the direction of Beer Brezel.

Beer Brezel was situated in a narrow, cobbled street, full of sex shops and music bars. From about 200 metres he saw a flashing neon light advertizing the Brezel above the doorway. He slowed his pace slightly so that he could survey the general lie of the land. If he needed to make a quick exit for any reason, he wanted to make sure he had an escape route.

The street was about 180 metres long with exits at each end only. The first was from the direction in which he had come and the other was about 100 metres beyond the Bar Brezel, up a slight gradient. As he walked along the street he noticed several girls dressed for business, loitering in the doorways of their respective clubs trying to entice in passers by. It was still comparatively early, and, because it was midweek, trade was slow.

The Bar Brezel had a single wooden door on the left of the building. On the right hand side there was a drinks menu showing prices. Beer was ten marks for a 200 cl glass, well above the going rate of four marks in a respectable bar. John didn't bother looking any further. He knew if he talked to a hostess it would probably cost him at least a bottle of champagne. He drew in a deep breath and entered cautiously. As he pulled the door open, a burly bouncer stepped forward from behind a large red curtain and directed John inside. The bar was poorly lit with low, red lights. The walls were covered in a heavy flecked red paper, reminiscent of that used in curry houses back in England. It was an L-shaped room with a bar on the left hand side. There were a few customers engaged in conversation with some of the hostesses. John headed for the bar and, as he did so, several of the girls pushed forward to meet him. He waved them away and took a seat on a barstool in the corner with his back to a pillar.

'Ein Bier, bitte,' he said to the barman, who had also been sitting on a barstool prior to John's arrival. He too was a big man, aged about 60, with a huge walrus moustache. His face was pock-marked and reddened from what appeared to be years of drink, which had clearly taken their toll. He poured the beer and took John's ten marks in return. As John took a sip, the barman returned to his stool, his eyes fixed on one of the big screen TVs dotted around the walls. He was watching a porno film. John didn't take much notice of the movie. Porno films had always bored him. Another screen was playing a music video. He looked carefully around the room. The hostesses who weren't entertaining were seated. They were watching John with interest. Eventually one of them got up. Her hair was an outrageous peroxide blond, cut in a short, spiky punk style. Her white-powdered face was heavily made up and, in place of her eyebrows, large black pencil lines, shaped like a stretched diamond, were laid horizontally above her eyes. Her lipstick was bright red. A lacy white basque emphasized her bosomy figure, and beneath her short black hotpants stretched white suspenders supporting white fishnet stockings. As she tottered towards him in black patent boots with precariously high stiletto heels, John tried his best not to laugh out loud.

'Hello mein Liebling,' she said as she offered her hand. 'Are you English?'

'Yes,' retorted John, very abruptly.

'You buy me a drink,' she demanded.

'Okay, you can have anything you like as long as it's beer,' John responded, worrying about his expense account.

He knew he was pushing his luck and he grimaced as she said rather curtly, 'I don't want a beer, I only drink champagne. You buy for me?'

John knew he had little alternative but to buy her what she wanted. He pulled some money from his pocket and asked the barman for a bottle.

An ice bucket, containing the champagne and a glass, was pushed towards John. 'Will you pour it or shall I?' he asked, in a deep guttural voice.

'I'm paying enough, so you can do it,' John instructed.

He turned to blondie and raised his glass. 'Prost, and what's your name?'

Blondie introduced herself as Sylvana. It wasn't long before she had told John almost all her life history. She was from Rumania and had come to Germany to seek her fortune after the Wall had come down. They chatted for about 15 minutes, with John interjecting with an occasional 'yeah' or a 'right' in his London twang. He wasn't much interested in what she had to say; he was just hoping that Njeri would appear.

A short time later Njeri emerged from behind a door that was situated at the far end of the bar. She was tall and strikingly beautiful. John realized why Sean had been attracted to her; any man would be. He looked towards her but she just stared blankly back at him. Her face was puffy, particularly around the eyes, her expression vacant. He beckoned her to come and sit with him. She hesitated. John soon realized that Sylvana's presence was preventing Njeri from approaching him. He leant forward and told Sylvana to take a walk. 'But I want to be with you!' she protested.

'Well, I don't want to be with you!' he replied bluntly. He gestured to the barman that he wanted her out of the way. Before the barman could move, the big minder strode over and whispered something in Sylvana's ear. Her expression quickly changed from one of annoyance to fear and she moved away.

Njeri was soon at his side.

'What are you drinking?'

'Champagne,' instructed Njeri to the barman as John winced, already feeling the pain of James's sharp tongue. He handed over the money with an expression of resignation.

Njeri took her glass and sipped it slowly, as if bored with the whole proceedings. John studied her closely. Her eyes were red from crying. She looked in pain.

'Well, say something then,' she said. 'Now I am here you might as well talk to me.'

'Is there somewhere we can go that is a little more private?' John mumbled. He was embarrassed that it might have appeared that he was trying to proposition her.

'Upstairs, but that is going to cost you,' she said.

'How much?' said John, worrying about his expense account again.

'Five hundred marks minimum,' she said, lifting her glass and taking his hand. 'Bring the bottle with you,' she instructed and turned and headed for the stairs.

John felt rather sheepish as he trailed behind her, and self-conscious. As they climbed the stairs he tried not to notice her backside wriggling in the tight mini skirt. She led him to the third room on the right. It was dimly lit. She went straight to the bed and lay down.

'Come on, let's get it over with,' she said flatly.

'Do you always speak to your customers like that?' enquired John. 'Aren't you worried about them complaining to the management?'

'I'm past caring. They can do what they like to me. Other than killing me they can't do worse than they have already,' choked Njeri. She started to remove her clothes.

'Hold on!' said John, and touched her shoulder gently. 'Let me explain why I'm here. I'm a friend of Sean, in fact I'm working for him. I've come to find you and take you away from this place.'

'Why didn't he come himself? It just proves he doesn't care for me, sending you instead.'

'Wait a minute,' John interrupted. 'He does care for you, but he can't come at the moment. James and Sean are on a mission down in the Black Forest. I can't go into detail, now, but they could both be in grave danger.'

'Oh no, I'm sorry,' Njeri said, and began to cry softly. The tears rolled down her cheeks and she started to shake uncontrollably. John took her in his arms and held her tight. He felt a bit awkward and began to tell her not to worry and that everything would be okay.

As Njeri lifted her head from John's shoulder, she wiped away the tears with the back of her hand. 'You can't take me away from here on your own; it's too dangerous. The girls in here are watched constantly. You've only seen one minder but I tell you there are at least five others, either in a room behind the bar or lurking close to the building on the street. They all have walkie-talkies, so if any of the girls tries to leave before the place closes, all hell breaks loose. Recently, a customer persuaded one of the girls to leave with him. They made it to the street but the customer was dragged away and badly beaten up. He was lucky they didn't kill him. The girl, who was from the Czech Republic, was brought back and locked in one of the rooms down in the cellar. We never saw her again. Her body was later dragged out of the sea down in the docks. She had been strangled and badly beaten, according to police reports. That was a severe warning to us. We are not allowed any newspapers, but one of the other girls, who has a bit of a thing going with Ludo the barman, got the information from him. I tell you, John, all the girls here are terrified. The place is run by the Russian Mafia.'

'Well, we'll have to do something about that, won't we?' said John angrily. 'I won't risk trying to take you out now, or we could both end up dead. If what you say is true, I won't be able to deal with six men on my own. I'll have to come back with Sean and James and a few of the other lads. It may take some days. In the meantime, you will have to deal with your problems here in the best way you can. I'm sorry.' He got up to go.

'I'm sorry to have to say this, but haven't you forgotten something?' Njeri asked, holding out her hand.

'Oh yeah.' John blushed with embarrassment and fumbled in his pocket. He gave her the 500 marks that she had asked for earlier.

'Please make sure that when you see Sean you tell him nothing actually happened,' urged John.

'Don't worry. I'll tell him you were very, very good,' she said cheekily, fluttering her eyes provocatively.

John squeezed Njeri's hand to reassure her. 'I'll be back with the cavalry, I promise.'

As he left the room, Njeri straightened her clothes before returning to the bar downstairs. John had gone by the time she had taken up her place to wait for her next customer.

John hurried along the street, anxious to catch the next flight to Stuttgart. He wanted to be in on the action to help Sean and James. From Stuttgart he would have to drive down to the Black Forest to link up with Dieter's men. He looked at his watch. It was 22.10. He had no idea if there was a late plane. He needed to call the airport. He didn't want a wasted trip and to have to sleep at the airport. He hailed a passing taxi and ordered the driver to take him to the nearest phone kiosk.

'I'll tell you where I want you to take me after that – and make it quick,' he ordered in his best German.

CHAPTER 43

Fritz was spot-on with his estimated time of arrival. The forest track widened slightly and, just ahead in a clearing, Sean could see a log cabin. It had two rooms and a small verandah. Leaning against the railings were two heavily armed men and to the rear were more men, also heavily armed. They all carried machine guns and a pistol in a holster on their belts.

Jochen issued a command to the men on the coach and about half of them, around twenty-four, filed up to the verandah where they were each issued with automatic rifles and a spare clip of ammunition. Sean wondered why only half were given guns. He reasoned the other half must be new recruits like himself, who hadn't completed their training.

'No gun for me, then?' Sean enquired of Jochen.

'No chance,' snapped Jochen. 'We still don't trust you but if you prove yourself this weekend you will have one on the next exercise.'

Sean had been studiously watching the log cabin. Eventually one of the doors opened and James appeared, flanked by two guards. He was handcuffed to another man who looked to be of Turkish or Middle Eastern origin. He was much shorter than James but very rotund. He was sweating profusely. James began looking around, surveying the situation. His gaze fell on Sean but he showed no sign of recognition. He looked very alert in spite of his ordeal. If he remained handcuffed to the other man and there was a chase, it would seriously reduce his chances of escape. One of the guards gave James a push with the butt of his rifle. Quick as a flash James's left fist flew out and hit the guy square on the jaw. His gun clattered to the ground and he fell back clutching his face. Several of the other guards jumped back and took up the firing position, aiming their guns at James and the Turk. The men began shouting in German. The Turk dropped into a crouching position, pulling the right side of James down with him as he tried desperately to cover his head with his hands. James tried to haul him to his feet, but he was too heavy and had begun to shake uncontrollably, shouting in a language that Sean didn't understand.

Jochen stepped forward and pointed his pistol at James's forehead. 'One more move like that from you, nigger, and I'll blow your head off,' he screamed at James in English.

'No you won't,' said James calmly. 'Your bosses won't be too pleased if you kill me and ruin the chance of a chase.'

Jochen hesitated for a moment; he felt awkward in this situation. The

Schwarzer had out-manoeuvred him in front of his men and he didn't like it. James's professionalism, acquired through years of training, had enabled him to remain calm in a crisis. Talk about a cool customer, thought Sean.

'Okay, nigger, you and the Turk can go for a walk to stretch your legs, and no funny business. There will be many guns trained on you.'

He stepped back and ordered James to move. James had another go at hauling the Turk to his feet. This time it worked as the man had calmed down somewhat. 'Come on, Abdul, we need to walk for a while,' he said. As they moved forward, the Nazis stepped aside and let them pass.

'You've got five minutes,' shouted Jochen, turning to head back to where Sean was standing. He said to Sean, 'When the chase starts, Engländer, you'll be the one to kill the Schwarzer. In that way, we will see if you hate black people as you claim you do – or whether you still love them like that bitch whore of yours we killed in Frankfurt.'

The anger rose in Sean and it took every ounce of self-control not to hit Jochen or show any emotion. He clenched his fists at his sides and drew in a deep breath. It was the first time any of these bastards had mentioned Akinyi and he was shocked.

'What time is the chase, then?' queried Sean.

'Six o'clock we start. We'll separate the two of them. Abdul will get a head start on the Schwarzer and then we will follow three minutes later. You'll stay with me and when we capture them we will expect you to do your duty.'

'So can we sleep now?' Sean asked. It was 23.00 hours. Seven hours before the chase was due to start.

'Ja, you can sleep until 04.00 hours and then you will be on guard duty with Kurt.'

The forest floor was cold and damp, so Sean went up on the verandah and sat with his back against the wall of the room in which James was being held. He knew he would find it difficult to sleep in an upright position, but he hoped he could at least catnap until his guard duty with Kurt.

In spite of the dampness, many of the men curled up and went to sleep on the ground. Some made low-level beds from small twigs and branches, while others slumped down against the trees. Overall the men had scattered in small groups within about a 100 metre radius. The guards with guns took up a position outside the perimeter.

Sean assessed the situation. He counted eight armed guards. Each of their partners stood unarmed, obviously the new recruits. Sean began working on a plan of attack. He knew that some of the off-duty men also had guns, but James had taught him that, even though the odds might be stacked against you in a dangerous situation, it was sometimes better to use the element of surprise and make a move when it was least expected. He decided to wait until he was on guard duty with Kurt. Sean hoped they would be asked to relieve the guards on James's room. If they were given that particular duty, Sean reckoned he could take out Kurt and then free James and Abdul. From there James could take command and together they could make a run for it, he hoped, without disturbing the rest of the camp. A potential problem was Abdul, who might have neither the physical stamina nor the courage to cope with such an exhausting and dangerous challenge.

Sean hoped that Dieter had succeeded in following them, and that the Special Forces units were in place to mount a rescue operation. He drifted off to sleep.

CHAPTER 44

Surprisingly enough, Sean slept well. He was eventually woken up roughly by Kurt. 'Come on, Engländer, we've got work to do.'

Sean rubbed his eyes. He had leant on his left side as he slept and his body ached from being in an awkward position. He stood up to stretch his limbs. He wanted to be sure that his reactions were quick enough to take on Kurt when the opportunity presented itself. His hopes were rewarded when they were ordered to relieve the guards to James's room. It was now only a matter of time before he made his move. He needed to be sure that the guards and the others they had relieved had fallen asleep. He waited half an hour. He glanced at his watch; it was 04.30 hours. He had manoeuvred himself to be on Kurt's blind side and was contemplating the best way to knock him out without making a noise and waking the rest of the camp. He tried hard to remember what James had taught him at training camp. He needed a weapon or a club. His eyes scanned the verandah; there was nothing suitable. Should he rush Kurt in the hope that he could overpower him and club him over the head with his own rifle? He dismissed that idea as unrealistic as Kurt would surely cry out and warn the others. His only option was a karate chop to the back of the neck. He made his move. Creeping forward stealthily, he reached his target and hit him as hard as possible with a downward swipe of his hand. Kurt tumbled almost silently to the ground. Sean couldn't believe his luck. He grabbed Kurt's rifle and, just for good measure, cracked him over the head with the butt. He then checked that the safety catch was in the 'on' position before scanning the camp and doing a head count. The eight armed guards were still in their original positions, their unarmed comrades sitting diligently beside them. Some of them were chatting, some seemed bored and others were dragging on cigarettes. But none seemed to have noticed what had happened.

The next thing Sean needed to do was to get rid of Kurt's body before it was spotted. He tried the door to James's room, turning the handle slowly before pushing it open gently. As he moved sideways through the doorway, a guard jumped up unexpectedly inside the room. Sean reacted quickly, surprising himself at his own speed. He automatically swung his rifle butt up across the guard's face, and jumped on him. The guard crashed backwards against the wall, taking the full weight of Sean's body. He was completely winded and, before he could recover, Sean swung an uppercut to his chin, knocking him senseless and cracking the bones in his hand as he did so. The pain was excruciating. It felt as if he had broken all his fingers.

By this time James was on his feet. He grabbed the second rifle almost instantly and took up a position by the doorway, dragging the handcuffed Abdul with him. 'Quickly, Sean,' he whispered. 'You'd better get back to the verandah before you're missed.'

'This is killing me, James.' He shook his hand furiously. 'I'll be completely useless from now on.'

'Well, bloody well use your left hand to pull the trigger if you have to,' James hissed. 'But first of all get these cuffs off me. The guard has the key in his pocket.'

Sean stepped across the apparently lifeless body and rummaged in his pockets, eventually finding the key which he threw to James. He returned to the verandah, taking up his previous position.

Meanwhile James had unlocked the cuffs and pulled Abdul to his feet. Sean had left the door slightly ajar so he could continue to talk to James.

'How many guards are there, Sean?' he whispered.

'Sixteen in total on duty at the moment, but only eight of them are armed. There's a further 16 asleep, of whom at least eight have automatic rifles.'

'So there's only 32 in total?' queried James.

'No, about 50 came down in my coach and there were another ten heavily armed men already here when we arrived. But I don't know where they are now.'

'What's in the room opposite?'

'I'm not sure. I think it might be an armoury because they issued the rifles from there,' replied Sean. 'I didn't see anyone go in, but they could have done so when I was asleep. I'll drag Kurt's body into your room, James, and then it's up to you what we do next, but I'll need some help, I can't grip anything with my right hand.'

James crept out and the two of them moved Kurt into the room. As they got inside James felt for a pulse.

'He's still alive, but well and truly out for the count. You don't know your own strength, Sean. What the hell did you hit him with?'

'Just a karate chop to the neck as you taught me – and then the butt of the rifle.'

'It must have been the rifle then,' James joked. 'He's going to have a very sore head when he comes round. I doubt he'll be too impressed with you.' James began to tie him up and then moved to the other guard. He bound and gagged both of them, trussing them together.

By this time Sean was back on the verandah. Abdul began asking James all sorts of questions. His English was poor, but James calmed him down as best he could. James then moved back behind the doorway.

'Our friend Abdul here will slow us down a bit, but we've got to take him with us, Sean. If we leave him here they'll almost certainly kill him when they find out we've gone.'

'Okay, it's not a problem for me, but remember, James, my hand is useless. The best thing I'm going to be able to do is run and that's about it.'

'Don't worry, my old mate, we'll soon all be home safely,' James said, with confidence.

Sean then told James that Dieter and his men and a team of US Special Forces were possibly in place around the camp, or at least in the vicinity.

'We have to get through the cordon of guards, and then it won't be long, I hope, before we meet up with our own guys,' said Sean.

'And what about John? Where is he?'

Sean explained that John had gone to Hamburg to find Njeri, but that he hoped to be back in time to join Dieter and his men.

'Let's try the other room. Two guns against 42 or more are not good odds,' said James.

'You first,' countered Sean, pointing James in the direction of the door.

James moved across the verandah. Meanwhile, Sean had his back to him so that he could see out over the camp. There was still little or no movement from any of the guards. Sean clutched his rifle in his left hand and supported the stock with his right wrist. James gently turned the handle of the door. It creaked slightly as he pushed it open, but it was hardly discernible. The room was about the same size as the one in which he had been held prisoner. In the right hand corner was a man curled up on a bed, asleep. Further away another man was lying in a sleeping bag on the floor. Neither had woken. James crept quietly across the wooden floor. He was soon at the bed and, as he was about to stick the muzzle of the gun into the man's face, he pointed to Sean to do the same to the man in the sleeping bag. They nudged the men awake, and even in the half light could see the look of surprise and fear on their faces. The safety catch was off and it was the nearest Sean had ever come to threatening a man's life. James quietly commanded both men to get up slowly. As they moved, Sean noticed that it was Jochen on the bed.

'You bastard, Sean Cameron. I knew I could never trust you,' he hissed. 'Mark my words, you will never get away with this. My men will kill you all.'

'Shut up!' breathed James. 'Right now – on your knees, and then lie down with your arms outstretched.'

The other man looked awkward as he tried to struggle out of his sleeping bag.

James instructed them to take off their belts. As they did so he tied Jochen's hands behind his back. He ripped a sheet from the bed and tore it in two, using one half to bind his feet. He then moved quickly to the second man and did the same. He looked at his watch. It was 05.00 hours. 'Come on, Sean, we haven't much time. I'll just gag these two and then I'll tell you what we're going to do.'

He quickly gagged them while Sean watched in awe.

James left nothing to chance. Sean could see why people claimed the SAS was the best regiment in the world.

James took Jochen's pistol and Uzi sub-machine gun, picked up the spare clips of ammunition and turned on Jochen's torch to look for more weapons. He knelt down and counted six pistols and four more automatic rifles. He checked them for ammunition; all had a clip in them, and the boxes of ammunition were still sealed. 'Come on, Sean, we need to get Abdul and we also need to drag the other two guards over here.'

After they had done this, and out of earshot of Jochen, James continued. 'If Dieter and his men are close by, we will hole up here until they arrive. If we start firing it will alert them, but we won't shoot until your ex-comrades do so. I suspect Jochen will have arranged to be woken at 05.30 hours to prepare for the chase at 06.00. We've probaby got 15 minutes before all hell breaks loose.'

'You mean we are not going to make a run for it?' queried Sean.

'It doesn't make sense to do so, now. Abdul will slow us down and, as you say, your right hand is virtually useless. We are better off making a stand here. At least we've got plenty of weapons to take them on, if we have to.'

As they moved into the other room, Sean looked quickly across the camp. It was still quiet. Abdul helped them to drag the guards back, and they pushed them into a corner of the room with Jochen and his subordinate. Jochen was still squirming on the floor. The anger was apparent in his eyes. James gave him a prod with his boot and re-checked the bindings and gags. They were still tight.

At 05.30 one of the guards started to walk towards the cabin. Sean had repositioned himself on the verandah, the rifle in his left hand.

'Where's Kurt?' the man asked, as he stepped on to the verandah.

'Oh, he just went inside to talk to Jochen,' Sean pointed in the direction of Jochen's room. 'He wants a word with you as well.'

The man looked quizzically at Sean. 'Why have you got a rifle? Recruits aren't normally given one.'

'Kurt said it would be okay for five minutes while he talked to Jochen. Go and ask him,' Sean responded.

'Kurt, it's Jurgen,' the man called. 'Are you there?'

Sean had to move quickly. He lifted his rifle, released the safety catch and pointed it at the back of Jurgen's head. 'Drop your weapon and get inside now,' he commanded.

Jurgen half turned, but Sean pushed the muzzle of his rifle further into his neck. It worked and Jurgen moved hastily through the doorway to be met by James, whose rifle was pointed directly at him.

'Down on the floor!' he said.

Jurgen obliged and James went through the same process of tying him up, eventually dragging him into the corner with the others.

'At this rate there's not going to be any room left in here for us,' said James jokingly. He turned to Abdul. 'Start unwrapping those boxes of ammunition, and, by the way, have you ever fired a gun before?'

'Nein, nein, no gun for me,' Abdul stammered fearfully, mixing up his English and German.

'Well, you can keep an eye on these jokers,' James commanded, pointing at the group of hostages. 'Just tell me if any of them makes a move.' He turned to Sean. 'Go back on the verandah and stay there till I tell you to move. We'll stay quiet for as long as we can, but it probably won't be many minutes before at least one of the guards gets inquisitive and comes over to have a look.'

CHAPTER 45

Dieter and his men had kept track of the coaches. The first coach had gone in the direction of Munich and, although he could spare only two cars and four men, they had done a good job in following it.

His other team had been allocated the task of following the coach Sean was in. They used a small fleet of vehicles which constantly overtook one another or pulled off and on the Autobahn at various intersections, so that no one vehicle was seen specifically to be following the coach. It wasn't critical to always have the coach in their sights, as they were able to monitor its progress from the tracking devices in Sean's boots. Dieter had remained in the tracking van a few kilometres behind the coach. Occasionally they would lose contact when the van dropped back too far, but once they accelerated it soon picked up the signal again. Dieter was satisfied with the monitoring system.

When the coach eventually stopped and the men alighted, teams of four-wheel-drive vehicles were dispersed at a safe distance around it. Dieter had also kept in radio contact with Captain Johnson, who was controlling the American Special Forces team. Both units were strategically placed to cut off any escape by the neo-Nazis and, more importantly, to rescue James and Sean. Some of Dieter's men had spent the night watching the log cabin and were restless for the action to begin.

As the sun came up, Dieter's men checked and double-checked their weapons. They were on full alert from 05.45 hours.

Shortly after 06.00, the morning silence was broken by the sound of gunfire echoing from deep in the heart of the forest. At first there was the single crack of an automatic rifle followed by short, sharp bursts of rapid fire.

As soon as he heard the gunfire, Dieter started issuing orders. All the teams were in radio contact but had maintained almost complete radio silence in case their frequency was being monitored.

'Move in slowly, and if you encounter any of the neo-Nazis give them a warning to surrender. If they don't lay down their weapons, shoot to kill. I don't want any casualties in my teams! From now on, I want complete radio silence unless any of you need to give vital and urgent information, understand?' The teams responded one at a time, 'Roger, we copy and out.'

The gunfire continued. Up at the log cabin, all hell had broken loose. A hail of bullets had ripped into the thick cabin walls. James was doing most of the firing from the cabin. Sean struggled to take any reasonable aim, using his left shoulder. Sighting with his left eye was difficult. Eventually he changed back to his right shoulder. Fortunately the trigger was so sensitive he didn't need to put much pressure on it, but the pain in his hand had become almost unbearable.

James had instructed Sean to shoot at two particular groups of guards. Meanwhile, James had loaded all the automatic rifles, emptying one magazine at a time and then changing to the next rifle until he had exhausted all five. Abdul took over the task of reloading as James changed weapons. The intensity of the firing must have led the neo-Nazis to think there were several snipers in the cabin and they returned fire intermittently. Suddenly, after he had exhausted the first five magazines, James stopped firing. He went to the back of the cabin, untied Jochen's ankles and dragged him to his feet. He then removed the gag from his mouth.

'Okay, Jochen, you are going to tell your men to lay down their weapons. They are completely surrounded by a team of Special Forces and they have no chance of escape.' He pushed Jochen through the doorway, pointing his rifle at the back of his head.

Jochen spoke loudly and clearly in German. 'Do not give up. Never surrender. You must die for your cause.'

'Shut up!' James shouted. 'Tell them what I told you to say.'

'Never! They will eventually get you, Schwarzer. We Nazis do not run away from battle.'

In the next second, Jochen took a dive forwards and rolled away to the right, missing the top step of the verandah. A hail of bullets hit the door frame and James ducked. He sprayed a short burst of fire in Jochen's direction. Jochen kept low, finally making it to safety behind a pile of logs.

'Schnell, schiessen. Die Hütte!' he screamed in German. 'Get me out of here.'

A torrent of bullets hit the window next to James, splintering wood everywhere. This time the rifles were joined by a number of sub-machine guns. The sound was unmistakable.

The heavily armed guards had obviously returned. Sean and James were pinned down. They could now only hold the Nazis at bay. They prayed that Dieter would arrive soon.

All went quiet for about five minutes. In the east the sound of a helicopter broke the silence. It came in fast, swooping across the camp and banking away.

'That will be the signal from Dieter that they've got our exact position. It'll all be over soon,' said James calmly.

The helicopter peeled away to the right of the camp. The Nazis fired at it aimlessly, but caused no damage. While their attention was distracted, James took careful aim and downed two of the guards. He wasn't shooting to kill, but hit them both below the knees. They crumpled to the ground, writhing in agony.

By this time Jochen's arms had been freed by two of his men and he was back in command. He held an Uzi and was barking orders to his men.

'Be prepared, Sean,' warned James. 'They will try to rush us soon. Stay in position and only shoot if you can get a clear shot at your target. From now on, you've got to start putting them down.'

'Right,' said Sean. He didn't fancy shooting to kill and he didn't have James's skill in being able to place a wounding shot accurately. He could only hope that none of the shots were fatal, knowing it was a case of self-preservation. Another volley of shots hit the cabin. James and Sean both ducked below the windows. James threw a pistol to Sean.

'Tuck that in your belt and use it if they get very close.'

James raised his head and peered out. By now some of the guards were within 50 feet of the cabin. He shouted to Sean. 'Put your rifle on automatic and keep them pinned down. I'm going to try and pick a few more of them off.'

He stood up, and as Sean let rip with his rifle on rapid fire, James took careful aim and one by one he downed the advance party. He stopped firing. Eventually a man's voice on a megaphone broke the short interlude. It was Dieter.

'You are completely surrounded. You have one minute to throw down your weapons and put your hands in the air.' He paused. 'One minute, do you hear!' He paused again. 'This is the police and we have army back up. You are outnumbered.'

Dieter's men fired a short burst in the air. 'The next bullets are for you,' he threatened.

Dieter waited another minute. He deliberately began to count to 60. 'One, two, three, four, five, six, seven . . . ' He didn't have to count any further as, one by one, the men rose and began throwing down their weapons. Jochen, defiant to the end, was the last to give up.

Very quickly Dieter's men moved forward. They frisked the neo-Nazis for further weapons, before snapping their wrists in handcuffs. They were then herded to the centre of the camp, where police vans had arrived to take them away for interrogation. Sean, James and Abdul stepped out of the cabin. Abdul had the biggest smile that Sean had ever seen in his life. They walked down and greeted Dieter.

'A helicopter will be here in five minutes to take us back to Frankfurt,' he told them. 'A lot has happened in your absence. I'll fill you in on the flight.'

CHAPTER 46

As they flew back to Frankfurt, Sean's mind turned to the new changes in his life. He wanted to arrange an appointment with General Sundberg to see Major O'Keefe, and was lost in contemplation of his next move.

Meanwhile, Dieter was absolutely delighted. A major neo-Nazi cell had been infiltrated. The operation had been a complete success. They had captured 42 men, who would very quickly be locked away in a remand centre near Frankfurt. Those who had been wounded would be taken, under heavily armed guard, to a military hospital. The next step would be to have the men interrogated, and it wouldn't be long before they extracted further information. A good percentage of the 42 men would talk. Dieter put a call through to Sundberg on the helicopter radio. He, too, was absolutely delighted with the success of the operation and also had some good news for Sean.

'Mr Cameron, Major O'Keefe is due to fly into Wiesbaden near Frankfurt this afternoon. He has asked specifically to see you.'

Sean shut his eyes and took a deep breath. He was getting closer to his goal of finding Akinyi's killers and also to that of finding his daughter. He opened his eyes, and in his excitement gave James the high fives. They were both physically and mentally exhausted, but pure adrenaline was keeping Sean awake.

At 11.00 they touched down at Frankfurt and were whisked away in one of Dieter's cars to the Officers' Mess at Wiesbaden, where they showered and changed and then tucked into a hearty brunch.

They had almost completed their meal when Sundberg's secretary, Sandra, walked in.

James rose immediately. 'I think I owe you a big thank you,' he said. 'I understand it's because of your quick thinking that I am alive.' He gave her a hug.

She smiled and kissed him gently on the cheek. 'Oh, it's nothing,' she said, a little embarrassed.

'This is my friend, Sean Cameron. Sean, this is Sandra Green.'

She smiled. 'I've heard a great deal about you, Sean.'

'And James tells me you are very interesting yourself,' said Sean, grinning.

Sandra flushed slightly. 'I must go now, I have an important appointment. I'll see you later, I'm just glad you are both back in one piece.' She turned and left.

The two friends took their seats again.

'It's a good thing it was Sandra and not any other woman that you asked out to dinner, James. Otherwise we would never have found you,' Sean smiled. 'Still, we'd better keep that part of the story secret from Yolanda, I think,' he said, mockingly.

'I've got nothing to hide!' James protested.

'I think he protests too much,' said Sean, looking at Dieter. They continued their brunch in silence.

Sean eventually broke the silence. 'My appointment with Major O'Keefe is at 14.30 hours, but in the meantime, James, have you heard from John?'

'Yes, he will be here shortly. He missed the last flight from Hamburg last night, so he flew down this morning. He's kicking himself for missing out on the action in the forest.'

Five minutes later John arrived. He greeted James and Sean and pulled up a chair at their table.

James called the steward to arrange another breakfast. While he was waiting for it to arrive, John gave them a detailed account of his visit to Hamburg and how he had found Njeri in a bar in the red-light area.

'To get her out is not a one-man operation,' he said, 'but four good men should do it.' He explained about the minders. 'I can't be certain, but I think the bar is run by the Russian Mafia and we must be very careful not to upset them.'

'Well, you and I can go in,' interrupted James. 'And I'm sure Dieter will lend us a couple of his men as back up. It shouldn't take long. We should be in and out in less than ten minutes.'

'What about me?' queried Sean.

James looked at him with disdain. His right hand was in plaster. An X-ray had shown that he had fractured two of his fingers and the knuckle on his middle finger. 'You will be no good to us with your hand like that if the going gets tough. You will have to wait until we bring Njeri back. We'll fly to Hamburg after your meeting with O'Keefe and we'll sort it out either tonight or tomorrow,' James said, authoritatively.

Sean was disappointed. But in a curious way he was also pleased, because he did not want to find Njeri in what would almost certainly be a compromising situation.

CHAPTER 47

Sean was feeling nervous when he arrived for his meeting with Major O'Keefe. Sandra greeted him and directed him to General Sundberg's office. He knocked on the door.

'Come in,' called a deep voice.

As Sean entered, Sundberg rose from his desk and, noticing Sean's right hand in plaster, shook his left hand.

A tall, middle-aged, distinguished looking man in an American Air Force officer's uniform was standing by the window. He had black hair, slightly greying at the temples, and wore aviator-style spectacles. He was, perhaps, a little younger than Sean expected. He turned to greet Sean and offered his hand.

'I am Major Adrian O'Keefe. General Sundberg has told me your incredible story. I think we need to talk.'

'I'll leave you guys to it,' said Sundberg, beating a hasty retreat.

O'Keefe beckoned Sean to take a seat at Sundberg's conference table. As they sat down opposite each other, O'Keefe was the first to speak.

'Mr Cameron, tell me what you want from me and my wife? I hope you are not considering taking Samantha away. She has been with us now for two years and is very happy. We adopted her from birth and it is as if she's our own blood. We both love her dearly and couldn't imagine life without her.'

It was clear that O'Keefe's feelings ran deep. Sean tried his best to reassure him. 'Don't worry, Major. First of all you can call me Sean and, second, let me make it quite clear that I have no wish to take her away from you and your wife. When I heard the news that I had a second daughter, I desperately wanted to see her, and to be a father to her. But during the last few days, in spite of everything that has happened, I've thought long and hard about this extraordinarily unusual situation, and I know in my heart that if you treat her well and she is happy with you – and I can see that for myself – it would be foolish to attempt to take her away.'

O'Keefe felt a sense of relief. Until their meeting, he was unsure what to expect from the man who claimed to be his daughter's biological father. However, he seemed a reasonable enough kind of guy. 'Listen, I give you my word of honour that we treat Samantha very well indeed.' He paused. 'By the way, my name is Adrian,' he said warming to Sean.

'What I would like to do is to visit you at your home to meet her,' suggested Sean. 'You can tell her I am a friend of the family. If I am satisfied that she is happy and well, I won't cause any trouble. Because I loved her mother very much and believe that it is my duty to ensure her well-being, I should like to see her as she grows up, perhaps on her birthdays or during the school holidays. You can make me a godfather or guardian in the event of anything happening to you or your wife. How does that sound?'

O'Keefe said nothing for a moment.

Sean looked out of the window. He could see James, John and Dieter deep in conversation. He wondered what they were discussing.

Finally O'Keefe spoke. 'I must speak with my wife first about your request. Personally, I don't object to your meeting Samantha and I am sure she won't either. But if she does, then I must support her. If she thought she was going to lose Samantha it would kill her. We tried desperately for years to have our own child, but after several miscarriages and an ectopic pregnancy, we gave up trying and decided to adopt instead.'

'That brings me to my next question,' said Sean rising. 'But first, do you mind if I open the window? It's a bit stuffy in here.'

'No problem, I was thinking the same myself,' O'Keefe said, loosening his tie slightly.

'Are you prepared to testify that Dr Matthias sold Samantha to you?' asked Sean, suddenly changing the subject.

Again O'Keefe paused. 'If my wife and I were granted immunity from prosecution and Samantha wasn't named in any resulting court case,' he paused again. 'And if I have an absolute cast iron guarantee that there will be no publicity for my family, then I will do it.'

'I'm sorry if it seems like I'm attaching conditions,' said Sean, 'but put yourself in my shoes.' He hesitated. 'I can tell you I was devastated by the death of my fiancée Akinyi.' Sean swallowed hard and cleared his throat. His voice wavered with emotion as he began to talk again. 'That a scumbag like Matthias should take my daughter away as my girlfriend lay dying, is not only immoral, but goes against everything the Hippocratic oath stands for in the medical profession. To think that he made money out of her simply makes my blood boil,' he said, bitterly.

O'Keefe felt momentarily guilty and put a fatherly hand on Sean's forearm. 'I must apologize if I am inadvertently guilty of causing part of your pain. One could say that if it were not for people like me and my wife the likes of Matthias would not be able to operate. We had no idea of the circumstances in which Samantha was born. We were told her parents had been killed in a car crash.'

Sean interrupted. 'My moralizing was not directed at you, Adrian. I understand perfectly well and accept the reasons why you adopted her. I would probably have done the same myself, had I been in your position.

Now, please tell me about Samantha.'

O'Keefe said she was a beautiful little girl. He told Sean about her first footsteps, when she cut her first teeth and when she uttered her first words. Sean sensed the pride in his voice and saw O'Keefe's eyes well with tears. It was obvious that O'Keefe had strong feelings for his adopted daughter.

Half an hour later General Sundberg returned to his office.

'I guess you gentlemen are just about through. I'm sorry, but I need my office back. I have a staff meeting in ten minutes.'

'No problem,' they both said in unison.

'Sandra has arranged some tea in reception.' He offered his hand, 'Thank you, gentlemen, I wish you both the best of luck.'

'No, it's you whom I must thank,' responded Sean. 'Your help has been invaluable.'

O'Keefe, too, was grateful. 'Thank you, General, for your time and courtesy – and most of all for the introduction. It's been a pleasure to meet Samantha's real father, I can now see where she gets her resilience from,' he joked.

Sandra was in reception where tea and biscuits were laid out on a small table.

'I would like to call my wife; is there an office or a private room I could use for five minutes?' O'Keefe asked.

'Yes, of course,' she said, with her usual efficiency.

'Down the corridor, second on the left,' she called, as he began walking.

Sean spent the interim minutes chatting to Sandra. It turned out her parents were English and that she had grown up in America as her father worked for CNN in Atlanta, where she had been educated. On leaving school she had gone to a secretarial college and her first assignment was a temporary job with the US Air Force recruitment office in Atlanta. From there her position had become permanent and she'd eventually joined General Sundberg's staff, rising to become his personal assistant three years previously.

O'Keefe was back within five minutes. 'I've just spoken to my wife, Gladys, and she says it's okay with her for you to come and meet Samantha. I am back in Mildenhall in four days, so you could visit us then. Shall we say Saturday at three o'clock?'

'That's terrific,' said Sean, greatly relieved. 'I have some pressing business to attend to in Hamburg, but I should be back in the UK by then. I look forward to it.'

O'Keefe handed Sean his card. 'Give us a call if you can't make it or if you are going to be late.'

'Don't you worry, Adrian, I'll be there on time. This is one appointment I won't miss.' He got up to go. 'Thanks for the tea, Sandra.' He turned away and walked towards the exit. Minutes later he had located James, Dieter and John, who were still chatting in the car park.

'About time too,' said James. 'We've got a plane to catch.'

They had managed to hitch a lift on a transport plane out of Wiesbaden at 17.00 hours. Two of Dieter's men were already at Wiesbaden when James, John and Sean finally turned up. They introduced themselves as Bruno Netzer and Max Hartel.

Both had worked for Dieter since the inception of the Justice '89 unit. They looked as hard as nails, with not an ounce of superfluous fat between them. Bruno had a small scar on his left cheek. Both had closely cropped hair, cut in a military style, with lightly tanned but rugged looking faces. On the flight to Hamburg, John and James briefed them on their plan of attack at the Bar Brezel. They touched down just over an hour later. Dieter's men flashed their I.D. cards, enabling them to clear airport security swiftly.

It was drizzling as they left the airport and made their way to the hotel. The car journey passed almost in silence.

CHAPTER 48

James, John, Bruno and Max went off, leaving Sean in the bar of the hotel. He now had an anxious wait.

John had briefed James on the layout of the Bar Brezel and the street in which it was situated. They had hired a car and Bruno was chosen to drive, because he had been police trained, had exceptional car control and could have competed up to rally standard, or on the race track.

As they arrived in the square, just to the north of Albrechtstrasse, Bruno manoeuvred into a position where he could see almost the full length of the street while remaining in the car. He jumped out with the others and stood a few yards from the car with the Brezel in full view. He remained near the car in preparation for a quick getaway.

The others walked single file down the street. Max stopped at another bar entrance that was almost opposite the Brezel. He began browsing through the menu card on the wall. It, too, was a 'Red House', selling incredibly overpriced drinks. As he continued to browse, one of the girls came out and engaged him in conversation. She offered her services but Max politely declined. He leant back against the wall and made small talk with her to pass the time, while keeping one eye on the Brezel.

Shortly afterwards, John and James entered the Brezel separately. Nothing had changed since John's last visit. The disco music was still loud, porno videos were playing on the bank of monitors on the far wall and the barman was in his usual position. Remembering the last time, John wondered why he wasn't bored to death with the porno movies.

James sat down near the doorway that led upstairs. John had drawn a small plan, indicating where the door was in relation to the bar. It wasn't difficult to remember, as the place was small, and his description of the interior layout had been good. James would congratulate him on their return to the hotel; he couldn't have produced a better brief himself.

John strolled nonchalantly to the top end of the bar and climbed on to one of the bar stools. He had hardly sat down when the peroxide blond, with the diamond-shaped eyebrow liner and squeaky voice, made a beeline for him.

'Hello.' She sounded as if she had inhaled a ballon-full of helium gas and spoke very quickly. John figured she was on 'speed', but managed to stifle his laughter. It brought back memories of his previous visit.

'Hello,' he countered. 'And where is your friend the Schwarzer?'

'Ach, she's upstairs getting screwed by another customer. They've been at it for about an hour, so she should be down soon but, hey, what about me? I promise I will give you a good time,' she giggled.

He smiled, not wishing to upset her. 'I'm sorry, but blonds are not to my taste.' He turned to the barman. 'Hey, Ludo, how about a beer? And, I guess, one for my friend here.' He grimaced, expecting another order for a bottle of champagne.

'Just a beer for me this time,' she squeaked, perhaps thinking that she had more chance of succeeding with him if she was less extravagant with her choice of drink.

John breathed a sigh of relief and took a swig from the bottle.

Meanwhile, James had been accosted by two gorgeous-looking Thai women, who shrieked with laughter as he countered their proposals with amusing one-liners. One of them jumped up, sat on his knee and put her arms around his neck.

John laughed to himself. He could see that James was embarrassed. If Yolanda could see him now!

James ordered a bottle of champagne and three glasses. His companions giggled excitedly as he popped the cork and the champagne fizzed into their glasses.

John cast his eyes quickly around the room. One minder was stationed at the door and he could see the butt of a pistol jutting out from behind his left lapel. There was no sign of any other minders. He sipped his beer slowly.

The bar was filling up with a few more customers.

Eventually Njeri appeared through the doorway from upstairs. A fat little man of about 60 had his arm around her waist. The pair of them looked ridiculous. She hadn't noticed James sitting behind her. He was partially screened by the Thai girls.

John watched her closely. She was staring straight at him, but showed no sign of recognition. She was either pretending very well or she was so high she didn't know where she was. He studied her face. Her eyes were completely blank, staring straight ahead and she looked unsteady on her feet. It became obvious to John that she was drugged up to the eyeballs.

The old man, who was clearly drunk, released his grip around her waist and stumbled towards the door, mumbling to himself. The minder stepped forward and grabbed him before he fell. He lifted him off his feet and dumped him unceremoniously out in the street.

While that was happening, John seized his opportunity and moved towards Njeri, grabbing her. 'Come on,' he said. 'We're off.'

At first she was taken by surprise but then something inside her head sparked a hint of recognition. She realized she knew John but couldn't remember where from. They headed towards the exit.

As the minder closed the front door he turned and confronted John.

'And where do you think you are taking the Schwarzer?' he said, reaching for his pistol.

John was too quick for him. He had already drawn the gun he carried in his belt. He pointed it directly into the minder's face. 'I'll take that,' he said as he grabbed the pistol.

The sudden appearance of the guns terrified Njeri and she began to scream, which brought two more burly minders into the bar from behind the door, just to the right of James. Expecting reinforcements, James had held his position. He, too, had drawn his pistol, in readiness for any trouble and it was lying on the seat beside him, the Thai girls quite oblivious to it.

As the minders ran past him towards John and Njeri, James jumped to his feet, sending one of the Thai girls sprawling across the low table and spilling what remained of the champagne. The ice bucket clattered to the floor. The girls began to scream, shouting obscenities at James for being so clumsy.

The girls' screams stopped the two minders in their tracks. They turned to be confronted by James, who by this time had assumed the stand and fire position, his pistol cocked and ready.

'Drop your guns and put your hands behind your head. Now!' he barked.

Neither man moved.

'NOW!' he ordered again, with even more steel in his voice. He fired a shot, narrowly missing the bigger minder's ear and shattering a few bottles behind the bar. Realizing he meant business, the minders hastily dropped their weapons and raised their hands behind their heads. Suddenly, Ludo charged James, swinging a baseball bat high in a full arc. James ducked, catching his would-be assailent with a left hook to the right ear. Ludo screamed in pain, dropping the bat as he tumbled to the floor. In the commotion the customers and the other hostesses dropped to the ground.

'I'm off,' yelled John, grabbing Njeri.

'Lie down! Arms behind your heads! Don't move!' James ordered the minders. They duly obliged; their bosses didn't pay them enough to perform any heroics. He grabbed their pistols and backed towards the door.

John signalled to Max as he and Njeri came out of the bar. Max remained in position, with his pistol in his right hand, waiting for James to exit.

John was half walking and half running, dragging Njeri along with him. 'Here, Bruno,' he called. 'Take Njeri to the car and start it up.' He then adopted Bruno's previous position and waited.

Bruno pulled Njeri to the car and bundled her unceremoniously into the back seat before moving swiftly behind the wheel to start the engine. It roared into life.

James ran out of the bar slamming the door behind him. 'Let's go, Max,' he called. 'Let's get out of here.'

The two of them moved backwards up each side of the street, still pointing their pistols at the front door of the Brezel Bar. Moments later two of the minders came rushing out of the bar carrying machine pistols. There was a burst of fire in James's direction. It was way off target. Max and John replied with a volley of fire which saw the minders duck back into the bar as quickly as they came out. James chuckled and the three of them ran to the car, causing a few startled passers-by to jump out of the way.

James and John climbed into the back with Njeri, and Max sat in front beside Bruno. James tapped Bruno on the shoulder, signalling him to move off. He put the car in gear and slipped into the traffic. There was silence for a few minutes as they caught their breath. John was the first to speak.

'I think Njeri needs to see a doctor. Look at her arms and those needle marks. It looks like she's been shooting up heroin.'

James felt her pulse and looked into her eyes. Her head lolled back as he did so. 'Put your foot down, Bruno. We need to get her to a hospital and quickly. Does anyone know where the nearest one is? After all our efforts, we don't want to lose her now.'

'Don't worry, I've worked in Hamburg before so I know where to go,' said Bruno confidently as he accelerated.

After five minutes of weaving in and out of traffic they reached a hospital. On arrival at casualty, Njeri was put on a stretcher and taken to intensive care.

James telephoned Sean at the hotel with the news. He arrived half an hour later.

'How is she?' he asked. He looked ashen.

'It's okay. We got her here just in time. It seems she's been given a massive dose of heroin. The doctor reckons she will be fine in a couple of days, but they'll need to keep her in for observation.'

'Can I see her?'

'She's sleeping now, but the doctor said you can go in. I'll wait here.' James touched him on the shoulder reassuringly. 'She's going to be okay, mate.'

Sean entered Njeri's room. She looked so small and vulnerable lying there, her thin, dark face and arms contrasting sharply with the pure, white cotton sheets. He was surprised at the number of drips attached to her, and God knows how many tubes. As he leant over to kiss her gently on the forehead, he could feel her shallow breath on his face. He sat down in the chair next to her bed and took her cold, limp hand in his, gently squeezing it. 'Dear Njeri,' he whispered. 'My dear Njeri.'

CHAPTER 49

It was Friday afternoon when they touched down at Heathrow. Sean had collected Njeri from the hospital that morning and they had driven straight to the airport. Njeri looked drawn after her ordeal and thinner than Sean had ever seen her. She held his hand tightly throughout the flight, refusing to let go.

John and James had returned to the UK on Wednesday, and immediately James had travelled home to be with Yolanda and the kids.

Back at his house in Richmond, Sean packed for their journey to Hereford to stay with James and his family. It was like old times as they drove up the A40 from Gloucester. He had arranged for Njeri to convalesce with James and Yolanda for a couple of weeks, but he couldn't stay; he had more pressing things on his mind. He didn't want to be late for his first visit to see Samantha.

After an early night Sean left at five o'clock in the morning, travelling across country to Mildenhall. There was very little traffic on the road during the first part of the journey and he arrived shortly after 3 p.m., having stopped only for fuel and a coffee. The latter part of the journey had been frustrating because some of the roads had been very slow and winding, with little opportunity to overtake if he got stuck behind a lorry or a caravan. Unfortunately, this had happened frequently.

On arriving, Sean entered by the main gates. The O'Keefes lived in officers' quarters on the base. As he pulled up at the barrier to the USAF Airbase, a corporal approached him and saluted.

'I've come to see Major and Mrs O'Keefe. Can you direct me to their quarters, please?' Sean asked politely.

'What name, sir?'

'Cameron, Sean Cameron.'

'Wait a moment please, sir, while I arrange a visitor's pass for you.'

The corporal returned to the office. Sean could see him through the window. He said something to his colleague behind the desk and pointed in Sean's direction. His colleague picked up a phone and spoke for a few minutes before putting it down, during which time the corporal had been busy writing out Sean's pass. He returned to the car. 'Can you show me some form of identification please, sir, so that I can confirm your identity to my sergeant?'

'Certainly,' Sean said, producing his passport and handing it to the corporal. By this time he was getting impatient. He was anxious not to be late for his appointment with the O'Keefes.

The corporal examined it carefully, looking first at Sean and then at the photo in the passport. 'Thank you, sir. Everything seems to be in order. Here is your pass. Please pin it to your lapel. The CO would like to see you first. If you can follow that military police car, he will escort you to General Spencer.' He pointed to the car parked on the left on the other side of the barrier and saluted. He stepped back and then paused. 'Just a moment please, sir, but can I ask you a question before you go?'

'No problem,' responded Sean, trying to be as friendly as possible in spite of his obvious impatience.

'I hope you don't mind me asking but I follow rugby, and I just want to know whether you are *the* Sean Cameron who used to play for Scotland?'

'I am,' responded Sean. 'But isn't it a bit unusual for an American to be following rugby?'

'Well yes, sir, but I used to play for my college team, and I now play for the local team here. Do you mind giving me your autograph before you go? I watched you on TV scoring many tries for Scotland and the Barbarians.'

Sean obliged, quite taken aback. He smiled as he did so. 'Of all the unlikely places to sign an autograph,' he said as he grinned, shaking his head and taking his passport back at the same time.

The automatic barrier went up and Sean moved forward slowly, pulling up behind the police car. They moved off and in less than two minutes had stopped outside an office block. The MP left his car and came over to Sean.

'Follow me please, sir, the General is expecting you.'

Sean got out of his car and walked slowly behind the MP. They showed their passes at reception and negotiated a long, poorly lit corridor to the General's office. The MP knocked hard on the door.

'Come in, come in,' a voice responded.

The General stood up as Sean and the MP entered. The MP saluted and stood to attention. The General returned the salute.

'At ease, soldier, and thank you. Please wait outside.'

The soldier saluted again, turned and marched out.

'Please sit down Mr Cameron, this won't take long.' He pointed to the chair in front of his desk – an exact replica of General Sundberg's. It must have been standard government issue for ranking generals, thought Sean.

The General began. 'Mr Cameron, I understand you have come to see Major O'Keefe and his wife.'

'That's correct.'

'Well, Mr Cameron, I am sorry to be the bearer of bad news, but Major O'Keefe and his wife were killed in a car crash in the early hours of yesterday morning.'

Sean was stunned and rose from his chair. His legs wobbled and he slumped back down again. He stared at the General. He was almost paralyzed. 'But how? Why? ... Surely you are kidding me?' he stammered.

'Mr Cameron, do you seriously think that I would kid you about something so serious?'

'I'm sorry, I wasn't thinking. But what about Samantha, their daughter? Was she with them?' gasped Sean.

'No. Fortunately she was safely at home with a babysitter.'

Sean's mind was racing. 'Where is she now? Can I see her? You know who I am?'

'Yes. I've spoken at great length with General Sundberg about you. I've also spoken to my wife, who runs the officers' wives club. She discussed you at length with Gladys O'Keefe last week.'

'Can I see Samantha now?' said Sean impatiently.

'Naturally you will appreciate that she doesn't understand that her parents have been killed but, given the circumstances, I think you might see her for a little while. My wife is presently looking after her until a decision is made about her future. Please come with me.'

Sean followed him as they left the office.

'My driver will take us to my house,' the General said.

The waiting MP stood to attention again and saluted.

'Please escort us to my house, soldier,' General Spencer commanded. 'Certainly, sir.'

With the Police car in front and the siren wailing, they soon reached the General's house, which lay just outside the complex. It was a large, white mansion with a sweeping horseshoe-shaped drive. At the entrance, the MP on duty pressed a button and the gates opened automatically, letting the cars through. The General's driver held the car door open as they both alighted to climb the well-polished steps to the front door.

'Margaret,' the General called as they entered. 'We're home. Where is Samantha?'

'In here, honey.'

Sean followed the General into the drawing room.

The room was elegantly decorated with two large comfortable leather sofas. A child's tape of nursery rhymes played in the background. Margaret was standing at the fireplace. Behind her, and tugging at her skirt, was a small child with short, black hair braided in an African style. Her skin was a light coffee colour and she had large, beautiful brown eyes, just like her mother's.

The General kissed his wife gently on the cheek and introduced Sean. They shook hands and Sean offered his hand to Samantha. She turned shyly away and hid behind Margaret's skirt. Margaret was a big woman and Samantha was soon lost among the ample pleats.

'Hey, sweetie,' she said encouragingly with a smile, 'Don't be shy. This is a good friend of your Momma and Poppa.'

Samantha shuffled and peeped out from behind the mass of material. She gave Sean a big smile before shyly turning away again. Sean's heart melted; not since Louise was a small child had he experienced such heart-felt emotion.

'Go on, Samantha. Off you go and get some toys from the toy box,' Margaret said gently. 'Victor and I need to talk to this nice man.'

Samantha skipped away happily.

Margaret had prepared afternoon tea and Sean, hungry and thirsty after his long drive, tucked in.

'We hope you will stay with us tonight,' said Victor.

'That's very kind of you,' said Sean. 'But I don't wish to impose on you; I can stay at a local hotel.'

'No, no, we won't hear of it; we insist,' interrupted Margaret. 'The maid has already prepared a room.'

'Yes, and we will be able to discuss Samantha's future,' added Victor. 'The funeral is being arranged for next week, probably on Wednesday. It would be good if you could stay for that.'

'Thank you, General, of course I'll stay, and it will be nice to spend some time with Samantha.' He paused. 'What caused the accident?'

'Well, Adrian and Gladys were returning from a dance in Bury St Edmunds. It was around one o'clock in the morning. It had been raining and the roads were very greasy. According to the police report, and a statement from the driver of the car following them, a large van pulled out from a side road at speed. It was full of members of a pop group returning from a gig. Adrian was travelling too fast for the weather conditions and had no chance to brake in time. The van hit them on the passenger side, killing Gladys instantly. The car slewed off to the right and struck a tree. Adrian suffered multiple injuries and had to be cut from the wreckage. He died in the ambulance on the way to hospital.'

'What about the people in the van?'

'Amazingly, they only required treatment for minor cuts and shock. The driver was breathalyzed and found to be just over the legal limit. He was arrested and released on bail.'

'What's going to happen to him?'

'He was charged with being over the limit and causing death by dangerous driving. He'll probably go to prison.'

Sean leant back in his chair and closed his eyes. Why did the good people always have to die? he asked himself.

'Mickey Mouse, Mickey Mouse,' a little voice spoke. Samantha had come back into the room and was clutching a huge Mickey Mouse doll, almost as big as she was. She handed it to Sean and ran off giggling.

Over the next few days Sean played with Samantha. He took her for walks and found that she particularly loved the swings and slides. It reminded him of the time he had spent with Louise before his divorce. Although he enjoyed himself immensely, he had a heavy heart. He mourned for Akinyi, who should have been with him and Samantha.

Victor and Margaret were marvellous, extending kindness and hospitality. Neither of the O'Keefes had any living family so Samantha's future was of the utmost importance, and had to be decided upon quickly and carefully. Sean discussed many matters in some depth with the General. Legally, Sean had to prove paternity. This was going to be a tedious task and blood and DNA tests were necessary to start the process.

The funeral was on Wednesday in the air force chapel. The O'Keefes were buried with military honours and on each of the coffins – draped with the Stars and Stripes – was a little posy of yellow orchids from Samantha. The service was deeply moving. Samantha sat close to Margaret, clutching her arm or hand. She didn't understand what was going on, but there wasn't a dry eye at the graveside. Everyone was visibly moved by the plight of the pretty little girl who had just been orphaned.

On Thursday morning Sean said his goodbyes. He was sad to leave Samantha, but he needed to visit Louise, whom he hadn't seen since his return from Germany. He was completely traumatized, both by the events of the last few days and by the shattering experiences of the last two years.

CHAPTER 50

Three months later, Sean and James were sitting in Dieter's office in Cologne. Dieter was in a buoyant mood. Sean had never seen him openly happy. He had always appeared to be such a serious person, but now he had cause to celebrate.

'Thanks in part to you two – and the rest of my team – we have smashed the biggest neo-Nazi cell this country has seen since the end of the Second World War,' he enthused. The Chancellor is delighted. At last Germany has received positive international press coverage on our efforts to crack down on extremist Fascist activities.' He poured them a coffee and then offered champagne. Sean declined but James accepted.

'What of Meissner?' enquired Sean. 'Was he involved?'

'He was up to his neck in it. After we made our arrests in the Black Forest, we got one or two to implicate him.'

'And what of Jochen and Fritz?' asked James.

'Fritz has disappeared completely and Jochen was the biggest surprise of all. He sang like a bird. He knew he was looking at a long term in prison and agreed to testify, subject to immunity from prosecution.'

'So what's happened to that snake Meissner?' said Sean, recalling vividly his shaven head and pince-nez spectacles.

'Two days after Jochen testified, Meissner was arrested at his office. He denied everything. It turned out he was one of the driving forces behind the neo-Nazi movement in Germany. According to some of his colleagues, he deliberately did little or nothing to track down Akinyi's killers. Any suggestions to follow a new course of enquiry were disregarded, and new evidence that came to light was conveniently lost.'

'Can you put together a strong case against him? Have you enough evidence?' asked James.

'Jochen's statement will put Meissner and Schneider away for a very long time. However, we shall have to call you both as witnesses at the trial.'

'When will that be?' enquired James.

'The trial starts next month.'

'Well, we are available if you need us,' said Sean, hoping that at least one chapter of his recent stormy life was about to close. He looked forward to the day when he could become Samantha's full-time father. 'And what of Akinyi's killers? Have you made any arrests?' he added.

'Yes, you will be pleased to know that we have arrested two of the three prime suspects in a series of raids in which we rounded up a total of

70 neo-Nazi members. The remaining members of the cell have dispersed and gone further underground.'

'And the third?' said Sean. 'What happened to him?'

James was by now on his second glass of champagne. Dieter topped up his own glass before answering. 'He was killed in a shoot-out with the police during an abortive bank raid in Hanover.'

'Phew,' sighed Sean. 'He sounds a really a nasty piece of work.'

'Well, it saves at least one more of them rotting in our prisons at taxpayers' expense,' said Dieter.

'But what about the two they arrested? What's happening to them?'

'They were charged with Akinyi's murder and are due to stand trial very shortly. If they are found guilty they are looking at life imprisonment,' replied Dieter.

Sean breathed a huge sigh of relief, confident that justice would be done at last. 'That's wonderful news, but what's the situation regarding Dr Matthias and Dr Peterson?'

'Another stroke of luck, really. It has nothing to do with my unit but, because of your involvement in the Nazi case, the Chancellor ordered a top-level enquiry into the profile and background of key personnel at Meissner's station. The purpose was to establish that there were no more Nazi sympathizers among them.'

'That doesn't tell me about Matthias,' said Sean, slightly agitated.

'Sorry, but I'm coming to that. The investigation into the Matthias case was carried out by one of the department's top inspectors. He put Matthias and the clinic under surveillance for four weeks, after which every visitor was followed and interviewed. All were promised immunity from prosecution, against any charge of seeking to adopt illegally, if they cooperated with the authorities. The tragedy of their cases was much the same as the O'Keefes'. The visitors were childless couples who had tried desperately for years to have children of their own.'

'But did they make statements that would help in the prosecution of Matthias and Petersen?' asked James.

'Yes, all of them will be used as witnesses, but the real key to the whole case is the statement from Matthias's mistress, Beatrix Snell. She and Matthias had a big fall-out.'

'Why was that?' queried Sean.

'For years they were having an affair, but he always refused to leave his wife. One day she discovered he had started a new affair with a much younger woman. She went crazy and got her revenge by reporting him for professional malpractice to the German Medical Council. The Council immediately contacted the police to seek their assistance. When the police explained that they already had him under surveillance,

Matthias was immediately suspended from his duties at the hospital and closed down his clinic.'

'Didn't that scare him off and leave him with enough time to cover his tracks?' asked Sean.

'No. The police already had a watertight case against him. They arrested him a short while later and obtained a writ to seize all his assets.'

'Has he managed to get bail?' asked Sean.

'No way, his crimes are too serious for that. He's been charged on at least 15 different counts and, if found guilty, will go down for a very long time,' said Dieter.

'And what of his assets?' said James. 'What will become of them?'

'Some will be used to pay back some of the unfortunate people who were currently on his waiting list for a child – and who had already paid a deposit.'

'And the remainder?' asked Sean.

'A proportion will go towards the costs of the case, and anything remaining will be donated to a children's hospital,' concluded Dieter, rising from his chair. 'Well, gentlemen, it looks like we have managed to solve more cases than we ever expected. I'll have to let you go now because I've got a lot of work to do, if you don't mind.'

James and Sean stood up.

'We know when we've outstayed our welcome,' Sean said as he smiled at Dieter. 'Come on, James, let's go,' and he shook Dieter's hand.

James also shook Dieter's hand. 'See you at the trials, old friend.'

'Oh, there is one last thing before you go. Do you remember the barman at the Junction Bar?' Dieter asked.

James and Sean looked at each other, puzzled that Dieter should ask about the barman.

'What relevance does he have in all of this?' said James, the first to speak.

'He was arrested with the others in the Black Forest. It turned out he was quite a senior member of the local neo-Nazis, and reported on our meetings at the Junction Bar. I recognized him instantly when he was brought into my office, and I interviewed him myself,' said Dieter.

'I remember him now,' said Sean. 'You are right about surveillance, James. You warned me about the dangers of meeting in the same place more than once.'

'What will happen to him, Dieter?' said James, realizing that he couldn't afford to let his standards drop when he started his security company. It had taught him a very valuable lesson for the future.

'Oh, he confessed to being a member of the neo-Nazis and made a statement. He'll probably get a year or 18 months, but probably no more than that.' He looked at his watch. 'Gentlemen, I must ask you to go now,' and he smiled.

CHAPTER 51

Sean's parents had arranged a very special family dinner party to mark the end of Sean's heroic mission to win justice for Akinyi and Samantha. It was the biggest party they had had for a very long time. Sean's entire family – brother, sister, *et al* – were dining together that night, along with James, his wife Yolanda and their children. Best of all, Louise was sitting next to her little sister, Samantha, and proud to be looking after her. Sean had won custody. His DNA and blood tests had proved conclusively that he was Samantha's natural father, and Beatrix's evidence had confirmed the facts about her birth.

'So Meissner and Schneider each got 20 years,' Sean's father said towards the end of the meal.

'Yes, it's wonderful, and, best of all, Akinyi's killers got a life sentence,' said Sean. 'Matthias was also charged as an accessory to Akinyi's murder. Although he wasn't involved in the attack, and it cannot be proved that he caused her death by inducing labour, several eminent doctors gave evidence to state that it is just possible she might have survived her injuries. As a result, Matthias pleaded guilty to manslaughter and was sentenced to ten years in prison.'

'That would have affected the sentences passed on her murderers, Roth, Müller, Bauer and Schmidt. I know Grunefeld was killed in the bank raid in Hanover,' said James.

'Yes, it certainly did,' replied Sean. 'Müller was found not guilty of murder due to insufficient evidence, and the lawyers for the other three claimed that they were not entirely responsible for her death as a result of evidence from other doctors.'

'You mean it created some doubt?' asked Sean's father.

'Yes, but they were found guilty of manslaughter after the judge directed that they were primarily responsible for her injuries. I think the jury's verdict confirmed this, and that's why he handed out such severe sentences.'

Matthias and Petersen were struck off by the German Medical Council and also imprisoned, Matthias for 10 years and Petersen for eight. Beatrix Snell got a two-year suspended sentence and had left court in tears of relief. She was the one person Sean felt sorry for. At the age of 49, her career and life were in ruins, destroyed by a man who had taken advantage of her love for years.

The international press had a field day. Sean and James had their faces splashed all over the media. In England, in particular, they were hailed as conquering heroes. Several newspapers had sought exclusive rights to their stories. They were big news and had been approached by film companies to make a film of their lives. They declined all offers, asking only for the media to donate some money towards a children's orphanage in Kenya.

Victor and Margaret became Samantha's 'adopted' grandparents. They had looked after her until the end of the Matthias trial, when she was legally handed over to Sean. Lawyers had rushed through a request to a High Court judge to issue a new birth certificate, stating that Sean and Akinyi were her parents. Sean's pride was evident. He looked across the table at Samantha and Louise. Louise was growing up to be a beautiful child. She was confident and happy with her life, even though she would have liked to have spent more time with her father. She knew he loved her and would always be there if she had a problem.

While they were having coffee, Samantha climbed down from the table and walked over to Sean. He lifted her up on his lap and she promptly fell asleep. Sean held her in his arms for a short time before carrying her upstairs to bed. After tucking her in, he went back downstairs.

James had gone to sit on the patio and Sean joined him. He needed some fresh air and time for contemplation. He looked up to watch the stars twinkling in the clear night sky. Sean savoured the quietness for a few moments until James broke the silence.

'Well, mate, where do you go from here? What are your plans?'

'I'm returning to Kenya with Samantha. Akinyi would have wanted to bring her up there. I think it is very important that she grows up knowing about her culture and her mother's country.'

'But what about all the problems there – the political unrest, the violence, the robberies, the poverty? How can you bring her up safely in such an environment and, more importantly, what will you do for a job?'

'I agree that it may be difficult. Corruption and jealousy are both cancers that appear to be slowly strangling the country but, as with cancers generally, some are treatable and can be cured. It is up to individuals not to give up hope. I don't know whether I will be able to cope with it – all I can do is go there and try my best. If it doesn't work out, I can always come back here and start again. I've got to give it my best shot.'

'I admire your optimism, Sean, and I wish you luck, but what would Akinyi have thought about it all?'

'She was very radical and had no patience with things as they were,' said Sean. 'For example, she wanted to get rid of tourism in Kenya as it exists at the moment.'

James frowned. 'But isn't tourism one of the biggest earners for the country?'

'Yes, that was my argument, but at the moment it is not on Kenya's terms. Most of the large hotels and tour companies are owned by local Indians or foreigners: Germans and Italians. They all take most of the revenue out of the country, and very little is being ploughed back. Akinyi's plea was to invest in Kenyans to help them start up their own businesses.'

'But you can't just throw the foreigners out!' said James, logically.

'They don't have to. Tourism is at an all-time low at the moment. If it continues to drop, the hotels will either close down or be bankrupted, and the investors will leave. If the Kenyan government does not combat the huge rise in violence and disease, there will be massive social change. There are so many people employed in tourism and related industries that there will be major unemployment with few opportunities for alternative work. The hotels and the tourist industry will survive only if investment in hotels and other leisure facilities is made affordable and available to Kenyans – and not just to rich Europeans.'

'This is all a bit too political for me,' said James, shaking his head and changing the subject. 'What about Njeri? What will become of her?'

'She left for Kenya two weeks ago. I offered to pay for her ticket and to give her £5,000 to start a hair and beauty salon attached to a small hotel on the north coast of Mombasa. She would do well at that.'

'I can't believe you gave her that amount of money after all the things she did to you, Sean. Do you seriously think she will invest the money wisely? It is surely more likely she will return to her bad old ways.'

'Wait a minute. I only said I *offered* her the money. I didn't say she accepted it, did I?'

'Well did she or didn't she?' asked James, exasperated.

'No, she refused. She told me she had managed to save a lot more than that while she had been working here.'

'You mean while she was on the game?' exclaimed James.

'I guess that's where she got it from. I'm not sure whether she will invest it wisely, only time will tell. However, I genuinely believe she will make a go of it. She certainly has the ability.'

'Finally, Sean, tell me what you plan to do for a job?'

'For a start, I'm going to invest in transport. I'm going to buy two *Matatus*, which are small buses, and employ drivers and touts to work for me. Transport is a money-making industry in Kenya. Second, I'm going to act as a marketing consultant to the tourist industry – I think I can apply my expertise in that field. But first I am going to take my two daughters on a month's holiday to Mombasa before I start work. We are going to fly to Kenya next week. But what about you, James? What are your plans?'

'Well, I still intend to start my own security company, providing body-guarding, security advice and surveillance services to anyone who requires them – companies, governments or private individuals. I think I can use my expertise doing that,' James said and grinned. 'You never know, Cameron, I might even employ you for some of the operations!' This time he laughed. 'Since our media exposure, I've been inundated with job offers to act as security advisor for a whole host of projects. There is probably enough work to keep me busy for the next ten years.' He paused. 'Tell me one last thing, Sean. Why Kenya?'

'I guess it's just got into my bones. I've heard all sorts of stories from many people about Africa; it seems they either love it, or hate it. It may simply be a romantic notion, but I believe I've found a place where I truly belong.'

'Haven't I heard that somewhere before?' asked James. 'I seem to recall Akinyi saying that she didn't feel she could settle in to a European way of life.'

'Yes, indeed. Both Akinyi and Njeri didn't know where they belonged, but for distinctly different reasons.'

'What were they?' questioned James.

'Well, the reasons are complicated and would really take a long time to explain. In a nutshell, Akinyi had a very good education, both in Kenya and in Germany, but at home she couldn't get paid enough for her skills because of the socioeconomic and political attitudes in Kenya. She desperately wanted to return to her country and contribute to the country's well being, but she was not valued by the Kenyan government on an equal basis with Europeans. The government would rather pay an expatriate a lot of money to do the same job that a Kenyan could do for far less, so that it becomes impossible to build the foundations of a great country with the skills of its own people. Although Akinyi was able to get a well paid and satisfying job in Germany, she encountered such racism that she had a very bad time. For example, even though she could speak perfect German, she still suffered gross prejudice because she was black. She could not blend into the environment like a white immigrant. In Germany, black people stand out like sore thumbs. The Germans themselves were often amazed that, as in Akinyi's case, a black person could be so well educated and, to some extent, speak better German than they could themselves.'

'And what about Njeri?'

'Njeri didn't know where she belonged, either. She was from a less privileged background than Akinyi. Her parents couldn't afford to educate her in the same way and, as a result, she ended up as a bar girl because there was little or no opportunity for her to get a well-paid job. Also, her father disowned her because she got pregnant at an early age and brought shame on the family. The tourists she met often treated her and other girls like whores. Maybe they were whores, but nine times out of ten the girls didn't want to do the terrible things that white male tourists forced them to do. Njeri had aspirations similar to any European girl. She wanted a good job, a house, car, and so on, but the Kenyan government couldn't provide the opportunity for her to obtain such things working in a normal job. She dreamed about coming to Europe, where she thought the streets were paved with gold, but, of course, the harsh reality was different. Her relationship with me failed, but that was probably due more to my shortcomings than hers. When we split up she knew of no way to survive other than to resort to what she had been doing in Kenya. In Kenya she could control the way she went about procuring men, however, in Germany she was forced into the sex trade by bastards whose only interest was making money, and lots of it. How could she ever feel she belonged to the country in a situation like that?' said Sean.

James shook his head.

'When I discovered that Njeri had joined an escort agency, I was absolutely horrified. I spoke to various friends about it, without telling them the situation related to me and Njeri.'

'What did they say?' asked James.

'Incredibly, most of them shrugged their shoulders and said it was no big deal these days. Can you believe that, James?' said Sean shaking his head.

'Well, I must admit, that does surprise me, but there's no point dwelling on it, Sean.'

There was a moment's silence.

'Getting back to our earlier conversation, as a black man I can empathize with Akinyi. I, too, have often felt dislocated from the society I live in, and have felt that I'm not British, even though I hold a British passport and have spent all but five years of my life in this country. However, from a very young age I've been determined to make a success of my life in this country.' James looked at his watch. It was 2.30 in the morning. 'Come on, Sean, I think it's time for bed. We could go on talking about this for hours.'

Sean remembered he had to get up early in the morning to be with Samantha. 'Before I go, James, I really cannot thank you enough for all your help. I will forever be in your debt.'

'Don't even mention it; I would do it again tomorrow if I had to. But before you go to bed, Sean, just tell me about yourself. I've known you for many years and never thought you would succumb to alcoholism. You've always struck me as such a well-balanced person who could handle most problems.'

Sean pursed his lips and looked agitated. 'You're right. I have always appeared to be a cool, calm person, but Akinyi's death just blew me away. I should have talked to you or Smithy, or any one of my friends, but I've always felt that grief is a very private thing and I thought I could handle it on my own – clearly I couldn't. I'm not a chemical alcoholic. My alcoholism was caused purely by the problems in my head. When I start drinking again I'm sure I'll be able to control it. I am happier now than I have been in a long time, and the added responsibility of bringing up Samantha will help.'

James didn't share Sean's confidence. 'You should be extremely careful if you start drinking again, Sean.' he warned, offering no further advice.

They got up and shook hands, their close friendship even more securely bonded than before.

'You know what, James. One of the first things I noticed when I was in Kenya was the absolutely massive potential for developing a stable and buoyant economy.'

'What do you mean?'

'Well, if you look at things from a practical point of view, every single person in the country wants everything that we have in the Western world. They want nice houses, fridges, cars, TVs, good jobs, and so on. The irony is that if the government – and this includes those corrupt groups that keep the government in office in order to retain most of the wealth for just a few people – broadened its outlook and adopted a fiscal policy to generate wider prosperity with greater consumer spending power, it could make much more money. The potential market for capital goods is immense, and the same is presumably true for other African nations.'

'Sean the politician next, I think?' James laughed and slapped Sean on the back.

One week later, almost three years after his first trip to Kenya – and several lifetimes – Sean, Louise and Samantha touched down at Jomo Kenyatta International Airport in Nairobi. They were the last to leave the plane.

As they stood at the top of the steps, Sean looked around. 'Here you are, Samantha, you're home at last, in the land of your mother. It will become very precious to you.'

As he looked over towards the terminal he saw Njeri standing at the viewing gallery next to the arrivals hall. He shook his head and smiled wryly. The image disappeared.

'Samantha,' he called. 'The sun is shining. From now on I am going to call you by your Luo name, *Achieng*, for sunshine. That's it, *Achieng*.' He smiled at Louise and gripped her hand.

'Ach-i-e-n-g, Achi-e-n-g,' Samantha giggled, as she and her sister climbed down the steps in front of their father.

Sean hesitated for a moment. 'Achieng,' he called.

Samantha turned. 'Yes, daddy. What is it?'

'I think your mother would have liked that name.' He nodded, giving her a wide smile of approval.